RELENTLESS

MASON FAMILY SERIES

BOOK FOUR

ADRIANA LOCKE

UMBRELLA
PUBLISHING INC.

To my readers.
May this book give you a little dose of the sunshine that you give me each and every day.
With love.

Also by Adriana Locke

My Amazon Store
Purchase Signed Copies

Play Me Series
Play Me | Try Me | Show Me

Brewer Family Series
The Proposal | The Arrangement | The Invitation | The Merger | The Situation

Carmichael Family Series
Flirt | Fling | Fluke | Flaunt | Flame

Landry Family Series
Sway | Swing | Switch | Swear | Swink | Sweet

Landry Family Security Series
Pulse

Gibson Boys Series
Crank | Craft | Cross | Crave | Crazy

The Mason Family Series
Restraint | The Relationship Pact | Reputation | Reckless | Relentless | Resolution

The Peachwood Falls Series
Tempt | Truly

The Exception Series
The Exception | The Perception

Dogwood Lane Series

Tumble | Tangle | Trouble

Standalone Novels

Sacrifice | Wherever It Leads | Written in the Scars | End Game | Like You Love Me | The Sweet Spot | Nothing But It All | Between Now and Forever

For a complete reading order, visit www.adrianalocke.com.

To receive a text alert for new releases, text BOOKS to 740-206-6969. US only.

Synopsis

"I had to sneeze."

I should've taken her insurance information and driven off like any reasonable CEO with places to be would.

She crashed into my car, for heaven's sake. Because she *had to sneeze.*

What did I do? I didn't get in my car and drive away if that's what you're thinking.

Nope. I stuck around. I could suggest I stayed because she needed help, but the truth? She was really, *really* hot.

We became fast friends. Then friends with benefits. Before I knew it, we were involved in an illicit office romance that had me fumbling through a drawerful of panties to get a Post-It.

It was supposed to be easy—a fling, if you will. A dashing millionaire hero (*adjusts tie*) and a beautiful (stubborn, frustratingly independent, hell-on-wheels) damsel in distress. (Don't tell her I said that.)

It wasn't supposed to be forever, but we did want a happy ending. (Pun intended.) We could've made it work, too.

But one of us overcomplicated things with the *L-word*. And the other? They omitted a truth that changed everything.

Chapter One

Shaye

I just had to sneeze.

My breath rushes in and out in quick succession, yet somehow isn't enough. I open my mouth to drag in more oxygen so I don't pass out.

The last thirty seconds are a muddled mess. I try to sort through them—there was the sneeze, *that* I remember—but it feels like trying to make sense of a huge ball of yarn that's been batted around by a kitten.

I grip the back of my neck. The pain is immediate, as though someone flipped a switch and—*voila!*—the discomfort begins. I wonder vaguely if it's due to the impact or from the shadow of someone coming around the side of my car.

Crap.

Something tells me to find my insurance card. *Please, let me have my insurance card.* I reach for the glove compartment, figuring it's where the responsible version of me would've put it, and glance up into the passenger's side window just as the person who I rammed with my car appears.

My hand falls to the seat next to me, covering a ketchup stain from an errant fast-food cheeseburger. It flew out of my hands last week during an impassioned concert I put on at a red light.

"Sometimes" by Britney Spears just gets to me.

As does the stranger at the window.

I'm not sure what I was expecting, but this wasn't it. It wasn't blue-green eyes that remind me of the ocean in postcards from faraway places peering back at me. Or sun-kissed skin. It definitely wasn't beautiful lips and a jawline that's squarish and bold.

I fall back into the seat as a surge of adrenaline rolls through me—my wits frazzling more by the second—and try to keep my composure. *I just hit a man's car.*

He watches me quietly, licking his lips as if he's having a hard time comprehending the situation. It gives me a moment to regroup.

A quick once-over puts him in his mid-thirties. He's ludicrously handsome. Brown hair kissed with a touch of blond is cut short to his head and styled as though he rolled out of bed looking that handsome. A deep-blue Polo shirt is stretched across broad shoulders. Lines around his mouth and eyes lend an approachability, a warmth to his features.

Let's hope that's true.

"I just had to sneeze."

I say it before I can think about it, which is unfortunate. My insides shrivel as the look on his face changes from concern to ... *surprise? Confusion? Judgment?* I don't know which it is, but it's clear he's thrown for a loop.

"Look, I'm not any happier about this than you are," I say, glancing at his dented Range Rover. "Actually, my insurance rates are going to go up, and that's devastating." I look at him again and gulp. "Okay, *devastating* might be a stretch, but I'm not looking forward to it."

He blows out a breath. I swear I smell peppermint.

"Are you okay?" he asks.

I think he means it like, *Did you hit your head or something?* but I can't really tell.

His voice is honeyed and sympathetic—not at all the cool and annoyed tone I predicted. *Sadly.* Irritated would've been easier to accept when I replay this scene in bed at three in the morning.

"Are you all right?" he asks again.

Nope.

"Me? Oh, yeah. I'm fine. I think. I mean, just a little pain in the back of my neck ..." I clasp my hand over the area. "It's probably just ... stress."

Stop talking, Shaye.

His brows pull together. "Why don't you step out of the car so we can figure out what to do?"

I reach for the glove box again. "My insurance card. You probably want that."

"Why don't you ... Let's make sure you're okay before we get into the insurance and stuff, okay?" he asks gently.

A quick scan of the glove compartment proves that the responsible me was not present the day I got my card from the insurance company. And I know for certain I didn't download the app like they suggested.

Who needs an app when I have a paper card? I don't need another dumb app.

I distinctly remember thinking that.

Dammit.

I sit back in my seat again—a little taller this time. I'm going to have to fake having my life together.

"My card is missing in action at the moment," I admit. "But I have insurance. I swear."

He holds his hands out as if the movement will calm me somehow. "It's okay. Let's start here—what's your name?"

"Shaye. My name is Shaye Brewer."

"*Shaye.*" He says it as if he wondered what it would sound like in his voice. "Okay, *Shaye.* I'm Oliver Mason."

Oliver Mason. Good lord—even his name is sexy.

"Hi."

I mentally kick myself. *Hi? Really, Shaye?*

"I really am sorry for ... that." I shift my eyes quickly to the location of our cars kissing and then back to him again. "It was an accident."

"Because you sneezed?"

"Yup."

His lips dip at the sides as though he's fighting a smile. His eyes don't fight it, though. The sides crinkle, the irises light up, and the blues and greens mix into crazy pools of color that are almost hypnotic.

"I sneezed four times, actually," I tell him, my guard slipping thanks to his I'm-not-going-to-lose-my-shit-over-this demeanor. "Most people do twos or threes. I always do fours."

He breaks. A wide, knock-me-off-my-feet grin splits his cheeks. It renders me breathless but, unfortunately for me, it does not render me speechless.

"Four times in a row is basically a blackout," I ramble on. "It's terrifying. This has always been a big fear of mine and now it came true."

"Fear of talking too much?" he teases.

My face flushes as I glance in my mirror at a car passing behind me. "No. Sneezing and getting into an accident, but thanks for that."

His chin lifts to the sky, and a full, friendly laugh slips through the air. My body sags in relief. The pain in the back of my neck becomes a distant memory.

"I talk too much when I'm nervous," I say, grimacing.

He grips the top of the window with one hand, his eyes still twinkling. "I was just kidding. I've never considered the dangers of sneezing and driving before. You have me wondering what other hazards lurk that I haven't thought about."

"There are tons of lurking hazards." I tap at the air vent by the display. "Ever wondered if a snake climbed in your engine at night? And then it occurs to you while you're driving that it could pop out one of these?"

He shakes his head, clearly amused. "I have not. I am also fairly certain that is impossible if it makes you feel any better."

"Well, if you're right, it does. But what's your expertise in this area?" I narrow my eyes. "Do you even know anything about cars?"

He rewards me with a laugh again. "Get out of there so we can survey the damage and decide what to do."

"So, that's a *no* on knowing anything about cars," I say as I climb out of the car.

A burst of wind greets me as I step onto the pavement. The contact of my shoe with the ground catapults me back into reality, causing me to look at the front of my car again. *I so don't need this headache.*

Oliver walks around the car and stands beside me. He's taller than me by a handful of inches, probably hitting six feet without shoes. He stands tall and confident, his body long and lean like an athlete but without the bulk of one. And, for the first time in a long time, I feel a crackle of attraction to another person.

I must've hit my head.

"Well, that's disappointing," I say, focusing on the mess in front of me and not at the man at my left.

"That depends on what you're looking at."

I don't look at him, but I don't have to in order to know he's looking at me. His gaze is heavy on my cheek.

A chill fires through my body as I try not to read into his words or the way they—*he*— oozes sex appeal.

"My bumper is definitely not supposed to be touching the ground," I say and then force a swallow. "That's pretty disappointing."

He switches his attention from me to the cars. "On the other hand, I'm pretty sure my mechanic can just pop my panel out, and I'll be good to go."

"Good for you."

Knowing nothing about car repair except for the fact that it's not cheap and the state of my front end is ... hanging, all I see are dollar signs. Dollar signs that I do not have.

My stomach tightens as reality sobers me a little more.

"So, what do you want to do about this?" he asks.

Cry?

"I don't know," I say. "What do you do in an accident?"

He moves to get a better look at the damage. "According to Georgia law, we don't have to involve the police unless there's an injury, death, or property damage over five hundred dollars."

"This is not the first time you've been in this situation, I gather."

"What can I say?" He grins. "I was a mischievous teenager and I have four brothers. It's a recipe for disaster."

"Four brothers? Your poor mother."

He laughs. The sound is easy and comfortable, as if we're discussing the weather or family stories and not property damage. I don't really know what to make of that.

"Well, there's no injury and no death, but I have no idea on the amount of damage. Do you?"

"Probably fifteen hundred or so."

Shit.

"That is," he says, pausing for effect, "if you take it to a random mechanic and get ripped off." He slips his hands into his pockets. "My mechanic, though—I bet we could get him to do it for less than five hundred."

A-ha!

I twist around and square my shoulders with his. "So, what you're saying is that we estimate the damage is less than five hundred dollars, so we don't have to call the police."

"That's what I'm saying. We don't have to call the police if you don't want to. I don't plan on turning mine into insurance. If you are, we need to call the cops for a report. The insurance will want that."

I'm not reporting this to anyone. Involving the police sets us up for tickets and I'd definitely be getting one. I also have no interest in getting this fixed for five hundred or fifteen hundred if it's not totally necessary.

"Let me ask you this," I say, rocking back on my heels. "Can I drive it like that?"

"How far do you have to go?"

"Not far."

He bends at the front end and inspects it. He peers beneath the busted plastic or whatever a bumper is made out of and fiddles with things.

I stand behind him and watch. My mind takes off, sprinting away from the accident and straight into bed with Oliver. I'm visualizing his rough palms grazing over my body and the taste of his lips against mine. The way my name sounds when it comes through clenched teeth—

"Oh!"

He stands abruptly, catching me off guard. I jump back and clutch my heart.

He dusts his hands off and grins. Amusement is written all over his handsome face.

"I have an idea," he says, heading to the Rover.

Me too, but it's probably not what you have in mind. It was nothing to do with getting my car *engine running.*

He opens the back of his SUV and digs around. I use the opportunity to catch my breath.

The whole day has been a whirlwind of fuckery. I stubbed my toe climbing out of bed. The water heater decided to go out two minutes into my shower. The staffing agency I have been using to fill an employment gap had me booked for a weekend afternoon shift downtown. When I showed up to the address they gave me, so did another woman —the *right woman*. She stayed. I was sent home.

The day did not get better from there.

Clearly.

I sigh and look up as Oliver stalks toward me with zip ties dangling from his hands.

Oh, good grief.

Two possibilities fire through my mind at the exact same time. I didn't know that was possible, but it happens.

One is that he's going to tie my hands a la Christian Grey. *Now that I think about it, he has that businessman-with-a-backstory vibe going on.*

The other is that he's going to secure my wrists together and perform a citizen's arrest. It seems possible. He somehow knows the law.

Then it hits me.

He's a cop.

I'm not sure whether to run or offer myself up. Getting detained could go either way, depending on the final destination—police station or Red Room.

Oliver stops a few steps away, his gaze turning wary as he reads my expression. "I was going to try to tie your bumper up with these, but if you don't want me to ..."

My shoulders slump and I sigh. Relief is mixed with disappointment. "Oh."

His gaze narrows. "I feel like I missed something."

"I was thinking about what you were going to do with those zip ties."

His eyes darken. "Oh, really?"

"But tying up my bumper sounds like quite the plan," I say, adding a laugh as if that will somehow erase the thinly veiled reference that we both know exists. "Zip ties are strong. I bet I won't even need a mechanic, huh?"

His lips twist into a smirk.

"I once used them to hold up a clothes rod in my closet," I babble, desperate for him to let it go. I haven't flirted in a million years. My flirter is broken. "And I zip-tied my shoes onto my feet one night. Long story."

"I bet."

I smile in hopes it distracts him. "So, about the bumper?"

"Yeah. The bumper." He crouches down, keeping an eye on me. "Come here and hold it up."

I squat next to him, doing my best to keep the scent of his cologne at bay. It's persistent. Before I know it, the notes of tobacco and amber are flirting with my core.

It doesn't take him long at all to fasten the bumper ... somewhere. All I know is that it isn't touching the pavement anymore and that's good enough for me.

He wipes his hands down the front of his jeans as he stands. "That should hold pretty well for a while. But you do need to have someone take a look and make sure nothing else is broken."

"I will," I lie, ignoring the roar of a truck on the road behind us.

The wind kicks up, ruffling the edge of my shirt. But as I stand next to Oliver, I absorb the calm, sturdy energy rippling off him. It's nice. I wish I could bottle it up and take it home with me.

His eyes search mine. "I wasn't kidding about my mechanic. I'd be happy to have him take a look at it for you, if you want."

"I've already caused you enough problems for one day."

He smiles. "We could schedule it for tomorrow then. We could grab lunch while it's being looked at."

Suddenly, I don't know what to say.

He's been so kind to me, despite the situation. I could never tell him how much I appreciate that. But not only am I not getting my car fixed—tomorrow or any other day—I also have a laundry list of things that require my attention. Lunching with a gorgeous stranger is anxiety I don't need to worry about for the next twenty-four hours.

Who am I kidding? I'd replay that scenario for days and overthink it every time.

"I'm sorry for all of this," I say. "But I need to get going."

"Oh. Okay," he says warily. "You will get that checked out, right?"

I nod. "Yeah. Sure."

I turn toward my car door.

"Should we exchange contact information?" he asks. "Just in case? I'd like to check on you in a day or two and make sure you're all right."

I grab the handle and pause.

My heart betrays me. It beats harder, obviously affected by this gorgeous specimen named Oliver Mason with four brothers and a miracle mom. My body double-crosses me too, tingling from my hairline down to my toes. *I'd like you to make sure I'm all right too, Oliver Mason,* it cries.

I take a moment to breathe.

I haven't been attracted to anyone in so long. At first, it was because of the divorce. Six years of a marriage that blows up in your face will make you a little bitter about relationships. Then it was that my husband died before we could sign the papers. I wasn't in love with Luca anymore, but there's something about being a widow and not a divorcee that screws with you a little bit. And when you're suddenly saddled with a load of debt that your ex was supposed to take with him? That's fun—with every drop of sarcasm that will fit into the word.

Here I am, buzzing with an energy that's taking me by surprise—something I haven't experienced in years—on a day when it's apparent that I have no time nor space in my life for such luxuries as lunch with a cover model. This kind man doesn't need any more of my crazy.

"I'll be fine," I say, pulling the door open. "If you need my contact information for your insurance company, I use the local branch of Beach Bureau Insurance. They know me there."

He furrows his brow. The sun shines from behind him, illuminating him like a hero in a movie. His lips part and I hold my breath, both hoping he says something and wishing he won't.

He doesn't.

"Goodbye, Oliver," I say.

"Goodbye, Shaye ..."

His words drift off into the air as though maybe I'll capture them and volley them back again.

But I don't.

I climb inside my car and pull away before I can change my mind.

I don't even look back.

Chapter Two

Oliver

"It's about time you made it."

My youngest brother, Boone, launches the words in my direction before I have a chance to close the door.

The birthday party for Rosie, the little girl who my brother and his fiancée are in the process of adopting, has all but ended. There are three cars in the driveway, belonging to my mother, Boone, and his soon-to-be-wife, Jaxi.

"I'm sorry the car accident that I was just in inconvenienced you," I say, setting my keys on the table in the entryway.

"A car accident?" My mother appears out of thin air, clutching a glass of water with lemon. Her free hand touches her chest. "What are you talking about, Oliver?"

Boone stands in the living room off the foyer with his chin pointed at the ceiling. It's clear he didn't tell our mother about my fender bender.

This is going to be fun.

"Didn't Boone tell you, Mom?" I ask, widening my eyes for effect.

"Tell me what?" Mom looks at me, then at Boone, before settling her gaze on me once again. "Boone didn't tell me what, Oliver?"

"I'm late because a car slammed into me on the way over here."

Her hand drops to her side. "You're kidding."

I shake my head.

"Are you all right?" She looks me up and down. "Why didn't you call me?"

I look past her at Boone. "I told *him*. I figured he'd tell you."

She gives me a quick once-over as only a mother can. Apparently satisfied that I'm in one piece and no worse for wear, she pivots in a tight circle.

I smile at Boone over her shoulder. He rolls his eyes in return.

"How dare you not tell me, Boone Michael?" Mom says.

"Ooh, middle name. You're in trouble," I tease.

She snaps me a warning glare before turning back to Boone. I try my best not to chuckle but fail miserably.

"He was fine," Boone says as if the entire conversation exhausts him. "You would've just worried. *And he was fine.* Did I mention that?"

"It's my job to worry." She flips him a pointed look before turning her attention back to me again. "Was anyone hurt?"

Just my ego.

"Everyone is fine," I say, pressing a kiss to her cheek. And then, before she can poke any deeper, I head into the kitchen.

Even if I didn't know that Siggy Mason was here before I came into the kitchen, I would've known now.

An assortment of leftovers is in warming trays along the counter. I peek inside and find meatballs, egg noodles, and mini corn on the cob. There's a sliced pork loin because it's Boone's favorite and a big pan of mashed potatoes with golden butter melted on top.

On the island is a charcuterie board of cheeses, fruits, vegetables, and nuts. Mom has made these since we were kids. It amuses her that they're trendy now.

My hand shakes as I reach for a cracker. It's the slightest tremble. I toss a cracker on a plate stacked next to the board.

A long exhale whispers past my lips.

My insides still buzz from the adrenaline of the accident. My body still hums from the excitement of *her*.

Shaye Brewer is the epitome of what I love in a woman, what I'm attracted to. She's beautiful, of course, but in an effortless way. Her smile is contagious. She drips with an exceptional degree of warmth, a unique charm that has me wondering if we've met before.

Except I know we haven't. I would remember her.

As it is, I know nothing about her but her name. *Who is she? Where does she work? Is she married?*

I fill my plate with vegetables.

She has to be married. It's the only logical reason that she refused to give me her number.

Getting phone numbers is never an issue for me. Hell, I routinely get digits without asking for, or wanting, them.

The first time in ages that I want one? Naturally, I don't get it.

I chomp down on a carrot.

"Easy there," Boone says, coming into the room. "You might break a tooth."

I set the carrot down and feel my shoulders drop. The tension from the afternoon releases just a bit at being called out.

"How was the party?" I ask, hoping the change in topics will change the direction of my mood.

Boone slides up and on a barstool. "Solid ten out of ten. Fun fact should you ever need it—kids don't need petting zoos at their birthday parties. They're happy without it."

"Doubt I'll ever need that bit of information."

"You never know." Boone shrugs. "Mom was hell-bent on getting a donkey and a monkey and God knows what else, but Jaxi insisted that Rosie would be fine. Jaxi was right."

He smiles proudly.

"Where is the birthday girl, anyway?" I ask.

"In the bath. She has dog slobber and pink icing in her hair, and Jaxi was afraid she was going to fall asleep before she got it clean."

I smirk. "That's like the kid version of waking up in Vegas."

Boone laughs. "You know, I thought the same damn thing."

I laugh too as I spin a carrot in a blob of ranch dip. "Where is everyone else? I know I'm late, but I thought people would still be here."

"This is the beauty of preschool-aged parties. It's just family, and when kids get cranky, people leave." He motions toward the food spread. "When Mom is involved, we could feed an army and still have food left over."

"That's the truth." I lean against the counter. "Did Dad show up?"

That's all it takes for Boone's laughter to diminish. His jaw sets.

"I'll take that as a no." I bite off the end of the carrot. "What's his excuse this time?"

Boone shifts in his chair and releases a breath that's filled with disappointment.

I get it.

Our father has been a no-show at most family activities lately. It's not his lack of appearances that's surprising. Actually, that's the most consistent thing about him. The fact that he hasn't bothered to call any of us, particularly me, with any sense of regularity that's concerning.

And annoying.

"Mom said he took Gramps golfing in Myrtle Beach for a few days." Boone shrugs as if it doesn't bother him, but I know better. "I didn't press. Fuck him."

"Boone ..." I swallow back what I really want to say. It won't do anyone any good. "Let's reserve the *fuck him*s for non-family members. Okay?"

"He misses everything, Ollie. I bet he's seen Rosie twice since she came into our world. He doesn't call to play golf on the weekends or invite me to poker with the guys. Nothing."

Boone's face falls.

I toss the rest of the carrot back onto my plate and lean against the counter.

As frustrated as I have been with our dad for a few months now, I've never been more irritated than at this moment.

Growing up, Dad was hard on us. He pressured all of his sons to do everything and to do it all well. We were to exceed expectations, and we did. Holt, Wade, Coy, Boone, and I were All-Star baseball and football players. We took music lessons. We got excellent grades. His demands were irritating, but I could deal with them. We all dealt with them and saw the reasoning behind them. He wanted us to win. To succeed. And we all have—without question.

Even Boone.

But seeing the pain on my little brother's face because Dad is too busy fucking off to support him? That I can't deal with. That I don't understand. But I can't say all of that because it'll rile Boone up, and that will make matters worse.

"It's his loss," I say, trying my best to keep my tone free from the anger beginning to roll through me. "I know that's a cliché thing to say, but it's true."

"I know."

Boone rests his elbows on the island and, for the first time in his life, the levity that's always close to the surface with him is nowhere to be seen.

"Has Mom said anything about him not being here?" I ask. "Is she pissed too?"

He shakes his head. "I don't know. You know Mom. She's not about to show a split in the Mason household. She'll ride out a unified front until the end."

"Yeah."

I sigh. I don't know how or why Mom does it. I'd hoped things would be different when Dad retired a few years ago and that he would spend all of the time he typically spent in the office with her. She deserves that. Only, he didn't.

Instead of taking Mom to dinner, or helping Boone navigate fatherhood, or having Sunday dinners with his kids, he gallivants all over creation. He plays poker. He enters into fishing tournaments. He plays golf like I used to play travel baseball—like it's a fucking job. I get that he wants to enjoy his life. I just wish his enjoyment didn't come at our expense and that it didn't leave Mom on her own so much. I know she's blazed her own trail in life with her jewelry shop and all of that, but I think she's lonely.

"Anyway," Boone says with a grin, "on to more important matters—what did you get my girl for her birthday?"

"You're gonna love me," I say, grinning back.

His smile falters. "When you say things like that, it usually means I'm not gonna love you."

"I couldn't resist."

I scoop up a huge dollop of ranch on another carrot and toss it in my mouth. I watch him squirm while I chew. *Slowly.*

After I swallow and take a long drink of water from a bottle I find in the refrigerator, I put him out of his misery.

"I got her a battery-operated Escalade that she can ride in," I say, popping my collar. "It has a fucking radio in it and everything."

"Okay. That's cool."

"You're damn right it's cool. I'm determined to take over the favorite uncle role from Wade."

Boone rolls his eyes. "Well, good luck with that. I'm still trying to make her like me more than him, and I bought her a fucking puppy!"

I can't help but laugh.

"Boys, I'm heading home," Mom says, poking her head around the corner. "I have a big meeting in the morning about getting my jewelry into gift bags at a big music event in Nashville."

"Good luck," Boone tells her, hopping off his stool.

"If you need anything, just call." I walk across the room and kiss her cheek again. "Love you, Mom."

She pats the side of my face. "I love you, boys."

"We love you too." Boone kisses her other cheek. "Thank you for coming."

Mom's smile softens. "I wouldn't have missed it for the world." She looks at Boone and then back at me. "I'm so proud of you both. All of you, really."

"Nice of you to include Wade, although that wasn't necessary," Boone jokes.

I laugh as Mom taps Boone on the nose.

"Be nice," she tells him. "I'm going to tell my beautiful granddaughter and daughter-in-law goodbye. You two behave. And if you ever withhold information from me again, Boone ..."

Boone sticks out his lower lip. "I'm sorry, Mommy."

She laughs. "You're too cute for your own good. Good night, boys."

"Bye, Mom," I say.

"Good night, Mom," Boone says too.

She grins and turns away to find Jaxi and Rosie.

I head back to my plate on the island. Rosie's laughter filters down the hall as she apparently sees her Iggy, the nickname she uses for Mom. It's followed by Mom's voice mixing with Jaxi's.

This is a very different house than it was a few months ago when the only decorations were stacked ramen containers and the only sound was a sports channel that Boone forgot to turn off as he fell asleep when he should've been getting up for work.

"How does all of this feel?" I ask before taking a drink of my water.

"All of this what?" Boone asks, getting situated on the stool again.

"This." I look around the room, screwing the cap back on the bottle. "You're getting married. You basically have a kid. You own apartment complexes, for crying out loud. You even come into the office. *Regularly*. I've known you for almost thirty years, and I've only been certain that you're my brother for the last month."

"Very funny."

"I'm being serious." I drag a slice of bell pepper through the ranch. "Are you okay with all of this? It's a lot all at once."

I glance at him from the corner of my eye. He smiles softly.

"Yeah," he says. "I can't imagine my life any other way. She's ... my reason. *The* reason. It's like I fucked off for so long because I subconsciously knew that there was no point in getting serious about anything until Jaxi came along. That sounds stupid, I know."

The pepper crunches as I snap it in half. "It does."

He laughs. "You'll know someday."

"Eh."

I pick up another piece of bell pepper as my mind goes to Shaye. "I'm not sure I'll ever go the love and marriage route."

"I said that too."

I mean it though.

My brothers are starting to settle down. First, it was Holt. Then Coy. Now Boone. I'm happy for them. They've all found women who complement them in the best way. Women they can trust. Women who make them better men.

I'm just not built that way.

It's not that I don't want to be. *I've tried.* Every time I've attempted to trust a woman—or anyone besides my family, really—I've been reminded why I don't.

"You'll change your mind," Boone says smugly.

"I doubt it."

He picks up a napkin and folds it in half and then in half again. "You'll find someone you can't stop thinking about and, before you know it, you'll realize you'd do anything for her. I mean, I got a job, so anything is possible."

I can't help but laugh.

"And if that's not proving a point, I don't know what is." He looks up at me and laughs too. "So, is your car all messed up? Did you have to file an insurance claim? What's happening with all of that?"

My insides are jolted awake, and I squirm.

"Actually," I say, picking up the water bottle again just to keep my hands busy, "my car is fine. Mostly. No big deal."

My lips twitch. They want to smile in response to the vision of Shaye's reaction to the zip ties.

Boone, like the nosy little brother he's always been, furrows his brow.

"And?" he prods.

"And what?"

"And what aren't you telling me?"

I should blow him off and redirect him to something else. Something that doesn't involve Shaye. But he's astute enough to read the situation and will ultimately get his way. He's maddening like that.

"Just spit it out," he says.

I take a deep breath. "It turns out that the woman who hit me was hot."

Boone smirks.

"Like *super fucking hot*," I say, the words pouring out of my mouth like a broken dam. "I asked for her number. I even proposed it like I wanted to check on her and make sure she was okay."

He raises a brow. "You had to ask her for her number?"

"Yeah. And, get this—she didn't give it to me."

Boone's eyes light up. "She turned your ass down. You got shut down. *The* Oliver Mason got sat the fuck down."

"Oh, hold up." I hold up a hand. "It wasn't like that."

"That's what that is, Ollie. When a woman refuses to give you her number, she's turning you down."

I cross my arms over my chest. "She's probably married or something."

"Keep telling yourself that."

I will.

I set the bottle on the counter. "Is Rosie going to be out of the bath anytime soon?"

"She's out cold," Jaxi says, coming into the room. Her shirt is damp, and a dollop of icing is embedded in her hair near her ear. She looks completely and utterly happy. "Hi, Oliver."

"Hey, Jax."

"I didn't know you were here or I would've tried to keep her up," Jaxi says, wrapping an arm around Boone's waist. "She passed out on me as I was helping her get dressed. Her and Fluffy the puppy are snuggled up in bed."

Boone frowns as he peers down at his lady. "I thought we were using the crate at night."

"You go take the dog away from her."

"Not a chance." Boone laughs, nuzzling his cheek into Jaxi's hair. "You're the mean parent. I'm the fun one. Remember?"

"I absolutely do not remember that."

I shake my head at their antics as I set my plate into the sink.

"Well, if the princess is already asleep, I'm going to get out of here," I tell them. "Her present is on the porch. Boone will have to put it together."

"Gee, thanks," Boone says, rolling his eyes.

"I told you that you're gonna love me," I say.

Boone groans. "You should've avoided the car wreck and got here with that thing while Wade was here. He loves building shit."

"Again, I'm sorry my accident inconvenienced you." I make a face at him.

"You wouldn't have been on time anyway," Boone protests. "We were giving her the puppy when you called."

I sigh. "I lost track of time. My office is a fucking wasteland of shit not getting done and I got neck-deep in reports. I'm sorry—for real. I should've come straight here from the house."

"Thank you for coming," Jaxi says as she untangles herself from Boone. "I appreciate you being here."

"We're family. It's what we do."

I pause to take in my youngest brother. I can see a blip of sadness about Dad not being here and it causes my chest to tighten.

"Hey, Boone," I say.

He raises a brow.

"Fuck Dad." I punch him in the arm as I walk by.

"See you in the office tomorrow," he says.

He's smiling when I turn around.

"That's still so weird coming from you," I say.

He grins as he hops off the stool. "Holt said that human resources is interviewing for your executive administrative assistant position tomorrow and he'll see if he can find someone to work for me too." His grin grows wider. "I'm going to have my very own secretary."

I roll my eyes. "Welcome to the big leagues, kid."

His laughter follows me to the door. I give them both a little wave before stepping outside into the cool evening air.

I make my way to my car, my stomach rumbling from the lack of an actual dinner and wonder why I didn't just box up some food from the party. But as soon as my gaze lands on the damage to my Rover, my thoughts whisk away from food.

My body turns its attention elsewhere as my conversation with Shaye filters through my brain.

"I was thinking about what you were going to do with those."

I groan as I climb into my car. "Shaye, you have no fucking idea."

The engine comes to life with the push of a button.

"No fucking idea," I repeat as I put the car in reverse and back down the driveway. "And that's wholly irritating."

I slam the car into drive, leaving a blast of rubber on the road behind me.

Chapter Three

Shaye

"I'm sorry I'm late," I say to no one in particular.

The storage area to The Gold Room is a wreck. The supplies that were delivered on Friday still sit in cardboard boxes—well, most of them. Some of them spill over onto the floor. Pantry items are askew on the large metal shelves along the wall and something wet with a blue shine has pooled under the shelf where we keep the dish soap.

"This is wonderful," I mumble, trying not to break my neck on the slick surface.

I hang my purse in the locker with my name spelled out with children's magnets and then slam it. The sound must echo through the kitchen because Nate's head pops around the corner.

"Thank fuck you're here," he says, annoyance embedded on his handsome features. "I was getting ready to come looking for you."

I smile because he would've done exactly that.

Nate Hughes is good people. We met at a bar—ironically not his bar, The Gold Room. It was late one night a few months ago and I was at an impasse. Tequila sounded like an acceptable answer. It was as good of a solution as any in my clouded, this-may-as-well-be-total-rock-bottom moment. Nate and his brother, Dominic, just happened to be there. Before the night was over, Nate had quietly labeled me as one of his tribe—a ragtag bunch of misfits, for the most part—and offered me a part-time job.

I accepted. The rest is history.

"I would've left to avoid this mess too." I wrinkle my nose as I look around the room. "What the hell happened here?"

"Murray." Nate gives me a pointed look as he fills the doorway with his broad shoulders. "He was in one of his moods and tried to start shit with Paige over a fish sandwich. Things got a little ... heated."

Imagine that. "And messy, it appears."

The corner of his lip twitches. "It's not as bad as it could've been. I didn't break his face."

I shake my head. We both know he'd never hurt Murray. Murray is like a son to him, despite the fact that Nate's not actually old enough to be his dad.

"I fired him," he says, as if this shores up his point. "I love the guy, but he can't act a fool to Paige. I won't have it."

"So he'll be back, when? Tomorrow?"

"Probably not until Friday." He smiles sheepishly. "He'll be out of money and full of apologies by then."

"You're weak, Hughes. Weak."

He laughs and steps into the room. "Forget Murray. How are *you*? Any broken bones? Do I need to go hunt anyone down?"

My skin tingles as I think about Oliver.

It's such a shame that the universe wasted a perfectly good meet-cute on me.

"I'm fine," I say. "My car is currently held together by zip ties though."

As if on cue, images of Oliver and his unintentional smolder fires through my brain. I wonder vaguely if I'm always going to have a Pavlovian reaction to the word *zip ties*.

My stomach clenches.

There could be worse things to endure.

"I'm fine," I reiterate.

Nate's brow furrows. "Okay. Want me to look at your car?"

"Nah," I say, taking a waist apron off a shelf. "It'll be fine."

I tie the apron around my middle and ignore Nate's piercing gaze. He doesn't say a word but he doesn't have to. I know what he's thinking.

Nate's irritation over my refusal to accept help from anyone is no secret. His heart is as big as his shoulders and rebuffing his attempts to help never goes over smoothly. But I love that about him.

"Hey, I have some good news for you." I fiddle with the ties at the small of my back. "Your girl here has a job interview tomorrow. And that's a damn good thing because the temp job the staffing company told me they had for me—the one at the Creamery? They made a mistake."

"That sucks."

"Yeah. But the good news part of this is that one of the resumes I sent out over the past couple of weeks panned out and I have an interview in the morning."

Nate smiles. "That *is* good news as long as that means I won't lose you around here."

"I'm not going anywhere. This is the only night job I'll ever have."

"Good."

I laugh as my hands fall to my sides. "Trust me when I tell you that working two jobs—three if I can find a third that can coordinate with the other two—is not where I wanted to be at thirty years old. I'll require this second job for the foreseeable future."

He takes a deep breath almost as if he already regrets what he's about to say and Nate Hughes regrets very little of what comes out of his mouth.

My nerves fizzle back to life as I open my locker. I don't need more lip gloss but I also don't need to stand in front of him like a target waiting to be shot.

Just as I put the cap back on the tube, he sighs.

"Dominic told you that Camilla could help you," he says warily.

I fire a glare over my shoulder. "Stop."

"Come on, Shaye. Think about it."

I slam my locker again. It causes the *y* magnet to fall to the floor.

I level my gaze with my boss. *My friend.* I know he means well. His heart is as big as his shoulders. But I just wish he'd stop.

Nate's features soften as he marches over my line in the sand. I've drawn it more than once. My problems are *my problems*—whether they actually are or not. Tangling money with friendships is never, ever a good idea.

Not ever. In the history of evers.

"Dom's girlfriend is loaded," he says. "And Camilla has this intense need to help people—which I don't understand. If I had her money, I'd just live on an island by my damn self and roll around in it."

"Oh right. Sure."

"I would."

I press my lips together. "Nate, you aren't loaded and you give free ham sandwiches out like you own a pig farm. Don't try to sell me that *I'd just live on an island by my damn self* bullshit. We both know that isn't true."

He tries to stay stone-faced but it doesn't last. Finally, he cracks. "Fine. But this isn't about me or ham sandwiches. It's about you and the way you refuse to let someone give you a loan that will never miss the money."

I turn on my heel and start picking up the mess scattered across the floor.

"Will you at least think about it?" he asks, coming up beside me and picking up a box. "You work yourself to the bone. You live in a neighborhood that's getting shittier by the day—no offense."

"None taken."

He puts the box on a shelf before leaning against it. "And you are paying a debt that's not even yours."

I grind my teeth together and stare at him.

I can't be mad at him for speaking the truth. But I can be pissed at the way hearing it out loud makes me feel.

My blood runs hot with anger but my chest squeezes in pain. It's the worst kind of pain too. It's the kind of hurt that comes from so many places that you know you'll never be able to fix it. There's no antidote for it.

Nate takes a step toward me. "No one deserves to be saddled with a one-hundred-thousand-dollar bill that they didn't run up."

I reach for another box. "I went along with it, so it's mine. Plain and simple."

"It's not that plain or simple."

"Okay, true. But no one else needs to have the burden thrust on them. I'm not making this someone else's problem."

"Luca sure as hell made it fucking yours."

I tuck the box at my side and face him head-on. The bridge of my nose tickles like it does just before my eyes start to water. I pinch it with two fingers.

Of all the friends to find at the end of a shitty day, I'm thankful that I found Nate. But he doesn't always get that when you're used to doing life on your own, it's hard to rely on others—even kind souls that chose you as family.

"Nate, buddy, I appreciate your big-brother act and all but—"

"It's not a fucking act, Shaye." His voice is as solid as a rock. "You have no one in the universe to go to bat for you. My bat is big enough to take care of you too."

I know how he means it, but I can't resist. It's a good way to defuse the situation and avoid tears.

"How many women have you used that line on?" I tease, dropping my hand from my nose to my side.

He sighs in frustration, but smiles nonetheless.

"Look," I say, putting another box on the end of the shelf, "I'm fine. I'm going to be fine. Everyone has to work for a living. I'll just be working two jobs until the day I die."

I watch him out of the corner of my eye. He wants to argue with me. But, slowly, I watch him relent.

Thank God.

"Speaking of working for a living, let's get to it." I find a towel perched on top of a stack of cups. "Is Paige still here?"

He nods. "Yeah. The dining room is pretty slow though. Would you mind cleaning this up? I can circle back in a few and help you, but I need to run a couple of errands."

"Go. I'm good. It'll be easier if you stay out of my way."

"You just want me to stay away so I won't talk to you."

"No," I say, tossing the towel on the floor next to the spill. "It's just a fortunate side effect."

He chuckles. "I wonder why I like you sometimes."

"Same, Nate. Same."

He flashes me a boyish grin and disappears through the doorway.

I kneel and gather random lids that are scattered under the shelves. The process gives me a moment to collect my thoughts—and emotions—too.

My heart is still tender. I massage it absentmindedly as I think about what Nate said.

You have no one in the universe to go to bat for you.

I force a swallow down my throat and set my jaw in place. My teeth ache as I clamp them together in a form of determination.

Nate is right. I have no one on my side in the world. And I'll be well served to remember that.

The only two people I've ever really trusted to be on my side one hundred percent are my mother and Luca. Both were a mistake.

Mom took Luca's side when we split, accusing me of being spoiled. She refused to understand that Luca had been so careless about our finances that I struggled to pay the utilities most months. She wouldn't hear about him shoving me against a wall when I threatened to leave or taking my keys with him to work so I couldn't go anywhere. She didn't care that I didn't love him anymore and that I wasn't sure he ever really loved me.

And, when he crashed his car and died? She blamed that on me too.

We haven't spoken since.

I put a stack of lids into a box at my side and let my hand rest on the edge. The cardboard bites into my wrist.

It's sad that I feel more comfortable alone in life than with my family. It hurts my heart. But admitting the truth is the first step in moving on from trauma. At least, that's what I read.

"I'm going to be fine," I say quietly, pulling my hand back from the box. "I'm in control. I'm in the driver's seat."

My lips break out into a half-smile, half-grimace as I think about the last time I was in an actual driver's seat.

Oliver's smile slips into my brain, sweeping out thoughts of Mom and Luca.

I sit back on my heels. A sigh topples from my lips.

My arms cross over my chest and I snuggle into my shoulder, unable to remove the grin from my face. I search through our interaction—not with the fine-tooth comb I will use tonight, I'm sure—and try to find something, anything to indicate that he was annoyed. Or irritated. Or frustrated.

And I come up with nothing.

Could he really be remarkably handsome and unwaveringly kind? Does that kind of guy really even exist?

I drop my arms and shrug. Who knows? Not me and I never will. By the time I get my act together, all the good men in the world will be scooped up.

My knees scream as I get to my feet and get back to work, but that can't matter. As Nate pointed out, I have an enormous debt to pay. And, as they say, *life goes on*.

Well, debt does, anyway.

Chapter Four

Oliver

"That's never going to work." I rub my forehead and listen to Greg, our construction manager, deliver his spiel over the phone. "Look, I don't mean to cut you off here, but that's simply not going to work."

My leather chair squeaks as I lean back and gaze out of my office windows. The sun is shining brightly just above the buildings to the East. I love watching it rise—slowly inching its way into the sky like a lazy yawn. Some people meditate. Some go to church. I watch the sun rise.

But not today.

Today, I missed it. It's evident in my mood.

"I'll tell you what," I say, taking advantage of Greg's pause, "email me a bullet point list of everything you just said and I'll go over it with Holt today. I don't think it's going to work, but we'll see what he thinks."

"Will do. I know it's more than we bargained for, but I don't see another solution."

"There's always another solution, Greg."

"I can't find it for the life of me."

That's why I'm the boss. "Then we make one."

"Okay, Mr. Mason."

Greg's voice is defeated, which wasn't my intention. I want our guys in the field to feel confident. Confident people do better work. But I don't have the time, nor the energy, to coddle anyone today.

"Email me," I tell him. "I need to go."

"You got it. Goodbye, sir."

I end the call and sit up, my chair screaming again. The sound grates on my nerves. I unlock my computer screen to send an email to my assistant to buy me a new one when I realize I don't have one. Or, rather, I do but she's overwhelmed.

Irritation sweeps through me like a wildfire.

I punch a couple of buttons on my desk phone.

"Yes, Mr. Mason?" Toni, the head of human resources, asks.

"Good morning, Toni. I need an update on the administrative issue in my office, please."

"Yes, sir. Not a problem." Papers shuffle in the background. "We are in the process of hiring you an executive assistant. We'll leave Kelly to oversee the office as a whole and we'll move Miriam over to assist Holt. Also, I'm on the lookout for an EA for Boone, too. Someone *tough* is what Holt suggested."

The plan soothes my displeasure enough to stop the start of a migraine behind my left eye.

"I have a few candidates coming in this morning," she says. "Here's hoping they are as good in real life as they are on paper."

They never are. "Yeah. Okay. Thanks, Toni. Please keep me in the loop."

"I will, sir."

I lift the handset and then sit it back down.

My chair squeaks *again* as I lean back and try to center myself. The morning has been a shit show with problems from job sites that Greg can't handle, issues with contracts from the legal department, and the disarray in the front office.

And I missed the sunrise.

I sigh.

My gaze falls to the stack of papers—contracts, purchase orders, invoices—that need my signature. It's not as easy as it used to be. *Just as harried, but not as simple.* When our former secretary retired, everything fell apart. Suddenly, no one knew anything despite all the training in the world. The day she left felt like the first day of work for everyone else.

We've never recovered.

Miriam and Kelly do a decent job, but they aren't equipped to handle three Masons in one office now that Boone has decided to actually work. Miriam and Holt get along well, so he'll use her exclusively. Kelly is great but we don't really vibe on a level that will work out on that kind of EA level.

The light on my desk phone flickers and a buzz resonates through the room. Holt's extension flashes on the screen.

I press the speakerphone button. "Yeah?"

"Did Greg call you?" he asks.

"Yeah."

"You sound optimistic."

"It's not gonna work, Holt. There's no fucking way. By the time you factor in—"

"I know." He chuckles. "How much coffee have you had today?"

I glance at the three mugs on my desk. "Enough."

His chuckle grows louder.

"This version of you is annoying," I tell him, plucking the top file off the stack at the corner of my desk.

"What version?"

"The …" I grimace, even though he can't see me. "The *happy* one."

The bastard laughs even louder.

"Call me back when you're a prick," I tell him. "It makes me feel better about myself when I'm the nice one."

"Just go see Wade. That'll fix it."

My lips turn upward. "At least you're still logical."

"I'm a *happy* logic. That's what a good woman will do for you."

Just like that, I grimace again.

There's so much to be vexed about in that sentence—some of which I might've worked out in sunrise therapy this morning.

I tug at my collar. Happiness. A good woman. The concept that my life is lacking in any way—it's all annoying and it's been annoying well before Holt called me this morning.

A bubble sitting in my stomach kept me from finding any peace all night.

I snacked. I worked out. I snacked again.

A shot of whiskey never hurt anyone and it didn't hurt, nor help, me last night. The hot tub wasn't the answer. My sheets were nestled at the foot of my bed in a giant ball when I woke up this morning.

Throughout all of this, one voice filtered through my brain.

"Goodbye, Oliver."

Out of everything Shaye said to me yesterday, this was the one sentence that ricocheted through my brain. It was almost a taunt, a challenge—even though I don't think she meant for it to be.

I think she genuinely was concluding our interaction as if we will never see each other again.

And why would we? We're two strangers who met in a freak sneeze accident that may be the first of its kind.

But, then again, maybe that was some kind of universe interference? Maybe we were supposed to meet. It certainly feels like it.

I scowl at myself for unearthing this line of thinking. It's stupid. It's pointless. It's a waste of damn time.

My fingers strum against my desktop.

"Are you?" Holt asks, shaking me out of my reverie.

I shift my weight and refocus. "Am I what?"

"Never mind. Obviously, you're not."

"Okay. I'm not."

He laughs, which amplifies my irritation again.

"I heard you had a car wreck yesterday," he says, a smile buried in the words.

I roll my eyes. "Word travels fast."

"What can I say? Boone is quick."

I roll my eyes.

"Naturally, I also know that the woman refused to give you her number," he goads.

"She was married."

Even though I don't know that to be true, it seems like the fastest way to shut him down.

It also makes me feel better.

That one little possibility—that I have no reason to believe due to no mention of a husband and no ring on her finger—is my saving grace. And not just for my ego.

It's what dampened the burn inside me to find her.

A hand goes to my head and I scratch at my scalp.

I've fought all morning not to think about Shaye. Each time she started to slip into my mind, I shoved her right back out. But now that Holt has placed her in the forefront of this conversation, the nugget in my gut that I fought with all night is back.

"You being quiet is concerning," Holt says.

"Yeah, well ..."

I frown.

My thoughts remind me of a hurricane, tumbling over themselves so fast and hard that it's impossible to make any real sense of it. I don't know why I keep thinking about her. This isn't a problem I encounter often. Or ever. I can push a woman out of my brain and focus on work like the CEO that I am.

Sure, she was gorgeous. And funny. And charming in an entertaining kind of way. It also probably didn't hurt that she didn't fawn over me. I like a chase as much as the next guy. But, in reality, I'm sure it was just the fact that I'm not sure if she was okay or if she got her car checked.

Yeah. I'm sure that is it.

"I'll give you a pass," Holt says. "What are we doing about Greg?"

I blow out a breath. "I don't know. I think we need to go out there and take a look at the Jewell site and see what he's overlooking. There has to be a better way to get in and out of there."

"Probably a good idea. You free around four?"

I fiddle with my keyboard until my screen awakens. My calendar is splashed in front of me. "Yeah."

"I'll drive. Meet me in the parking garage at four."

"Okay."

"Also," he says, "I was just in Toni's office. She's interviewing a handful of possible assistants this morning for you. I told her to weed them out and send you copies of any of the resumes that might work."

I open the folder in front of me and take out an invoice. "Yeah. I talked to her this morning."

"One more thing." He clears his throat. "The Landry family sent an invitation over on Friday for the annual Landry Charity Gala."

"Can I just send a check?"

"Negative. Blaire and I are going since her brother, Walker, will be in town for it. That means you have to go too."

I scan the invoice in front of me. I slap my signature in bold, black ink in the red box, thus approving payment for a new accounting software system.

"You're the family representative. I think that gives me a pass," I say.

"This is good press, Ollie."

"This is a pain in the ass," I mutter.

He sighs. "It's Saturday, so make plans. I'll see you at four."

The line clicks, and he's gone.

I glance up at my computer screen as a purple-colored box magically appears on my calendar.

Landry Family Gala—Saturday, 6p.m. EST

"Fucker," I mumble.

My stomach growls, desperate for something other than more coffee. I check my watch and see that it's nearly lunchtime.

I toss my pen on my desk and reach for the phone but pause. My hand dangles in the air.

In another time, before the administrative mess in our office, I would've asked my assistant to order me lunch. I wouldn't have to tell her what I wanted or where from. She'd know. But as my gaze flips to the door that separates my office from the reception area, I know that time has passed.

"I can't work like this," I say to an empty office. "I need help."

I grab a mug of cold coffee and march to the door.

"Good morning, Mr. Mason," Kelly says from her perch at the large black marble desk that faces the elevator. "Can I get you anything?"

"No, thank you, Kelly." I nod to the other two women standing at her desk. I also ignore the hearts in their eyes. "Hold my calls, please."

"Of course, sir," Kelly says.

I hit the button on the elevator and try not to acknowledge the weight of their eyes on me. As soon as the doors open, I step inside and punch the floor for human resources.

My stomach growls again as I descend to the fourth floor.

The doors pull apart, and I step into the lobby. Genevieve smiles brightly from the front desk.

"Hello, Mr. Mason," she says.

"Is Toni in her office?"

"Yes, sir."

"Thanks."

My coffee sloshing in the cup, I head down a long hallway to the right. Offices pass on my right, and two large conference rooms are on my left. As I pass the second one, my feet falter.

I step closer to the half-closed blinds and peer inside the room.

My body knows what, or whom, I see before my brain registers it.

I draw in a quick, heated breath as goose bumps prickle my skin. My stomach knots. My heartbeat picks up in to a frenzied pace.

Sitting at the table is her. *Shaye.*

I shift my weight from one foot to the other.

Her chestnut-colored hair falls in loose waves around her shoulders instead of the messy bun she wore yesterday. Her lips are a pretty pink. From this angle, her cheekbones look wildly high and the apples of her cheeks round and rosy.

She focuses on a piece of paper in front of her.

What is she doing here?

"Mr. Mason?" Toni's voice says from somewhere to my right. It snaps me back to reality. "Can I help you? Genevieve said you were on your way back to see me."

Shaye moves, her head beginning to turn to face me. I step away from the window toward Toni.

"Is that where you're holding interviews?" I ask, jamming a thumb toward the conference room behind me.

"Yes."

A hot swallow passes down my throat and drops into an acidy stomach.

My mind races, calculating possibilities that this woman would randomly show up in my life twice in as many days.

Surely, that's a harbinger. Hopefully, a good one.

I ignore the scream in my brain that's as loud as my squeaky chair—the one telling me that I know better than to do what I'm about to do, that it's against every rule I've ever made about work—and do it anyway.

Chapter Five

Shaye

"Calm down," I whisper, chastising myself.

My insides bubble as I try to ignore the hum of energy coursing through my body. I take a long, deep breath and blow it out in the steadiest exhale I can muster.

Am I anxious? Is it the anticipation of the interview that's getting to me? Is it the desperation? Regardless, waiting for Toni Brooks to arrive is getting to me.

The paper handed to me by the sweet receptionist sits in front of me. It lists the job duties of the executive assistant role, the hours required, and a salary window that's dependent upon experience.

It all looks great. The experience is an easy checkoff. I'd work twelve-hour days at this point if they needed me to. And the salary? I'd work happily for half of what they're offering.

This job appears to be everything I've hoped to find. *I just have to convince Ms. Brooks that I'm the person they need.*

The sound of the door opening catches my attention.

"Good morning, Ms. Brewer." A woman dressed in a crisp white button-down tucked into a neat black pencil skirt walks toward me. "I'm Toni Brooks."

I push my chair back and stand. "It's nice to meet you. Thank you for the opportunity to interview with you."

She shakes my hand and then sits across from me. I, too, take my seat.

"I'm sorry to keep you waiting," she says, setting a folder down and then clasping her hands together on top of it. "I had an impromptu meeting a few moments ago, and it put me a touch behind schedule."

She presses her lips as if she's trying to hide a smile.

"Of course," I say, speaking slowly so I don't ramble.

"Tell me a little bit about yourself."

I clear my throat. "I worked as an EA for five years, most recently for Monroe Companies here in Savannah. I managed the schedules and communications for the CEO, as well as coordinated travel, assisted in various special projects, and prepared information for meetings with staff."

Toni smiles.

"I'm a good communicator, can juggle multiple tasks at once, and I'm discreet and professional. Always," I say, straightening my posture. "I take pride in my work and approach all projects with enthusiasm and optimism."

A bead of sweat trickles down my spine. *I hope I wore deodorant.*

Toni nods. "That's great. Now tell me a little about *you*, Ms. Brewer."

I squirm in my seat. My mind races as I try to figure out what she wants to hear.

"Don't overthink it," she says nicely. "Just tell me a little about yourself. Give me an idea as to how you, as a person, would fit in here."

Toni's eyes shine with sincerity. I still don't know how to answer this question, but I have to say something.

"Well," I say, tucking a strand of hair behind my ear, "I just turned thirty a month ago, and I've found myself at an *interesting* place in my life. I'm not where I thought I would be, if I'm being honest. Not that I ever really knew where I would be. I wasn't the kind of little girl who knew what she wanted to do with her life when she was ten. My mom thought I was going to be a vagrant, I think."

I force a swallow. I know I'm word vomiting, but I can't turn it off.

"I'm motivated," I say, trying to read Toni's reaction. "I love setting goals and exceeding them. I'd love to find a business where I can settle down and meaningfully contribute. Make a home, so to speak. And then go to my actual home and rest a little bit."

Toni's head tilts to the side. "Thank you for your honesty."

"You're welcome."

She watches me for a long moment, and I fight an urge to squirm. I can't tell what she's thinking—only that she's thinking *something*.

Finally, she picks up the papers in front of her. "I want you to meet someone." She gets to her feet. "Just sit right there, please."

"Sure."

My face heats as I watch her leave the room.

The song overhead reminds me of the Dua Lipa song that's been stuck in my head all morning. I try to focus on that and not how I might have just ruined my chance at this job.

I knew the *Tell me about yourself* question was loaded. It's some magic trickery that interviewers use to get to know you. I've read dozens of articles about it and how to prepare an answer ahead of time to dazzle them.

"Now tell me a little about you, Ms. Brewer."

I had it until that moment—until it turned to *me*.

My eyes fall closed. I consider emailing Mr. Monroe, my old boss, and asking if he's looking for anyone. He liked me. I'm sure of it. He just couldn't wait on me to get my shit together after Luca passed away almost three years ago. I couldn't blame him for that.

The door handle clicks as it swings open.

I heave in a deep breath. But instead of settling me down and helping me prepare for the second part of the interview, something else entirely happens.

My senses are overloaded with the warm scent of amber and tobacco.

I gulp.

With every cell in my body on high alert, I turn my head toward the door.

I gulp again—this time harder.

Oliver Mason, the man I hit with my car only yesterday, is standing in the doorway looking like nothing less than a magazine cover. A pair of khaki pants hug his thick thighs, and a leather belt showcases his trim waist. A black button-down shirt shows off his broad shoulders. A plaid tie with subtle hints of yellow ties the entire look together.

He shuts the door behind him, keeping his eyes trained on me.

I can't help but look anywhere else.

The air crackles around us, getting thicker and hotter by the second. He's one item in the room, but somehow, it seems like he fills it. Everything else takes a back seat to his presence.

"Hello, Shaye," he says, wrapping his voice around my name.

"Hi, Oliver." My statement is much more a question than a statement. It's a *why in the world are you here* more than a hello.

He walks to the table and stops at the chair Toni was sitting in. He grips the back of it with both hands. There's no confusion in his eyes— just pure confidence.

Damn.

"I ... I'm confused," I admit.

His lips twitch.

My brain scrambles to understand this situation. How could I run into this man again? It's not possible—not by coincidence.

Then slowly, it occurs to me.

"You *are* a cop, aren't you?" I ask, lifting my chin.

His brows pull together.

"I thought it yesterday with the zip ties." My face flushes as—*snap, snap snap!*—the pieces fall in place. "But then you played that off really well, and I didn't think much more about it. Because I haven't done anything wrong. I'm a law-abiding citizen. I only went along with not calling the police yesterday because *you* suggested it. So, if you're here to arrest me for leaving the scene of a crime ..." I swallow back a lump in my throat. "Please don't. I have enough problems."

His lips part, and a solitary laugh escapes them. "What on earth are you talking about?"

The confusion on his face seems genuine.

I slink back in my chair. "I mean ... I've watched crime television. It's not beyond the realm of possibility."

The smile that breaks across his face leaves me speechless. It's wide and refreshing, and I wonder how anyone can think with him around.

"Don't you think it's much more plausible that I work here?" he asks.

"I bet that department doesn't get much done," I mutter to myself.

His gaze picks mine up and holds it midair. It causes my stomach to flip-flop.

He grins again. "What was that?"

"Nothing."

He pulls out a chair and sits down, relaxing back into the seat and crossing one ankle over his other knee. It's like he has all the time in the world.

"Where's Toni?" I ask, glancing quickly at the door.

He shrugs. "Hopefully doing her job. That's what I pay her to do."

"I ..."

That's what I pay her to do.

My mouth closes.

He bites his lip, clearly amused, as I begin to sort through the situation. It's a clumsy process full of possibilities and disbelief, and by the time I work everything out, Oliver is downright entertained.

Finally, I lean forward against the table. My cheeks are on fire, and my palms are sweaty.

"So, what you're saying is ..." But I can't get the words out. It still feels too unbelievable.

"I'll help." He leans against the table too. I think he's teasing me by mirroring my posture, but I'm not sure. "Do you remember my name?"

"Oliver Mason." *I've only thought about it a dozen times since yesterday.*

"Good. Now, did you happen to see the words printed on large, copper-colored letters on the arch above the entrance when you arrived here today?"

I nod. Slowly. "Mason Limited." I suck in a breath. "So that would make you ..."

"CEO." He considers this. "Co-CEO. My brother Holt and I share the position. But I'm much better at it than he is."

"Oh, good God."

He laughs.

I sit back again, needing a bit of space. "You're telling me that I just happened to show up to a job interview at a company that you own on the day after I hit you with my car?"

He sits back too and shrugs. "Seems like it."

"How is that possible?"

"Crazier things have happened," he says, the words slightly defensive.

"Okay. Like what?"

It's a rhetorical question, but he seems to take it as a challenge. His brows pull together, and a smile ghosts his lips. He looks entirely too comfortable.

"Well, Pepsi had the sixth biggest army in the world for a hot minute," he says easily as if he has this kind of information poised and ready to go.

"Pepsi? The soda company?"

He nods.

"Huh," I say, mostly because I didn't expect him to start giving me examples.

"A woman survived the sinking of the *Titanic and* both of its sister ships," he says, the words a breeze. "Think about those odds."

I don't think about anything. I just look at him.

"Franz Ferdinand escaped one assassination attempt," he tells me. "Then his driver took a wrong turn, and they wound up in front of a random assassin who killed him."

I cock my head to the side and try to orient myself to this conversation. "I ... that's some bad luck." That's all I can come up with. I still haven't gotten past the fact he's here.

"For all of us. That started World War I." He watches me closely. "With all that being said, the fact that you showed up today isn't all that preposterous, is it?"

I frown. He makes it hard to think with his face and his body and apparently his brain now too.

"Toni tells me that you're highly qualified to be my assistant," he says and then runs his tongue around the inside of his cheek.

"*Your* assistant?"

He nods. I wait for him to laugh or chuckle—for someone to pop through the door and yell, "*Gotcha!*"—but none of that happens. He just strums his fingertips against his knee and watches me like a CEO.

I take a deep breath. Slowly, my heartbeat returns to its natural rhythm. I imagine coming to work and dealing with him all day. True, there are worse ways to spend a solid eight to ten hours a day, but I'm not sure I'm equipped to deal with it—*with him.*

"Should we talk salary?" he asks.

The room begins to spin—or maybe it's the walls that seem to close in on us, I'm not sure. I grab the sides of my chair.

I redirect my attention toward a painting to the right of Oliver's head. It's some abstract art piece with streaks of paint dotting the canvas as though someone took a paint brush and flicked them in that direction. It's not nearly as interesting as I make it out to be.

"What kind of position are you looking for?" he asks, changing tactics.

"Something stable." I gather my courage and let my gaze find his again. I can almost feel my brain cells misfire. "Something challenging."

So far, so good.

Oliver slides the paper from Genevieve toward me. "Have you had time to look at this?"

I nod.

"Is this in your wheelhouse?" he asks.

I scan the list of job duties again. "Of course. I've done all of that before. None of it would be a problem."

"That's great. I think you seem like a good fit for us."

I raise my hand to my lips, touching them briefly, before dropping it back to my lap.

"You've asked me one question—two, maybe," I point out. "Excuse me for saying this, but how do you know I'd be a good fit here?"

"First instincts." His features remain perfectly calm. "I've been in business long enough—had enough assistants and co-workers—to know when I have chemistry with someone and when I don't. It's imperative that exists between two people who will work as closely together as I will work with my assistant."

Fair enough.

"And I think you and I will work together very well," he says, his voice growing deeper.

His gaze sears into me. It's so heavy, so hot, that I have to look away.

He's right, of course. There is a definite connection between us. It's a ripple of energy present every time we're together. And while I'm sure chemistry is necessary in the executive office, I'm not sure it should feel like this.

A job interview shouldn't borderline feel like a date. It shouldn't feel like we're about to walk outside, get in his car, and go to dinner. And it sure as hell shouldn't feel like we're one errant look—one misfire of the energy between us—away from being naked and sweaty on this conference room table.

I take a deep breath. Oliver's attention sits squarely on me. It's perfectly professional on the surface, but the heat that lies just beneath the exterior crackles. *He wants me here.* Or does he just want me?

Can I do this?

I can't do this.

I need a real, bill-paying job again. My savings are depleted, all extra expenditures have been cut, and the piddly life insurance from Luca has been gone for a while. I'm up shit creek without a paddle, but is this the paddle I've been looking for?

As I look at Oliver sitting across from me and feel a tingle in my belly, I'm not sure that Mason Limited is the right answer.

I have to be honest with myself. I'm *very* attracted to him. It would be so much easier if I wasn't.

Oliver takes a pen out of the container on the table and scribbles on the back of the job description. Then he slides the paper toward me again. The number written is exactly in the middle of the salary window —an amazing offer. Not at all where I thought it would be.

He raises a brow. "That's our offer. Start time would be as soon as you're able."

I blow out a breath. "That's very generous."

"Of course, we will reassess it on your first review," he says. "We need great people to be able to do great things. We pay our employees fairly."

My smile wobbles. "Mr. Mason," I begin, unsure about what to call him now, "I appreciate your faith in me. But I'll need a bit of time to think about it."

He wasn't expecting this. His lips press together, his brows tug into a mass in the middle of his forehead.

"I can get back to you in a couple of days," I offer.

He nods curiously. "Sure. Not a problem." He pauses, watching me carefully before rolling his chair back. "Do you have any questions for me? I'm happy to answer any questions you may have."

I shake my head and get to my feet. "No, I think I'm clear on everything. Thank you for taking the time to talk to me today."

"Here." He hands me a business card as he stands. "Call me. My personal cell number is on there. If you have any questions at all, let me know. I'd be happy to discuss anything you might need to talk through."

His fingers brush against mine as I take the black card from him. It sends a zip of electricity through my body. He holds my gaze a moment longer than necessary, the intensity infiltrating my defenses and settling deep inside my core before turning toward the door.

I wait as he pulls it open, letting the cool office air inside the room. We step into the hall but turn toward each other instead of going our separate ways.

He smiles. My heart flutters in my chest.

"Do you need me to see you out?" he asks.

"I'll just ... go out the way I came." I look over my shoulder and see the receptionist watching us from her desk. "Genevieve is waiting on me, I think."

He glances over my shoulder and then back at me. "Genevieve needs to mind her own business."

I laugh, relieved at the effortless way the easiness between us returns.

He dips his head and peers into my eyes. "I think we could be a good team, Shaye."

"Maybe."

He smirks and shakes his head. "Fair enough. Talk soon."

"Goodbye, Oliver."

I nod and give him a little smile before turning on my heel. My eyes meet Genevieve's. She whips her head back to her computer screen and pretends not to have been watching.

But I get it.

Oliver Mason is hard not to stare at.

I have a half of a notion to turn around and stare at him again too.

Chapter Six

Oliver

"How the hell are we going to pull this off?" Holt plops a finger onto the set of plans spread out on the hood of his truck. "This project is a nightmare already. Leave it to Boone."

"So we're blaming this on Boone?" I ask.

"Yeah. Why not?"

"Hey, I'm not saying I'm ever against blaming shit on Boone," I say with a shrug. "I just wanted to be clear."

"Yes. We're pinning this on him."

"Cool."

We exchange a smile.

Holt and I face a large dirt lot. We purchased this parcel from the Landry's last year for a new retail area. After some permit issues and a few tweaks to meet accepted green building methods—an agreement we made with the Landrys when we bought the property—we're finally ready to approve the final design.

In theory. It's not coming together.

Nothing is coming together these days.

My mind goes to Shaye immediately. It's only vaguely left her all day. I'm not sure what I'm most frustrated by—the fact that she didn't accept my offer or the fact that I offered her the job to start with?

It's a bunch of fuckery either way.

"How far was the survey off?" Holt asks.

It takes a lot of effort to refocus my mind.

"The front of the property is about fifty yards narrower than we originally thought," I say. "So instead of going to the east with this whole arm of the building like we planned, Wade had to go up and back with the design."

"But it leaves all of this as wasted space." He motions toward the edge of the property. "I mean, Wade didn't have much to work with—I get that. But I don't like it."

I slide my sunglasses off. "Tell him that. *Please.*"

Holt chuckles.

I walk toward the property line, leaving my brother at the truck.

The boots that I changed into when we got here crunch against the earth. Puffs of dust billow at my feet and infiltrate my nose.

It's honestly one of my favorite parts of our business. Sure, sitting in an office with floor-to-ceiling windows is great. The adrenaline of signing a multimillion-dollar deal is pretty damn awesome. But getting outside, smelling the dirt, feeling the fresh air on my face, and knowing that I get to decide how to transform this space in the universe makes me feel like a kid again. It reminds me of playing with Tonka trucks in the backyard. It's what gets me up in the morning.

I stop walking and face Holt. "The entire vibe changes with the new design. It feels ... crunched. It's even more obvious being out here ..."

Holt nods. "I'm with you. It's worse than I thought. And now I see why Greg was saying we're going to have to try to get permission from the property owner to the east to use their land, or some of it, for staging and ingress and egress."

"That never ends well."

"I know, but what else are we going to do?" Holt asks.

"Fuck if I know. We can't come in from the west because of that damn neighborhood two miles down. Did we ever figure out what all that is about?"

"Apparently, someone who lives there is on the city council. There's supposedly some shady shit that might get leaked before the next election cycle, and he's going out of his way to make good with his constituents by keeping the noise and dust down," Holt grumbles. "Fucking politics."

"I hear ya."

Holt walks across the property and stands next to me. We take in our surroundings.

"There's a right-of-way over here," Holt says, turning around and facing the property line. "Could that help us in any way?"

"It's a gas company right-of-way, so no. We don't want anything to do with that."

The wind picks up as we take in the area. Tiny pieces of dirt and sand are tossed into the air. They dance around us, making Holt sneeze. *Once.* Not four times in a row.

I stifle a chuckle as a warmth erupts in my core.

Shaye.

I can't decide if she's a blessing or a curse.

She frazzles me. I can't seem to figure out what to do with her, yet I feel *a need* to find an answer. She just sits in the back of my mind. She's the elephant in my head.

I can't put my finger on it. Yes, she's gorgeous, but I meet a lot of beautiful women. Sure, she's amusing, but since when is that my Achilles' heel? I absolutely want to fuck her, but it's more than that. I want to have dinner with her. Talk to her.

It's almost as if I don't have a choice. She keeps showing up in my life, and I keep doing things like offering her a job.

I rub my temple.

"You okay?" Holt asks.

"Yeah."

"Liar. What's wrong?"

I drop my hand. There's no sense in lying to him. He can read me like a book.

"Do you know the girl who hit my car yesterday?" I ask.

He nods.

I bite the corner of my lip. "Guess who showed up in the office today?"

A slow, uneasy look sweeps across Holt's face.

"It's nothing like that," I say. "She was answering Toni's ad for EAs."

"And you think that's random?"

I don't look at him. I can't. I know when I tell him that I do think it was a coincidence, he's going to think I've lost my marbles.

Hell, maybe I have.

"Shaye seemed as surprised to see me as I was to see her," I tell him.

He makes a face. "I don't really like this, Ollie."

I spin around to face him. "*Why?*"

He's taken aback by the gusto in which I fired that question. So am I. But it's already done. All I can do is ride with it and not overthink it.

He takes a step back. "Easy there, little brother."

"I'm sorry. I don't mean it like that."

I sigh and look away again. *I just don't like you insinuating that she is setting me up.*

He shifts his weight. I hear the pebbles crunch with the movement.

"You know that I trust your judgment more than anyone in the world," Holt says. "So, if you think this is a random act of kindness by the universe, then I'll buy it. I'm with you."

My lips twitch.

"I mean, hell—I met a woman in the airport and then at a business meeting. What are the odds of that?" he asks, bumping my shoulder with his.

"Oh, the woman who won't marry you?" I tease.

I wait for Holt's explosion. It takes one-half of a second.

"If Blaire doesn't give me a date soon, I swear that I'm going to set it my damn self." Holt blows out an exasperated breath. "My patience is wearing thin."

I laugh, relieved at the change in topics.

"What would she do if I just organized a wedding?" he asks, his face pink with irritation. "Mom would totally help me. I would just buy her a dress, hire a preacher, reserve a church, send out invitations, and tell her to be there. What would she do then?"

My laughter gets louder. "First of all, I'd go easy on bringing Mom into this. Second ... I don't know. I kind of like it. I mean, I've never imagined you as a wedding planner, but I'm game to watch this shit show."

Holt misses the humor. "I'm serious. I don't know what she's dragging her feet about."

He starts to walk, and I follow for the sake of conversation.

"Maybe she's not dragging her feet," I offer. "Maybe she just wants it to be perfect."

"I'll give her perfect. I'll give her anything she fucking wants."

I smirk. "What if she wants our family to have a private jet?"

Holt tosses me a sharp look, making me laugh.

"On a more serious note—no, I am serious about the jet. We need one," I say. "But on *another* note, it might be hard for her to think about planning a wedding. Both of her parents are dead, right?"

He nods.

"And her siblings are where—in Indiana? Illinois? Iowa?" I pause. "Why do all the Midwestern states start with an I, anyway?"

"Illinois, and I see your point." He chews on his bottom lip. "You know, I've always thought we'd get married here by default. But maybe you're right. Maybe I'm an asshole for not thinking about that."

He stops walking. I do too.

"It might be something to consider," I say.

He hums as if he's in the process of doing just that.

I look into the distance, settling my gaze on the top of a grove of trees.

Holt has always been my best friend. We've done absolutely everything together. From sports to clubs to college, I followed in his footsteps throughout my life. Now that he has Blaire, our lives aren't on the same trajectory for the first time.

I'm not sure what to make of it. It's a natural progression, I know, and I'm happy for him. He loves Blaire. But this is where our trajectory separates. It's where his best friend is someone else, and sometimes ... I feel alone.

I kick at a rock as Holt hums again. As he ponders future wedding locations, I let my mind wander to past engagement proposals—namely, mine.

Kendra Pickler was the only woman I ever considered making Mrs. Oliver Mason. We met in college. She was a business major. She was wickedly intelligent, fun to be with, and had lips made for blow jobs. She hinted for months about getting married around our one-year anniversary—far too soon, by my estimation. There were bridal magazines on the coffee table, only half hidden by *Forbes*. Her email was left open with ads for jewelry stores. Her best friend even dropped Kendra's choice in gems—a princess cut diamond, preferably at least two carats— while pretending to be buzzed on mimosas.

I took the bait. Why not? It was probably love. I figured that my family liked her, and I couldn't find anything too annoying or problematic about her. She adored me.

So I bought the diamond. Mom designed the setting on a gold band, just as the best friend ordered. I rented a boat, hired a caterer, and invited all of our friends for a sail at dusk.

Then—with said ring—she went and got knocked up by my dad's business partner, and the rest, as they say, is history.

Holt clears his throat.

"What?" I ask, taking a deep breath to rid myself of thoughts of the past.

"Nothing. You just checked out for a minute."

It's my turn to hum. It's better than admitting what I was thinking about.

I start to walk and, this time, it's Holt that follows along.

"What did you do about what's-her-name?" Holt asks.

"Shaye?"

"Yeah. *Shaye*. She showed up for an interview. What happened?"

"Well ..." I lick my lips. "I offered her a job."

Holt whistles through his teeth.

"What's that supposed to mean?" I ask.

"Again, I trust your judgment. But I'm going to ask it anyway—are you sure this is a good fucking idea?"

Fuck if I know.

"I mean, yesterday you were a little ... To use a Siggy Mason word, *smitten*," he says cheekily. "And today you're offering her to be essentially your right fucking hand in our family business. Should you fuck where you feed?"

My head whips to the side, and I laugh. "What?"

He shrugs. "I don't know. It was supposed to be a play on *shit where you eat,* but it got lost in translation."

"That it did."

"You know what I mean, though."

I do. I know exactly what he means.

The offer was purely based on her credentials. I'm not totally out of my gourd. I scanned her resume while Toni went in to talk to her and recognized the name of her last employer. Miles Monroe is an old family friend. He gave her a stunning reference filled with praise and said he was sad to have to part ways with her.

I didn't have time to press the issue for details. Toni walked back out.

Offering Shaye the job was a game-time decision, but it wasn't made on the fly. She has the experience. She has the recommendations. We have chemistry—something that is essential for an executive and his assistant.

But that's the problem too. We have chemistry. And Holt suspects it.

"I'm not fucking anyone at the moment," I tell him. "So fucking where I feed isn't a problem."

"And if that status changes?"

I blow out a hasty breath. "I don't know, Holt. I don't even know if she's going to accept the offer. She said she'd think about it and let us know."

We pause at a washout. The air is thick and heavy like it's about to storm.

"What happens if she accepts?" Holt asks. "Do you think you can work with her and keep it professional?"

"Yeah."

"I mean, I could hire her to work for me. And then—"

"No." I shake my head. I know I answered too quickly but it's too late to do anything about it now. "I can keep it under control. I got this."

He looks me right in the eyes. "Do you really? Because your whole vibe about her is different than anyone since Kendra."

I groan at the sound of her name.

"Nah, it's even different than Kendra," Holt says. "I don't even think you liked her."

"I did, actually."

"Okay, maybe you *liked* her. But you didn't *love* her."

I look at him like he's crazy. "How would you know who I loved and didn't love?"

"Because you let her go."

"She was having someone else's baby, dumbass. Someone else, might I add, who caused our family a lot of fucking embarrassment."

I clench my jaw and exhale.

"I think Dad enjoyed knocking out Charles Gamby," Holt jokes. "And Mom was thrilled when they closed that cigar side business. She thought it was a waste of time for years."

"Glad I could help."

Holt clasps a hand around my shoulder. "Be honest with me. Weren't you a little relieved when all of that happened with Kendra?"

I still. I've never admitted that to anyone, not even Holt. I've never said it aloud to anyone either. Not even the mirror. But a little part of me did feel a sense of relief the morning after Kendra told me the truth. I felt guilty about it, but relief was there in spades, too.

"I'm going to be honest with you, Oliver. I think you knew that Kendra was fucking around, and you let it happen. That's what I meant. You put very little time into that relationship, and you couldn't have been blind at events when she was talking up random men." He shrugs. "You don't have to admit shit to me but just know I know."

I want to argue with him, but I can't.

Holt drops his hand. "Hey, if you want to hire Shaye—do it. Just be clear minded about it. Family first. Always."

"Always."

We exchange a grin.

My shoulders sag, and I turn away from my brother, happy to have this conversation concluded. As I peer into the distance, I observe a dip in the trees that piques my curiosity.

"Hey," I say, pointing toward the drop-off. "Is there a road out there? Or a driveway? Do you see that?"

Holt shrugs.

"Who owns that?" I ask.

He shrugs again. "I have no idea. Why?"

"Because," I say, moving to try to get a better vantage point, "that's another potential access point. Greg didn't mention this."

"Right. And if we owned this back chunk ..." Holt says, his voice raising.

"Consider the redesign." I use my hands to help explain. "Instead of going up because he can't go east, Wade could expand north, and ... the options are endless."

"I wonder how many acres that is?"

I turn back toward the truck. "Let's go take a look."

Holt follows me, staying a few feet back.

I slip my phone from my pocket and take a quick glance at the screen. There's one missed call ... from Kelly.

I breathe a sigh that's equally filled with relief and disappointment.

Chapter Seven

Shaye

Water droplets splash onto the countertop and down the front of my shirt.

Leftover scrambled eggs from this morning fight against the current but eventually drop into the garbage disposal. It growls as it eats the debris. The sound is a little more metallic than it used to be, like metal-on-metal.

I turn off the disposal and the water. My favorite hand towel embroidered with lemons that I got on sale at Marshall's is soft on my hands as I dry them.

The kitchen is filled with the soft glow of the sun's setting rays. It's my absolute favorite time of day in this house, specifically this time of year. I walk to the window overlooking the backyard and soak in the warmth.

The fence separating my backyard with the house behind me will eventually fall down during a storm. I'm surprised it's still standing. The yard is tiny and uneven, and the overhang on the back stoop creaks when the wind picks up. Still, I love this little house and its cheap rent and chipped paint because it's mine.

At least until my lease runs out.

I toss the towel on the counter.

My body fills with a peace that I've welcomed in my life in lieu of the sadness and anger I used to feel. It isn't sunshine and rainbows in my soul, but it's not fire and brimstone either. My best friend, Lisbeth, says the rainbows will come. I just need to give it more time.

I say she's more of an optimist than me.

The doorbell jolts me out of my head.

"Coming," I call out as I walk around the corner of the kitchen island.

"Hurry up! This is heavy!"

I yank the door open and nearly get trampled by Lisbeth Kline. Her cheeks are flushed as she rushes in like a bull, her arms loaded with bags.

"What in the heck are you doing?" I ask with a laugh.

The bags hit the floor with a thud.

"I said I would take a couple of bags of lettuce. I didn't say you could bring me all the food you've ever bought," I say.

"I went ahead and cleaned out my fridge *and* my deep freeze." She wipes a chunk of blond bangs off her forehead. "You know how I do when I get going. It was supposed to just be perishables that would, well, perish while I'm in Florida for a week. But then I thought it was a good time to just go all-in. I mean, I am going to see my parents after the wedding. You know how hard Mom makes it for me to leave once I'm in Ohio again."

I take in the number of containers in front of me. "Tell me this is it. There's not more in your car, is there?"

"This is it. But we better get it in your freezer before it melts."

I help gather the bags from various department stores filled with frozen food items and carry them into the kitchen.

"I need a grocery store monitor," she says, setting the bags on the island. "Or at least one of the new fancy refrigerators with a camera so you can see inside it while you're in the dairy section."

I laugh. "Or, you know, you could just make a list."

She scoffs at me like I just asked her carb-loving self to go gluten-free.

Lisbeth pulls out boxes of Hot Pockets, cartons of milk, and bags of frozen pearl onions from a Macy's bag.

"When are you leaving?" I ask, putting the items away.

"In a few days," she fake cries. "Why did I have to RSVP to this damn wedding, Shaye? And why won't you come with me?"

"You RSVP'd because you and Lydia are friends. And I'm not going because I'm not throwing away that much money on a destination wedding that's not my own. Also, *I* wasn't invited."

"But you could be my plus-one."

"No."

She rolls her eyes.

"But weddings are fun. I mean, I think they are," I say, taking a half-gallon of unopened orange juice from my friend. "I've never actually been to one."

She makes a face. "They are usually fun. This one held a lot of promise until *The Break Up*."

I make the same face back to her.

"I wish I could say that I wasn't dreading seeing Thomas and the starlet who shall not be named," she says, her grip clenching so hard on the bundle of bananas in her hand that I think I'll have to throw them away. "But let's be real."

Lisbeth is right. It would be futile to even try to play the devil's advocate.

Her ex-boyfriend, Thomas Raines, is the talk of professional baseball. He's leading the league in a variety of statistics—a fact that I know because he's a hometown boy. But Tommy is also the talk of every rag magazine in the world because he was caught with his fingers literally inside the starlet at an award's show earlier this year.

While probably great for YouTube replay numbers, it wasn't so good for Lisbeth's relationship with Tommy.

It also doesn't bode well for their mutual friends' wedding.

"I think you should go and enjoy yourself," I tell her. "You obviously learned an important side of Tommy that you didn't know before it was too late. Let the starlet find out on her own. This is definitely your win."

"I just wish I weren't going alone."

"So find a date." I toss the carrots into the crisper. "There are a million guys you could call."

"Yes. True. But I don't want to have to entertain someone. I don't want to have to be nice to them. I'm going to be pissy and self-conscious, and having to dance around someone else's feelings doesn't seem doable."

I raise a brow. "But going alone does?"

She shrugs.

We work silently for a few minutes, trying to find room for all of Lisbeth's groceries in my refrigerator. I pause every now and then and examine items. *Beet juice shots? Okay.*

"You really don't want to go?" she asks out of nowhere.

"No." I laugh at her. "I can't. I ..." I set a box of ice cream on the counter and try not to smile. "I got a job offer today."

Her blue eyes light up, and she raises her hands up in the air. "You did? Why didn't you lead with that when I walked in? We could be celebrating right now."

I force a smile and turn back to a bag of frozen peas.

My insides go bananas as I let my mind flip back to the interview this morning. It feels so amazing to have hope that I might be able to turn things around. It's the light at the end of a disastrous tunnel that I've been begging for.

But, then again, it has my stomach in knots because I don't know how to navigate this anymore.

"Where is it?" Lisbeth asks, oblivious to my inner turmoil. "Is the commute awful? You can always sleep over if it's closer to my place, you know."

"I'm not sure I'm taking it, actually."

"Why?"

The million-dollar question. Or, at least, a hefty-salaried question.

I take a deep breath. "Do you know the guy who I hit yesterday?"

She nods.

"Well ..." I blow out my breath. "It's for him. As his executive assistant."

It's as though the room gasps, waiting for an explanation. Lisbeth leans back as if the distance will help her understand.

"*Okay*," she says slowly, her lips threatening to split her cheeks. "This is an interesting development."

"It's an odd coincidence. That's what it is."

"Or kismet."

"*Or a coincidence.*"

She sets her jaw and tilts her head. "You said he was *hot*—a word you don't throw around lightly. That leans this entire situation into the kismet realm."

I scoff.

"What happened?" she asks. "Like you just walk in, and he's sitting there?"

I abandon the ice cream on the counter and sit at the kitchen table. I might as well get comfortable. Lisbeth and I have been friends for almost ten years. There's nothing she doesn't know about me and vice versa. She loves a good kismet story, and I can tell by the look in her eye that she thinks that's what this is.

Poor girl.

"The interview has been scheduled for three days with a woman named Toni," I say, using the time to replay the scenario for the six-thousandth time today. "I'm sitting in a conference room, and Toni comes in. She sits down for a few minutes. We chat. It's going well. Then she leaves, and a few minutes later, Oliver walks in. We were both dumbfounded." I narrow my eyes, trying to hide the way my heartbeat just picked up. "Well, *I* was dumbfounded. He seemed to be surprised but less ... shocked."

I think back to the way his eyes widened ever so slightly and how a grin tugged at the corner of his mouth. He was definitely pleased to see me. But shocked? No.

My stomach turns itself inside out.

"So," Lisbeth says, poking me along as she sits across from me. "What happened? What did he say?"

"He ... he sat down. We talked a little bit. I accused him of being a cop and—"

"What?" she shrieks.

"I mean, isn't that really Occam's Razor here?"

She snorts in frustration. "No. No, it isn't, Miss Conspiracy Theorist."

I shrug at the accusation. It's not totally wrong.

"So you accuse him of being the po-po, and he still offers you a job?" Her eyes widen. "*The* job? His trusted confidant job?"

"Well, yeah. I think that's a little over the top in the description, but basically."

She crosses her arms over her chest, smirking happily.

"Don't look at me like that," I say, pointing a finger at her.

Her smirk deepens.

"I didn't take it," I admit.

"And why the eff not?"

I rub my forehead with the palm of my hand.

"I'm ... thrown off," I tell her before dropping my hand. It hits the table with a thud. "Can I do the job? Absolutely. Do I need it? One thousand percent. Is it an amazing opportunity? Clearly. But ..."

I look at my best friend and silently plead for help. She reaches across the table and puts her hands on mine.

"Look, I know this is a lot for you at once," she says softly. "A new job is enough to freak anyone out. But you chose this guy to be your first crush since Luca—"

"It's not a crush. And I didn't *choose* anything."

She brushes me off without a thought. "If you weren't panicking a little, I'd worry." She withdraws her hand.

"I am. Don't worry."

She laughs.

"I feel so ... clumsy," I tell her. "Let's set aside the fact that this guy, *Oliver*, might be my new boss. Let's just consider him a guy who asked me to have lunch with him only yesterday, okay?"

"Okay."

"I don't know how to do that. I don't know how to navigate the dating waters, Lisbeth."

"Yes, you do. It's been a long time, I know, but you know how to do it. You weren't born yesterday."

"I might as well have been. I only dated one guy before Luca, and I was nineteen. I mean, besides the three blind dates you've set me up on this year, that's it—and those went *so well.*"

She giggles at the mention of the awful dates she arranged. I roll my eyes.

"I just keep getting thrown into this guy's life and"—I shrug—"if I take this job, I *need* it to work. I have to get a grip on my life so I can move on. I can't work for him and feel myself tingle in all the right places—or wrong places, depending on how you define the word."

"I think you're getting ahead of yourself."

"Probably." I sigh hastily. "You're probably right. I mean, who am I to think that he even sees me like that?"

She laughs. It's loud and chirpy. "Oh, he does."

I look at her like she's nuts.

"*Shaye.*" She says my name with exasperation. "You're beautiful. You have the prettiest hair in the world. Your eyes tell stories. Your body is banging, my friend, and you're funny and smart. So, yeah, I'm absolutely positive he's attracted to you." She grins. "I was just saying that ... who knows? You might get to know him and hate him. The chemistry might fizzle. Maybe he has rules about dating co-workers. You don't know."

Suddenly, she seems less crazy-pants.

My shoulders sag as I let her words of wisdom soak in.

I know I'm jumping the gun with some of this. My mind is definitely ahead of reality. But I want this so bad, I need this so much, and it feels too good to be true. Naturally, my mind wants to sniff out all the ways it could go wrong instead of focusing on the ways it could go right.

"Just relax and do what's best for you. Today, maybe that's taking the job," she says.

A chill rushes through my body. I close my eyes and breathe.

"Maybe you're right," I say. "I don't know."

I open my eyes as her sweet smile gets sharper.

"Maybe I'm right," she repeats. "And tomorrow, maybe it's taking his dick—"

"Hey!" I protest, but not without a giggle.

She laughs too. "If he's hot enough to flip your switch *and* he owns Mason Limited, keep your options open. Be smart."

I get to my feet and roll my eyes.

"Don't look at me like that," she says, standing too.

"I *am* being smart. I'm well aware of the fact that my judgment on men is broken. Maybe Oliver Mason is a sociopath or a narcissist. He could be married and a total scumbag."

"Nope."

I turn to face her. "Nope what?"

Her face sobers. "Don't write this job off already. Don't write him off already. Don't write *you* off already. You're defaulting to your mother's voice in your head."

"Yeah ..."

"Listen to me, Shaye Marie—your mom is fucked up. God love her, but something went wrong with her parenting gene. You gave that woman so many chances to be in your life and be the person she should be, and she failed you every time."

"I—"

"I'm not done." Lisbeth smiles softly at me. "We subconsciously absorb what we hear our moms say and do. Somehow, because it comes from them, we assume it's right and true. But in your case, it's not. You know that." She makes a face until I smile. "You're leaving all of that nonsense behind, okay? All of the negativity and blame she placed on you was projection. She was projecting her shortcomings onto you. That has nothing to do with you in all reality. Right?"

Her words hit the soft, vulnerable spot in my heart. I want to hope she's right. I want to think she's telling me the truth and not doing best-friend duty and telling me what I want, even need, to hear. But I'm not sure.

"Right," I say, my voice not as confident as I'd hoped it would be.

"Good. Now, I'll break it down for you. Take the job." She brushes her bangs out of her face again. "You need the money. You have the skills. You obviously vibe with this guy. So take the job and get back on your feet. Give yourself a little room to get to know yourself again." She reaches out and presses her hand against my arm. "This is the break you've been praying for."

For the first time in a long time, a blossom of hope begins to flutter in my belly.

This is the advice I'd give Lisbeth if the roles were reversed. I'd tell her to take the job and I'd mean it.

She dusts her hands off as if she just solved world hunger. "Now that decision has been made, go find your wine bottle opener. We're going to celebrate your new job."

I want to backtrack, but I know the conversation with Lisbeth will never end if I argue. I'm also not really sure how I can construct an argument against her.

So, I head toward the drawer for the corkscrew. Might as well give in. And rejoice, because she's right. This is the break I've been praying for.

I hope.

Chapter Eight

Oliver

A fire crackles in the fireplace across the room. The flames dance, sending shadows across the walls.

I stretch, my bare feet slipping against the black Egyptian cotton sheets that I love. They make me feel like I'm climbing into a cave at the end of a hard day. And today was *definitely* a hard one.

I drop my phone next to me. The screen is lit up with the farming game I downloaded by accident and now play when I can't sleep. Who knew little digital chickens and cows could be so relaxing?

Most nights, anyway.

My muscles ache from the workout I decided to get in just before bed. My head hurts from trying not to lose my shit fifty-eight times at the office. My stomach is sore from twisting itself into a knot every time I thought about Shaye during the past twelve hours.

And that was a lot.

I fling my arms to my sides, smashing the pillows I use to box myself in when I lie in bed. The soft thump is barely audible over the noise in my head.

Feeling like I'm teetering on the verge of losing control is a new and unwanted sensation. I always have my shit locked down. I'm the Mason that keeps my cool, operates on an even keel. I'm even better at it than Wade because he operates without emotion altogether. I know how to balance it.

But, today, my emotions might have gotten the best of me. I might have been impulsive. And the fact that I don't regret it—despite feeling like I would—is concerning.

I rip the blankets off me. Cool waves of air from the ceiling fan flirt with my skin. It's not enough of a distraction to take my mind off my problems.

The biggest issue is that I really think she would do a good job. Monroe out-and-out praised her work ethic and efficiency. But is it smart to work with someone who I can't stop thinking about outside of the office?

Probably fucking not.

"Ugh," I groan, sitting up on the side of the bed. I bounce my legs as I try to work out what I'm going to do if Shaye accepts the job.

And what I'm going to do if she doesn't.

"Which would I rather?" I ask myself, my voice slicing through the stillness of the room. "Would you rather have her work for you or sleep with her?"

A small smile slips across my lips.

"Both."

I punch the rust-colored bedding and stand.

My reflection in the circle-shaped mirror hanging over my dresser is not my best look. A five-o'clock shadow dusts my jaw, and my hair looks like I've run my fingers through it all day.

Probably because I have.

I want to blame my brothers for this conundrum. Watching them settle down has to have infected my brain because I don't do this. I'm not the guy who gets confused about women.

That's Boone.

Rather, it was.

Maybe I am the one now?

I scoff at my thoughts and flex, watching my muscles pop in the reflection.

"Don't lose your shit," I chastise myself, letting my arms drop to my sides. "Stay calm. This, too, shall pass."

Even though I'm the one who uttered the phrase, it makes me smile. It was one of my grandma Annabelle's favorite sayings, and something about hearing it out loud helps me re-center.

I start toward the door to make a sandwich when my phone buzzes. Confused, I climb across my bed and grab it from under the comforter.

A text from an unknown number is on the screen. I sit and unlock the phone.

My heart thunders in my chest as I try to override my hope that it's Shaye with the likelihood that it's a bot text about my nonexistent car warranty.

I press the green text app and hold my breath.

> Hi, Mr. Mason. This is Shaye Brewer. It's late, but I wanted you to know that I will be calling human resources in the morning to accept your offer. Thank you for the opportunity.

"*Fuck me*," I groan and fall back on my bed. A million thoughts scatter through my mind. I hold the phone above my head and read her words over and over again.

I will be calling human resources in the morning to accept your offer.

The knot in my stomach that I've battled all day loosens. Maybe it's just because I'm now focused on the text and the fact that a decision has been made—she's my new EA—and not on the what-ifs or what-will-bes.

Or maybe it's just that I get to see her again.

I shove to a sitting position. My finger hovers over the audio button.

"I have to call her," I rationalize. "I need to welcome her to the company and see if she has any questions."

It's enough of a justification for me.

My thumb hits the audio button, and the line begins to ring.

"Who needs human resources?" I joke as I wait for her to pick up.

My heartbeat pounds as the phone rings once, twice, three times. I pull the phone away on the fourth ring to make sure I called the right number. Just as I look at the screen, the line clicks.

"Hello?" Her voice is sweet, albeit kissed with a tinge of confusion.

"Hi, Shaye. It's Oliver."

She clears her throat. "Oh. Hi, Mr. Mason."

"Please, call me Oliver."

I jump to my feet, my body unable to contain the need to move. I don't overthink me asking her to call me by my first name—something I only allowed my first secretary to do, and that was because she knew me as a kid when she was working for my father. I just go with it.

"I got your text," I say. "I just wanted to reach out and see if you had any questions."

Lies. All lies.

She hesitates. I hesitate.

This is not going well.

"Well, since you reached out," she says, choosing her words carefully. "What time do you normally start? Or what time would you want me there?"

"I'm there way too damn early. I can't sleep, so I always just roll in around four or so. But if you could be there around eight o'clock, that would be terrific. Toni gets there around then too, so I'm sure you could just meet her there in the morning. I need you to start as soon as possible."

"Eight is great. That rhymes."

I think she smiles. I can't see it, but somehow it translates through the line.

"I'm really excited," she says, an ease in her voice that I'm happy to hear. "I went to your company's website and googled you a little. You're involved in a lot of really interesting things."

I lift my chin. "I think so. We're slowly expanding into other areas of the country, but Georgia and the southern United States will always be our home. My grandfather started Mason Limited out of his garage, and it's really important to my family to keep our roots here."

"I love that."

My lips part into a proud smile. "I love it too."

"So it looks like there are a lot of Masons around the office."

"Yeah. My older brother Holt and I are co-CEOs. Our youngest brother, Boone, works in the office too. You'll meet them both tomorrow. Wade doesn't work for Mason Limited but is in and out of the office all the time. He has an architecture firm that falls under the Mason umbrella. And our other brother, Coy, is starting a label."

"A music label?"

"Yeah."

"Oh. Okay." She laughs. "I'll never keep you all straight. Your pictures look almost identical."

"It'll get easier. Just wait until you meet them all. You'll see. I'm the handsome one. And the smart one. And the charming one."

I can't say it without smiling, and her laughter makes me smile even harder.

I sit on the edge of the bed again. My muscles relax, and the need to pace and move diminishes. It's a let-down of a day's worth of adrenaline.

"And which one of you is the conceited one?" she teases.

"Boone. He's the baby of the family. It comes with the territory."

She giggles. "I think the babies of families take a lot of unwarranted flack."

"Oh, so you're the baby of a family too, huh?"

"Nope. Only child right here."

"I dreamed of that most of my youth."

Her amusement swirls through the phone. "It's not all that it's cracked up to be. There comes a day when you realize that *you* are your family. But it's fine," she says, seemingly catching herself from a conversation I don't think she wants to have. "Anyway, I can't wait to meet Boone. Should be fun."

The tone she uses indicates that she's circling the conversation around toward the end. And, although I should go along with it because it is the right answer, I'm not ready.

"Wade is the one to watch," I say before I can stop myself. "He's so smart that he's practically a wizard. But he has absolutely no personal skills. None. Zero. The only people who like him are our mother, who has to on account of that fact alone, and Boone's daughter, Rosie. But she's five years old. She doesn't know better."

"He sounds lovely."

I chuckle. "Yeah. Lovely."

"So he's the real brains behind everything, huh?"

My jaw drops. "No. That's me. I told you."

"I guess I'll just have to decide for myself," she says, a hint of smugness in her tone.

"Just remember who your boss is, huh?"

"Good point." She laughs. "I will lie and tell everyone that you're the wizard."

"Hey!"

"What? You said Wade was the wizard! If I say it's you, I'm lying. I'm just repeating the information you gave me."

I shake my head, amused at her playfulness. "You shall not ever, ever repeat that I said that about Wade. That was completely off the record."

"I'll try to remember that."

"You do that." I run my hand through my hair, unable to stop smiling. "How is your car? Did you get it looked at?"

There's the briefest pause. It might be quick, but it's full of hesitation.

"Oh, not yet," she says quickly. "I've been really busy. I'll get to it this week."

I furrow my brow. Something about the way she says it has me second-guessing her promise.

"Did you get yours checked out?" she asks. "I'll pay you for the damage out of my first check since it was my fault."

"Nah, it'll be fine. I haven't even called to get it into the shop, to be honest."

"I still feel really bad about hitting you. For what it's worth."

I stand as the knot begins to pull once again in my stomach. It's fast and tight, and I rub my belly with one hand while I begin to pace around the room.

"It's not a big deal," I tell her. "Please don't worry about it. Shit happens."

"Shit happens to me a lot."

"It happens to all of us, Shaye."

She hums, but I think it's in disagreement.

I pace around my room, running a hand through my hair again. I don't want to get off the phone with her. A plethora of questions are on the tip of my tongue, a million things I'd like to ask her.

Every time we talk, she becomes more interesting, and I realize what a problem this might be if I don't get it in check.

I take a deep breath. "Okay, well, I guess I'll see you in the morning."

"Oh. Right. Absolutely. I'll be in the office at eight sharp."

"Feel free to reach out if you think of anything else you need to know."

The vibrations between us change. The easiness is replaced with an awkwardness that I loathe. I want to show her that I don't want to end the call. But that probably complicates things.

"Thank you for the call. I'll see you tomorrow. Goodbye, Oliver."

"Good night, Shaye."

She sucks in a quick breath before the call ends.

I make quick work of saving her number to my contacts list and then toss my phone on the bed.

I walk over to the window and drag open the blackout curtains. The backyard glows from the lights in the pool and the pool house. I usually find it soothing to look out and reflect on my day.

But not tonight.

Tonight, I'll just start counting down the minutes until tomorrow.

Chapter Nine

Shaye

"I got this," I whisper, pushing the button for the elevator. "Settle down."

I slide my palms down my black trousers and avoid Genevieve's stare from behind. She was really sweet this morning and helped me find Toni—who was clearly not expecting me. But Genevieve's excitement on my behalf at working for Oliver Mason *personally* was a little more than I could handle.

My nerves are nearly shot as it is.

The onboarding process with Toni went well. She gave me a quick tour of the building and introduced me to key staff. It all went swimmingly. But as soon as I finished my paperwork and headed toward the elevators, my anxiety surged again.

The elevator dings, and I step inside. My black heels hit a staccato against the floor. I press the button for the fourth floor.

I grip the thin strap of my purse at my shoulder and look up to see Genevieve's smiling face. She offers me a little wave; my hand does a version of a wave back. I try hard—*really hard*—not to absorb the excitement rolling off her in waves.

Breathe in, breathe out.

The doors roll to a close, and the elevator begins its ascent.

I watch the numbers light up. There's a slight pause on the third floor, but a man in a suit jacket tells me he wants to go down, not up, and apologizes for the slight inconvenience it causes me. I tell him it's fine and clutch my purse tighter.

My brain races faster than the elevator and, by the time I reach the fourth floor, I simultaneously decide that this is both the worst and best thing I've ever done.

What was I thinking? Surely, there must've been an easier way to climb out of the hole I'm in. *Working closely for the one man who I've felt an attraction to in years? I thought* that *was a good idea?*

I force a swallow down my throat and try to temper the thundering of my heart.

Ding! The door opens and a woman with long red hair greets me with a smile.

I step out of the elevator and onto the shiny floor. The room is airy and smells faintly of lavender. Under normal circumstances, the scent of lavender helps me calm down.

Today is not a typical day.

A long black desk made of some kind of stone faces me. There are two closed doors behind the desk, one near each corner of the room. Two more doors—one on each side wall—are open with the lights off. There are two more on either side of the elevators.

I glance swiftly around the room as if Oliver might suddenly appear out of thin air. I can't decide if I'm excited to see him or if I'm dreading the moment. It's a wild mixture of apprehension and unreadiness that makes me a little unsteady on my heels.

"Good morning," the redhead says, getting to her feet. "You must be Shaye. Toni said you were on your way up."

"I am." I give her my best smile. "It's nice to meet you."

"I'm Kelly."

She comes around the side of the desk. Her body is slim and

wrapped in an emerald-green dress. With her red hair and green eyes, it's a stunning package.

"Welcome to the team," she says.

"Thank you."

My eyes dart around the room. The four cups of coffee I had this morning—double my usual intake—aren't doing me any favors. My hands are shaky as I take my purse off my shoulder.

"Hey," Kelly says, a laugh buried in her tone. "Relax. Don't be nervous. You're going to do great."

I blow out a breath as my shoulders drop. "Is it that obvious?"

"A little." She smiles. "First-day jitters are normal."

I wonder if being awake, dressed, hair and makeup done, and being overcaffeinated by six thirty in the morning is normal, but I don't ask.

"On my first day here, I vomited in the first hour," she says, wincing. "I blame the bagel that I got at this sketchy place in my neighborhood, but it might've been nerves. *Maybe*."

I laugh.

"So, you know, don't do that, and you're ahead of me."

"I'll definitely try not to," I tell her. What I don't mention is the bubble of bile sitting at the top of my throat. "It's been a long morning already."

"I know that this can be intimidating ..." She smiles knowingly. "The Masons are truly the best bosses I've ever worked for. They can be loud and expect a high level of efficiency, but they're good men, and they employ good people. Trust me."

The phone on Kelly's desk begins to ring. She sighs.

"Give me just a moment. This office is understaffed and it just gets busier." She moves gracefully around the desk again and picks up the phone. "This is Kelly."

I turn away from her and take in a long, deep breath. The chaos in my brain and body settles slightly thanks to Kelly's genuine words—and I know they're true. If I doubted them at all, I wouldn't have accepted Oliver's offer.

Trust your gut.

I take another cleansing breath and try to adjust my focus from my anxiety to what I have to do—work. I spin in a slow circle and take in the reception area. It's masculine and sophisticated, decorated in blacks and grays with copper-colored accents. The windows to the right of each door are covered by blinds from the inside. Soft music plays overhead—some kind of instrumental that's not really noticeable until you listen for it.

"Sorry about that," Kelly says. Her heels click against the floor. "Okay, from what Toni told me, you're Oliver's executive assistant. Is that correct?"

I nod.

"That's his office." She points at the office behind her desk on the right. "And that one is yours. They connect on the inside, which you'll see shortly. The offices to my left are Holt Mason's and his EA, Miriam's."

"Okay."

"One of the offices back there is Boone Mason's. He's ... he's fun. Keeps things lively. The other is used for meetings." She stifles a smile and motions for me to follow her. "Let's get you situated before Oliver gets out of his meeting."

My gaze lingers on Oliver's door as I follow Kelly to my office. She flips the lights on and steps inside.

The first thing I note is the prominent, deep-colored wood desk. *Nice.* Behind it, a cabinet is set up along one wall, and another connects to the two on one side, forming an L. As Kelly noted, a door on the other wall is closed that apparently leads into Oliver's office.

I fight off a surge of anxiety that threatens to creep up my spine.

Two chairs face the desk, and a coatrack stands next to the door. Besides a piece of art in the same vein as the one in the conference room yesterday, there's nothing else to note except a computer and a stack of folders.

"Take a look around and get comfortable," Kelly says. "There are office supplies inside the desk. If there's anything you need that you don't have, let me know. There are some files on the desk with basic project information, a few things that just came in that need Oliver's attention—that kind of thing. It would probably help you to skim over that. It'll give you a good feel of what's to come and then I'll come in and check on you in a little while."

"Sounds good. Thanks, Kelly."

"Absolutely." She glances over her shoulder at the phone that starts ringing again. "Oliver and Holt should be back any time now. I expected them already, to be honest."

"It's fine. I'll just get settled."

She gives me a final smile before scooting off toward her desk.

I blow out a breath and sit in the brown leather chair. I pull open the large bottom drawer on my right and plunk my purse inside.

My heart races as I give myself a second to become acclimated to my new setting. It's reminiscent of my office at Monroe Companies, yet a level or four up. Every detail from the light fixtures—a sleek modern chandelier in my office—to the faint flecks of gold in the otherwise dark tile seem intentional. Even though I had nothing to do with it, it gives me confidence.

I can do this.

Riding the wave of confidence, I ignore Oliver's office door and turn to the computer instead.

The log-in information Toni gave me works and I start clicking around on various icons. There are already a couple of emails from Toni with copies of things I signed downstairs, as well as one from Kelly with a list of names and numbers of people I might need. I find the calendar and take a quick glance at Oliver's schedule. Everything is color-coded. I don't know who is responsible for the hot-pink notes, but they're hilarious and very needy, from what I can tell. Also, whoever controls the olive-green notes doesn't seem to find Hot Pink funny.

"These have to be Oliver's brothers," I whisper, looking for a color key and coming up empty.

I do a little more investigating on the computer, checking out the shared drive as well as the systems that the company uses. It's all pretty standard. That's a relief.

My attention shifts to the stack of papers on my desk. I'm sorting through them, familiarizing myself with things, when a knock raps softly on the door to my right. I glance up from a memo about a project called Greyshell and bite back a gasp.

Oliver leans against the doorway. A pair of dark denim encases his thighs. A bright white button down that looks soft and silky is fitted over his chest. On top of that is a steel-gray blazer that hangs open.

His hair is perfectly coiffed in an *I just rolled out of bed, or I took fifteen minutes on this look* kind of way. My mind shifts to the fifteen minutes option because visualizing *Oliver* and *bed* at the same time is not the way to start my day.

Or, rather, it is but not when I work for him.

"*Oh,*" I say, the single word somehow becoming multi-syllable.

He lifts a coffee cup to his lips and takes a sip. He watches me over the brim, his eyes twinkling.

I kick myself for just reacting and not being prepared for him to look this delicious. It's not like I didn't know. What I didn't account for was the way his gaze feels welcoming, nearly caressing me from across the room.

Don't go there, Shaye.

It's wishful thinking ... because, let's face it, it's been a while.

And it's wrong thinking ... because you need this job.

My mind scrambles for a way to deal with this obstacle. I'm immediately reminded of a tactic I learned in a communications class—pretend your audience is naked.

No! Don't do that!

My eyes pop open wide as I try to think of something to say. I have to move this situation along before he thinks he made a very bad mistake in hiring me.

"There was a note in here ..." I rummage through the files and pull out one on the bottom. My palms are damp. "I think this might be urgent."

"What is it?"

I skim the letter once again and block out the warmth in his voice.

"It's about green building materials. It looks like a guy named Greg inquired about a company's products, and this is their response." I look at Oliver. "I think it got buried."

"Greg is our construction manager. Can you send him a copy of that directly and then scan it in the project file? There should be a list of project numbers somewhere for you."

"I'll figure it out."

He smiles.

I wait for him to say something more, to lead me into the area of conversation that he wants to have. I sure as hell don't know what to say.

Instead of saying anything, he walks into my office and stands across from my desk. The whole room seems to shrink. The lavender in the air is long gone, and the faint scent of amber takes its place.

Oliver watches me as if he's unsure of how to proceed too. We just feel each other out with the safety of my desk and two chairs between us.

"Did Toni and Kelly get you sorted?" he asks softly.

"Yes. They've both been amazing. Thank you again for this opportunity ... Oliver? Mr. Mason." I flush. "I'm not sure what I'm supposed to call you in this setting."

"Oliver. There are *a lot* of Mr. Masons around here, even though I'm the most important."

I laugh, my shoulders relaxing as I recall his jokes from last night. "I remember that conversation."

"He's so full of shit." A man steps into my doorway, filling the space. He's a younger version of Oliver with lighter features but the same bright smile. Mischief is written across his face. "*I'm* the most important one around here."

Oliver scoffs. "You just started working here, Boone. How can you possibly be the most important?"

"I've just started coming to the office. I've *always* participated. Actually, I've been the unofficial Employee of the Year now for years. I have the two biggest projects attributed to me." He beams. "You always seem to forget that."

"How could I? You don't let anyone forget that," Oliver says, shaking his head. He blows out a breath and turns back to me. "Shaye, this is my youngest brother, Boone. Boone, this is my assistant, Shaye."

Boone walks in and extends a hand. "It's a pleasure to meet you, Shaye."

I give his hand a firm shake. "The pleasure is all mine."

He lets go of my palm but leans in. A smirk kisses his lips. "If you get bored or need to escape work, I have candy."

"Thanks," I say with a laugh.

Oliver rolls his eyes. "Boone, leave her alone. Don't taint her with your bullshit."

Boone winks at me before pulling away. "Someone is jealous that other people, *meaning me*, have to work a fraction as hard in order to get double the output." He pats Oliver's shoulder as he returns to the doorway. "It's okay, Ollie. I understand."

I settle back in my chair and feel my heartbeat even out. The banter between the two of them—and the mood they create—helps my nerves. And every time Boone calls him Ollie, I wobble a little bit on the inside. *Ollie* is so darn cute.

Like the man himself, unfortunately.

"Ignore this guy. I warned you about him," Oliver says, unable to maintain the serious look on his face. He breaks into a smile.

"You did," I say to Oliver. "He's the one you called a wizard, right?"

Boone's jaw drops. "You called me a wizard? Ollie! That's awesome."

"No, I fucking didn't. I was talking about Wade," Oliver says. As soon as he says it, his shoulders slump. "I can't believe I just admitted that out loud. Don't tell him."

"Oliver called *me* a wizard," Boone repeats, ignoring Oliver's explanation and looking quite pleased with himself. "*A wizard.*"

"No one has ever called you a wizard unless they were talking about bullshit wizardry or something," Oliver says. "Now settle down."

I watch the fireworks between the two of them. It's so fun.

They banter back and forth, Boone extolling himself and Oliver dismissing each and every bit of praise Boone lauds on his own shoulders. I can't imagine what it's like when all of the brothers—*How many are there? Four? Five?*—get together.

And if they're all this attractive ...

I gulp at the thought.

Just like that, an edginess creeps back over me.

"Get to work, you slacker," Oliver tells Boone, laughing. "I need to go over a few things with Shaye, and you're distracting us."

Boone faces me. "Remember, I have candy. I also have good music playing in my office."

"I'll remember."

"I'm also the crazy pink color on the calendar, so if you need a break, just pencil yourself a meeting with me. I'll be your cover."

I laugh. *Boone is Hot Pink. Makes sense.*

"Noted," I say. "Thank you, Boone."

He smiles. "I need to go get some work done because, regardless of what this guy says about me, I do work." He pats Oliver on the shoulder again. "Have fun."

I'm not sure what he says after he turns away from me, but Oliver punches him in the arm. Boone grabs the spot with his other hand and disappears from sight.

Oliver turns back toward me and shakes his head. And at this moment, I feel as though I've found my footing. The man in front of me is a bit of a goof. He may be CEO, and I'm sure he's very serious when he needs to be, but in each of our interactions so far, he's shown that he's a man I can work with. He's intelligent, kind, warmhearted ... maybe even fun.

I think we'll vibe well together.

And watching him with his brothers? I raise my eyebrows at him.

"See?" he says. "Baby of the family."

"I think he's nice."

"A nice big pain in my ass."

Even though the words are pointed, I don't believe them. I don't believe he thinks that either. There was too much tenderness between them.

Oliver takes another sip of his coffee. He watches me, his forehead marred. I could sit and watch him all day. He's somehow even better looking in this lighting. But sitting and staring at my boss like a piece of meat isn't going to do either of us any favors.

I clear my throat. "Is there anything you'd like me to do first? There's a lot here to digest, but if there's something pressing, please let me know."

"Why don't you join me in my office, and we can go over a few things?" he says after a short pause. "I know Kelly is going to steer you in the right direction this morning, but I'd like to give you a lay of the land first."

Don't read into that.

"Yes. Of course," I say, blocking out the voice in my head trying to scream things about innuendos.

Oliver turns and disappears inside his office.

I grab a notepad and a pen before getting to my feet. I straighten my blouse.

"You're doing great," I say, blowing out a breath. "You got this."

I lift my chin and follow him into the other room.

Chapter Ten

Shaye

Holy shit.

I wasn't ready. The little pep talk I gave myself before walking into Oliver's office wasn't enough. Then again, I'm not sure if I could've been prepared for this vision.

This vision of power.

A large, stately desk with a white marble top sits toward the back of the room. Two leather chairs face it. Behind the desk are floor-to-ceiling windows with unparalleled views of the ocean.

A fireplace with faux logs, complete with a mantel adorned with a few framed photos, anchors one wall. A sofa in a deep velvety blue is placed in front of it. On the opposite wall facing the fireplace is a bar with a gold mirror hanging over it.

And, in the middle of it all, stands an Adonis with a furrowed brow and a hint of a smirk. Maybe it's that we're in his defined space—I don't know, but it's different in here.

More private.

More real.

More official.

I try to tell myself to play it cool—to keep it together, for the love of God because I need this job—but it's too late. I bet he can see my heartbeat pound through my blouse.

"Close both doors, please," Oliver says.

I shut both the door to my office and the one to the main lobby area. *Breathe, Shaye.*

"Our offices can remain open to each other throughout the day if that works better for you," he says, looking at a piece of paper.

Probably not. "Okay," I say instead.

"I do prefer to keep a barrier between my office and the reception room." He looks up. "I've had people walk off the elevator right into my office before."

"Are we talking about Boone?"

Oliver sets the paper down and laughs. "Yes. Mostly." He sits in his office chair. It squeals with the movement. "Have a seat."

I sit across from him, the cool leather seeping through the thin fabric of my pants and into my skin. It's enough of a shock to my system that I shake off the apprehension of the moment and focus on what I came here to do: work.

"Are you cold?" Oliver asks, his brows raising. "I keep it so fucking cold in here because it keeps me awake. But I can warm it up."

He starts to stand, his chair squalling again. His brow furrows.

"No, I'm fine," I say, motioning for him to return to his seat. "I think the adrenaline of my first day is starting to wear off. I always get cold after I go into fight or flight."

"You were in fight or flight? About working for me?" He sits down and grimaces as the chair squeaks through the air.

"Well ..." I smile sheepishly. "Maybe that was a slight exaggeration. But it is a little overwhelming to walk in here."

Oliver cocks his head to the side, running his thumb over his bottom lip in thought. I rip my eyes away from his mouth and pick up my pen instead. It takes only a second to make a note to research a good chair for him.

"I have a question," I say, raising my gaze to his. I'm momentarily silenced by the intensity in his eyes, so I clear my throat. "What time do you want me to start? I know it was eight today, but I'm unsure if that's the usual starting time or what."

He leans back in his chair. "I wanted you here early today so we could get started. My day is usually a shit show by nine. If you would've started any later than eight, I wouldn't have had time to see you at all."

I force a swallow at the implication in his words. *Was he looking forward to seeing me?*

Of course, he was. You're his assistant.

I wipe my palms on my pants again.

He rests his elbow on the armrest and runs a finger down the side of his face. I have to fight the urge to follow the motion instead of looking him in the eye.

"Does eight work for you?" he asks.

"I'll be here at whatever time you need me."

"Eight it is then."

"Sounds good," I say, making a note of that on my pad.

"We have a meeting the first Friday of the month at six o'clock."

I recoil. "Six? I'm not that much of a morning person."

He grins. His eyes flicker into a deep shade of green. "Guess you're going to have to adjust."

I grin back, the playfulness in his tone helping me relax. "Guess so. Are they the only ones we have regularly?"

"For you? Yes. There will be a variety of others I'll ask you to attend. We keep track of all of that on the calendar. Have you gotten access to that?"

"I was looking through it earlier. It's quite colorful."

"You are Orange, I believe. I'm Purple."

I write that down. "May I ask who is Olive Green? Because Olive Green and Hot Pink have some ... interesting conversations there."

Oliver rolls his eyes and sighs. "Olive Green is my brother, Wade. Should've been me since I'm Oliver, I know. But someone fucked up."

We laugh. A comfort between us settles the bubble of uneasiness in my stomach and reminds me of our interaction at the accident. It was easy, despite the circumstance, and if I hadn't walked away with such a good vibe from him then, I wouldn't be here right now.

"You met Boone, otherwise known as Hot Pink," Oliver says. "Wade is his exact opposite."

"Oh, yes, Wade the wizard, right?"

"Yes." Oliver leans forward, lacing his thick fingers together on his desktop. He smiles. "Speaking of wizard, way to throw me under the bus with Boone."

I grin. "Sorry. I got confused."

"You did not." He laughs. "You wanted to watch me squirm."

My shoulders rise and fall as I play coy.

"I will get you back," he teases.

My stomach warms, and the heat flows through my veins. *I'll look forward to it.* Visions of Oliver and zip ties rush through my brain. A flush creeps across my cheeks. I keep my head down and doodle a flower in the corner of the notepad while I wait to return to a normal color.

"What time do you go home? Or do I go home, I guess?" I ask, coloring in the center of the flower.

"You can leave around five, depending on what we're in the middle of."

I nod. And gulp as I force errant thoughts out of my head.

"I stay until ..." He laughs, leaning back in his squeaky chair again. "I work too much. I don't get out of here until six or seven most nights."

My gaze lifts. "Even though you start at four?"

He smiles ruefully. "I see my whole family here, so it's not like I'm locked away in some castle. I have lunch with my mother once a week. I usually play golf with my dad a couple of times a month ..." He grimaces. "Touchy subject. But the point is that work and family life come together here for me. It's not as bad as it sounds."

I make a face.

"What?" he asks.

"Oh, nothing. I was just thinking that no matter how much you love your job, being there for twelve, thirteen hours a day for five days ..." I take in his reaction. "You're here *six* days a week, aren't you?"

He holds his hands out in defense. "What? I like my job."

"You need a hobby. Here—I'm writing that down. Find Oliver a hobby," I say, writing those very words in all caps across the top of the paper.

He laughs as he watches me.

"What do you do for fun?" he asks. "What are your hobbies, Shaye?"

The pen hits the paper with a thud.

I think about lying to him and making up something crazy. How fun would it be to say that I scuba dived on the weekends or flew planes? I'm *this close* to telling him that I skipped stones on the water in my free time but stop when my gaze catches his.

My lips are parted, but my fabricated hobbies don't come through. I know he'll call my bluff.

"I don't actually have any hobbies," I say. "But that doesn't mean that *you* shouldn't have any."

"What's good for the goose is good for the gander. Or maybe that should be reversed?" His forehead wrinkles. "Which is the boy—the goose or the gander?"

"I have no idea."

We laugh, the sound of our voices blending together in easy waves.

One solid knock rips through the room before the door behind me opens, and two men walk in.

"Sounds like you two are hitting it off," one of them says. He approaches me with a hand extended my way. "You must be Shaye."

Oliver groans. It's amusing.

I take the stranger's hand, keeping one eye on a watchful Oliver. "I am. And you are?"

"I'm Holt. The CEO."

"Co-CEO, thank you," Oliver says pointedly at his brother. "Shaye, these are my brothers. That's Holt, which you now know. The other one is Wade. Wade, this is Shaye."

Wade looks much less interested in chatting me up. However, he shakes my hand dutifully.

Holt and Wade are nearly exact copies of Oliver—and Boone, for that matter. They all vary in the slightest degrees. Holt would be the older one of the group, if I were to make a snap judgment, thanks to the lines around his eyes and mouth. Wade, in my estimation, might be the most interesting. There are stories behind those walled irises. I'm sure of it.

Oliver, on the other hand, is a blend of the two—an exquisite one and the best looking.

By far.

I have no idea how people get any work done around here. It's no wonder Genevieve just sits at her desk smiling.

"It's nice to meet you both," I say, maintaining my composure despite the company.

Wade sits in the chair beside me. A wave of expensive cologne ripples through the air. "Are we getting work done today, or are we having orientation?"

"Wade, why do you have to be a dick?" Oliver asks.

"Let him orientate, Wade," Holt says, his words bordering on caution.

"It's all right," I say, taking a deep breath.

They all look at me.

I push a strand of hair behind my ear and focus on Oliver.

I need to win them over—show them that I belong here. There's an undulation of something between them—about me—that I sense but can't put my finger on. It was there in Holt's *Sounds like you're hitting it off*, it was thick in Wade's *Are we working today?*, and the vibrations pulsed through the office with Holt's thinly veiled warning to let Oliver be.

Assistants are probably befuddled by them, at least at first. I need to show them I'm not ... even though I kind of am.

I sit up straight. "Wade is right. Oliver has a full day scheduled, Holt has a briefing with Boone about Greyshell at one, and Wade has an appointment in forty-five minutes. He might need to hurry things up in here."

I hold my breath. Wade's head whips to mine.

"How do you know that?" he asks. "How do you know where I need to be in forty-five minutes?"

"You're Olive Green, right?" I ask.

A slow smile spreads across his handsome face.

"I took a brief look at the calendar this morning," I tell him. "I saw it. There was a note that you should take your Brekker sketchbook."

Wade looks dumbfounded as he turns to face his brothers. "Why are we wasting her on you guys?"

I beam.

"Shaye is *my* executive assistant," Oliver says quickly.

For whatever reason, this makes Holt laugh. Oliver fires him a warning look.

"Shaye," Wade says as sober as a judge, "when these two idiots—three because Boone is also in this office—push you over the edge, you have a standing invitation to work for me."

"Why, thank you, Wade. That's nice of you." I glance at Oliver. "I'm hoping things will go swimmingly with Oliver."

Wade scoffs. "I wish you the best of luck with that."

Holt taps on Wade's shoulder, and Wade gets to his feet.

"We just wanted to come by and say hello," Holt says. "Welcome aboard, Shaye."

"Thank you, Holt," I say.

They walk to the door and, with a soft thud, it closes behind them. I stare at it for a long moment.

Four incredibly, ridiculously *nice* men. In one place. At the same time. *Who knew that was even possible?*

Oliver's chuckle greets me as I turn back around in my chair. His arms are crossed over his chest, and he's wearing a playful grin on his face.

"What?" I ask.

He looks at the door for a moment before shaking his head. His tongue rolls around his mouth as his hands drop back to his side. He sits up.

"Nothing," he says. "Brothers."

"They seem delightful."

He snorts. "Yeah. *Delightful.*"

An alarm goes off on his phone. He picks it up, reads the screen, and shuts it off.

"I have a meeting downstairs—" he says.

"Marketing at eleven. Do you need anything for that?"

He smiles at me. *And I really do like his smile.*

"No, thank you. Grab a coffee from the kitchen—it's on the same floor as HR—if you need one. Make sure you review the welcome packet Toni gave you," he says.

I nod.

"Kelly will help familiarize you with the computer systems, and I think there is an intake form that you'll need to complete this morning. Again, Kelly will help you with that," he tells me.

"Easy enough."

He fiddles with his tie. "Otherwise, I'll be back upstairs in a few hours, and we can head up to legal. You'll be communicating with them a lot, and I want to make the introductions."

"Okay," I say, following his lead and standing.

He comes around the corner of his desk and stops a few feet in front of me.

Our eyes lock, his irises shifting colors again—deepening—as he takes me in. If we were in another place—any other place—at another time—besides the office in which we both work—I'd raise on my tiptoes and kiss him.

At least, I think that's what I would do. It's been so long. But the version of me that lives in my head and plays out fictional romantic interludes believes that's what would happen.

My mouth goes dry, and my lips are downright parched. But as the reel of the make-believe kiss we'd share finishes in my head, I scamper back to reality and the fact that he's *my boss*. And no matter how kissable he is or what I wouldn't give to lean in to this feeling—the one that feels pretty and desired—I don't.

I can't.

Because life is about priorities and having a roof over your head is a big one. So, too, is ensuring that you don't give people the ability to screw up your life.

Kissing my boss would surely put me at risk for the first one. It would definitely be wading into the waters of the second.

"Let me know if you need anything from me today," I say, my voice a little raspier than I would like.

His eyes darken, but all he does is nod.

I lift my chin and give him my best-practiced smile. Then I turn on my heel and escape into my office.

Chapter Eleven

Shaye

"So, how did it go? Tell me *everything*."

I laugh at Lisbeth's gusto. "What? No hello?"

She groans through the telephone. "Hi, Shaye. How are you? How's the weather? How's your mother—no, don't answer that one."

I laugh again. "Today went ..." Well? Swimmingly? "Great."

"*Mm-hmm.* If you think you're getting off that easily, you do not know me, friend."

Steam from my pasta carbonara rises in front of me, distracting me from Lisbeth's demands.

"Shaye!"

"Sorry," I say, pulling my face away from the plate. "I made dinner."

She gasps.

"I know, I know. I just felt like celebrating." The smile that has been painted on my face all evening stretches even farther across my cheeks. "It went *so well*, Lis."

My friend cheers. The sound is so loud, so shrill, that I jerk the phone away from my ear.

"That makes *me* so happy!" She cheers again—more softly this time. "Tell me *all about it.* What did you decide to wear? More importantly, what did *he* wear? Did you have a bunch of one-on-one meetings with the door closed?"

I twirl pasta around my fork and try to gather my composure. The last thing I want is for this conversation to turn into something that today was not—namely, a love story waiting to happen.

"I wore black pants and that cream-colored blouse that I wore to dinner with you when your parents were in town," I say.

"Great choice. Great choice."

It's a good thing Lisbeth can't see me. Otherwise, she'd be hyping herself up over my grin that just turned stupid.

My fork spins around and around as my brain focuses on Oliver standing in my doorway today. The way the denim hugged his thighs. The bright white T-shirt that gave his gray blazer an air of approachability.

How his smile seeped into my skin and warmed me from the inside out.

"And ...?" Lisbeth prompts, pulling me out of my daydream.

"And Oliver looked awesome," I say before filling my mouth with pasta.

"No one uses that word anymore, for starters. Secondly, I know you. I know your vocabulary. Dig deeper, Shayester. *Describe him to me.*"

I snort, wiping my mouth off with a napkin.

"I hope you didn't do that," she says, stifling a chuckle.

Quickly, I take a sip of water. "No. I didn't make that ungodly sound at work today."

"That's good."

I roll my eyes.

"You had a good day then?" she asks. "I'm being serious. It went well?"

I sit back in my chair and feel a semblance of peace drift through my body. Even with my ability to pick apart any given situation—even if it happened twenty years ago—and still find something to either be embarrassed about or worry over, I still feel good about today.

"Yeah," I say, blowing out a breath. "It did. I was super nervous this morning, but once I got there, it felt … natural."

My gaze drops to a stack of folders I brought home with me. The idea of sorting through them, getting them organized, making notes of all the things that need to be done—the things that should've been done and are overdue—fills me with excitement. I pondered that while I made dinner. I certainly never felt this way when working for Monroe Companies. Sure, my position there wasn't that much different from what I'm doing now, and Mr. Monroe always treated me so respectfully, but I was never this motivated to do the work.

I get up from my seat. "It's really weird. I walk in, and everyone is so nice to me. They all made me feel so welcome. Toni, the woman I interviewed with, had everything ready to go first thing this morning with a smile on her face. Kelly, she works on my floor, told me about her first day to help me relax. And every one of the Mason brothers were just …" My cheeks ache from grinning. "They're so different, yet so much the same."

"Ooh. Brothers? Tell me more."

I laugh. "Holt is the co-CEO, along with Oliver. He seems like he keeps them all in line. And Boone is a riot. I like him already. Then there's Wade. He seems annoyed with the rest of them. Think … stupidly hot, glasses-wearing architect."

"I think—*hook me up, please?*"

I laugh again.

"I don't want to go to this wedding, Shaye." She groans at the new topic. "I've been trying to talk myself into packing or at least making a list of what I need to take, and I just can't."

"So don't go. Your situation has changed since you RSVP'd. No one will be upset with you if you sit this one out."

"Ha. Then you don't know Lydia."

"I know that if she's your friend, she won't want to torture you."

"Let's just say that there's a reason you are my best friend and she is not. Besides, I already gave you all of my food," she jokes.

I pace around my table, side-eyeing the stack of folders next to my carbonara. My fingers itch to dig through the reports and papers. To be useful. To be helpful.

To impress.

A burst of energy courses through me as I recall the look on the Mason faces earlier today when I rattled off all of their schedules. That felt great—like I was valuable. I haven't felt that way in a long time.

"Want to come over and eat some of your food?" I ask her, trying to tease her into compliance. "I made carbonara. We can eat, and you can grill me about work, and I can tell you just how awesome you are and how every guy at that wedding will be trying to get your number. *Oh!* Come over, and we can plot out every outfit for the events at the stupid wedding. You'll have everyone looking at Tommy with pity."

She hums as though she's considering it.

"Sounds like fun, right?" I take a bite of the pasta, slurping the end of the noodles up for effect. "This is delish, if I do say so myself."

"I do love me some carbs ..."

"I know."

She sighs. "I want to come over, and I should, probably. But I know you have other things to do besides coddle me."

"I coddle no one."

"*Sure.*"

It's my turn to sigh. "Just come over, Lis."

"No. I won't. You have an entire day of badassery you need to revel in. And I know you, and you'll want to prep for tomorrow—"

"Not true," I interject as my gaze lands on the files again.

"It *is* true. You can't lie to me. I'm your best friend."

I rest an elbow on the table and smile. "That you are."

"And that's why I'm going to keep my butt at home and wallow in self-pity. You deserve to bask in your greatness today. I couldn't live with myself if I dimmed your sparkle."

I brush a strand of hair out of my face and then motion toward a pretend aura of glitter floating around me. "I am sparkling today."

Lisbeth laughs. "Girl, I know it. I'm so proud of you."

I'm so proud of you.

I lower my hand to the table slowly.

No one has ever really said that to me. Maybe my mother when I was a tiny girl over something small—I don't know. I can't say I recall Luca ever being especially excited about anything I ever did. My father, whomever he was, wasn't even proud enough to stick around for my birth.

Lisbeth's words roll around my head and then over my heart. It's not the first time she's used those words. She's been proud of me a few times over our friendship. She uttered that phrase when I told Luca I wasn't ready for children. She said it again when I filed for divorce. I'm sure she said it when I didn't curl up in a ball and disintegrate into the carpeting when Luca died, and then my mother basically disowned me. But this is the first time she's said it—anyone has said it—over something ... *happy*.

There's a decided difference.

Sometimes making a huge decision can feel like moving mountains. But making a choice to be happy is altogether harder.

And that's what taking this job was—a choice to be happy. Or, at least, to put myself on the path to find happiness.

"Okay," Lisbeth says. "I'm going to get off here and convince myself to do something productive."

"If you need help picking out clothes, FaceTime me."

She laughs. "I will. But I'm probably going to turn *Game of Thrones* on for the hundredth time and wish that Jon Snow was my lover."

"Sounds like a good use of your time to me."

"Me too." She pauses, and I know she's grinning. "Call me if you need me. Or if you think of any details you forgot to mention or decide you want to give me about your day. I don't wanna pry, but I got very little information on Oliver, so I will expect you to rectify that as soon as you're comfortable ... meaning that you have a week to cough up the goods."

"There are no goods!" I laugh. "Keep living in your little fictional world, darling."

"I fully intend on doing just that!" She laughs along with me. "Talk later."

"Bye."

"Goodbye, Shaye."

I end the call and set my phone next to my plate.

I take a deep breath and let it out in a steady stream. The act is soothing, dropping me back in reality with a soft landing. Shoving my plate aside, I pull the stack of folders in front of me and open the first one. *Jewell* is written on the cover sheet.

The file is thick. Oliver's notes are scribbled on half-sheets of paper, along the borders of others, and on sticky notes that have fallen off their original locations. I take a bite of my dinner and flip through the pages.

It's fascinating. There are reports on everything from the soil composition to solar panels production to man-hours required for moving dirt. I flip through each report, every purchase order, sketch by sketch, awed at what this company does.

At what Oliver does.

Each piece of paper has his signature on it, a note somewhere, and a contact name or the price of materials. The care that he's taken on every single element of this project is inspiring. The CEOs I've known in the past have mostly written off this low-level grunt work and passed it along to others. It's inspiring to see someone pay such time and attention to detail like this. *Admirable.*

My phone buzzes beside me, and I pick it up without looking at it. "Hello?"

"Hello, Shaye."

The voice is not Lisbeth's like I predicted. It's low and thick and confident. *Sexy.*

I sit up straight.

"I hope I didn't disturb you," Oliver says.

"Me?" I pass a swallow down my throat. "No. Not at all. Is everything all right?"

My brain switches to panic mode, and I sort through my day, trying to figure out what I might've forgotten or might've said that would justify a call at home after hours.

Shit.

"Yes, everything is fine," he says. "How did your first day go?"

"It was great. Fine. Thanks." I pull my brows together. *Surely, he's not calling me to ask about my day.* "How was yours?"

It's a dumb question, but I can't take it back. I cringe instead.

"Mine was good. Thanks for asking," he says, his voice kissed with a smile. "I peeked around your desk this evening. I love how organized you are."

"Thanks," I say, biting my lip to keep my cheeks from splitting.

"I, however, am not quite as organized. I can't seem to locate a file called Jewell. Do you happen to know where it might be?"

My face heats as I spring to my feet. My eyes are glued on the folder in front of me.

"I do, actually," I say, gulping back a wave of trepidation. "I brought it home with me. And now, on second thought, that might not have been a good idea. I just wanted to get to know things a little better, and I didn't think it would be a big deal. Most things are on the computer these days anyway—*wait!* I'm not saying there's anything wrong with not accessing them via an online portal because—"

"Shaye?"

I suck in a hasty breath. "Yeah?"

"Relax." He chuckles. "It's fine."

"Are you sure? Because I feel like a twit."

I stare out the window. The moon hangs high in the sky, a sliver of silver amongst the stars. It would be a beautiful moment if I wasn't ready to puke.

The squeal of his chair breaks the silence.

"There will be no feeling like a ... twit? Is that what you said?" he asks.

"Yes. A twit."

"I'm not sure what that is, but it sounds awful."

The corner of my lip curls up. "It is."

"Well, none of that," he says. "I'm actually impressed you took files home."

The heat begins to drain from my face. My stomach relaxes a little.

"I find all of this fascinating," I admit. "Monroe Companies does a fraction of what Mason Limited does. They are one little piece, and you are the whole puzzle."

"That's been said."

I can hear the smile in his voice. I blush in response.

"Do you need the file?" I ask. "I can bring it to you. I don't live far from the office."

My words hang in the air. My insides twist at the offer, and I'm not sure if I want him to take it or not. Would I love to see him? Yes. But also ... no.

It's a conundrum.

I glance down at my yoga pants and What The Fucculent shirt.

"Could you? I hate to even ask you to do that." He groans. "Maybe you could just screenshot a few things and—"

"I can bring them to you. It's not a big deal. Honest."

He pauses. "I can come pick them up."

"No. Let me bring them to you. I have nothing going on."

"You're positive?"

"One hundred percent." I nibble on my bottom lip as I glance at my pasta. "But ... I'm in leisure clothes."

"*Oh?*"

I still at the tone of his voice. Suddenly, my heartbeat is all I can hear. "I'm just saying that I'm not in work attire, and I'm not changing. So I can bring you this file, but I'm in yoga pants."

His chair screeches again. "I don't think that's a problem at all."

I gulp. "Good."

"Good."

"I'll see you shortly then?"

He pauses. The line goes quiet. Despite the silence, the connection is filled with an intensity, an anticipation of what comes next.

"Thank you, *Shaye*."

The way he says my name sends a shiver bolting down my spine. I part my lips and take in a quick breath—and hope to the heavens he can't hear it.

"Goodbye, Oliver," I say as smoothly as I can manage.

"See you soon."

I end the call.

Chapter Twelve

Oliver

"Fuck you very much," I say, my fingers flying across my keyboard. "Oliver."

I sit back and review the email that I just composed. The *Regards* closing I used instead of the one I typed out loud seems to be a good choice.

I hit send.

Blowing out a breath, I sit back and look out the window.

The sky is filled with hundreds of bright stars that twinkle from the heavens. Cars scoot around on the roads below, and Shaye is in one of them.

My lips twitch as I consider the fact that she's on her way to me—*to the office*. My immediate frustration at not finding the file quickly diminished when I realized that she might have it. And while I do regret that she has to trek to the office so late on my account, I also ... don't.

I rub my chin.

I can't decide if Shaye is a blessing or a burden. On the one hand, today exceeded my expectations. She was quick, efficient, and eager to learn. That's a trio that's hard to find. But every card has two sides, and this situation is no different. All of that ability is housed in a tight little body with a glowing personality—neither of which I can ignore.

Sure, I work with beautiful women on the regular. I'm always able to put them in a box. Dangerous. A competitor. High-maintenance.

That one is too clingy, and this one expects too much.

Shaye, unfortunately, doesn't fit in a box.

As Holt reminded me yet again on his way out of the office this afternoon, Shaye is now our employee. *Family first.* If I'm going to have her in our business, I need to be cognizant of our relationship—keep it on one side of me. Keep it in one of those boxes that I can't seem to get her in.

My phone buzzes on my desk. I scoop it up, hoping it's Shaye. The name on the screen says it's not.

"Hello?" I say.

"Hey, son." Dad's voice barrels through the line. "How's it going?"

My body tenses. I lean forward and place one elbow on my desk as if it'll somehow bolster me for this conversation.

"I'm good. You?" I ask.

"Same old, same old."

In the course of a normal conversation with the old man, I'd volunteer information about my day. I'd tell him about Shaye or about the predicament on the Jewell project. I might ask him to meet me somewhere for a drink and he'd oblige. This, however, isn't a normal conversation.

I hoped that when he finally called me that I wouldn't feel as irritated with him. Maybe time would've softened my reaction to him missing Rosie's birthday or that Mom would've called and smoothed it over like she's done before. *He's a grown man, Oliver. He has a life outside of me.*

My fingertips strum against the desktop. "Did you just get back to town?"

"I got in yesterday," he says. "Did some golfing up north. Did a little fishing. Pretty good time."

"Glad to hear it."

"Is there something wrong?"

I blow out a breath. The sound rattles through the phone. I sit back in my seat and feel a shot of adrenaline push through my veins.

"Yeah, actually," I say. "I'm a little pissed off that you missed Rosie's party."

He scoffs. "She's a kid. She didn't miss me being there."

"Maybe you're right. But maybe your kid, Boone, did."

"Oh, come on, Oliver. Don't try to guilt-trip me about missing a little girl's birthday party—a little girl I just met, mind you."

I spring forward, chair squealing. "That *little girl* is your grand-daughter."

"She's not my blood."

The pressure building at the top of my head feels like it's going to blow. My jaw falls open as a response fit for my father eludes me.

"I'm sure your mother got *the granddaughter* a very nice, very expensive gift," he says, sarcasm thick in his tone.

It takes everything I have to keep my composure. "I'm sure that you are missing the fucking point, Pops."

"Did your mother get to you too?"

"Did my mother ..." I clench my teeth together and exhale—for my own good as much as his. "I don't know where you were going with that, but it would behoove you to leave Mom out of this conversation."

"It would behoove *you*, Oliver, to remember who you're fucking talking to."

I get to my feet. My free hand goes to my tie, jerking it free from my neck. "I know exactly who I'm talking to."

"I've already been hassled by your mother about this whole party bullshit, and I'm not about to do it again with you," he says, the statement more a warning than an information bulletin.

"Fine. Let's leave the party out of it. When is the last time you talked to Boone?"

"I don't know. He hasn't called."

"And it never occurred to you to check on your youngest son? The one who's going through a bunch of shit right now and might, I don't know, need his dad's advice? Or at least to know that he's got his dad behind him?"

"If he needed me, he'd call."

I run a hand through my hair and face the windows again. "Maybe he just expected more from you. Maybe he expected a little support without having to ask for it. Hell, maybe *I* expected more from you."

"You know what? I raised you kids. I did right by all of you and your mother for the past thirty, forty years. I paid my dues. You're grown-ass men who can handle yourselves. And if you can't, well that's not my fucking problem anymore."

I force a hot, tense swallow. His words ring through my head on repeat—ricocheting through my mind like a bullet fired from an enemy.

Only it's not an enemy. *It's my father.*

My lips part to follow up with a question or a comment, but nothing comes out. My brain fails to find an appropriate response to the admission from Dad that he has been choosing to detach himself from our lives.

No. *He's chosen.* Past tense.

I've suspected this is the case. Things have been slowly changing with him over the past year or so—less calls. Less appearances. Less normal Dad shit that he's done my entire life. Even though I've thought something wasn't quite right, it still stuns me to hear him verbalize it. To admit he's *paid his dues.*

What the actual fuck?

"What's going on with you?" I ask him. "Where is all of this coming from?"

"I'm tired. I'm tired of all of this. I've spent my entire life making choices that benefit everyone else, and as soon as I decide to do a few things for me, everyone's pissed." He sighs. "At what point do I get to live my life, huh?"

I look around my office—the one that used to be his. I remember sitting on the old brown leather sofa he had against the back wall, listening to him finishing up his day. He'd set the phone down or dismiss his secretary, and then smile at me and say, *"Let's go tell Mama how pretty she is."* I recall coming in the door with Holt, the two of us sent here by Mom for fighting, and listening to an hour-long speech about how family is everything. It feels like yesterday that Wade and me, wet behind the ears, helped map out our very first project together with Dad at the helm.

What the hell happened?

"You're the one who preached to me my entire life that family comes first," I tell him, massaging my chest where his invisible bullets landed. "Family *is* life. Did you forget that?"

"That's just a bunch of rhetoric."

"Is it?" I slide a hand in my pocket and lean against the wall. "I don't think so."

"You're still young, Oliver. You still view the world through a pair of rose-colored glasses. Just wait until you get to be my age and have a bunch of grown kids who still need you and a wife who still expects you to come home for dinner. Let's see what you have to say then."

I imagine that scenario. I pretend I'm him. I envision having a son like Boone who became a husband and a father overnight—and how proud I'd be. Having your eldest son take over for you like Holt and I did? Priceless. And then having Wade, a fucking genius, branch out your company into a brand-new area?

Does it get better than all of that?

It's everything he's said he's always wanted, the pinnacle of a life he planned from an early age. And now he has it. He achieved it all, and somehow he's unhappy?

With us?

It stings. His words, his confessions burn the center of my heart. The man who I've always looked up to, the man I tried to emulate considers me an inconvenience?

"I think I'd be pretty happy with my life," I tell him, my voice hollow. "Your kids are great. Your wife is amazing."

"My wife is a pain in my ass."

I shove off the wall, my eyes nearly bulging from my head. *How dare he.*

"I don't know if you've forgotten, but Mom is a big part of why you were successful in the first place. Slow your roll when it comes to her."

"What is it with you and your mother?"

"I don't know. Respect?"

He snorts angrily. "You always have had a problem with women, haven't you? Hell, the last time you buddied up to one, it cost me my cigar business."

Fire floods my body.

"What the hell is wrong with you?" I boom.

He sighs as if this conversation is boring him.

"Look," I say, my voice wavering with the anger coursing through me, "you wanna be a dick? Fine. You can go to hell."

"Easy there, son."

"No, we're past that," I tell him, my body shaking with fury. "Maybe Mom makes excuses for you. Maybe Boone chooses not to say shit when you let him down. But me? I'm not going to stand here and watch you hurt everyone who loves you. And I'm sure as hell not going to listen to you throw the fact that *your* partner fucked *my* fiancée in my face. So, no—*go to hell*. I mean it."

The line clicks. He's gone.

I stare at the screen in disbelief before tossing the phone on my desk. It rattles around, spinning in a circle, before coming to a stop next to my keyboard.

I rub my hand down my face, trying to rationalize what just happened. It's as though I've been blindsided—hit with a two-by-four when I wasn't looking.

What the hell is wrong with him?

My face is hot, my body tense, as I pace around my office.

I'm simultaneously shocked and saddened, hurt and horrified. Regardless of my suspicions, I never expected *this*. It's so out of character for him, so ... odd.

But if that's the way he feels, fuck him.

I stop moving when I realize that the door to Shaye's office is closed. It was definitely open a few minutes ago.

Curious, I walk across the room and knock gently.

"Come in," Shaye says.

I open the door, and my dad is completely forgotten.

Holy. Fuck.

Chapter Thirteen

Shaye

"What are you doing?"

Oliver's voice is borderline incredulous as he takes in the scene in front of him. I shrug, my shoulders bobbing up and down in a sheepish gesture.

He furrows his brows. "Is that an office chair?"

"Okay, maybe I overstepped just a little," I say, getting to my feet. "But your chair is very, very squeaky, and I noticed that you winced every time it squealed."

The wrinkles in his forehead slowly disappear.

"I did some research on office chairs. There's a lot more information out there about them than you might think," I say, watching a grin tickle his lips. "And as long as you don't have any back issues that I don't know about, I think this one is worth a shot."

I grab the back of the frame and send the chair spinning in a circle.

"It's top rated," I say. "Very similar to the one you had. It's quiet as a church mouse, and best of all, I used a coupon." I make a face. "A digital one on Amazon. I'm not spending my weekends clipping coupons or anything. I'd starve first."

I hold my breath and await his reaction.

It was a gamble to order him a chair without his consent or request. I knew that going into it. Chairs are *so* personal. But he was clearly annoyed with his—*I* was annoyed with it from the office next door—and he was too busy to interrupt. Also, if I were a betting woman, I'd bet by the looks of disarray and how far behind things seem to be running that ordering himself a chair was the last thing on his mind.

So I did it. I took a risk. And I hope he likes it ... or at least isn't upset over it.

He reaches for my masterpiece. "Did you put this together?"

"It came in after I left, I guess. Prime shipping is magical. Anyway, you were on the phone ..." I bite my lip as a cloud rolls over his features. "It took all of ten minutes. You just shove this shaft into this hole and ..."

I force a swallow as the cloud swiftly moves from irritation to something else entirely.

I tuck a strand of hair behind my ear. "Anyway, it was simple."

"May I?"

"Oh, sure. Of course." I shove the chair toward him. The sound of the rollers against the floor seems intrusively loud in the small office. "If you hate it, I can send it back."

He pulls it in front of him and sits.

His tie is gone, the top button of his shirt undone. Knees spread, hair wild, and lips curled into an undeniable smirk paints a picture that will be very hard to forget.

Focus, Shaye.

I gulp. "Do you like it?"

He stretches back and moves around, the chair bending and flexing with him. Quietly.

"It feels nice," he says. "I just can't believe you got me a chair."

"Hey, you pay me to make your day more efficient. There's nothing worse than working in a crappy chair." I ponder that for a moment. "There are worse things, actually. But having a bad chair is near the top of the list."

We watch each other, separated only by the corner of my desk. My office is filled with the presence of this man. I wait for a moment of discomfort—a moment where I feel smaller, somehow. A switch in the scenario that makes me feel less powerful or itchy to get some air.

It doesn't come.

"Here's your file," I say, knocking on the top of the folder with my knuckle. "I'm sorry if it inconvenienced you."

He toys with his bottom lip thoughtfully.

"I also brought you dinner." I look over my shoulder at the Tupperware of carbonara I scooped out just before I left my house. "I'm not the best cook in the world. Don't get your hopes up. But I made way too much and figured that you might not have eaten if you were still here at this hour …"

My voice fades away as my gaze falls on Oliver again. His hand has fallen to the armrest, and his eyes are lit up like a child seeing a gift that they weren't expecting.

"It's just carbonara," I warn him again.

His eyes lift to mine.

I still, the edge of my desk biting into my yoga pants as I relax in his gaze. I find myself blowing out a breath—almost sighing—as my body realizes that we won't be fighting or flighting anytime soon.

It's safe here. No need to be ready to defend myself or flee.

"You have single-handedly salvaged my night," he says, his voice throaty.

I smile. "That's better than destroying it."

He smiles too. Leaning forward, he rests his elbows on his knees. The movement sends a whiff of his cologne through the air.

"Did you happen to hear any of my conversation before you closed the door?" he asks, his smile faltering a little.

"Not really. It seemed like a very personal call, and that's none of my business."

I pick a piece of nonexistent lint off my pants.

In truth, I did hear bits and pieces of Oliver's conversation but only because his voice was raised. He seemed angry and frustrated. There were notes of sadness, too. Although I know he's human, it's hard to imagine Oliver not in control of a situation to the point it affects him that way.

When I look up at him, he hasn't moved. He's still watching me. I expect him to say something, to change the subject—to blow off the call as something trivial and march forward with the Jewell file.

But he doesn't.

And the longer we sit across from each other, the more I feel prompted to say something. To ask.

I shift against my desk. "I want you to know that I'm a really good listener. I'm not prying, and I'm fully aware that your private life is yours. I'm also not being nosy," I say in a rush, my nervousness getting the best of me. "I just know what it's like to have something going on and feeling like you have no one to objectively listen to you. I mean—"

"*Shaye*." He grins.

I bite my bottom lip.

"Thank you," he says.

"The chair was no big deal."

His grin stretches across his cheeks into a full-blown smile. "Yes, thank you for the chair. And for dinner. And for the file. And for ..." He shrugs. "I don't know. I'd say *being you,* but I haven't known you long enough to really know who *you* are in that capacity yet. Right?"

The last word, the question, hangs in the air.

"I'd like to think that I'm the person you'd thank for being herself." I laugh softly. "I've never had that happen before. Seems cool."

He laughs too. "So, who are you, Shaye Brewer? Besides the obvious."

"Besides the chatterbox, non-coupon cutting, fairly competent in the executive assistant realm?" I joke, hopping up on my desk and letting my feet swing.

"I somehow think that's a very under-serving description of yourself."

"Me too. I'm also a decent, probably slightly below average cook."

He chuckles and relaxes back in his chair. "Slide that carbonara over here while you talk."

"Yes, sir." I push the container, a plastic fork, and a bottle of water his way. "Do you have any allergies I should be aware of in the future?

Peanuts? Shellfish? Even though there's no way I'm ever making anything with shellfish."

He opens the Tupperware. "Not a shellfish fan?"

"Not an anything-that-was-ever-in-the-water fan."

"You're missing out." He scoops up a forkful of pasta. "But no, no allergies except to bullshit."

"Ah, I happen to share that particular affliction."

He takes a small, measured bite. His eyes widen. "Oh, *that's good.*"

Internally, I beam. Externally, I try to remain unaffected.

"I thought you said you couldn't cook?" he asks, gathering another bite.

"I can cook the basics decently well. It's edible."

He shoots me a look as though I'm being silly and wraps his lips around the fork. My breath hiccups as I watch the soft yet determined way he slips his mouth over the utensil.

My body heats, my face probably flushing an embarrassing shade of crimson as I equate watching this man—*my boss*—eat to porn.

"It's very good," he says, setting the container down. He reaches for the bottle of water. "I was starving."

"Which explains why you think it's good," I joke. "When was the last time you ate?"

He takes a drink. "Lunch. Did I have lunch?" He screws the top back on the bottle. "Maybe breakfast. Hell if I know."

"You have to take better care of yourself."

His smile is warm. "You sound like my mother."

"She sounds like a brilliant person."

He laughs and sits back in his chair again. "My mom is pretty brilliant. She raised five sons and started her own jewelry line and takes care of everyone in the family."

"So, that's where you get it, huh?"

His lips drop back into a thoughtful line. His head cocks to the side.

"I mean that you seem to have a lot of those qualities too," I say quickly. "You're a businessman. You're smart. And I can tell that your brothers respect you tremendously."

He feathers his chin with his thumb. "It's a mutual respect."

"I can't imagine having a family like that."

He drops his hand and straightens himself in the chair. "Tell me about yours."

I bite my lip and smile around it. It's more of a wince, an internal sob about discussing a topic that you'd rather fight a bull than discuss. But the longer I fidget on my desktop, the more intense his determination for me to answer gets.

I search wildly for an acceptable starting point into an explanation that is both politically correct and honest. Telling the truth—that my mother is heartless and my ex-husband was abusive and now deceased—feels like it would paint me in an unfavorable light.

"My family isn't like yours," I say carefully.

He snorts. "That might be a good thing today."

I swing my feet again, watching the slight golden thread in my Hey Dude shoes catch the light. He's expecting me to say more, to explain, but I don't know how to do that.

"You don't really want to talk about it, huh?" he asks.

I look down at the floor. "Well, there's nothing to really gain from that conversation. It's also mildly mortifying to go in depth about your family's dysfunction when the person you're talking to has ... *your family.*"

"We ..."

I look up.

He sighs. "Honesty is the one trait that I value most. It's above loyalty and integrity and generosity." He shakes his head. "No. The importance of honesty is that it is an element in all of the others. Right? You can't have integrity or truly be devoted to someone else if you're not honest with them."

"True."

He moves around in his chair. "So, I'm going to be honest with you. And I'd like to think that you'll be honest with me too. Always."

"Of course. That doesn't mean that I want to spill my family secrets to you," I say with a nervous laugh. "But it is refreshing to hear that honesty means so much to you. It does to me too." My mind flips back to Luca and my mother. "It doesn't for most, sadly."

He leans forward and looks me in the eye. The contact isn't physical, but it might as well be. The weight of it is heavy.

"The conversation I was having when you came in tonight was with my father." He stills as if the admission is new to him too. "Growing up, Pops was my hero. I wanted to be just like him. I wanted *to be* him. He was the master of his universe, you know? He was exactly what I thought made a man a man."

My feet stop swinging. "And now?"

He blows out a breath. "And now I'm not sure what the fuck is going on with him."

If Oliver were a friend, if he were Lisbeth, I would know what to say. I'd offer an explanation—midlife crisis, maybe?—and a possible solution—have you talked to him? I'd also make sure my friend knew it wasn't their fault.

But Oliver isn't my friend. He's my boss.

"What?" he asks.

I give him a curious look. "I didn't say anything."

"No, but you were thinking something. What was it?"

"I was just thinking ... I don't know how to respond to that—to what you just said. Do I offer you my sympathies and tell you that it isn't your fault? Do I suggest reasons for his behavior? I mean, I work for you. We aren't friends."

Despite the fifty words I spoke, only three of them seem to hit us. *We aren't friends.*

Oliver recoils from the statement, looking vaguely hurt. I flinch from the taste of them too.

It's true, we aren't friends. *So why does that sound so cumbersome?*

"That was rude," he says with a compressed chuckle.

"You know what I mean."

He peers at me for a long moment. "I think we should be—friends, I mean. Wouldn't it make things easier between us?"

I force a swallow down my throat. "I don't know. Would it?"

"My brothers are my friends, and it's easier to work with them than anyone else."

That makes sense. But I'm not sure if it makes *enough* sense to override the warning flares being shot by the logical section of my brain.

He sighs. "Look, Shaye. I'm going to circle back to the whole honesty thing, okay?"

I nod warily.

"I've felt like you and I could be ... *friends*," he says before clearing his throat, "since you ran into me with your car."

"I ran into *your car* with my car."

He laughs, his eyes twinkling. "I don't want to stifle our ... *rapport* with each other by stuffing us into a professional box." The laughter wanes, but the smile stays. "Sure, we need to be professional. But I want us to be honest and open with each other. Who knows how well we'll work together if we allow ourselves that space?"

A bolt of energy races through me as I absorb his words. I know what he means. People who get along and can trust each other do work together better. I've seen it in action. But there's an edge to his words that slices through the rational side of me. It bleeds into the irrational, the illogical side. That's the side that is reading way too far into things.

I squirm. "Okay. Yes. Friends it is, then."

"Friends it is."

He grins. I think he wants to say something else, but he doesn't.

My phone buzzes next to me. "That's my reminder to take the trash cans at my house to the road for the morning."

He stands. "Let me walk you out."

"You don't have to do that," I tell him, but my body fills with a warmth that's so hot it almost makes me wiggle.

"Some fresh air will do me some good."

He flashes me a wide, disarming smile as we head for the door. All I can do is smile back.

Chapter Fourteen

Shaye

Ding!

The elevator doors part, and Oliver and I step inside.

"Don't think that I don't realize how you sidestepped the question about who you are as a person," he says, shoving a hand in his pocket.

"Did I?" I bat my eyelashes at him. "I didn't realize."

He bumps me with his elbow as the doors close. "Sure you didn't."

I fight off a physical reaction to the contact. "Our conversation just kind of went in another direction. How is that my fault?"

The elevator wooshes as it lowers us to the parking garage. I hope the sound and motion distract him, but it doesn't.

"You don't like talking about yourself too much, do you?" he asks.

"There's not a whole lot to talk about."

I stare straight ahead, waiting for the ping that will announce our arrival. It will be a good diversion.

Unfortunately for me, the sound rings through the elevator car, but Oliver is undeterred.

"I highly doubt that, Shaye," he says.

A gust of wind barrels through the parking area. It's so strong that it catches me off guard. I take a step, but the wind takes advantage of my momentary imbalance and knocks me to the side. I land against Oliver's arm.

Instantly, his arm goes around me. His hand cups my waist, steadying me with his sturdy grip.

It all happens in an instant—before either of us realizes what is happening.

My gaze flips up to find his already pinned on me.

The heat of his gaze steals my breath, the intensity of his touch silences me.

I can't pull away. I can't lean into him. I'm frozen in an awkward-yet-not-awkward position that I can't do anything about.

I'm electrocuted—held to the spot by an invisible connection that has my body lit up from the inside out. It's been so long, so incredibly long since I've felt anything like this. All I want to do is close my eyes and pause time; enjoy being held without the weirdness that will ultimately come from this errant step.

But this is the real world, and there are no remote controls to stop the bad.

Sadly.

"Oops," I say, planting a hand on his chest. I start to push off, to get back to my own two feet, but I don't quite have the strength, or the desire, to disconnect myself from him yet. Instead, I stare into his eyes. "I didn't mean to fall into you."

He grins but doesn't move a muscle either. "It's a thing with you, isn't it?"

"What?"

His hand clenches a bit tighter on my hip. "You just keep running into me."

"At least there's nothing to zip tie this time."

His eyes darken. And then as if he just realizes that he's essentially holding me in his arms in the parking lot, he frees me from his clutches.

I stand, wobbling a second as I get myself together. *How did it feel more comfortable in his arms than it does out of them?*

Oliver straightens his shirt and heaves a deep breath.

Goose bumps shoot across my skin, reminding me of the particulars of the situation.

I need to say something. I can't stand the silence in all of its trickiness, and if I don't say something, who knows what might come out of his mouth?

"My middle name is Lilliana," I tell him. "It's after my grandmother."

His hand falls slowly back to his side. He looks at me cagily.

"I like the color blue," I say. "Deep rather than light. My favorite food is macaroni and cheese. The blue Kraft box, if I get a choice."

The corner of his lips turn up.

I start to walk toward my car. He follows beside me.

"My favorite movie is *Steel Magnolias*. I was obsessed with that movie growing up. I named my cat Ouiser when I was nine," I say.

He nods but doesn't respond.

"I always thought that I'd have a daughter and name her Shelby Lilliana someday," I say, pushing a strand of hair out of my face. "I was stuck on a boy's name, though. Drum lent itself to a lot of jokes, and I was never a big fan of Jackson." We stop at the front of my car. "I was always convinced he was cheating on Shelby."

"I've seen that movie."

"You have?"

He nods. "My cousin Larissa loves it. That and *Fried Green Tomatoes*."

"Oh! I love that one too!"

Oliver grins. "You'd love Riss then."

The wind picks up again. I turn my back away to shield myself from the dust being thrown around the parking lot.

"What else is there to know about you, Shaye?" he asks.

It might be the softness of his voice. It could be the smoothness of his tone. Still, it could be the way my name feels so intimate wrapped around the twang of his voice. All I know for certain is that the simple question feels a whole lot more complex than it should.

I raise my eyes to meet his. In a flash, my shoulders fall.

All I see in Oliver's eyes is sincerity—an honest-to-goodness request to get to know me as a person.

I search his features, looking desperately for a sign of deceit. *What does he have to gain from this? Would answering it put me at a disadvantage? Do I trust him?*

Uncertainty bubbles inside me. The possibility of lowering my guard and being open with this man sends a spike of adrenaline surging through my veins. But the fact that I'm even considering it, something I haven't done for anyone in a very long time, tells me that maybe it's okay to open up.

Just a little.

"I don't know my father," I admit, my voice just a notch above a whisper. "My mother and I don't really see eye to eye. About anything." I swallow past the lump in my throat and look at the ground. "I haven't talked to her in three years."

I focus on a bubble gum wrapper that has landed at my feet.

"That's a long time not to talk to your mother," Oliver says

"Yeah." I bend down and pick up the thin waxy paper. "She took my husband's side in our marriage and then blamed me when he died."

The words fall from my lips and land in the space between us. This is what absolute silence sounds like.

As if Oliver should have something to say about that, Shaye.

Oliver shifts his weight from one foot to the other.

"I know that sounds like I'm a terrible person," I say with a sigh. "I mean, whose mother does that? It paints me in a really bad light, but—"

"But nothing."

My attention snaps to him.

His eyes are narrowed, his lips pressed into a firm line.

"I feel like I should explain," I tell him.

"If you want to, then sure. I'll listen. I'd love to know why your mom took someone else's side in your marriage. It would justify my anger right now."

I lift my chin.

"But there's really no explanation needed for your pain, Shaye. And all I really care about is you."

The bridge of my nose pinches as a swarm of emotions gathers in my chest.

The wind swirls around the two of us. The sound of the air rippling through the concrete and light posts act as background noise for the cacophony of my thoughts and feelings struggling for attention.

And all I really care about is you.

I know he doesn't mean it—not in the way it sounds. I'm positive he just means that I'm his employee, and I'm the only person involved in the situation he knows.

Still, no one besides Lisbeth has said that to me. Ever. And to hear someone say that, regardless of how they meant it, renders me speechless.

Oliver studies me with the most tender look in his eyes. "I hope you have someone to talk to."

I nod, still unable to formulate words.

"You said you're an only child, right?" he asks.

I grin at him. "You remembered I said that."

"Of course, I do."

A small, disbelieving laugh escapes my lips.

"And your husband died?" he asks carefully.

"Yeah. He did." I give myself a second to walk through this conversational door. "We were getting divorced anyway. It just wasn't final yet. He had a car accident and didn't make it."

He shoves his other hand in his pocket. "I'm sorry to hear that."

"It was three years ago. Not that three years somehow erase the trauma and all that comes with it, but time makes things more manageable." I shrug. "It's hard to explain that to someone who hasn't experienced it."

Oliver leans against my car. The halogen lights above give him a warm, orange-y glow. He stares off into the distance, choosing his next words.

"I haven't lost someone like that. Just grandparents. *But,*" he says, letting a sigh surround the word as if he doesn't quite want to transition into the next part of the sentence, "I was engaged once."

"You were?"

He twists his lips. "Yes."

"Can I ask what happened, or is this too personal of a topic?"

He looks at me. "Do you want to know?"

I think about it before answering. "Yes."

"Her name was Kendra. She was having an affair that I didn't find out about until after I asked her to marry me. Something that she and her friends all made clear that she wanted."

"Ouch." I frown. *I think it's clear she's a fucking fool.* "She sounds like a bad apple."

"She was a rotten one." He smiles as he leans up and away from my car. "Rotten to the core."

"Luca, my husband, was rotten to the core too. I often wonder if he was always that way, and I just didn't see it or if he rotted while we were together."

He slips his hands out of his pockets. "What you're really wondering is if you're to blame somehow for it. If he was rotten before, then you just didn't see it. If he changed while you were together, maybe you had a hand in it. Am I right?"

I exhale sharply.

What he said is absolutely true. It's a deep, dark fear that I only let myself consider in the middle of the night. I've never admitted that to anyone before—not to Lisbeth and not to the therapist I saw for a few weeks after Luca's death.

Oliver's question, coupled with the complete lack of blame in his eyes, is like a button has been pushed.

What you're really wondering is if you're to blame somehow for it.

It's hard when the people you love—your husband and your mother—both blame you for all the wrong in the world. That you're responsible for everyone's unhappiness. If only you did a little better, were a little *more*, then you wouldn't have handprints around your neck from being shoved against a wall. That if you could love better, your husband wouldn't be on the prowl and your mother could be proud of you.

But Oliver's not suggesting I was responsible. He was angry on my behalf ... for my mom's behavior. And from the short amount of time I've known him and watched his interactions with others, my guess is he definitely wouldn't blame me for Luca's actions either.

Oliver takes a step and turns to stand directly in front of me. He stares into my eyes, fights silently with me so that I allow him to see me without the guard I struggle to keep up.

"I don't know you that well, Shaye, but I know that you need to stop blaming yourself for whatever happened with your husband."

How is that possible not to feel responsible?

As if Oliver's pushed a button to disengage the guilt and feelings of responsibility for all the ways my life has been fucked up, my bottom lip trembles. My eyes wet with tears that I refuse to shed.

"Sometimes people get fucked up," he says. "Sometimes people pretend to be one thing when they're really another."

I nod, a strand of my hair falling into my face.

Oliver reaches out, his eyes glued to mine, and brushes it away.

"My father is currently fucked up," he tells me. "I don't know why. I know it's nothing that my family has done to him. But when you watch us and think we have it all together, just know that isn't true. We're all the same at the end of the day. We're all just people trying to do their best."

My heart squeezes in my chest. I wish I could wrap my arms around him and bury my head in his chest.

But I can't.

"Thank you," I say instead. "Honestly. That means a lot to me."

He nods. "Of course."

I clear my throat. "I better go. My boss wants me back here tomorrow morning at eight."

He grins, taking a step back and giving me room to turn. I open my car door and climb in.

"Thank you again for the file and food and chair," he says, gripping the top of the doorframe. "I really appreciate everything."

I search his eyes. I should drive off and give him a little wave and get back into the role of his EA. But when I see the openness, the vulnerability staring back at me, I don't.

"Thank you for saying all the things you did," I tell him. "I think we're going to be good friends."

His lips twist at the words. "Yeah." He dips his head in the car and surveys the interior.

"Don't make a comment about the straw wrappers, okay?"

"I wasn't going to say anything." He grins. "It just looks like you collect little white strips of paper."

I laugh. "Why is it never, '*Oh, you don't litter! What a nice person!*'"

He laughs too, his attention landing back on me. Moment by moment, the laughter stops, and something else takes its place. It's thick and hot and almost dizzying.

His Adam's apple bobs in his throat.

"I better go now," I whisper, starting the car.

I reach for the seat belt. As I turn to grab it, my hand touches his shoulder. The connection of our bodies is the spark that's been missing.

His eyes zap to mine, the pupils wide. I open my mouth to apologize or make a joke, but neither thing happens.

Instead, Oliver leans in—almost as if he's unable to stop himself—and cups my cheek in his hand. His palm is warm and smooth. I lean into it, my body already in overdrive.

Something inside me screams to stop—that he's my boss and I can't screw this up—but it's overridden with the pounding of my heart and the desire pooling in my belly.

Oliver's lips touch mine for a lingering, a touch-too-long but a touch-not-long-enough moment.

My eyes flutter shut. The contact isn't enough to quell the surge of need rolling through me, but it's enough to rocket me back to the present.

Oh, shit.

"Oliver ..." I stumble around for words.

He hangs his head. "Fuck."

"Look, that probably just—"

"Complicated things," he says, cutting me off. His eyes shine with sincerity. "But I'm not sorry. I've wanted to do that since the day I met you."

I half-laugh in a response riddled with shock. "Really?"

"Really." He touches his mouth where my lips just graced. "I hope it doesn't make things weird for you. If it does, I take full responsibility."

I sit back in my seat and try not to burst at the seams with ... happiness? Excitement? Lust?

"I just hope it doesn't affect my job," I tell him. "I really need this job."

"I assure you that this won't affect your job."

"Good."

"Good."

I reach for the door handle. "I better go. You have work to do."

He steps back. "Good night, Shaye."

"Good night, Oliver."

With a final grin, I tug the door shut.

I reverse carefully, ensuring not to hit anything in my haste to leave. It's difficult, but I don't look back as I pull away.

It's even harder not to let my brain get the best of me.

Did I want that kiss? Absolutely.

Would I do it again? For sure.

Is it in my best interest?

Abso-freaking-lutely not.

Chapter Fifteen

Oliver

"You're early." My mother sticks out her cheek for a kiss. "To what do I owe this change of habit?"

I hold my tie down with one hand and place a quick kiss to her cheek. Then I sit at the table across from her.

The dining room of Hilary's House, my mother's favorite restaurant in Savannah, is bustling. It's the typical weekday crowd. Women coming from private tennis lessons, men hashing out contracts over lunch, and a handful of tourist couples lured in by the heavy local traffic fill the tables at the small establishment.

"Sometimes you just have to get out of the office," I say with a tight grin.

I'm saved from my mother's curious look by the waitress.

"What can I get for you today, Mr. Mason?" Lola asks.

"Grilled chicken breast with asparagus, if you have it. If not, I'll take broccoli. Iced water with lemon. Thank you."

I try not to look at her. It gets tricky when she salivates over me with my mother sitting inches away.

"Mrs. Mason?" Lola asks, brushing my bicep as she turns.

"Bring me a Cobb salad and an iced tea, please," Mom says. "Thank you, Lola."

"My pleasure. I'll be back with your drinks," she says.

Lola leaves us quickly, for which I'm both grateful and disappointed. I'm glad she's gone; I have zero interest in humoring her advances today. On the other hand, the prospect of being at my mother's behest isn't exactly settling.

Mom takes her linen napkin and folds it. She places it on her lap, watching me with a knowing look.

Shit.

I sigh, resting my elbows on the table.

"Oliver?" She lifts a brow.

I pull my hands back to my lap.

"I thought I'd taken Boone out to lunch for a moment," she teases.

My jaw drops in faux shock. "Are you telling me that I've taken you to lunch every week for the last four, five years and you take that little shit out and pay for it?"

She laughs, her eyes twinkling with mirth. "Like you would let me pay."

"You're damn right I wouldn't."

She reaches out and pats me on the arm. "That's why you're my favorite. Don't tell the others."

I roll my eyes as I lean back so Lola can set my drink in front of me.

"Thank you, honey," Mom tells her.

Lola looks at me, but I only give her a small nod. No need to give her an opening for polite mindless chatter. Even that is more than I can give her today.

My head hurts. I slept like shit. Rolling out of bed a solid hour before usual—giving up on the prospect of getting any reasonable rest—I got to the office well before anyone else. But instead of being productive, I kept one eye on Shaye's door.

I'm not sure what I'm more fucked up about—that I did something I *should* regret or the fact that I *don't.*

The taste of her lips sits on my tongue even now. Her soft curves are fresh in my mind. But it's more than that. It's the weight of her smile, the vulnerability of the tears in her eyes, the truth of her words.

People don't share things like she shared with me—intimate, personal details—with just anyone. I know that. I don't share my fears and failures, not even with my brothers. But she chose to share them with me, chose to open her heart and give me a glimpse inside her wounds.

And now I don't know what to do.

My instincts are all over the place. The calm, rational part of my brain that I rely on to guide me through complicated situations abandoned me on this one.

I want to put distance between us. I can see how many ways this can go wrong, and I don't want to deal with the fallout of any of those circumstances. However, I have another urge just as strong in the opposite direction.

I want to care for her.

Imagining the pain she's in after the loss of her husband, the loss of her living mother—something I can't begin to wrap my brain around—and the loneliness she must face hurts my heart in a way that I can't fully rationalize. It's not just that she's alone that upsets me. I'd have that sympathy for anyone in this situation. It's more than that.

She understands betrayal from a parent. Is that what this is? What I feel?

There's an understanding between us. No pretenses. An instant, irresistible connection that I felt from the moment I laid eyes on her. And now that she's in my life, albeit not in the role that I contemplated that very first day, it doesn't feel like she got here by happenstance. It feels like she was placed here. For me. Perhaps in more ways than I first imagined.

And that's fucking crazy.

Shit like that doesn't happen in the real world. Even if I play devil's advocate—which I did hourly last night—and pretend Shaye is in my life for a reason, it doesn't solve the problem. It causes more problems.

What am I supposed to do? Date her? Be her friend?

"I think we're going to be good friends."

Right.

Through the fogginess of the situation, all I know for sure—the one thing that I feel deep in my bones—is that I now have a responsibility. I need to protect her from more harm.

But what if I am the harm?

"Oliver?" Mom's tone is stern.

I look up to see her watching me.

"What's going on, honey?" she asks more sweetly since she has my attention.

"What do you mean?"

She gives me a no-nonsense look. "We can pretend that I'm suspicious because you were here early, or we can chalk it up to Boone being your brother and tipping me off that there was something brewing. We could also just call it mother's intuition and leave it at that. Whatever makes you feel better."

"Fucking Boone," I mumble.

I pick up the saltshaker and tap it against the table.

If he didn't know something was afoot before, I'm sure the fact that I left the office at precisely seven thirty this morning made it apparent. But as much as I wanted to see Shaye this morning, I didn't. I don't want to see her until I know what I should say.

Which might be never.

"So ...?" she prods.

"So let's talk about Dad." I get settled in my seat. "We had a nice father-son chat last night."

Her face darkens. "So I heard."

She heard? What the fuck does that mean?

"What the hell is wrong with him, Mom?"

She smiles, but it's not a look written with happiness. Instead, the grin is almost a grimace, a tight-lipped gesture that makes me angry with my dad all over again.

"I know he's been ... slipping," I say, watching her reaction for any indication that I should tread more lightly. "He's been very disconnected for a while now. But last night? He was a total fucking dick—"

"*Oliver.*"

"What?" I lean forward and lower my voice. "Our shared DNA doesn't save him from being labeled an asshole, *Mom.*"

Her eyes narrow. "No, but his behavior doesn't give you an excuse to lower your standards either."

"I apologize." I blow out a hasty breath. The last thing I want to do is give her additional stress. I'm sure she has enough already. "Dad crossed a line last night."

She opens her mouth to speak but doesn't. I'm not sure if the words she planned to use were a lie and she reconsidered them, or if she can't find them to use at all.

"I'm not sure what's going on with him," I say, "but he needs to check himself before he does damage that he can't fix."

I lean back as Lola places our lunch on the table. Mom has a quick exchange with the waitress before turning her attention back to me.

Her chest rises and falls as she lifts her fork. "I think he's already done that."

There's a coolness to her words, a resolution, that lands hard.

Her fork dangles in the air, her eyes fixed on mine as she gives me a few moments to absorb the aftershocks of her statement.

I lean forward, forearms on the table, and hold my breath.

"Your father and I are separating, Oliver."

Her tone is practiced, controlled. Her emotions are in check, as always. Her features are neutral and intentionally passive as she waits for me to react.

But I can't. I can't react. I can't say anything because I really can't believe what I'm hearing. Sure, Dad has been a prick, and Mom shouldn't put up with it, but ... *my parents are separating?*

My head spins as I sit back and try to work around this bomb that was just tossed onto my lap. In a split second, hundreds, if not thousands, of images and thoughts and concerns and emotions rip through me.

As the seconds tick by and my mother's fork still hangs in the air, I snap back to reality.

I reach for her hand. "Mom."

It's all I can say as her shoulders drop. Her fork finally lays on the edge of her plate. She places her hand in mine.

The mask that she wears as the matriarch of the family slips ever so slightly. There's a ripple in her green eyes, a wave of uncertainty that looks so strange on the woman who is always in charge.

"Mom," I say again, my voice raspier than before. "Are you all right?"

"Yes, Oliver. I'm fine. I'm not at my best right now, as you may imagine, but I will be stronger for it in the end."

"Have you told my brothers?"

She shakes her head. "It was decided on last night. No one knows but you." Her grin is wobbly. "You are my test dummy."

"Gee, thanks."

She slips her hand from mine, but not before patting my forearm.

Mom sits back in her seat and composes herself again. Where she finds her strength—the will to press on in the face of what must be a devastating turn of events for her—is beyond me.

"This has been a long time coming," she says. "It's no one's fault."

"Okay. For one, this is me you're talking to. Not Boone or Coy. You can speak frankly."

She almost smiles. Almost.

"Second, I don't want you to feel like you have to explain anything to me. This is your marriage. I mean, it affects me—yeah. I'm curious. I won't lie. But I can imagine that some things would be ..."

"Better off discussed with a friend. I agree." She waves Lola off for refilling our drinks and waits for her to leave. "It's important to me that you have whatever relationship you want with your father. Your relationship with him is independent of mine."

"There won't be a relationship to have if he doesn't get his shit straight."

She makes a face as if she agrees but won't verbalize it.

My brows pull together. Dad told me he'd paid his dues and wanted to get on with his life, whatever that means. *But is there more? What's missing?*

"May I ask what *you* think his problem is?" I ask.

"That's the million-dollar question." She sighs. "I don't know, Oliver. I have suspicions, but they're just that. I don't feel right discussing those with you because they aren't facts."

"Well, at least tell me you got a good lawyer."

She grins. "I'm not ignorant."

My muscles relax a little.

The idea of being at my mother's house—*will it even be her house now?*—without my father around or, worse yet, congregating elsewhere hits me all at once. Just like that, the tension in my body resurfaces.

"I want you to know that I didn't make this decision lightly," she says.

"But it was your decision, right? He didn't spring this on you like he sprung his attitude on me last night, did he?"

"No. His attitude last night is what sealed the deal for me." She picks up her fork again and spears a piece of lettuce. She doesn't look at me. "I heard what he said to you last night. I was in the kitchen and didn't mean to eavesdrop, but his voice carries."

All of the things Dad said—*"My wife is a pain in my ass", "At what point do I get to live my life, huh?", "I paid my dues"*—ricochet through my brain.

My heart cracks open as I watch my mother fight hard for me not to see the pain in her eyes.

"Mom ..."

She presses her lips together and shakes her head.

"Mom, really, I—"

"None of that was new information to me," she says, her voice wavering. "I've been aware of this for some time now."

"Then why? Why did you stay with him? Tell me you didn't stay with him because of us."

She pokes around her plate as if the Cobb salad will give her the words to use. All I can do is sit and wait and hope she's really as calm about this as she's making herself out to be.

Her strength in the face of such adversity reminds me of another stoic woman I know. My shoulders soften as I consider the similarities between Shaye and Mom.

Strength, for sure. Class. Grace. A respectability that is hard to find.

Mom lifts her eyes to mine. I'm relieved to see clarity in her irises.

"I've had an amazing life, Ollie. It was more than I ever could've dreamed. I had a great husband for the majority of the past few decades and still have the five most handsome, brilliant sons that God could've given me."

I take a sip of water, mostly so I don't interrupt her flow.

"Things with your father haven't been great for a couple of years now. It was around the time that he had that falling out with Gamby—"

"Over Kendra and me."

She nods carefully. "Something happened to him around that time. I don't know what it was. I'll never know. But he hasn't been the same."

I sit back in my chair and try to wrap my head around this.

"I kept telling myself it would get better," she says. "And it wasn't terrible. I'm not painting your father to be an awful person because he's not. Our relationship just disintegrated, and I've flirted with the idea of separating off and on since Christmas."

My foot taps the floor. My need to get involved in this and fix it is overwhelming. Talking myself down from launching full-force into the middle of this family drama and taking charge is one of the hardest things I've done in a while.

Almost as hard as not kissing Shaye.

The thought makes me smile in spite of the situation.

"I'll be honest with you," she says. "It felt like—feels like—a big risk to divorce your father."

"Why would you think that? You'll be fine."

"Because staying married is the safe route. I know what to expect. I know the ways in which it can go wrong, and I know that I'd survive that."

My jaw drops. "That's no way to live a life, Mom."

Her smile falters. "Well, I chose to risk it. To see if there was something even more wonderful on the other side of the fear."

I listen to her articulate her thoughts—her sadness slowly replaced with a sense of excitement. Of possibility. By the time I've finished my chicken breast, she's laid out her plan for me in precious detail. And I marvel. This woman is the epitome of resilience.

Knowing I need to return to the office is frustrating because I hate to leave her now. As Mom carefully places her fork on the table, I know she's aware of the time too. Beneath her veneer of calm, though, is the fact that she hasn't touched her lunch. And that concerns me.

"Can we get a box to go?" I ask Lola as she walks by.

"Sure. Be right back," she says.

I turn back to my mother. "You're taking that salad to go. Make sure you eat it."

She laughs.

"I'm not kidding," I say, taking out my credit card and exchanging it for the to-go container when Lola returns. "And if you get lonely—"

"I'll be fine. I'm going to Coy's house next to break the news to him."

"Want me to go with you? I can clear my schedule—"

"Absolutely not." She exhales. A hint of the burden she feels is evident, and it hurts my heart. "You go on about your day. And please don't mention anything to Holt, Wade, or Boone. I want to be the one to tell them."

I nod. It'll be hard not to talk about it to anyone—Holt, especially—but I need to let my mother handle this.

She takes her napkin off her lap and places it on the table. "I'm a terrible mother. I didn't even ask you about what was bothering you today."

I take my card from Lola and scribble a tip. "You did ask me. I didn't answer you."

"Do you want to talk about it?"

I leave the receipt under my plate and put my card back in my wallet.

Do I want to talk about it?

I contemplate what I'd say if we did talk about it. That I met a girl who now works for me, and I kissed her last night—which probably was a mistake, but it really doesn't feel that way.

As I look up at my mom and consider telling her that, I know she'd listen. I know she'd give me advice. But there's no way in hell I could bring this up when she just unloaded *her separation* on me.

"It was just Boone making me crazy," I say, scooting my chair back and standing. "Just another workday at the office."

She doesn't believe me, but she gives me her hand and lets me help her up anyway.

We make our way through the dining room and across the parking lot, then stop under the warm afternoon sun next to Mom's car.

"Sometimes you have to go with your gut, Oliver," she says, patting my arm. "Remember that."

Before I can say anything—before I can ask her why that feels like intentional words of wisdom—she climbs inside her Mercedes and waves. Then she drives off.

I pivot and head to my car, my brain swollen with so many things to think about. As I hit the unlock button, my phone buzzes in my pocket.

> Shaye: Legal sent a report about Jewell. Marked urgent. Uploaded to file.

I stop next to my car.

> Me: I'll be there soon.

I wait for a response but don't get one. But that's fine. Some things are better off done in person, anyway.

Chapter Sixteen

Shaye

"He kissed you!?" Lisbeth's voice is so loud that I have to tug the phone away from my ear. "Why didn't you call me last night? Do you even love me?"

"Are you done?" I ask, shaking my head.

"No. No, I'm not. I gave you plenty of space last night, and you held back." She huffs. "This is not best friend behavior. Just so you know."

"So go be besties with Lydia," I tease.

"Yeah, hard no."

I fold the baggie that my now-eaten turkey sandwich was in and return it to my lunchbox. The sun is shining brightly, even for late afternoon, and the heat of the rays inside my car make me feel like I'm starting to boil.

"I was going to call you back last night," I tell her. "But I really needed a little time to try to wrap my head around things."

"You mean, around the fact that your boss kissed you."

I roll my eyes. "Yes. That."

"Well, I, for one, think it's great."

I pull my sunglasses over my eyes and crank up the air-conditioning.

Of course, Lisbeth thinks it's great. I knew she would. That's precisely why I didn't call her before now—because I'm not sure it's great.

The kiss was great. There's no denying that.

My face heats, and it has nothing to do with the sun.

"What did he say about it?" she asks, excitement dripping from every syllable.

"I'm not sorry. I've wanted to do that since the day I met you."

A chill wiggles through me as his words filter through my mind. I've thought about them a hundred times since then, wondered if his sentiments would change once I drove away. Because that's how things work sometimes. You think something is a great idea until you're removed from the situation.

Then reality hits.

I brace myself against the seat. "He said he's wanted to kiss me since the day we met."

Lisbeth squeals. "Okay, that's good. I—"

"I don't know if it *is* good, Lis." I sigh, my head falling against the headrest. "I think I'd feel very differently about it if he were someone else. Well, I mean if he were him but just not ... him."

"Not your boss."

"Not my boss at a job that has the capacity to literally change my life."

My best friend sighs. It's the sound of her daydreams falling back into reality.

I run a finger along the edge of the steering wheel, feeling the heat of the leather against my fingers. The warmth reminds me of Oliver's hand on my face and the heat of his lips against mine. The sturdiness of his body as he held me close.

If only ...

"How has he acted today?" Lisbeth asks.

A short, snappy laugh escapes my lips. Tension creeps through my muscles. "Well, I think he's avoiding me."

"Huh?"

My hand drops to the seat. "He hasn't come into the office today.

I'm not sure if that's normal behavior for him or not. I haven't worked here long enough to know. But I do find it suspicious that he's not here the morning after he kissed me."

"I'm sure he's not avoiding you, Shaye."

I hum. It's not in agreement or disagreement—just an uncertain middle ground that isn't very fun.

My stomach flip-flops as the anxiety that I've fought against so hard since last night takes over. The turkey sandwich sits heavily in my belly. My palms begin to sweat as I let the quiet of the moment invade my thoughts and pull me in a direction I don't want to go.

If Oliver is avoiding me—if he thought things through and realized he made a mistake—then where does that leave me? *"I assure you that this won't affect your job."* I want to trust him. I desperately want to believe those words and the man who I think he is.

But can I?

This company is even more important to him than the EA position is to me. What if he decides that kissing your employee is bad for business because, objectively speaking, it is?

What happens then? I start from scratch? I go back to scraping together every dime I can find to pay off Luca's fucking debt? Stressing every morning, noon, and night that I'm going to default on Luca's loan and my mother will lose her house?

I couldn't live with myself if that happened. We might not talk, and I might not even like her very much, but I refuse to default on the loan. If nothing else than for my pride. It would be the definite end to our relationship, and I'm not ready for that.

Not even if it's probably for the best.

"Stop." Lisbeth's voice is stern. "Stop right now."

"Stop what?"

This time, her sigh is filled with annoyance. "Your boss is clearly a successful businessman. He knows how to manage his life, Shaye."

"What's your point?" I wave at Genevieve as she walks toward the building.

"My point is that you are so sure he's going to decide you were a mistake that you're discounting all the possibilities! You're shutting doors that are wide open at the moment."

I bite my lip, worrying it back and forth between my teeth.

I'm not sure how to define the overwhelming notion building inside me since last night. Shame? Guilt? Both are probably true. But if I really, truly think about it, there's a little relief mixed in there too.

I messed things up. I knew better than to let my emotions get the best of me. Believing that the kiss could go anywhere without repercussions was yet another eye-roll moment for Shaye Marie Brewer.

At least I'm consistent at screwing up my life.

"You think," she continues, "that if you shut down any potential open doors that it'll somehow be easier than if he does it. Because you're convinced he will. You're not giving him a chance to fling those babies wide freaking open."

I laugh at the imagery. I also smile at the lifeline she's tossing my way. While I highly doubt that Oliver will walk in and decide that risking an office affair with his new EA is a smart gamble to take, I appreciate the faith she's putting in me. It helps to hear it.

God, I love her.

"Let him decide," she says. "If he can make decisions to keep a multimillion-dollar business running, I'm pretty sure he can adult his way through a kiss with a woman he's been attracted to since hello."

"You make this feel so romantic," I say as I shut off my car.

"Because it is. *It can be.* It might be if you don't friend-zone him."

I cringe.

"You've already told him you're friends, haven't you?" she asks. "You've already tried to head him off."

I don't answer.

"Shaye!"

"What?" I ask, grabbing my purse from the passenger's seat. "It felt like the right thing to do. It was the right thing to do. It gives him an out."

She fake cries into the phone. "How can someone with so much potential like you be so ..."

"Dumb?"

"I was going to go with self-destructive."

I ignore her and open the door.

The air is warm as I step foot in the parking lot. My car locks behind me with two quick beeps before heading into the elevator.

After a quick glance around to ensure I'm alone, I press the button to go up. "What would you have me do? I'm new to this. I'm scared."

"I know you are, but that's okay. Fear is good. It's healthy as long as you don't let it freeze you from growth."

"Well, okay, smarty-pants." I laugh. "I feel like you're taking psychology classes on the side now or something."

She laughs. "I've been reading about self-growth, and I have more to say."

The bell dings, and the doors open. I step inside an empty elevator and make the selection for my floor.

"You better talk fast because I'm on my way upstairs," I tell her.

The doors close.

"Shit. Okay," she says hurriedly. "Here's what you do. When speaking about work things, be a consummate professional. No flirting. No side-eyeing his body. No innuendos. But when you're alone—*and only when you're alone*—and the topic changes, and it's not work-related, be ... *you*. No. *Don't be you*," she adds in a rush. "Be a grown woman who's looking for a good guy to treat her well. Pretend ... Pretend you met him at the grocery store."

I make a face. "You meet guys at the grocery store?"

"You'd be surprised. I have a friend who had a guy find her phone in the bananas. He took her to Vegas, and ..." She growls. "We don't have time for this story."

The bells ring again, and the doors open. Kelly smiles at me from her desk.

"No, we don't because I'm at my office," I say softly.

"Pro, then go. Feel me?"

I laugh. "That's a terrible rhyme."

"But it works." She laughs too. "Now stop overthinking everything and just relax. See what happens. *Be open to the gifts of the world*," she says in her best Disney princess voice.

I shake my head and ignore Kelly's quirked brow. "Goodbye, Lis."

"Call me—"

I end the call before she says something silly ... or suggestive. I don't want to burst out laughing or blush wildly in front of my co-worker. Neither is a good look.

Scents of lavender fill the air but fail to whisk me off into a state of relaxation. Instead, my eyes drift to Oliver's closed door.

My brain gets a running start with all of the things that might mean. *Is he here? Is he actually avoiding me? Is he angry or frustrated or trying to work out how to let me go?*

I take a long, deep breath. My stomach tightens as I drop my phone into my purse.

"Good lunch?" Kelly asks.

"Sandwich in my car." I give her the easiest grin I'm able to dig up at the moment. "I know there's a lunch room downstairs, but I like to sit by myself sometimes."

"I feel you. Sometimes I race home just so I can lie in bed and watch twenty minutes of mind-numbing television midday. It's a great way to decompress."

"Ooh, what do you watch?"

"Whatever is on Bravo, usually. I'm a big *Housewives* fan."

The elevator dings behind us. I spin around, the sound practically reaching out and knocking me sideways, and hold my breath.

The doors open.

"Hello," Boone calls out, raising his coffee mug in the air in a salute of sorts. He walks into the room and stands beside me. "What are we talking about?"

"What shows we love," Kelly says, smiling brightly at the handsome man next to me.

My gaze snaps to Boone's, my nerves still riding high. I'm not sure if it was a good idea for Kelly to admit we were talking about *Housewives* instead of working, but it's done.

Boone takes a sip of his coffee. "I've been watching *Peaky Blinders*. Good show. Have you seen it?"

I shake my head.

"*Great* show," Kelly says, sitting back in her seat. "It gets better as it goes."

"I'm just on season three, so that's good to know."

Our conversation is interrupted by a ding behind us. We all turn toward the elevator.

I was more prepared when it was Boone.

My heart races as Oliver steps into the room. His gaze turns from his phone to the three people staring at him. He glances over Kelly and Boone until he's fixed on me.

I gulp and try not to fidget.

He looks glorious in a pair of chocolate-y tailored pants, a crisp white shirt, and a narrow tie that lays against his solid chest. A golden blazer makes his hair look lighter than usual and his eyes even greener.

His steps falter briefly before he tears his eyes away from mine. "What a welcoming party."

He smiles at Boone and Kelly. It's not the easy smile from last night or the one he couples with a laugh when it's just us in his office. It's practiced, rehearsed. There's something about that I find appealing—he didn't use that on me—but also nerve-wracking—maybe he's using it because *of me.*

"I was telling them that I'm watching *Peaky Blinders*," Boone says. "Ever seen it?"

Oliver shakes his head and moves to stand next to his brother.

My heart races. Despite the fact that Oliver's attention is on Boone, there's still an invisible cord between the two of us. It's as real as the drool hanging from Kelly's lips.

"I'll try it sometime," Oliver tells Boone. And then as if he's turning a page in a book to get to the good part, he raises his eyes to mine. "Let's go over that file from legal."

"Yes, sir," I say.

"If you'll excuse us," Oliver says, walking toward his office.

I give Boone and Kelly a quick smile and follow Oliver to his office.

Chapter Seventeen

Oliver

The door shuts behind her.

"How has your day been so far?" I ask, circling around the corner of my desk. I set my keys on top of a legal pad. They rattle as they come to a rest. "Thank you for the text about legal, by the way."

"Oh, of course. No problem."

I plant both hands on the edge of my desk and, hoping I have enough self-restraint to do it, I look up at her.

Damn, she's gorgeous.

Her hair is loose around her shoulders, her body outfitted in a black fabric that gathers at the side. It skims her curves, hugging her frame without encasing it. The look is capped off with a pair of heels that have a strap over her narrow ankles.

How are ankles sexy?

The only piece of her that isn't perfect is my doing—the glimmer of uncertainty she's desperately trying to hide in her pretty doe eyes.

I blow out a breath.

"Wade needs to cancel your three o'clock," she says, her fingers laced together in front of her. "Holt would like to see you as soon as you're available in regards to the Jewell update from legal, and someone named Anjelica called. She said that there's a contract for Hollis Hudson in your email, and she would like it reviewed as soon as *desperately possible*." She grins. "Her words, not mine."

She flips a switch from hesitation to confidence.

"I confirmed your attendance at the Landry Gala. Apparently, the original RSVP didn't get returned. There is a stack of invoices that accounting would like you to look at on my desk, and I filed the box full of papers sitting beside the sofa." She motions toward the spot on the floor that housed an overflow of filing for the past month. "I hope that's okay."

My chest rumbles with a disbelieving chuckle. "That's amazing, actually."

She lifts her chin. "Great. I just got back from lunch, so if you'll let me grab a few things from my office, we can go over the report from legal."

I hang my head, my hands still planted on my desk. "Just ... hold on a second."

"Oh. Okay."

I close my eyes and sigh.

We need to go over the report. It's important. But what's more imperative at this precise moment in time is the undercurrent of precariousness between us. It's the wobble in her gaze, the tightness in her smile that's barely there today but didn't exist last night.

It's my fault. One hundred percent.

I kissed her.

I meant it when I said I wasn't sorry, and I also meant it when I said I'd been wanting to do it since I first saw her. But what I didn't mean to do was make things between us uncomfortable. Or awkward. Or anything less than the brilliant easiness that we've experienced every other time we've been together.

Until now.

I open my eyes. "I told you last night that I want us to be open and honest with each other."

She nods, biting her bottom lip.

"And I need you to be honest with me right now," I say.

"Of course. About what?"

I cock my head to the side and look at her. We both know what I mean.

She takes a deep breath and walks to the chair facing my desk. "May I?" she asks, motioning toward the seat.

"Yes. Please do." I sit in my chair and watch her gracefully unfold herself onto the chair across from me.

She settles herself before her eyes reach mine. "If you don't mind, I'd like you to be clear about what you'd like to discuss."

Her professionalism throws me off. This wasn't the kind of conversation I was prepared—or wanted—to have with her. I wanted the banter, the back and forth that I look forward to with Shaye. The laughter and rambling and smiles that stick with me for hours after she leaves.

I sit back and run a hand along my tie.

But this is where we are. Now I have to figure out how in the hell to get out of it.

"I kissed you last night." I sit upright and let the statement hang in the air. "How do you feel about that today?"

She swallows. "Well, I would feel a little better if I knew how you were feeling."

Her words are measured, chosen carefully to guard herself from ... what? Me? Disappointment? I'm not sure.

The idea that she'd want to protect herself from me does something I don't expect—it hurts. A physical pain rips at my chest as I take in her resolution not to let me do any harm.

What did her ex do to her to make her so guarded?

I have so many questions. There are so many things I'd like to know about the woman who sits in front of me without any idea how hard it is not to touch her.

I don't want to rip her clothes off. *Well, I do.* But it's more than that. It's strangely so much more than that.

What's going on inside her head is just as interesting to me as what's going on under her dress. I want to know her past, what makes her laugh, and why she's so scared of getting involved with me.

Is it just me? Or is it everyone? Does she let anyone in?

"Truthfully? I'm sitting here wondering if all of our interactions will be as awkward as this one," I say.

She smiles as her shoulders sag. "Me too."

"I don't want it to be."

"Can I ask you a question?"

I nod. "Sure."

"Have you been avoiding me today?"

"What? No." I halt the rest of my sentence before I lie to her. Instead, I take a deep breath. "Yes. I have."

Her smile wobbles, and I instantly regret saying that. But it is the truth.

I clear my throat. "You've got me in a bit of a bind, Shaye."

"How's that?"

She has no clue what she does to me—how she twists me up and hijacks my thoughts.

I clear my throat again as I contemplate how to progress this conversation. I could tell her how interested I am in her, which would be the easy, mature thing to do. And the honest one. But if I do that, will it make things muddier? Will it put the two of us in this same space days, weeks, months from now—or worse?

I'm not sure. And I'm not entirely sure it matters.

My mom's advice trickles through my mind. *Sometimes you have to go with your gut, Oliver.*

My gut, so to speak, is contrary. It's all mixed up about what I should do, and I'm certain, very certain, that I could sit in this chair all afternoon and not be confident about the right way to handle this. *To handle her.*

"I'm going to be frank with you," I tell her.

She nods in agreement.

"I'm insanely attracted to you." I watch as a myriad of thoughts dance across her pretty face. "If you were a random woman, I'd beg for you to let me take you to dinner."

The smile that slips across her face is priceless. It's pride and shock and excitement all wrapped in one. It's a humility that's touched with joy. *It's not having a freaking clue.* It's guileless, and *that* is rare. Welcome.

"I'll be honest with you too," she tells me as her voice waves in the slightest way. "I'm attracted to you. But I'm sure you know that."

Her chin dips as she looks at me through her lashes. It's not a move, a trick to make her seem more innocent. It's a glimpse into her vulnerability, and *it's so damn hot.*

She shifts in her seat before raising her chin again. When she does, I can see a marked difference in her eyes, a look of resolution.

"I'm not sure what you meant by that kiss, if anything at all," she says. "I can't imagine that you go around kissing your employees. That should make things easier to understand, maybe, but all it does is confuse me more."

"I assure you that I've never kissed, touched, even winked at another employee in my entire life."

She nods and swallows hard. I'm not sure if my response helped or hurt the conversation, so I decide to answer her question—the one she didn't outright ask.

"I didn't kiss you with an intention in mind," I say. "There is no plan. There was no plan. It wasn't a step on a critical path schedule to get from here to there."

She watches me but doesn't say anything.

"It just happened," I admit, filling the space between us. "It was just a natural course of events—at least to me."

Shaye looks around my office. It's clear that she's thinking. She doesn't look bothered or scared ... or regretful, which is good. I sit quietly, my stomach in a tight knot, and try not to get ahead of myself.

I'm not sure how this will end or how I even want it to end. But if she's not in my life somehow in a week's time, I'll blame myself.

And be pissed about it.

Finally, Shaye looks at me again and smiles.

"My best friend tells me to be open to the gifts of the world," she says, amused by her own statement.

I smirk. "Are you calling me a gift?"

She laughs. The sound is music to my ears.

"Not in so many words," she says, leaning against the armrest. "I guess I've ... closed myself off since Luca, my husband, died. I probably did it before that if you can believe Lisbeth."

"Lisbeth?"

"My friend. The one with the line about—"

"Me being a gift," I say. "I like Lisbeth."

She giggles. "She'd like you too, I think."

"What's not to like?"

She pretends to consider the question, making *me* laugh. After my laughter fades and the two of us find ourselves staring at one another, she sighs.

"I liked your kiss, Oliver," she whispers.

My body heats as if a fire was stoked in my core. I smooth my tie down the ridge of my chest to keep my hands busy—so I don't shove away from my desk and wrap her in my arms.

"*But*," she says, dampening the moment, "I think it's probably pointless to do it again."

"Why is that? Because we have options. I'm the CEO, you know. I can have you transferred to work for Boone."

She snorts. "No offense, but I'd rather work for Wade. And he's already offered me a job, if you'll recall."

I was joking. There's no way in hell I'd let her work for one of my brothers. The idea of her being in the building—or next door, in Wade's case—and not available for me to drop in, talk to, check in on at a moment's notice would be a nightmare.

"I like you working for me," I say.

"Then kissing is *definitely* not something we should probably do again."

My temperature increases ... but not from lust. This time, it's from aggravation.

"You seem so sure about that," I say, my words confused. *Definitely not something we should probably do? Clear as mud.*

She blows out a long, hasty breath.

"If it's not about your employment—because I've promised you nothing will happen to that, then what is it?" I ask.

"I ..." She falls back into her chair. "Honesty, right?"

"Always."

"Okay, then." She takes a shaky breath. "I haven't kissed a man in a long time. I mean, sure, I've kissed a couple of guys that Lisbeth tried to set me up with, but it was more like a peck on the cheek after a mediocre dinner. But I haven't kissed someone and had it take my breath away in ..." She tucks a strand of hair behind her ear. Her eyes never leave mine. "In a *very* long time."

If she's trying to bewitch me, it's working.

My cock comes to life, pressing against my boxers. All I can think about is having this woman naked and under me—over me, next to me, wrapped around me like a fucking glove.

I drop my hand under the table and adjust myself.

"I have a lot on my plate," she says, watching me carefully. "*A lot.* A lot of things are still screwed up from my divorce or ... my marriage's end, however you want to phrase that. And I'm trying so hard to climb out from under the rubble."

"Maybe I can help you."

She smiles. "This isn't something you can help me with. It's all mine to fix, to repair. Mine to sort out." She sighs sadly. "I'm trying to walk a balance of moving on from all of that mentally while still dealing with it in a fiscal way. It's not easy."

I study her. The way her hair catches the light looks like she's wearing a halo. How she leans toward me with her shoulders, as though she's asking me to hold her. The way her lips stay parted so the conversation doesn't end.

My gut squeezes, pulling me out of the fantasyland of Shaye Brewer and back to reality.

She's telling me she's not in a place to deal with me. If I'm being honest, I'm not in a place to handle her anyway. I never will be.

Shaye is marriage material—porch-swinging, sweet tea-drinking, childbearing material. And I am not.

I can't be. I've seen too much.

People are fickle. Their needs and wants change. Hell, my parents are getting a divorce. My own father isn't even the same person he was anymore. It's how the world works. I tried to put on a pair of rose-colored glasses once and buy into the false promises of forever. She's currently married to Charles Gamby.

"So, you're not looking for a relationship," I say. "Is that what you're trying to say?"

"Yes. I think so."

I nod and stand, figuring it's a good stopping point for the conversation. Shaye stands too and waits for me to come around the desk.

"I can't argue with that." I stop in front of her, breathing in the floral notes of her perfume. "You have to put your needs first. That's the responsible thing to do. I respect that."

She sucks in a shallow, quick breath. The sound fires through my body like a bolt of lightning.

I take a step toward the door—needing to get her out of here before I do something she doesn't want—when my hand brushes against her.

The contact is light, a dusting of skin against skin. It should not feel like an electrical shock to my overworked senses, but it does.

I look down at her as she clamps her hand around my wrist.

Her pupils are dilated, filled with a plethora of emotions that I can't begin to sort. I just stand completely frozen and beg myself not to react.

Let her take control.

"What if ..." She swallows. "But what if putting my needs first means that I really want to kiss you again?"

Oh. Fuck.

My brain misfires, unsure if I've heard her correctly or if it's a case of hearing what I want to hear. Sparks shoot through my veins, heat balling in my stomach, and all rationale and gut instincts that suggest otherwise are buried in a pool of desire.

Her grip grows tighter as she gives my arm a gentle, hesitant tug.

"Oh, Shaye," I almost growl as I turn toward her.

"Kiss me, Oliver. Even though we shouldn't—"

My mouth crashes against hers before she can complete the thought, swallowing all the reasons we shouldn't.

I turn her in a circle so her back is against my desk and cage her in with both hands.

She doesn't fight, doesn't object—just parts her lips to allow my tongue entry.

My blood runs hot as I taste her. My body screams as I feel the softness of her lips. My brain loses control of the situation as I process how much she wants me.

A chill races down my spine as she reaches up and touches my face. Her fingertips press into my cheeks as she kisses me back.

I flick the stapler away from behind her with the back of my hand. It crashes against the floor with a clatter. My hands find her waist, and I hoist her up to sit on the edge of the stone.

"Oliver," she whispers as I dot kisses across her jaw. Her head falls back, and she moans, leaning into the kisses I plant down her neck.

Her hands dance across my shoulders, skim down my sides, and slip under my blazer.

I grip her legs and spread them for me. She yelps with surprise but doesn't argue. My palms sit heavily on her thighs, feeling her soft, muscled legs under my touch.

I'm going to burst. I can't make sense of this anymore.

My fingers trail up the inside of her legs as I kiss her again. Just before they reach the apex of her thighs, my phone buzzes.

Shaye pulls back, her eyes wide, and gasps.

Fuck! Fuck, fuck, fuck.

She tries to push me away, but I kiss her again, and she relents.

"Shh," I say, peering into her eyes. "Everything is fine."

"Are you sure?"

I reach over and press the speakerphone. My eyes never leave Shaye's. "Yes, Kelly?"

"Yes, Mr. Mason. I have Greg on the line for you."

"Tell him that I'll call him back in five minutes, please."

"Yes, sir."

I hit the button again, ending the call.

"Oliver ..." Shaye's cheeks redden. "I don't know what I was thinking."

I smirk. "Me either, but I like it."

She smiles but bats at my arm. I step back, and she slips off my desk.

"Is this going to work?" she asks, straightening her dress.

"Is what going to work?"

She looks at me like I'm stupid. "*This.* You and me. This job. All of it. I feel like I'm just digging myself deeper and deeper into a hole, and I'm supposed to be climbing out of it."

I give her some space and walk behind my desk. I pick up the stapler.

"I'll agree that we need to get ahold of the situation," I say, trying to forget the way her lips feel against mine before I grab her and kiss her again. Before I pull up her skirt and watch my fingers enter her heat like they desperately want to do. "What does that mean? I don't know. But we can't just go on and pretend we don't want that to happen when we're together."

She considers this as she combs her fingers through her hair. "So what's the solution? Do I have to go work for Wade?"

"Abso-fucking-lutely not."

She grins.

I run a hand down my face. *How can I salvage all of this?*

"What would make you feel better?" I ask.

She thinks for a moment. "I need to know that I can trust you."

"You can."

"That's what they all say."

"Except that my word is the most important thing to me," I say. "If we can't figure this out, you can go work for Wade. And I assure you that he'd love nothing more than to have you in his office and deny me entry. It would make his fucking year."

She laughs. "Okay. Also ... I don't know what you're thinking or expecting or hoping, if anything, but I just don't want anything serious."

"You just want to be fuck buddies? Is that what you're telling me?" I ask, laughing too.

"I mean, *kind of*?" She covers her face with her hands. "I need something easy. Something to get me back in the game, so to speak."

I'm thankful there's a giant desk between us because, if there wasn't, I'd have her bent over this motherfucker in two seconds.

"Can we just ... take it a day at a time?" she asks sheepishly. "No expectations. *No rules.*"

What a weird thing to say.

"Yes," I say. "I don't want anything from you that you don't want to give me."

Her eyes light up. A look of contentment stretches across her face. The same feeling spreads through my body.

"You control the shots," I tell her.

"Okay." She grins. "You need to call Greg back."

Dammit. "Yeah. I do."

"And I need to find the ladies' room."

I look her up and down and growl. It makes her laugh.

"You go do what you need to do and then come back so we can go over this legal file," I say, sitting down. "I'll call Greg now."

She nods and heads for the door. Just before she gets to the doorway, I call after her.

"Shaye?"

She turns around. "Yes?"

"Will you go with me to the Landry Gala tomorrow? It doesn't have to be a date or anything, if that worries you. You can go in whatever capacity you want. I just think it might be fun."

Her brow furrows for a long moment before she finally smiles. "All right. I'd love to."

"Great."

"Great." She smiles and turns, but just before she reaches the door, she spins back around. "Oliver?"

"Yes, Shaye?"

"This might be a stupid or presumptuous question, but would you have invited me if we hadn't … kissed before?"

As Shaye knows, I've wanted to kiss her since the moment we met. Taking her as a date to the gala would have crossed my mind regardless if we'd kissed or if she worked for me or anything else as long as I had met her. So a part of my answer is most definitely yes.

But I don't think that's what she's asking.

She said last night that she wants us to be friends. If I'm being honest, I could use one of those right now who isn't related to me. I like Shaye. I like her for more than her soft, kissable lips and willingness to kiss me. I enjoy her company. She makes me laugh. When I'm with her, my load feels just a bit lighter.

So, yes, I would have asked her for the privilege—or torture, depending on how you look at it—of having her on my arm.

"Yes," I say simply. "I would have. I would've asked you for the honor of accompanying me to the Landry Gala, and I'll be looking forward to having you beside me now that you've said yes."

The smile that lights up her face is dazzling. She dips her chin and disappears into her office, shutting the door behind her.

I lean back in my seat and take a long, deep breath.

A shot of tension curls around the back of my neck, and it has nothing to do with taking Shaye to the event. It has everything to do with it too.

"You probably just fucked all the way up, Mason," I mutter before grabbing the phone and calling Greg.

Chapter Eighteen

"So tell me about the Landry Gala." I half-grin, half-grimace at Nate.

He looks up from whatever he's doing at his computer and furrows his brow. "Why?"

"Oh, I don't know. Maybe because I'm going."

I mosey into his office and ignore the look of surprise—*horror?*—on his face.

Nate would never admit it, but he's proud of this space. His ex-girlfriend, Joy, did most of the decorating. I loved her. She was just a bit too much sunshine for him, I think.

He rolls his chair back and faces me. "You are going to the Landry Gala? The biggest event in Savannah?"

I plop down on the little loveseat along the wall. "That's what I said."

I smile as if it's a good thing, as if I'm totally relaxed about my upcoming appearance at *the biggest event in Savannah*. But Nate knows it's all a façade. He knows *me*, after all.

He leans his elbows on his knees. "Do I even want to know?"

"Oliver asked me to go with him. And it sounds fun. It's a *gala*," I say, fluttering my eyes at the romanticism of the word. "I've never been to a gala before."

"Because they're stupid."

I make a face. "You can't call it stupid! They raise so much money if what I've seen on the news each year is accurate.

"Yeah, they do. And they could just call their friends and ask for a donation too. Instead, they all get dressed up in fancy clothes and eat things like escargot."

I wrinkle my nose. "So eat a burger before I go? Got it."

He laughs. "Definitely eat first. And wear something fancy." His smile slips, and a twinge of concern takes its place. "Do you have something to wear?"

"No. But Lisbeth does, and she's volunteered to bring me three choices tonight to try on."

He shakes his head.

I bring my feet up and tuck them beneath me.

The setting sun outside Nate's office window casts a soft, warm glow throughout the room. It matches the vibe I've felt since I left the office this afternoon. *Even before then.* And a lot has to do with the scorching, panty-melting kiss Oliver and I shared earlier.

I don't think I've ever been kissed like that—hot, urgent, desperate. *Sweet, tender, honest.* Oliver made me feel wanted and desired and beautiful. The kiss reminded me that there's still a spark deep inside me that can be lit by the right person. I was afraid it might've been extinguished for good.

But most importantly, the one thing that fills me with a giddiness that feels incredible is the way his words gave me so much confidence in the thought of *us*. Or whatever that might be.

Nate picks up on it and leans back in his chair. "What?"

"What, what?"

"What's with all of this?" He makes a circle in the air with his finger. "You're ... *happy*."

I smile. "It's not a felony to be happy, you know."

"I know that. It's just weird."

"Just be happy for me!"

He rolls his eyes. "You're annoying when you're happy." Despite the words, he grins too. "Tell me why you're Little Miss Sunshine all of a sudden."

I wish I could.

If I try to put into words what I'm feeling—like maybe, just maybe, things might be starting to go my way—I'll jinx myself.

It's happened before.

Nate scowls. "I don't care how happy you are at Mason Limited—you are not quitting me. I'll fight him."

"You aren't fighting anyone, pretty boy."

"Me?" He lifts his arms that are dotted with tattoos and flexes. "I'm hardly a pretty boy."

My body bounces as I laugh. *And it feels good.*

I'd forgotten how nice it is to have a normal day. To have a day when things just magically work out and you don't have a knife twisting in your stomach every ten seconds. To spend an afternoon with a little spring in your step because hope is starting to drift in on the fog that's clouded your life for months. Years, even.

"You're right, though. I'm not quitting you." I blow him a kiss. "You'll have me for ... however long it takes to pay off a one-hundred-thousand-dollar debt. Oliver is paying me well, but not that well."

Nate narrows his eyes. "Oliver, huh?"

"Yeah. Oliver."

He nods suspiciously. "I get it now."

I put my feet back on the floor. "You get what?"

"Nothing."

"*Nate.*"

He shakes his head before holding it in his hands. His reaction to my sunshine, as he calls it, definitely puts a damper on my spirits.

I scoot to the edge of the sofa. "Nate."

He looks up and sighs. "Look, I'm happy for you. If anyone deserves to find a good, rich dude, it's you."

"His money has nothing to do with anything. Besides—"

"Shaye? Shut up." He smiles, but it's restrained. "I know you don't want him for his money."

"I don't know if I even want *him*. I just know that it's ... *fun* right now. It's nice to have someone look at you and not just see the mess behind you. It's like I'm a different person."

"There's nothing wrong with the you from before."

I reach for his knee and give it a little shake. "Thanks, pal."

"You know what I mean."

He knocks my hand away, making me laugh.

"This is the first guy you've taken a liking to," Nate says. "Just go slow. Be careful."

"Yes, Father."

He scowls. "I mean it. You have no dating experience, and you decide to date this guy."

My cheeks flush. "We aren't dating."

"Okay. You decide to *fuck* this dude."

"Nate!"

He rolls his eyes. "Okay. You decide to have a Pepsi with this guy—whatever you want to call it. I don't give a shit. But this guy is used to getting what he wants. And men like that—who practically rule the universe—can get out of pocket sometimes."

I think of Oliver *getting out of pocket*, as Nate suggested, and I can't see it. He's too kind. Too thoughtful. Too communicative. If I saw anything in him that even resembled Luca, I wouldn't have even taken the job.

"He's not like that," I tell Nate.

Nate stills, watching me closely. Finally, a hint of a smile threatens to part his lips. "I hope he's not. I hope he's your prince or whatever girls want."

"Thanks."

"But if he's not, tell him—promise him—that I will rip his throat out and feed it to him."

I jump to my feet and smack him on the shoulder. "You are a barbarian."

He smiles sheepishly. "You'll thank me for it when I'm protecting your virtue."

I rub the top of his head and head toward the door.

"You need anything? For the gala?" he asks, mocking me.

I turn around and look at him. My heart swells.

Nate can be a pain in the ass. He can be overbearing and disorganized and forgets to order the lids for the to-go cups. But he has the biggest heart of anyone I know. And that's why I trust him—why I've let him in despite the fact that I haven't known him for nearly ten years like I have Lisbeth.

Nate Hughes has proven to me time and time again that he's a good egg. I've witnessed him taking care of the people around him, putting himself last, worrying over whether someone has a safe place to sleep or if they're hungry. He had Murray bring me soup when I was sick. Changed my oil and saved me money. Gave me a freaking job when I needed one.

He's earned my trust by being one of the very, very few people who has never failed me ... or anything around him.

"Thank you," I tell him.

"For what?"

"I don't know. For giving a shit? For looking out for me?" I shrug. "For telling me to have a burger before the gala."

He grins. "It's my pleasure."

I lean against the wall. A clamor happens on the other side of it, and I hear Murray's voice shout from down the hall.

"Ah, Murray is back," I tease him. "That took longer than expected."

Nate faces his desk again and waves me off with one hand. "Take your sarcasm elsewhere. Some of us have a business to run."

I open my mouth but am interrupted by the door opening beside me. Paige sticks her head in the room. Her dark brown curls bounce as she looks around.

"Oh, hi, Shaye," she says, surprise written all over her face. "I didn't know you were here. You're not on the schedule, are you?"

"Not tonight. I work again on Sunday."

"I work tonight and tomorrow and *someone forgot to order lids again*." She winks at me before we both turn to look at our boss.

Nate's fist slams into his desk. "You're kidding me."

"Nope." Paige laughs. "Want me to run to Target and see if they still have some?"

Nate groans. "I guess. I don't know what choice we have."

"Well, we could just order them from the supplier ..." Paige giggles, ducking from a piece of wadded-up paper that Nate throws at her. "I'll go. See you later, Shaye. I'm taking money from the register for this, Nate."

"Just put a note in the drawer and then—"

"Attach the receipt," Paige says, finishing his sentence. "It's not like I don't do this every other week."

"Get out of here," Nate jokes.

The door closes softly. Nate's gaze lingers for a long second before he turns his attention back to his computer.

"She likes you, you know," I say, watching him closely for a reaction.

"Who?"

"Come on, Nate. Paige. She likes you."

He scoffs at me.

"What's wrong with her?" I ask, putting a hand on my hip. "She's cute. She's fun. She's a hard worker."

"Not my type."

It's not the words he uses but the tone he chooses that both piques my curiosity but keeps me from pushing. Instead, I twist the door handle and pull it open again.

"I just came by to check the schedule for next week and to tell you my big gala news," I say.

He doesn't look at me. "Don't turn into a pumpkin at midnight."

"That's the plan."

"It's a good one."

I roll my eyes and step into the hallway. My phone buzzes in my hand.

Oliver: I'll pick you up tomorrow night at six.
Does that work?

My fingers fly over the screen.

Me: Yes. Need my address?

Oliver: Already got it from your employee
file.

Me: Isn't that an invasion of my privacy? 🙄

Oliver: Not when I'm the boss. 😏 See you
tomorrow.

Me: I'll be looking forward to it.

I wait a few seconds for a reply, but one doesn't come.

It's just as well. I have things to do, and if he kept texting me, I would've stood here all night and bantered with him. *I can't help myself.*

I slip my phone in my pocket and practically skip out of The Gold Room.

CHAPTER NINETEEN

Oliver

"She told me not to tell you, but—"

"We know," I say, cutting Boone off.

He stops mid-step, the door to the conference room swinging closed behind him. The look on his face is confusion and surprise muddled with anger. He takes in Holt, Wade, Coy, and me around the long, marble table and then huffs.

"All of you know?" he asks, raising a brow.

"All of us." Coy kicks back in his chair and sighs. "Welcome to the club."

Boone's jaw drops in a display of frustration as he sits next to Coy. "I was the last one, wasn't I? Mom told me last." He says it like he's not sure how to digest that piece of information.

Normally, I'd joke with him and make some assholish remark about how he's the baby of the family, and she was probably afraid he'd cry. But this isn't a normal day, and it's nothing to joke about—not even with Boone.

Especially with Boone.

"How do we feel about this?" Holt asks, his gaze settled on our youngest brother. "Anyone heard from Dad?"

The other four of us shake our heads.

"Our parents' marriage is between the two of them," Wade says, his voice characteristically even-keeled. "If they want to end it...fine."

"Do you have no heart?" Boone asks. "Good Lord, Wade. That's cold even for you."

Wade makes a face at Boone. "*Please.*"

"I mean, that's our mother," Boone continues on as though he's five seconds from losing his cool in a childish spiral. "She—"

"*She* is going to be fine," Wade says. "I wasn't finished."

Boone crosses his arms and sits back in his chair.

Holt gives Wade a side-eye, silently asking him for the floor. Wade nods and looks at a piece of paper in front of him.

"I think we're all worried about Mom," Holt says, his tone soft thanks to Boone's temperament. *Normally called a tantrum.* "We'll rally around her, and she'll be fine. I hate to say it, but this is probably good for her. Dad holds her back."

"Good for her or not, I'll be seeing Dad," Coy says, his lips pressed in a thin line. "I want to know what's going on."

"Make that two of us," I say. "I'm curious about what's happening in that man's head."

Holt sighs. "I think we all want to know. But as Wade said," he says, carefully, "this is Mom's business. We have to make sure we don't overstep too much. We can't smother her. That's not her love language or whatever she calls it. Give her some space but make sure we check in and are there when she needs us. Okay?"

"Naturally. I'll be there for Mom, but I have no plans on talking to Dad." I'm still too angry with what he said about our family—especially considering what Mom heard him say about her. She's strong but not impervious. Especially to someone she's been married to for nearly forty years. "Someone can fill me in if they do."

"I'll call you," Coy says. The look he shoots me is in stark contrast to the ease of his words.

I nod.

Wade coughs. "Now that we have the emotional reaction done and over with, let's discuss how this might affect our business."

"It won't. It shouldn't," Holt says, picking up his cup of coffee. "He'll still have an advisory position, but we—meaning mostly Oliver and me as co-CEOs—only have to take anything he brings before us under advisement per his retirement contract. We aren't required to do anything other than read his emails or take a meeting with him here and there."

"We just keep paying him his retirement, and that's it?" I ask.

"Basically."

I nod. "Isn't it great that meeting with the advisory board falls under *your* CEO-ship?" I ask with a grin.

Holt laughs. "We'll see about that."

"The important thing here is that we continue with our work and day-to-day activities," Wade says. "I know things might be a little different on a familial level, but that choice isn't ours. We have to make the best of it."

"*Heartless,*" Boone mutters. "You're heartless."

Wade rolls his eyes.

Holt sips his drink and then sets the mug back on the table. I watch him glance around the room at our siblings, quickly assessing each one. It's one of his strengths—to read a room in an instant and know how to proceed. He's especially good at it with our brothers.

He engages Boone and Coy, bringing up Coy's new agent. Coy loves Anjelica. I like her too. She's smart as a whip and thinks well on her feet. Boone, on the other hand, is terrified of her. It's the perfect way to defuse the emotions in the room and work the conversation away from our parents.

It also gives me a moment to catch my breath.

The afternoon has been a whirlwind—an unexpected one, at that. It was hard to focus on my call with Greg and my meeting with Holt—the middle of which Mom decided to swing by the offices to tell him her news. Then I got to sit in my office with Shaye and Holt and go over the Jewell file and try not to pull her onto my lap or think about the heat of her skin.

Or the way her lips tasted.

Or the softness of her inner thighs.

I had to stay focused and try not to tip off Holt that things between Shaye and me are anything more than employee and employer—a task that was as easy as threading a needle with a cow's tail. A task that I'm not sure we successfully completed. It's hard hiding things from Holt. I've struggled with it my entire life.

But this time it's important.

I don't want to defend my relationship with Shaye to Holt before I know how to define it myself. I'm not even sure it *is* a relationship. Maybe it's a fling. Maybe it's going to blow up in my face, and I'll be looking for another EA soon.

I just don't know. And I don't want to hear him tell me how dangerous or stupid or irresponsible it is to have any sort of an affair with someone who works for our company.

I know. I just can't help it.

"Who is going to the Landry thing tomorrow?" Coy asks. "I got an invite but didn't RSVP."

"Jaxi has a staff meeting at the apartments," Boone says. "I'm staying home with Rosie."

We all look at Wade.

"What? I'm not going," he says. "I had my assistant send a check."

I grin. "What's your excuse?"

"That I don't want to go." He shrugs. "I don't feel the need to make up an excuse as to why I don't want to surround myself with a bunch of people and pretend to give a fuck about what they're saying. They really just want my money. We can do that without all the pretenses."

I chuckle. "*Heartless.*"

"I'm sending a fucking check," he says, shaking his head and ignoring Boone, who is pointing at me as though I'm right.

Holt laughs. "Blaire and I are going. Her brother was supposed to be in town, but he's not coming now for some reason. I can't remember why."

"Her brother ... Walker? Is that right?" Boone asks.

Holt nods.

"Walker is married to a Landry. Sienna Landry. Camilla's twin." Boone nods. "I always forget that."

The room quiets, everyone lost in their own heads. My stomach tightens as I mull over whether to tell them I'm going—and taking Shaye with me.

There are pros and cons to each choice. I could tell them all now and get it out of the way. But if I do that, they'll be suspicious.

Hell, they'll be suspicious anyway as soon as they find out.

But if I make them wait, I'll just have Holt to deal with. At a public event. It could buy me some time *and* give me a night with Shaye to figure out what things might look like between us.

"I—"

"Are you going?" he asks.

All eyes fall on me. I shift in my seat. *Now I feel like Boone, except without the youngest-child indulge-me face.*

"Yeah. I'm going," I say, picking up my phone and setting it on top of the folder in front of me.

Boone reclines back in his seat. A smug grin falls on his lips. "Alone?"

Mom's words from lunch zip through my memory. *We can chalk it up to Boone being your brother and tipping me off that something was brewing.*

I level my gaze on him. "No. I'm taking Shaye with me."

His grin pulls even wider.

Holt's gaze is heavy on the side of my face, but I don't look over at him. I don't look at Wade either. Both of them have things to say. It's my brotherly instinct.

Instead, I focus on Boone.

"Did Rosie like her car?" I ask, figuring that bringing up his daughter is the easiest way to distract him.

Unfortunately for me, it's not that easy.

"*Oh, no,*" Holt says. "We're not going to act like you didn't just say that."

Shit. Was hoping for a miracle that he'd let it go.

"Say what?" I ask. "That I got Rosie a car? What did you get her?"

Coy snickers from across the table. "I need to come to the office more often."

Holt is undeterred. He leans forward and looks me square in the eye. "You're taking Shaye to the gala?"

"That's what I said."

My words ooze a confidence I don't feel. Holt is astute enough to read through the façade.

"You just put that out there like she's your girlfriend or something—like we should expect it," he says.

"*Here we go,*" Wade mumbles.

"I put it out there like she's *my date,* which is what she is," I tell him. "What's wrong with that?"

The question is rhetorical. Every person sitting at this table knows what's wrong with that.

Mixing business and pleasure is a no-go ... unless you're Boone. And even he did it with a careful magic that only he possesses.

"Is she hot?" Coy asks. "I haven't seen her yet."

I fire him a look.

He holds his hands up at his chest. "All right. All right. I'll take that as a yes."

"She's *really* hot," Boone says, leaning toward Coy and whispering. "Hot enough that if I wasn't madly in love with Jaxi ..."

Coy snorts, his eyes trained on me. "Pretend you didn't hear that, Ollie."

I close my eyes and will myself to stay calm and not overreact.

My first instinct is to mark my territory and stake my claim to Shaye. But my second reaction—the one that's based on logic and not lust—is to let it go. Laugh it off. Pretend it's not a big deal because *it's not a big deal.*

Is it?

The truth is, it feels like a bigger deal than when I call a random woman who I've slept with a time or three and ask her to accompany me to an event. *It's Shaye.* Unlike a random woman, I'll see Shaye again. *Daily.* We'll work together day in and day out to accomplish tasks that benefit the rest of the people sitting around me.

There's also the fact that I don't know how this will play out.

Do I take her flowers?

Will we like each other once we've spent time together? Will we want to see each other again? What's the point of even getting mixed up with her in the first place, considering her end goals—whether with me or generally—aren't likely the same.

What am I doing?

Fuck.

Holt chews on his bottom lip. Finally, he sighs. "Be careful. Be smart."

"Use condoms," Coy says, smirking. "Baby shit is expensive as hell."

We all laugh as we get to our feet. Relief washes over me as the topic of Shaye seems to have been dropped by my brothers. I flash Coy a grateful smile as we push our chairs in.

"How is Bellamy feeling?" I ask.

"Very, very pregnant. But pregnant sex is the best. *The best.* Highly recommend. Ten stars. Will order again."

I chuckle. "Not what I asked, but thanks for the information."

He sticks his elbow in my side. "Hey, if the look on your face when *Shaye* was brought up means anything, you might know sooner rather than later."

The blood drains from my face. My palms get sweaty.

What the fuck is he talking about?

"I think you're ... no." I wave him off. "Not happening soon or later ever, probably."

My fuckhead of a brother just laughs. I make a note to buy his baby the loudest, most annoying gift I can find. Every year. For eternity.

"It's quiet in here," Coy says as we step into the hallway.

"Everyone has gone home." Holt leads us toward Kelly's desk. "I'm heading out too. I told Blaire I'd take her out to dinner tonight."

"I'm going to go check on Mom," Boone says.

"And I'm going to call Larissa and see if Hollis is back from Indiana yet," Coy says, pushing the button for the elevator. "He was supposed to be back this afternoon, but his flight was delayed."

Wade leans against the wall. "Did he find Harlee?"

Coy shrugs. "I don't know. I don't think so. Poor guy." He shakes his head. "If he doesn't find that girl ..."

"What if he can't find her?" Wade lifts a brow. "Shit happens, you know? What if something happened to her? Will he be okay?"

"I hope so." Coy frowns. "Man, that not knowing has to be killing him. Can you imagine having to wait months and months for a resolution—if there is one?"

The elevator dings, and my brothers step inside. The mood is somber as everyone contemplates Hollis's struggle with finding his little sister.

"I'm going to grab a couple of things before I leave," I tell them. "See you guys later."

They all utter various forms of goodbye before the elevator door shut.

I make my way to my office, ignoring the darkness in Shaye's. I gather my wallet and car keys and shut off my computer. I do all of the normal things to end the day. I do all of it while keeping half of my attention glued to the edge of my desk.

Where Shaye sat.

Where we kissed.

I stand behind my chair and stare at the spot her sweet ass occupied and try to convince myself I have this under control and know what I'm doing.

We're both adults. We'll figure it out.

But even as I think the thought—even as I say it out loud to try to make it seem more believable—I know it's a lie.

I don't know what I'm doing, and I don't know if we'll figure it out.

Does that make me want to stop? Does it dissuade me in the least from taking her to the gala tomorrow?

I grin. *No. No, it does not.*

Godspeed, Oliver. Godspeed.

Chapter Twenty

Shaye

"This feels good." I stare at my reflection in the mirror. "Really good."

The fabric of the champagne-colored dress that Lisbeth brought over—one of the three—fits me like a glove. The fabric is nearly stretchy and skims my curves. The little translucent beads make me sparkle in the most magical, subdued way.

I turn side to side, appreciating the way the off-the-shoulder design shows off my collarbone—something I didn't know was a thing until now.

"Turn around," Lisbeth says from behind me.

I make a slow turn, careful not to trip on the heels she's letting me borrow, and catch a glimpse of the back of the dress. The way the fabric dips and bunches into a dazzling drape at the small of my back is downright incredible.

"You look stunning," she says.

I swipe a lock of hair away from my face. My red lips break out into a wide smile. "Again, this feels good."

"The dress or ... this?" Lisbeth raises a perfectly arched brow.

Her question is clear. The answer isn't as transparent.

The dress does feel amazing. I feel amazing wearing it all glammed up. The last time I wore something this fancy was my senior prom since Luca and I got married in jeans and T-shirts to save money.

But *this*—being ready and waiting for Oliver Mason to pick me up —also feels pretty damn good.

"That's what I thought," Lisbeth says, hopping on my bed and propping herself up against my pillows. "And, for the record, I fully support this. All of it."

I turn back to the mirror and look at myself again. I'm radiant. I hate that word. I've never understood it when models utter it on television commercials. *You'll feel radiant*, they say as they whip their perfectly styled long hair away from the camera and pose.

Maybe I don't hate it. Maybe I just didn't understand it until now.

I straighten my shoulders and take a long, deep breath.

"What are you thinking?" Lisbeth asks.

"That I thought you were supposed to be at a wedding tonight."

She fake coughs. "Didn't you know I'm sick?"

I roll my eyes.

"I'm going in the morning," she says with a defeated sigh. "My flight leaves at ten. I told Lydia that I came down with something and would miss the first two days of the brouhaha."

I laugh and turn to face her. "It's a wedding, not a brouhaha."

"Feels like a brouhaha. But don't think I don't see what you did there—changing the subject on me."

I wrinkle my nose so I don't have to lie to her. It would be pointless. I did change the subject, and we were both here to witness it.

"This is ... a lot for you," she says, choosing her words carefully. "I mean that nicely."

"I know you do."

"And, as your best friend in the whole wide world, it's my job to make sure you're loved and supported." She grins. "So tell me what you're thinking? What are you feeling? Gush. Get goopy with me."

This time, I wrinkle my nose to express my displeasure.

She giggles. "I love you even though you refuse to talk about your feelings."

"I talk about them. I just don't get silly about them."

"It's fun to get silly about them. Pour your heart out. Cry a little. Eat an entire pint of ice cream and wallow in your feels. Get goopy, baby," she says with a grin.

It's my turn to laugh. "That should be on a T-shirt, but no, I won't. I'm good."

She groans as she sits up.

I take a bracelet out of my jewelry box and slide it over my wrist. It's a delicate strand of blush-pink and diamond-like gems. It's the only nice piece of jewelry that I own and, I only have it because my grandmother gave it to me just before she died. I was fourteen. Ma told me she'd given everything she had in her life to her only child—my mother. And she wanted me to have the one thing she'd held on to that was worth anything.

She also told me not to tell my mother that I had it. I never did.

I admire the bracelet and think about my feelings—the real ones. The deep ones. The ones that sit below the excitement of playing Barbie and waiting for Oliver.

The truth is that my emotions are all garbled. Half of them are on a high from his touch, his kisses, and the way he looks at me. The other half are cowering, waiting for the proverbial shoe to drop.

The only relationship I've had before Oliver—not that what Oliver and I have is a relationship—was Luca. And Luca started out like a storybook hero. He was a gentleman. He was kind. He showered me with gifts and compliments as though I was a prize he had won. That fairy-tale beginning ended like a Lifetime movie.

Even though I trust Oliver, and despite knowing that this whole adventure is good for me, I'm still a bit wobbly. There's more ... risk. And now that I've had a taste of Oliver's passion, added to that list is ... *me.*

"I'm not making the wrong decision about this, am I?" I ask, my heart beating so fast that I think I might have to sit down.

A flash of fear dances across Lisbeth's face. "What? No. Talk." She scrambles to the edge of the bed. "What's happening?"

"Nothing." I shake my head, my hair swishing against my shoulders. "I just ..." I close my eyes and compose myself. *I will not cry.* "Things have been so good, almost too good, and I've been playing with a bit of fire, don't you think?"

I open my eyes to see Lisbeth watching me.

"I think you're living your life," she says softly. "I think that's head and shoulders better than you were six weeks ago."

She's right—to an extent. I have felt more like the me that I used to be lately. But ...

"But it's because of Oliver," I say. "And if he has the power to make me happy, then he also has the power to—"

"No. You're wrong." She walks across the room and takes my hands in hers. "You are the one with the power, Shaye. Not him. You let him in. You controlled the access, and you did it because you saw something in him that was worth opening up for."

"I haven't really opened up to him. The thought of talking about Luca makes me nauseous." I slip a hand out of hers and place it on my stomach. "I don't think I can share any more than the very little I've said already."

She smiles sadly. "Then you don't, girlfriend. It's simple. You only tell your story to people who you find worthy. And Luca? He was never worthy. Oliver might be, but that's your choice to make. And *that* doesn't have to be tonight. Tonight is about enjoying being the belle of the ball."

Her words comfort me, massaging some of the tension out of my heart. Some—but not all.

"You'll still love me if I get fired, right? Or if this little game of risk I'm playing doesn't pan out, and I end up not able to make rent and have to hide from my mom and the creditors?"

She laughs. "I will love you no matter what."

"Okay." I force a swallow. "Cool."

"Cool." She laughs. "And, for the record, I'm proud of you. The you from the last few years would've shut down way before now. You're making progress, my friend."

"Yeah. Maybe I am."

I hope I am.

Lisbeth gives my hand a shake and then releases it. She steps back and takes me in once again.

"You're going to knock him off his feet, you know that?" she asks.

I just smile at her.

"Let's get you a spritz of perfume and make sure you have all the essentials." She picks up a bottle of Tom Ford's Black Orchid perfume and pumps two sprays in the air. "Walk through the haze."

I lift my chin like a model walking the catwalk and hold my breath. The mist lands gracefully across me as I strut to the other side of my bedroom.

It makes Lisbeth laugh.

"Black clutch or nude?" She holds two purses up in the air. "I prefer the black with the gold chain, but that's me."

"Definitely black."

She tosses the nude one on the bed and busies herself adding a compact, toothpaste tabs, and God knows what else to the black one.

"When he gets here," she says, adding a tube of the vixen red lipstick she used on me, "I'll hide in the bathroom."

"You don't have to do that!"

She makes a face at me. "Yes, I do. You'll answer the door and, once you leave, I'll lock up and go home."

"I ..."

My protest is diluted by the sound of the doorbell.

All at once, my body stiffens, my heart races, and my stomach pools with a downright uncomfortable heat. The dress is too tight, the shoes too high. The powder—or concealer or whatever Lisbeth put on my nose—makes my face itch.

"Don't. Panic," Lisbeth says, stepping in front of me. "Breathe."

I inhale and exhale, following the directions of her hands like some kind of mime.

"Again," she says, filling her lungs slowly while staring at me.

I start to do as I'm told, and then I remember that Oliver freaking Mason is standing on my porch. I blow the breath out so hard I cough.

"Don't die on me." Lisbeth pats my back.

I swat her hand away, swaying on the heels. "You are terrible in an emergency," I say, struggling to get an easy lungful of air down my now-raw throat.

"You were the one who called me in a panic."

I turn away and grab the clutch from my dresser. "Well, I'm still panicking. He's standing out there waiting on me."

As if in agreement, the doorbell rings again.

Lisbeth looks at me. "It's ready. *You* are ready. Go knock him dead —no! No dying. Just ... turn him on and dizzy the crap out of him."

Note to self: Lis is terrible when things get crazy.

I give myself one final look in the mirror before blowing Lisbeth a kiss. Then I head into the hallway.

My heels click against the hardwood as I make my way toward the door. With each step—each click!—my heart beats harder.

The knob feels cool in my hand as I wrap my palm around it. I take one final breath, ensuring I don't choke this time, and tug open the door.

And I realize instantaneously that I'm not ready.

Bright, blue-green eyes. Freshly shaven skin. Perfectly coiffed hair and a suit tailored to perfection.

Oliver is downright edible.

I grip the side of the door so I don't make a fool out of myself.

His gaze licks me up and down like a flame, leaving a trail of heat in its wake.

"*Oh, wow,*" he says, his jaw hanging open. "You look ... *beautiful.*"

"Thank you." I try not to let my cheeks split with the force of my smile. "You look dashing."

"Dashing?" He lifts a brow. "I was going for handsome, but I'll take *dashing.*"

I laugh. As I release the door, I notice a single pink rose in his hand.

"For you, my lady," he says, handing the stem to me.

The scent is heavenly—my favorite. I bring it to my nose and revel in the sweet, simple fragrance.

"It reminded me of you," he says, his cheeks turning a shade similar to the flower.

"Because I blush all of the time?"

He chuckles. "No. But that's true." He waits as I set the rose on the table inside the door.

"I have a friend coming by who will put that in water for me," I say, hoping Lisbeth overhears us.

He offers me his elbow. I take it.

"Back to the rose," I say as we make our way to his car. "It reminded you of me how?"

"Ah, yes. The rose. It reminded me of you because it was elegant and sweet yet it had a richness to it that made me want to touch it."

We stop at the passenger's side door. Instead of opening it, he turns to me. His eyes twinkle with mischief.

I hold my breath as his hand reaches my cheek.

"I have a feeling," he says, stepping closer to me, "that it's going to be a long night."

"Okay."

"And I would like to kiss you now instead of just when I drop you off so I don't think about it all night." He grins. "Would that be okay with you?"

My knees go weak as I watch this handsome man appear to be smitten with me.

What is happening in my life?

"I think it would be helpful to both of us," I whisper.

His grin is immediate and ravishing. He cups the other side of my face in his other hand and lowers his mouth to mine.

This kiss is slow, unrushed. It's sweet, chaste. But the vibrations rippling off his body—the way he stands with each foot on the opposite side of me—gives off a completely different energy.

It's a vibe I'm dying to explore.

He pulls away and opens the door.

Still breathless, I climb in the seat. Before he can close me in, I reach out and grab the end of his tie.

He grins. A glimmer of roguery is sprinkled across his features.

Gosh, he's handsome.

"Thank you for inviting me," I say, smiling coquettishly.

His breath is sweet, tinged with peppermint, as he drags his face closer to mine. "Thank you for coming."

"I'm always happy *to come*, Mr. Mason." My heartbeat thunders in my ears. But I continue, emboldened by the look of pure desire in his eyes. "Just thought I'd throw that out there."

He licks his lips but pulls away. A look of pure surprise washes across his face. It melts before my very eyes into a war of self-control versus unbridled desire.

It's so wickedly hot.

My own lips part so I can get fresh air and not pass out.

I don't know who I am with this behavior. It's not me. But ... *I kind of like it*. It feels powerful.

"I'm going to close this door before I throw you out of this car and make you prove yourself." His eyes hood. "You'll thank me later."

I don't respond, but I don't think I have to. Everything I want to say is written on my face.

And if everything *he* has to say is written across his. Tonight should be a lot of fun indeed.

Chapter Twenty-One

"I'll be in touch. It was good to see you, Harris." Oliver shakes hands with the distinguished-looking gentleman to his left. "Vivian—as always."

The woman nods politely at my date. She must be my mother's age, maybe a tad older, but is downright regal. Everything from her dress to her posture to her perfectly timed interjections in her husband's conversation with Oliver is admirable.

"It was a pleasure to meet you, Shaye," Vivian says, smiling warmly. "Thank you for joining us this evening."

"The pleasure is truly mine, Mrs. Landry," I say.

She takes her husband's elbow and gives it a pat. "Let's see if we can find Graham, darling."

Oliver turns to me. His eyes are a mix of liveliness and ease.

"What?" he asks, wrapping an arm around my waist. It's a natural movement, a gesture that anyone watching would think that he's done a thousand times. "Are you enjoying yourself?"

The gala, now in its second hour, is in full-blown revelry. Servers mingle with the guests holding trays of fancy hors d'oeuvres like Nate warned me about. A band, complete with a saxophone, plays upbeat music that fills the air with festivity. Laughter from various groups of sophisticated men and women fills in any gaps.

"What's not to love?" I ask, declining a fresh glass of champagne from a server. The two drinks I've had already plus the one in my hand are enough to take the edge off my nerves.

Oliver's fingers press against the exposed skin on my back. The contact sends a chill up my spine.

"Do you go to things like this often?" I ask him.

"Like this?" He chuckles. "No. There aren't many events like this." He takes a sip of his champagne and looks around the room. "This room is filled with some of the most powerful men and women in the country. See the man smoking a cigar near the ice sculpture?"

I nod.

"He owns a large hotel chain. Worth a few hundred million, I'd guess," he says.

"Oh, *wow*."

"Marius Blast, the man next to him, owns a bank. He was in *Forbes* last month. And the woman next to him runs an umbrella company that controls more assets than the two men combined."

I force a swallow down my throat. "That's ... That's one way to make you feel unaccomplished." I give him a tight smile. "Me, not you. I have no idea how much you're worth."

He grins devilishly.

"And I don't want to know," I say, trying not to let his sexiness distract me, though that task is virtually impossible. "Your business is your business. I just make the coffee."

He angles his head and gives me a look of disbelief.

"Okay, I don't make the coffee." I laugh. "But I'll add that to my duties if it makes you happy."

He smiles again, but there is no laughter. Instead, he brushes a strand of hair off my face. "You really aren't interested in how I compare to these people?"

It's an odd question for a myriad of reasons. Even if I could overlook the question itself, I would be stumped by the curious yet hopeful look in his eyes.

"No," I say, my voice soft. "Why would I care?"

He trails the back of his hand down my chin but doesn't answer me.

"In my lifetime, I've learned a few things," I tell him. "One of them is that money and relationships—*friendships*," I correct quickly, "never mix. In any capacity."

"*Friendships*. Right," he says, his brows furrowed. His Adam's apple bobs in his throat. "Good logic there."

It *is* good logic because money complicates things. And we *are* friends. Assuming we are more than that sets me up to have a broken heart. I'm not sure what part of that he seems to have questions about, but I don't have time to ask him.

Two men come up to us. Both men are older than Oliver, and both are extraordinary in their own way. One of them—the one Oliver addresses as Curt as he approaches, has a Sean Connery vibe. He's ruggedly handsome with a voice that could melt honey. I instantly like him. The other one is the man Oliver told me was Marius Blast.

Jet-black hair, a dimpled smile, and a suit that was tailored for his long, lean body, Marius is stunning.

"It is good to see you, Oliver," Marius says, extending a large hand.

Oliver shakes it with gusto. "Good to see you, Marius."

"And who is this beautiful woman at your side?" Marius turns slowly toward me. His eyes are a brilliant green that lack a certain warmth about them.

I instantly miss Oliver's arm around my waist.

"Curt, Marius, this is Shaye Brewer." Oliver faces me. He seems to want to say something, but the seconds pass with silence.

Oliver's associates look at us expectantly, also assuming more will be said. And with all of their eyes shifting to me as the subject of the conversation, my stomach begins to twist.

"I'm his executive assistant," I say. It's the first thing that I can think of to finish his thought. "It's a pleasure to meet both of you."

The words flow from my mouth in a nervous rush, and I have to clamp my lips shut so I don't keep talking. Oliver's lips form a hard, thin line as he turns away.

"Yes, Shaye is my executive assistant," Oliver tells them, his words clipped. "I thought it would be nice for her to come tonight and meet some of the people she'll be engaging with in her new role."

"Brilliant idea, ol' boy," Curt says, clapping him on the shoulder. "I knew you were fit for a CEO when you were this high." He holds his hand out waist level. "So many men—*people*, forgive me, miss," he says to me, "expect their right-hand *people* to work with other brands and businesses without knowing them. I've always said that it's easier to do business if you know who you're doing business with."

They banter back and forth, Marius contributing to the conversation here and there. I stand at Oliver's side, clutching my champagne flute and replaying the last two minutes.

Could he possibly be mad that I told the truth?

Oliver stands a few feet away from me. He glances at me from time to time, but the hand closest to me is now in his pocket. It's a small thing to notice, but everything with Oliver Mason is calculated.

This is too. I just don't know why. *I am his EA.* It's my job title. It's how he presented me to the Landry family. *"This is the lovely Shaye Brewer, my EA. I'm pleased for you to meet her."*

My body shrinks. There isn't room for the champagne and the tiny pastry with brie and mushroom that I tried on Vivian Landry's request. It was delicious when I ate it. It's less delicious as it threatens to become unreasonable in my stomach.

"Have you said hello to Tyra?" Curt asks. "She wasn't with me last year. I believe she was in Switzerland with our granddaughter Carys. She's here this year, and I know she'd love to see you."

I lift my chin, taking a deep breath to settle myself. *Maybe having a woman in the conversation will stabilize things?*

I prepare to take a step toward the table that Curt motions toward when Oliver turns around.

"I'm going to say hello to Curt's wife. I'll be right back." His face is free from emotion, but his eyes tell another story. It's just not one I can read.

"I'll be fine. I'll be ... here."

My heart pounds as he walks with Curt toward a table with three gorgeous women. Their heads all snap to Oliver, their faces awash in delight at the opportunity to score his attention.

I don't realize Marius is still standing next to me until he chuckles.

"Excuse me?" I ask, not sure what I missed to warrant a chuckle.

"Oliver—*your boss*," he says pointedly. "I think I've seen him with a different woman at every social engagement."

"*Oh.*"

My brain races. Logic tells me that I didn't know him at any of those social engagements, so why do I care? I was with Luca—married to Luca. I can't, shouldn't, feel any sort of way about Oliver's acquaintances.

Still, my gaze falls to his broad back and the way the ladies at the table laugh at something he says.

"Yes, Shaye is my executive assistant."

My spirits tumble.

"I don't suppose he can help himself," Marius says. "He's a hell of a guy."

"He seems to be, yes."

I take a sip of champagne to keep myself from saying anything else.

"Have you worked for him long?" he asks.

I sigh softly. "No. Not too long. We are just getting to know each other."

A woman with long, blond hair places her hand on Oliver's wrist. My breath hiccups in my chest as I pull my gaze from their interaction. It lands on a smiling Marius.

"I'm sure you'll like him. He's a nice guy." He swishes his champagne around in the flute as he watches me.

I steady myself the best I can.

Too many things stream around me, carrying me in an invisible current before I get swept away in another line of thought. *Oliver's kiss tonight. The way he alluded to something more after the gala. How he cooled off after the Landrys left us and then the awkwardness of meeting Curt and Marius.*

And now ... *this.* I glance over at Oliver. He's standing next to Curt and a woman in a long, brilliant red dress cut into a sharp V in the front.

I gulp.

Maybe it's the champagne. I place my glass on a passing server's tray and thank them. Marius sets his next to mine.

The music transitions into something lighter and jazzier.

"Would you care to dance?" Marius asks.

"Dance?"

I trip over words in my head as if they're steps in a dark hallway. My mouth hangs open, but none of them—the right nor the wrong ones—slip out. Instead, I stand in front of Marius Blast and look like a fool.

Thankfully, he doesn't make it awkward. "Yes, dance," he says with a big smile. "It's what people do at galas."

"Couples do, I'm sure," I say.

"Yes, definitely couples. But I'm here alone, and you are here with your boss who," he says, leaning closer and whispering conspiratorially, "is having a conversation with two women on the other side of the room."

"And I'm having a conversation here with you."

"And we could be having this conversation while dancing."

"We could ..." I turn my whole body as if I'm taking in the room when, in fact, I want to see what Oliver is doing. Curt is standing to his right with the woman in the red dress. On Oliver's right side—where I should be—is a bombshell.

Emerald-green dress and a stunning diamond choker. Her hair is long and red, and if she hasn't walked a runway at some point in her life, I'll be damned. A man with a large camera faces them, snapping their picture. *Perhaps he recognizes Oliver's ... friend. Maybe she came with him last time.* Or the time before that. And I bet her dress is brand-spanking new, straight off a designer rack.

I look down at my borrowed gown from Lisbeth. *I felt like a princess before.* My thumb strokes the bracelet from my grandmother. *I'm going to turn into a pumpkin well before midnight if I don't watch it.* I say a silent wish that I knew how to navigate these sorts of things.

I'm so out of my element. I don't know if I'm supposed to stand here and wait for Oliver because I'm his date or if I'm supposed to mingle and represent his company as well.

What is perfectly clear is that I must look like a fool to anyone watching—certainly to Marius. Surely, anyone paying a shred of attention would see that I feel self-conscious. Edgy. Embarrassed.

"Is that a yes then?" Marius asks.

"It's just a dance. Right?"

He offers me his arm. "It's just a dance."

Something feels wrong about taking his arm. But something feels wrong about standing by myself in the middle of a gala while my date has his picture taken with another woman.

It's just a dance.

Marius leads me to the dance floor, saying hello to a few couples as we pass. Finally, we make it in front of the band.

The lights feel hotter as Marius places his hand lightly on my waist and takes my other in his.

"Hey, relax," he says as we begin to move. "We're just dancing."

"I know." I take a deep breath. "So how's the family?"

He leans his head back and laughs. The sound eases my anxiety enough to make me able to breathe again with more ease.

"*The family* ..." He grins. "Well, my father is in prison for tax evasion."

"Ouch."

"And my mother is living her best life in Mallorca, which, it would seem, is odd, considering the first fact that I shared with you. But my mother handed him off to a twentysomething ingenue years ago and laughed all the way to the bank."

I'm not sure what to say to all of that, so I don't say anything at all.

Marius leads me across the floor, keeping his eyes trained on me. "What do you think of this little party?"

"I think it's really nice," I say as an uncomfortable fire runs up my spine. "It's been a nice evening."

"Nice, huh?"

"Yes."

My eyes dart around the room in an attempt to find the source of my discomfort. Oliver seems to have disappeared.

What's going on?

"I've never been to anything like this," I say, my nerves busting free of their constraint. "It's quite a spectacle."

"The Landrys do so much for charities that it's not too much of an inconvenience to attend. Plus," he says, squeezing my hip ever so gently, "you never know who you'll meet."

I hum in agreement. My palms start to sweat. Just as I'm about to excuse myself, my gaze is snatched by Oliver.

He watches Marius and me from next to the door, next to the man with the cigar. His lips are nothing more than a thin line. His shoulders stiff. His eyes are narrowed as he follows me—us—across the floor.

"Do you live here? In Savannah, I mean?" Marius asks.

"Um, yes. I do. I've lived here for a long time."

"Where are you from?"

"I was born in Oklahoma City," I say, pulling my attention back to him. "We moved around a lot when I was growing up."

"Same. New York City, Seattle, London—my parents got the itch to move every four or five years."

"I've never been."

My breathing picks up as I sense Oliver's proximity. I can't see him and certainly can't turn around and look, but I know he's close. I can feel him.

"To London?" Marius asks. "It's a lovely city."

"To any of them."

He furrows his brows. "Oh. Well, you should rectify that."

"Between my jobs at Mason Limited and The Gold Room, I find it hard to believe that I'll make it anywhere any time soon."

"Maybe you could—oh, *hello, Oliver.*"

Marius slows our movements and releases his hold on me. His hand slips from my waist as he drops my other one.

I take a deep breath before I look at Oliver.

And I'm glad I do.

His face is tinted a shade of almost pink that I've never seen on him before. His hands are clenched at his sides. His stare slices a hole through my dress, my skin, and bleeds into my body.

"I'm sorry," I say, the words tumbling from my lips. "I—"

"*I* asked her to dance." Marius squares his shoulders to Oliver. "She was left standing alone in the middle of the room. Certainly, you'd rather have me ask her than leave it up to chance."

Oliver's shoulders rise and fall. He rips his gaze from me to Marius.

Marius doesn't flinch. Doesn't react. He just smiles at Oliver.

"Thank you for your kindness, Marius," I say, hoping to defuse the situation.

"It was my pleasure, Shaye. Truly. Now, if you'll both excuse me, I have other matters to attend." He nods to Oliver before disappearing into a throng of people near the bar.

Oliver doesn't acknowledge him; his eyes stay pinned on me.

My heart pounds in my chest as I find my footing.

"He asked me to dance. I didn't know what to do," I say.

The band switches to a slower tune, prompting more people to file onto the dance floor. Oliver takes my hand and pulls me against him. Chest to chest, he rests his free hand in the small of my back.

We dance slowly. Oliver's body is taut. I'm sure mine is rigid too.

Oliver's hand flexes against my skin. "I'm sorry," he whispers into the shell of my ear.

The warmth of his breath causes me to shiver. I don't respond. I'm not sure how.

"I ..." He swallows as he pulls me closer to his body. "I didn't like that."

"Didn't like what?"

He presses his palm into my back. "I didn't like seeing you in his arms."

His words flood me with a cascade of emotions. So many, in fact, that I don't know where to start.

My grin is dopey, and I don't dare look at him and let him see it. Instead, I press my cheek into his chest and let him guide me into a circle.

"I never should've left you alone," he says, his words soft. "I don't know why I did that." His chest rumbles with a chuckle. "Nah, I do know why."

"Why?"

"Because you told them you were my executive assistant."

I jerk my head back and look him in the eye. Those beautiful blue-green orbs glitter back at me.

"I am your EA," I tell him.

One side of his lips turns up. "That you are."

I study him for a long moment. "I only said that—the truth—because you left it a question and they were looking at me for an explanation."

"Well, you gave them one."

"What did you want me to say?" I ask as the saxophone kicks in behind us.

The sultry, smokiness of the music descends over the dance floor, adding a sexy undertone to the room. Oliver's body relaxes as he tugs me even closer—so close that taking a full breath is difficult.

But I'm not complaining. Not even a little.

Breathing in his cologne, feeling the firmness of his body, listening to the grit of his tone, which is laced with a familiar layer of desire, has every cell of my body firing. *For him.* This might be a complication, and I might wake up tomorrow morning and regret everything, but right now—in his arms—I only want one thing: *more.*

More of him. More kisses, touches. More promises. More laughter and more feeling like I'm worthy of a man like Oliver Mason. *More than being left alone while he flirted with other women.*

It's not that. Not really. I've never equated my worth with a man's opinion. But seeing him want me, respect me, *desire me* in the way I do him, makes me feel less like the struggling mess of a human I've been lately and more like the person I want to be.

Oliver holds me close to him, and our bodies sway back and forth to the music. My eyes flutter closed, and I let the thumping of his heart carry me away into a world that's probably not real, but I welcome with open arms.

At least for now.

"Do you want to know what I wanted you to say?"

His words—low and soft—bring me back to the gala.

"What?" I ask.

He takes a breath. "I wanted you to tell them that you were with me." He pauses. "That you were mine."

I lean back and look into his eyes.

He smiles hesitantly. "I know it's crazy. I have doubts that this is the right thing—but I wanted those fuckers to know that Shaye Brewer was with Oliver Mason and that they shouldn't dare look at you twice."

My skin prickles with goose bumps. The heat of his gaze travels through my body and pools between my legs.

I bite my bottom lip, unable to believe I heard him correctly. But then he smiles—a different one. The one I haven't seen him use with Kelly at work or the girl with the green dress tonight. He gives me *that smile,* and I know I heard him right. More than that, I want that too.

I hated being left to describe who I was to Oliver. And then left behind as he *socialized.* But there is no doubt in my mind now what, or rather who, Oliver wants. And this time, I don't mind being the one who has to step up. Ask for what *I* want.

"I think," I say, choosing my words carefully, "that if you want me to be yours ... you have to *make me yours.*"

He growls—the sound rough and nearly guttural. I'm still processing it when he releases me from his grasp. He takes my hand and nearly drags me through the ballroom.

"Where are we going?" I ask, my voice a combination of both a yelp and a laugh.

He doesn't answer me until we pause at the exit to let an older gentleman pass. Even then, his answer is brief.

"Your wish is my command."

He tosses me a wink before leading us to his car.

CHAPTER TWENTY-TWO

Shaye

"Where are we going?"

We've been in the car for a solid fifteen minutes. Neither of us has spoken a single word. The radio is off, our phones are muted—not one word from us or otherwise has been said.

Oliver tilts his head my way at my question. One arm extends over the steering wheel; his other hand plays with his bottom lip like he's thinking. Or planning. Or plotting.

The idea of what he might be considering fires a heat wave through my body. I clasp my hands in my lap and press lightly, hoping the ill attempt at relief will hold me over.

"If you're taking me home, we've gone the wrong way," I tell him.

He drops his hand away from his mouth and grins. "I know how to navigate Savannah. But thanks for the input."

"I was starting to have doubts since you didn't answer my question. I thought maybe you got confused and couldn't answer me."

"Patience really isn't one of your strengths, is it?"

"I don't know. I mean, I have been around you all night, and I have managed to be pretty damn patient."

He grins. "What are you waiting for?"

I grin back. "What do you mean? Why am I being patient, or what do I hope comes at the end of it?"

"I'm guessing that *you* hope you come at the end of it."

He leaves his gaze on me for one suffering, hot moment before turning his eyes back to the dark road ahead of us.

I'm underprepared for this. My flirting feels rusty, and the anticipation of being with him makes me fidget. It's been so long—so fucking long—since anyone has touched me, and even then, it was lackluster at best.

What if he finally touches me, and I'm all talk and no action? What if I've been throwing puns around like they're confetti, and then I forget how to have an orgasm in the first place? And I didn't bring a condom. *Should I have?*

I stare out the windshield and try to contain my thoughts.

"Or am I wrong?" he asks.

My head swings to his. "Wrong about what?"

"About you ... never mind."

Oh. I shift in my seat as I remember what we were talking about.

"If you're having second thoughts, I can turn around," he says.

"I'm not." The words come out fast and succinct. "I promise."

He laughs. "Good to know."

"It's just been a while."

His laughter fades. "How long is *a while*?"

"A while." I bite my lip. "I'm a little nervous. That's all."

"For someone who's been talking smack, this is an interesting turn of events." He does a quick once-over of me. "That's also a little hard to believe."

"Do I look like someone who just sleeps with random men?"

"Not what I meant." He fires me a look. "What I meant was that it's hard to imagine you going anywhere and not having men trying to take you home with them."

"Oh." I look out the passenger's side window so he can't see my face and smile. "Marius wasn't trying to take me home. Just for the record."

Oliver's laughter is loud and unexpected. I slide my gaze across the car to see his features alight with humor.

"My lady, he most definitely was trying to take you home with him," Oliver says, raising a brow in challenge.

"I beg to differ. He was the epitome of a gentleman."

"Marius Blast doesn't know how to spell gentleman."

"Then why did you leave me alone with him?"

The humor on Oliver's face slips away into the night. He regrips the steering wheel.

The swift change in his posture—the rigidity that forms across his shoulders—has me wishing I could take back the question.

But I do want to know. And before I fall into his arms or his bed, I deserve an answer.

"Didn't we already talk about this?" he asks.

I force a swallow. "Kind of, but not exactly. You said you left me alone because I said I was your EA. You didn't say why you left me with him."

He runs a hand down his thigh and exhales harshly.

I grab both sides of my seat and try to keep myself calm. The longer the silence between us, the more I have a need to fill it. But if I talk—if I help him wrangle himself out of this situation—then I might never have a chance to ask him again.

His forehead wrinkles. When he speaks, his voice is calculated and raw.

"My ex-fiancée met Charles Gamby, her new husband, at the Landry Gala," he says. "I should've known that night that something was amiss, but I didn't. I missed every freaking sign."

"That's sad."

He sighs ruefully. "It's not. Not really. My life has been infinitely better without Kendra." He glances quickly at me. "I can't imagine having her sitting beside me now."

There's a warmth to his gaze, to his voice, to the hand that reaches across the console and sits on my thigh. It's a warmth that I feel all the way into my soul.

"I'm glad she's not sitting here," I whisper.

He flexes his hand against the fabric of my dress. "When you were dancing with Marius, you looked up and saw me. I could see in your eyes that you didn't want to be with him. And while it's bullshit that I put you in that position—*I know that, I'm not proud of it, and I apologize for it*—it made me feel ... relieved."

"I don't like that you tested me, Oliver."

"It wasn't a test. A test would mean that I thought about it prior, and I didn't. I assure you." He nibbles on his bottom lip. "I like to think of myself as a man in control, but tonight, that slipped." He watches me out of the corner of his eye. "I wasn't leaving you alone to see what you would do, and it wasn't intentional to leave you alone with Marius. Trust me. But I was ... shaken, a bit, I guess. I reacted to the situation without thinking it through and that will keep me up at night for weeks. I didn't expect to get to the gala with you on my arm and ..."

His voice trails off, but a glimpse of a smile kisses his lips.

"And what, Oliver?"

"I needed to know that you were there with me and *not as my EA.*"

The grittiness of the tone catches me off guard. It's laced with an honesty, a vulnerability, a sweet rawness that hits my heart with the force of a cannon.

"And not as my EA." This sentence percolates through my brain, sending shock waves through my chest. *"And not as my EA."*

Holy crap.

He gathers the fabric of my dress in his hand, never taking his eyes off the road.

My breath hitches as his fingers dip beneath the fabric. His fingertips drag across my left leg. His touch is the weight of a feather, barely slipping across the sensitive skin of my leg—touching *here*, then *there* as it drifts toward the apex of my thighs.

I pant, my gaze lasered on the side of his face and the sharpness of his jawline as he toys with me. My legs part—offering him an opening if he chooses to take it.

And he doesn't.

He scoots my dress back toward the floor and pulls his hand away, leaving me breathless.

"You know what?" I say, fighting off a full-body shiver. "I'm starting to hate you."

He laughs. "There's a thin line between love and hate. Isn't that what they say?"

"Yes, but I never knew it was *this* thin."

He puts the car in park and kills the engine. "We're here," he says, motioning in front of us.

I look up and see the most statuesque home that I've ever seen. It's lit up with lights tucked beneath pristine hedges.

"Where are we, exactly?" I ask, withholding a gasp.

"My house."

I turn in my seat to look at him. His eyes are wary.

"You brought me to *your house*?" I ask. Even though I'm experienced in the art of dating, I know from Lisbeth's tales that men don't always take you back to their homes. There are a myriad of reasons, from what I'm told, but it's always a big deal to Lis when they wind up at a guy's abode.

Yet here we are.

Oliver grins. It's a new one to me. Not the uber-sexy CEO smile nor the sweet one that I saw earlier. This one is vulnerable and hopeful. This one melts my heart.

"Want to come in?" he asks.

I smile. "I definitely want to come in."

He laughs and climbs out of the car. I sit in my seat and say a quick prayer.

Please, let me know what I'm doing.

Chapter Twenty-Three

Shaye

"This is incredible," I say, the words barely a whisper.

The floor-to-ceiling windows in Oliver's living room showcase an unmatched view of the property below. I walk to them and peer out, taking in the pool, trees, and immaculate yard stretching as far as the eye can see.

"How far does that go?" I ask, pointing at a nonexistent spot on the horizon.

"Not as far as it looks tonight." He stands behind me, his body so close that his chest nearly hits me as he speaks. "There's a creek back there that winds through the trees. That's the property line."

"Can you see it during the day?"

"No. The trees are too thick."

I grin. "When I was a little girl, I loved playing in creeks."

"Did you?" he asks, seemingly amused by the admission.

I nod. "We had one behind our house. It wasn't huge or anything, but I'd spend hours back there messing around and trying to re-route it."

"Coy and Boone did that behind Mom's house." He chuckles. "They'd come in all muddy and Mom would threaten to strangle them. Of course, they would traipse through the house like the heathens that they are and get that shit everywhere. And Larissa would follow them, matching them step for step."

Images of a pint-sized Boone marching through a fancy house like this one with mud all over his shoes makes me laugh.

"It sounds like you had a nice childhood," I say.

"I did. I can't complain. What about you?"

"Oh, I can complain," I say, laughing.

He wraps his arms around me from behind. I don't expect him to do that, and it feels infinitely more intimate than him touching me in the car or dancing with him in a roomful of people. To my surprise, I relax into his chest and feel my body give up the stress it was holding—that it *always* holds.

"You know what I find funny?" he asks.

I hum.

"One minute, I can be ready to fuck you senseless. Then the next minute, I want to do this." He tugs me tighter against him. "I can't figure out what I want to do with you. You drive me crazy."

"I can't figure out what I want you to do to me either. What a conundrum."

I smile, knowing that he can't see my face. I feel his body tense behind mine.

"What do you mean by that?" he asks finally.

"Do I want you to fuck me senseless? Or do I want you to leave me with a guy like Marius so I can ensure that I keep my job?"

His body vibrates with a low, borderline-angry chuckle. "I assure you, Ms. Brewer, that the avenue to keeping your job is not to entertain any ideas whatsoever about Marius."

"So Curt is okay?"

"If you want decrepit old men, then he's your guy."

I rest my hands on his at my belly. "But what if that's not what I want? What if I want a younger, late-thirties, early-forties man with striking eyes and a tendency to leave me alone with men who ask me to sleep with them—"

"He did fucking not."

Oliver whirls me around and takes me in. As soon as he faces me and I can see the anger, surprise, downright fury written on his face, I can't contain myself. I laugh.

"You did this to yourself," I say, wagging a finger in his face. "You left me alone with him like an imbecile."

"You're kidding, right?"

"About what?"

"He didn't ask you to sleep with him?"

I consider screwing with him. It serves him right. But I don't want to intentionally make Oliver jealous and then end up sleeping with him tonight.

No, if this is where this is going and we end up in bed together, it will be because we choose to do that without any outside interference.

I cup the sides of Oliver's face with both hands. "No. He didn't. You're just going to have to trust me on that."

He searches my face for any thread of doubt before leaning down and hovering his lips over mine.

"Are you going to kiss me or not?" I ask him.

"I don't know."

"Oliver ..." I protest.

He laughs, scooping me up in his arms and marching across the room. My shriek—a response to the unexpected move—echoes down the hallway. My shoes brush against a lampshade on a table beneath an oversized painting of a shipyard.

The house is too dark to see too much; the doors coming off the hallway are closed. We finally make it to the door at the very end, and Oliver opens it with the flick of his wrist.

He swipes his hand against the wall and the lights come on. They're dim, glowing just enough to give me an opportunity to see where we are.

And holy cow.

He sets me on my feet. I venture deeper into the bedroom.

The room is grand, luxurious—fit for a king. The windows are floor-to-ceiling like in the living room. A dark wood, four-poster bed faces a fireplace that begins to flicker when Oliver pushes a button on a remote. Above the fireplace is a wood-beam mantel and, above that, a large television. A light-colored rug lays in front of a cozy sofa with pillows.

I look over my shoulder. Oliver is standing next to his bed.

His eyes are hooded. His breathing is shallow. His tie is undone, and he's watching me with one-hundred-percent attentiveness.

My dress shifts against the floor as I turn around and face him.

"My God, you're gorgeous," he says.

"I think you've said that already tonight."

He stalks my way, a grin playing on his lips. "Do you mind if I tell you over and over again? Because I think I'm going to find it difficult not to tell you."

I hum as he presses a kiss to the side of my neck. "I'd rather you show me, Mr. Mason."

He nips the skin just beneath my ear, making me jump. Only, when I do, he holds me tight and kisses me again.

The contact, the unpredictability—the overwhelming anticipation —has me breathing ragged breaths.

"I'm afraid," he says, kissing down my neck and back up again, peppering kisses between the words, "it would take all night to show you how beautiful you are."

"Well then, I guess it's a good thing I don't have anywhere to be."

His lips crash onto mine, taking me in a move of uncontrolled, relentless desire. My brain spins, my body aches—it's all I can do to be present and soak up the sweet, sweet attention of Oliver.

He works my zipper, dragging it down the center of my back. The fabric falls from my body and, as he steps back just enough to give it room to fall, it does. It becomes a heap on the floor.

Despite the crackling fire, the air is cool against my skin. Oliver, however, is undeterred. He kisses, touches—runs his hands over my body as though he must prove to himself that I'm here. *In the flesh.*

I unfasten the buttons on his shirt. With every one that pops free, an urgency increases to get this man naked now. I fumble with his belt; struggle with his pants. While I attempt to disrobe him, his kisses grow more frenzied. Hotter. *More intentional.*

He nibbles my lips. Kisses across my jaw. Plants a trail of kisses down my neck and over my clavicle.

My head falls back, my hair sweeping against my bottom as I give him complete access to me. He takes advantage of the moment as if he might not get it again.

His pants fall to the floor. He kicks off his shoes and socks and rids himself of his boxers. He shrugs off his shirt and tosses his tie on the bed and stands in front of me in all of his glory.

"*Damn*," I moan, trying to catch my breath.

His chest is sculpted, and his shoulders are thick and muscled. There is a distinct *V* in his abdomen that makes my head spin. His thighs are hard, and his cock is standing at attention, desperate for my touch.

He's too perfect, too fucking perfect to really process. Instead of reveling in the moment, my brain immediately starts to wonder what he sees when he sees me.

I look down, only to have his finger immediately touch my chin. He lifts my gaze to his and steps toward me.

"*Not here.*" That's all he says. Two words that I don't understand.

"You don't want me here?" I ask, fighting off a wave of defeat.

"No, pretty lady. You aren't doing *that* here."

I stare into his eyes and let his adoration seep into me.

"You're always waiting for something to go wrong," he whispers. "Looking for a way out."

You would too if you had walked a day in my shoes.

"Nothing is going to go wrong. There isn't a need for a way out," he says, taking my hand. "You are here because you are the woman I choose to be here. You are the one I want."

His brows raise as if he's as surprised as I am that he's saying this to me.

"You are a hundred things, Shaye Brewer. And while being beautiful is not one of the most important, nor is it the reason I'm fascinated by you, you are spectacularly gorgeous. If you're going to be in my bedroom, you're going to have to believe that." He presses a kiss to the tip of my nose. "It's a rule."

"A rule, huh?" I try to keep myself from beaming, but it's hard under the circumstances. "Thank you for saying all of that."

He smiles. "Thank you for being here." He walks toward the fireplace and flips a button. The flames dance slower, more methodically.

"Thank you for bringing me here."

"Thank you for coming," he teases.

I smirk. "I haven't. Yet."

He stalks toward me, making me walk backward until the backs of my legs hit the bed. His eyes are filled with seductive possibilities.

"Come here," he growls, cinching my waist with his hands. He lifts me and tosses me on the bed.

The mattress sinks with my weight. Pillows topple, spilling away from the headboard.

He climbs on the bed and hovers over me. Everything about the moment is dominated by Oliver. The scent of his cologne. The taste of his lips. The feel of his smooth skin and the heat rippling off it. The sound of his voice as he commands me to look at him.

I do. I rip my gaze from his delicious body and settle it on his eyes. The look he gives me melts me to the core.

He's as hungry for me as I am him, but there's something else. Something I can't quite explain. Reverence, maybe, or respect. Something that hits me so deep, so completely that I reach up and bring his face to mine.

He kisses me, as I ask, but breaks it sooner than I want him to.

Oliver rolls onto his side and places a kiss against my shoulder. His fingers trail over my chest, freeing my breasts from the white fabric of my bra. They sit on top of the lace—nipples beaded, and he takes his time caressing each one.

I lift my hips, my body begging for contact. He sees my reaction and grins.

"Impatient," he teases, letting his hand explore farther south.

"Frustrated."

"I like you sexually frustrated."

I narrow my eyes.

"Let me enjoy you," he whispers against my mouth.

I lick him along his bottom lip, eliciting a growl.

"Let *me* enjoy *you*," I whisper back.

Over my belly, along each side, he strokes every piece of me like it's a mission not to let a shred of my skin go without his touch. I can't complain ... yet I do.

"Oliver ..." I moan as he makes it to the apex of my thighs.

"Let's see how wet you are," he says as he slides my panties off.

"Oh, like that's a question."

He chuckles, dragging a finger through my slit. The contact against my overstimulated flesh is enough to make me yelp.

"How do you do this?" I groan, lifting my hips again. "How do you just sit there and touch me and not die for me to touch you?"

"Because ..." he says, placing a juice-coated finger into his mouth.

My jaw drops as I watch the finger pop free.

A fire burns deep in my belly so hot that I think the flames burst out of the top of my head.

"If you touch me," he says, drifting the wet finger across my stomach, "I'll come."

"Hey!" I laugh, batting his hand away. The cool air makes the dampness on my skin obvious, and it's just another thing I have to try to process at a moment when there are too many things to separate. "You're just being mean now."

"Am I?" He leans forward and wraps his mouth around one of my nipples.

My back arches, and my eyes fall closed. A moan worthy of a movie scene fills the room.

"Oliver ..." I reach blindly for his cock but come up empty-handed. "Dammit, Oliver."

He palms the breast he just mouthed with one hand and goes to work on the other. He licks, kisses, and puts pressure on the nipple with his teeth.

I yelp.

"I love watching you struggle not to fall apart." He grabs my legs, and in one quick move, he's between them. "Now you can come, my lady."

"Oh, fuck."

I ball the comforter up in my hands as he blows on my pussy. The steady stream of air against the swollen flesh is nearly enough to make me lose my mind.

"Watch me." It's an order, a statement requiring compliance. His tone gives no choice but for me to comply. "Don't look away, or I'll stop."

His hands pin the back of my thighs in the air as he situates himself between them. My legs framing Oliver's face is more erotic than any daydream I've ever had.

He sticks his tongue out and runs it up my slit.

"Oh, my gosh," I moan, sucking in a hasty breath.

His eyes are dark, broody, as he grins. And then he does it again.

My legs shake as he parts me, stopping at my clit to service it. The intensity of his tongue against my most sensitive part has my eyes rolling in the back of my head.

Immediately, his tongue stops moving.

"*Fuck*," I say, looking down at him with so much frustration that it's hard not to kick him in the face.

"Watch."

He lowers his face until I can only see his eyes. And then, in a moment I do not expect, he sucks my clit into his mouth.

"Dammit!" I all but scream, the intensity nearly painful.

Fire shoots through my body, curling and coalescing in my core. My legs shake uncontrollably.

He takes his hand off my right leg as I start to moan again. Just as I think the assault is starting to wane, he inserts one, then two fingers inside me.

"*Oh, shit*," I say, the words coming out in a broken scatter of a sentence.

"Look at me!"

I try—I try so hard to watch him between my legs. But every time I begin to focus, the pressure of his fingers pumping inside me and his mouth sucking at my flesh makes my eyes close again.

This is wonderful—insanely, mind-numbingly wonderful. I lay in a heap on Oliver's bed, clutching his blankets as if my life depends on it, and feel the fire burn through my veins.

It's a flood, a broken damn of orgasmic bliss that ruptures through me. Colors shoot through my vision like a fireworks display on the Fourth of July. The top of my head is light as if it's going to burst. The pit of my stomach is tight, clenched, as my body comes apart around this man's mouth and fingers.

"Oliver!" I scream, the potency of an orgasm something I'd long forgotten—if I ever knew to begin with. "Oliver! *Dammit!*"

He pulls his face away, taking advantage of his position, and watches me struggle to come back to earth.

His fingers slow, each motion more deliberate yet more controlled. Gently, he milks every last drop of pleasure from my body.

I fall back to the mattress. Sweat streaks my skin. I'm completely and utterly spent. *Mind. Blown.*

So that is an orgasm. Holy shit.

"That," Oliver says, sliding off the bed, "was worth every second of frustration you may have experienced tonight."

"Just tonight?" I wince as the words make me dizzy. "I've been thinking about this since you kissed me."

He leans over me, his face a few inches from mine. "I've been thinking about this since you hit me with your car."

I grin sleepily. "I hit your car with my car. Get it right."

He kisses me on the forehead. "Have you had enough?"

I lean up and kiss him, running my tongue around the inside of his mouth. He growls against my lips. The sound and vibrations send a shock through me again.

He pulls away. "I hope not because you just incited level two."

I laugh as he hovers over me. "That's all it took?"

"I have a feeling this won't be my best attempt at level two, but you have me ready to burst." He brushes a strand of hair off my cheek. "You are seriously amazing."

A blush creeps across my face, and I grab a pillow and cover it. There's something about being naked, fresh off an orgasm, and having Oliver tell me that I'm *seriously amazing* that makes me embarrassed.

"Oh, no," he says, ripping the pillow away from me.

I squeal in protest—a protest he doesn't pay a bit of attention to. He just grins.

He hops off the bed and procures a condom. He sheaths his cock, and then he's caging me in before I know what's happening.

"Shaye?" It's not just a question but a plea.

He's desperate ... *for me.*

My knees fall to the side. "Yes, please."

He lines himself up with my opening. At the same moment his lips land on mine, he parts my body with his.

"*Ooh.*" I sigh as he fills me.

"Shit." He rests his forehead on mine. "Dammit, Shaye."

"Does it feel good?"

He smirks. "*So* good, baby."

"So good, baby."

I hold on to his shoulders, wrapping my legs around his waist, and lift my hips. The words he just spoke echo inside my brain. He slides out of me before thrusting once again.

"*Oliver.*"

He grits his teeth, pushing and pulling, sliding through my wetness. I lock my heels just above his ass and squeeze him with my thighs.

Each movement, each thrust, builds me higher. Each flex of my muscles, each squeeze, sends him closer to his climax.

I watch his features—how his jawline pulses and the lines around his eyes crinkle. How his long lashes flutter with each blink and his forehead wrinkles as it shines with sweat.

My lord, he's beautiful. He's beautiful in every way. And as I lie beneath him, letting him pour himself into my naked body, I don't feel anything other than pure contentment.

This is exactly where I want to be.

I run my hands down his arms, feeling the ripples of his muscles as he holds himself up. He picks up his pace, pounding into me with the ferocity of a man who's on the edge.

I close my eyes and let my senses take over.

It takes all of three seconds to have me clinging on the edge of glory once again.

"I'm going to come," I warn him.

His entire body tenses. I can feel the head of his cock swell deep inside me.

"Me too," he groans as he pulls nearly out of me completely and then rockets himself inside. He's so deep, so wildly deep that I gasp.

"Ah!" I exhale, tightening my body around his length as his arms shake against mine.

"*Fuck*," he hisses, his back flexing against my heels that are dug into his skin.

Finally, my vision still blurred and my heart still racing, Oliver lowers himself on the bed beside me. We lie side by side for a long minute, catching our breath.

He laughs. "That was worth every ounce of self-restraint that I've used since we met."

I roll over, my body already aching, and lay my head on his chest.

He runs his fingers through my hair as I listen to his heart strum.

"Don't fall asleep yet," he whispers. "We need to get you cleaned up."

"Hmm."

My eyelids grow heavy, and I let them fall.

I vaguely remember the mattress dipping. A part of my brain recalls a damp cloth brushing against my skin. I dimly locate the moment that Oliver picked me up and tucked me under the blankets of his bed—against him.

My dreams fill with Oliver and dancing and sex. Lots of sex. And in each scenario playing through my head while I sleep is one line on repeat —"*So good, baby.*"

So good.

Chapter Twenty-Four

Oliver

Moonlight streams into the windows. The moon is so bright tonight as if it senses the battle I'm having with myself.

My fingertips dance along the ridge of Shaye's side. Her skin is warm and soft. Her body fits against mine like it shares the same mold.

I tried to sleep. I closed my eyes, I counted sheep—I even grabbed my phone and fed my virtual farm. But no amount of jumping ruminants or satiated cows can distract me from Shaye being here.

With me.

In my bed.

I stare at the ceiling, listening to her smooth breaths and feel the steady, rhythmic strum of her heartbeat against me. Her hair tickles my chest. One arm is stretched over me. Her ankle lays on top of mine as if it's some kind of security system.

It makes me smile.

It's also maddeningly confusing.

With every minute that passes, I expect panic to set in. I wait for the familiar sick feeling to elbow its way into my stomach. I brace myself for the alarm bells of my own internal security system starting to ring, letting me know that it's time to untangle myself from this woman and reset my brain. Reclaim my space. *My bed.*

I wait, watching shadows dance around my bedroom, and hold my breath.

Nothing happens.

If I lean in to the moment—allow myself to absorb the feeling instead of waiting for it to flee—I like it. *A lot.* Lying with her without tightness in my abdomen is relaxing. Not having to plot an exit strategy from this entanglement is refreshing. The absence of a mental bulletin that chastises me for the events of the past twenty-four hours—a state of mind that's always the case if a woman manages to make it to my bedroom—is satisfying.

But leaning in to this moment is dangerous. I'm not naïve.

Shaye stirs, her arm stretching before she settles into the blankets again. I hold my breath and look down to see if she's awake. She looks sleepily up at me.

"Hey," she says, her voice thick with sleep.

"Hey," I whisper back.

She tucks her chin to my side, resting her forehead on my chest, before rolling over onto her back. It takes everything I have in me not to grab her and haul her back next to me again.

"Have you been awake long?" she says, her eyes struggling to stay open.

"Nope. Just woke up."

She hums as her head nods subtly.

"It's the middle of the night," I tell her. "You can go back to sleep."

Her head turns against the pillows and she opens her eyes. Under the moonlight, she looks younger, more unguarded. It stirs something deep inside me.

I lean over and press a kiss against her forehead. She smiles.

"What's keeping you up?" she asks.

The question rolls softly off her lips. It comes across as a genuine thought, a natural inquiry. And I know that's intentional. There's a tilt to the words, a one-octave rise in the tone that tells me that she's thinking. She's curious. She's worried.

I move so that I'm on my side and facing her.

"It's hard to sleep when a beautiful woman is in your bed," I say.

She grins again.

"What's keeping you up?" I ask.

"Nothing. I just woke up."

"But you aren't going back to sleep, are you?"

She looks at me through her lashes, knowing I just read her like the sweet book that she is.

"I'm just thinking," she says.

"No. You're worrying."

"Yes. I'm worrying." She laughs softly. "You know me so well."

"So, talk to me. Tell me what you're worrying about."

She pauses and mulls over my request. Then she rolls onto her side to face me too.

I can see the trepidation in her eyes, the glimmer of uncertainty that she can't hide. I hate it. I hate everything about it.

After the night we had together, how could she possibly be worrying about anything? Didn't I make her feel good? Didn't I make her happy?

Doesn't she want to be here?

I take her hand in mine and lace our fingers together. I stroke the top of her hand with my thumb. She watches the motion as she thinks.

"Be honest with me," I tell her, bringing our interlocked hands to my mouth and kissing them. "Trust me."

As I set them back on the blanket, she sighs.

"I don't have a problem being honest. But the trust part is hard for me." She nestles into the pillows. "It's hard for me to just dive into this —whatever it is—headfirst. I worry."

"Why?"

"*You* are Oliver Mason. There's nothing I can do to you that would compromise that. But I'm ... *me*. I don't have the same level of mastery over my life that you do."

I stare at her. "Sweetheart, I don't understand."

She shifts around on the pillows. I release her hand so she can use it to get situated. It doesn't escape me that she puts some distance between us when she resettles, but I don't comment on it. I'm too focused on what she has to say.

"In every relationship I've had, it's always come down to a power struggle," she says. "To live in that space with the other person, I had to give up something. I had to give up me or at least pieces of me."

My chest aches as I listen to her. It downright hurts.

"My mom made it her mission in life to keep me in my place," she says, the words picking up speed. "I had little control over my life until I finally moved out and in with Luca. I probably moved in with him so soon to escape my home life, I don't know. I haven't explored that enough, I suppose. But it was always ridiculous curfews, punishments for the smallest offenses, and embarrassing me in front of my friends."

As she continues, her voice softens. Her eyes turn watery. Her hand finds mine.

I take her palm and give it the tightest squeeze I can give without making her wince. I want her to know I'm here, I'm listening—that she has me.

"And then Luca ..." She presses her lips together, her chest rising and falling. "It started off good. He was nice and thoughtful. But looking back, I can see where things went wrong."

I can't help it. I close the distance between us.

I reach for her and slide her across the bed until she's tucked beside me. I'm not sure if it's for her good or mine—or which one of us needs the connection more.

We lie together quietly. The only sound is the occasional hoot of an owl.

I rest my head against hers and give her the space I think she needs.

I also need a bit of time to try to rope in the emotions swirling inside me.

To be honest, I haven't wanted to know—to really know—a woman in a very long time. I don't even know that I wanted to know Kendra, really. I've had dates, one-night stands, but I haven't wanted their thoughts. Their hearts. To know what makes them tick, what makes them smile. Yet I want all of this from Shaye. I barely know her.

That fact is not lost on me. In fact, it sits obtusely on my heart as I feel her try to maneuver around whatever wound she carries. A wound I don't know. But as we lie together with nothing between us but the secrets we keep and the sheets on which we sleep, I understand that I'll never truly know Shaye until I know the scars on her heart.

I wanted men in the room tonight to know that Shaye was with me. Now I want Shaye to know that she has *me.*

"It's a bit of a messy story, so I understand if you don't really want the specifics. If you don't want to know, Oliver, it's fine. I won't burden you with—"

"No. I *do* want to know, Shaye. I ... I want to know you. It's just not the pretty pieces of our lives that make us who we are."

I give her a gentle squeeze and think about how my relationship with Kendra helped make me who I am ... and who I might want to be someday.

"I'd love to hear anything that you feel willing to share with me," I tell her.

She reaches up and places her soft hand on my bristly cheek. Smiles at me. *God, she's beautiful.*

"*Okay.*" She gathers her courage. "Things ... declined. With each step, he ... repositioned himself. I lost a little bit of my autonomy every time. When I moved in. Joint banking. When we got married."

I squeeze her tighter.

"It's not all his fault because I let it happen," she says, her voice cracking. "I wrote everything off and made excuses for him. The affairs, the debt, the abuse ..."

My body stills. I'm afraid to move. I'm afraid to look at her or touch her or breathe too hard.

Did she just fucking say abuse? Affairs, okay, fuck him for that. But abuse?

It's a good thing he's already dead.

"He'd yell," she says, sniffling. "He'd call me names. Made me quit my job because the boss wanted me—or so he said. He took away the checkbook because I didn't know how to manage money, yet he was the one that took out a one-hundred-fucking-thousand-dollar loan against my mom's house and made me sign the papers too."

Her tears are hot and wet against my bare chest. Her body shakes as she lets loose what must be a life's worth of pain. *Her mother. Her bastard husband.*

I hold her, biting back the explosion I want to spew into the room, reining myself in. I try to wrap my brain around what she's telling me, but I know that if I do, I'm going to have so many questions. It'll prevent her from talking ... and that's what she needs right now.

"I got you," I whisper, moving us both until she's on top of my chest. I wrap my arms around her and press kisses against her head.

My heart splits open with the weight of her words. The only bandage for me is that she's here—trusting me with this truth. Even though I know that she needed to do this long ago, the fact that she feels safe enough to do it with me makes me feel more powerful than any deal I've ever closed.

Finally, she sniffles and wipes her face with the back of her hands.

"Are you okay?" I ask, leaning back to get a better look at her.

"Yeah." Her voice sounds like it's wrapped in cotton. "I'm sorry for this. I don't know why I chose right now to break down."

I smile at her. "I'm glad you did."

She laughs and scoots off me. I hate to let her go, but I don't know what she needs. Maybe it's best to let her choose.

She pulls the sheets up around her. "I haven't talked about things like that with anyone besides Lisbeth. I don't like to let people see me cry."

"You're a pretty crier."

Her smile stretches across her tearstained cheeks. "That's probably not true but thank you for saying it anyway."

"It is true." I remove a chunk of hair that's stuck to the side of her face. "Can I tell you something?"

She nods.

"I have trust issues too." Admitting my weaknesses feels like a huge mistake, but it's the only way I think I can get through to her. "When your fiancée leaves you for a much older, much richer man and you realize she never really loved you at all, that stings. No, it hurts like a motherfucker."

"She's an idiot."

I smile at her. "I've been fucked over in a hundred business deals. My parents are now divorcing, which isn't about me, I know, but it does feel like ... if you can't trust your parents to stay together at our age, is anything even sacred anymore?"

"I'm sorry to hear that, Oliver."

"Thanks, but that's not the point." I lace our fingers together again. "The point is that this thing with you makes me worry too."

Her eyes search mine. "Why?"

"Because this ... *us* ... feels like it has the potential to be infinitely more important to me than Kendra or a business deal or my parents' marriage."

Her brows raise toward the ceiling, but she doesn't say anything.

"I've laid here all night and couldn't sleep because I was trying to wrap my head around you. Me. *This.*" I tug her close to me again. "I thought about last night at the gala and seeing you with Marius. I thought about having you in my house and in my bed. I thought about waking up and making breakfast and ..."

I peer down at her. She looks up, my apprehension reflected in her eyes.

"I don't know what we're doing, Shaye. And we both have every right to be scared as shit. But I don't want it to end. I want this to be the beginning."

"Of what?" she asks softly.

"Of whatever it becomes. To hell with your ex-husband and your mother and Kendra and—"

"And the fact that I work for you?" She sighs. "I love working for you. But if we ... if this is the beginning of something—"

"Don't you want it to be?"

A slow smile slips across her face. "Without a doubt."

I bend down and place a chaste kiss on her lips. "Then you work for me."

"Should I work for Wade?"

I flinch, making her giggle.

"Do you really fucking think that it would be easier for me to get anything done knowing you were in another office that I could just barge into?" I scoff. "*Please.*"

"Okay."

"Okay, what?"

"I don't know." She shrugs. "Okay, that I will try not to overthink this. And ... *I'll try to trust you.*"

A lot of women have said a lot of nice things to me in my life. Funny things, sexy things, interesting things. But no one has ever said anything as important as Shaye is saying right now. *Because trust comes with a price that both of us have paid before. And lost.*

My heart pulls in my chest as if I've just been deemed worthy of some great responsibility. It's baffling and a little disconcerting, but also, it's amazing.

"Come here, you," I say, pulling her on top of me again.

I hold her as close to me as I can. She wraps her arms around me and holds me as if her life depends on it.

Maybe it does.

Maybe we both depend on it.

"I have a question," she says, smiling against my chest.

"What's that?"

"What does level three look like?"

A band of heat uncoils in my groin as I flip her over in one swift movement. Her laughter pierces the air as she bites her lip.

"You want level three, baby?" I ask.

She nods.

I jerk the blankets off her and let my gaze feast on her naked body. The sweet curve of her hip, the roundness of her stomach, the fullness of her breasts—*it's all mine.*

A few things in the last twenty-four hours have struck me as odd. The fact that her dancing with Marius made me insanely jealous. Hearing her call herself my EA annoying me. Enjoying her in my personal space not shocking my system.

But the one thing that tops them all is this fierce, instinctive need to make her mine. I don't know where it comes from, and I don't know why. I only know that I'm powerless against it.

I just hope that I can figure out how to deal with it.

"What are you waiting for?" she asks, reaching for my cock. Her hand wraps snugly around it.

"I'm just trying to figure out what to do with you."

She leans up and kisses me. "Let's start here and figure out the rest together."

I lay her back and do as she suggests.

We'll start here and figure out the rest.

Together.

Chapter Twenty-Five

Shaye

> Me: Famished yet satiated. Interesting morning over here.

> Lis: Squee! Details!

> Me: As soon as I get home. 😌

> Lis: GIRL

> Me: Ha!

I yelp as Oliver slips behind me and nips at the back of my neck. I turn around to swat him, but he's already retreated to the other side of the kitchen.

His home is more amazing than I even realized. As the sun came up over the horizon and we untangled ourselves from one another, the beauty of his space became apparent.

Every detail is intentional—from the handcrafted soaking tub in the master bathroom to the imported Italian tile in the kitchen. The colors used throughout the house are calming and cozy, and random pops of color are displayed in what looks like a child's finger-painting canvas to the untrained—meaning, my—eye.

It works, nonetheless.

"Are you sure you don't want me to help you?" I ask him as he loads the dishwasher. "I feel lazy watching you do all the work."

"That's not what you said this morning."

My cheeks heat. "Well ..."

He laughs. "I want you to sit there and look beautiful."

"*Fine.*" I pull my legs up beneath the T-shirt I borrowed from Oliver for breakfast. "I guess I can manage."

He rinses out the pan we used to fry bacon and then wipes up the counter from the English muffins we toasted. The cheese is rewrapped and placed in a zipped baggie. The eggs are returned to the refrigerator.

He does it all in a pair of black boxer shorts.

"Do you cook a lot?" I ask him, trying to keep my focus on things other than the way his abs ripple with each movement. Or the way his ass flexes beneath his shorts. Or how his shoulders bend and flex and how my fingers want to touch them—to touch *him*.

"Sometimes. Why?"

"I don't know. You just seem really familiar with the kitchen."

He sprays off a plate. "Well, I live here. I designed it. Shouldn't I be familiar with it?"

"I guess so. I just ... I thought bachelors ordered a lot of takeout."

A laugh spills from his lips as he places the plate in the dishwasher. "How very sexist of you."

"It was, wasn't it?" I shake my head at myself. "You just surprise me, that's all."

He raises the dishwasher door and snaps it in place. Then he plants his hands on the white stone countertop and looks at me.

"I have a very nice lady who comes by once a week and makes sure things are clean," he admits. "I tidy up after myself just fine, but mopping and cleaning bathrooms—things like that—are hard to get to. I have to let some things go in order to be great at others."

"That's a nice luxury you have."

"What?"

"The choice of letting some things go in order to be great at others."

He tilts his head to the side and considers this. "I've never thought about it like that, but I suppose you're right."

"I'm always right."

He presses off the counter and dries his hands on a towel. I watch him.

Oliver is so different at home than he is at the office. I don't know what I expected him to be like here—if I had any expectations at all—but being so *casual* wasn't one of them.

I sit in my chair and watch him finish his chores—running the garbage disposal and wiping up a splash of juice that spilled when he grabbed me from behind. It's ... *lovely*.

It's lovely because it's so mind-numbingly normal. A man in his kitchen with a woman, making breakfast and cleaning up. He's not a powerful CEO here. I'm not his EA or a woman who happened to be brought here after a night out. We're just two people who chose to spend some time together, and it feels wonderful.

Comfortable.

Safe.

I lay awake long after he fell asleep in the early hours of the morning. I curled up next to him and held on to him, trying to convince myself that he's real. I'm really here. That this is real.

I prayed that I wouldn't regret opening myself up to him. I hoped that when I opened my eyes that the way he looked back at me wouldn't have changed over the night. I pled with the universe to please, somehow, let this situation be an anomaly in my life—let me have made the right choice for once.

Even though nothing about this with Oliver has felt like a choice. It's felt like the natural course of my life ... just heading in a positive direction for once.

"What are you thinking, my lady?" he asks.

I smile at him. "I don't think I've ever had a Sunday morning like this in my entire life."

"Really? What are your Sunday mornings usually like?"

He motions for me to get up and follow him, so I do.

We make our way lazily down the hallway. He tucks me under his arm as we enter a bright sitting room off the kitchen. White bookshelves line one wall, and a multitude of plants take up most of the counter that lines the other.

Two white wicker chairs face the windows that overlook an expansive field of grasses and flowers.

"So," he says after we sit. "Your Sundays?"

"Oh. Well, I usually sleep in, and then sometimes I go to Lisbeth's for brunch."

"You and Lisbeth are close."

I nod. "Sometimes I spend the afternoon in Forsyth Park with a book or watch a movie and sleep through most of it."

Oliver laughs. "What kind of movies do you like? Besides *Steel Magnolias*?"

My heart swells at the fact that he remembered what I'd said.

"I like girlie movies. Anything with Julia Roberts or Sandra Bullock. *Ocean's Eleven*—all of them— are good. *Jason Bourne*."

He seems surprised. "All excellent choices."

"Thank you." I laugh. "What do you do on Sundays?"

He rocks back and forth and gazes across the meadow. "I usually sleep in ... until seven," he says, watching me out of the corner of his eye.

"That is not sleeping in!"

He laughs. "It is for me."

"One of these days, I'll show you sleeping in."

"Didn't we sleep in today?" He holds out his hands. "It's nine o'clock."

I sigh. "No. Sleeping in means at least until ten. Maybe eleven. Twelve if you're really going big."

His eyes go wide. "You can sleep until noon?"

"Yeah. I've even slept until one."

He adds a dropped jaw to the mix. The whole look is more than I can take seriously. I swat at his shoulder and giggle.

"So I sleep in but apparently not to your standards," he says, running a hand through his perfectly mussed hair. "Then I usually go to church with Mom and Wade. And then we'll do lunch, or I'll come back here and work in the office for a while."

I shake my head.

"What?" he asks.

"You work at home on Sundays?"

"Yeah. That's how you get shit done. *You do it.*"

I lift my feet off the floor, and my chair rocks back and forth too.

We sit quietly, the sun warming my skin. It must be the fresh air that the plants give off—or maybe it's the large crystal in the corner of the room that sets the tone, but there's an intrinsically peaceful nature about the room.

"What do you want to do today?" Oliver asks.

I keep my gaze trained on the window. "I actually need to go home."

"Why? I thought we could go to the beach or go out to dinner somewhere nice."

This sweet man.

I give myself a minute to pretend having expensive dinners and afternoons at the beach are my life. That all I have to worry about is if I'd like seafood or steak, a movie in or a night out. It's a wonderful sixty seconds suspended in a daydream that stars me and Oliver and fancy evening dresses.

I sigh. "I have to work tonight."

"No, you don't."

"Yes. I do."

"I give you the night off." He bumps my hand with his. "See how that works? Now you're free to spend the night with me."

I turn my head and look at him. "I can't."

Despite the revelations that I've shared with Oliver, I haven't told him about The Gold Room. I haven't *not* told him that I work for Nate; it hasn't come up. I'm happy that I haven't given it much thought because now that the moment is here, I'm not sure it'll be smooth sailing.

Oliver's brow furrows as he tries to feel his way around this topic.

"Why the hell not?" he asks.

"Well," I say, stepping gently into this particular pool, "I have a second job."

This catches him off guard. He leans back as if it'll somehow help him understand the plain English that I just used.

"*Okay.*" He licks his lip, still unsure. "Where is it? What do you do?"

"I'm a waitress. I cook, too, and do dishes. And God knows I clean because Nate couldn't find his way around the place with a mop if he had to."

Oliver stills. "Who is Nate?"

"Nate is my boss. He owns the place." I squirm under Oliver's stare. "He's one of my best friends."

He nods, but it's more for my benefit than an actual understanding and acceptance of my statement. That much I'm certain.

"Do I not pay you enough?" he asks. "Because I swear I saw your employment offer, but if Toni—"

"You pay me enough. More than I expected and more than I made at Monroe. It's not that."

He shifts in his seat. "Then what is it, Shaye? How does my EA work as a waitress at a ... bar? Is that what you said?"

"Yes. It's called The Gold Room. It's nice. Nate just updated everything. I promised Nate that I would stay on for a while, and I don't go back on my promises."

My mouth goes dry. I'm not sure what Oliver's reaction is going to end up being. I'm not sure he knows either.

His fingertips tap against the armrest. In a painfully slow motion, he looks away from me and out the window.

"You and Nate are just friends?"

"Of course."

He rocks back and forth. "I want to be very clear about something that I didn't realize I needed to be clear about." He stops moving and looks at me. "But I do."

His gaze is intense, his eyes searching the depths of mine for a truth that I can't name. I just let him see what he wants to see because I have nothing to hide.

"What is it?" I ask, my voice steady.

"I don't know what the kids call it these days, but as far as I am concerned, you and I are exclusive."

My throat constricts as I absorb his admission.

Exclusive.

We're exclusive?

We're exclusive.

Holy shit.

His shoulders fall. "I want to give us the space to get to know each other, Shaye."

"I do too."

He looks relieved. "I don't want ..." He sighs.

My stomach roils, a mixture of anxiety and joy swirling together. The longer we go without saying anything, the more the anxiety overtakes the joy.

So I act.

"I don't know what's happening between us," I say. "I feel like we just met—"

"Because we did." He gives me a wry smile.

"And it feels like it in some ways, right? There's all this newness and excitement. Everything is fun, and it feels like there's so much potential."

He nods, caution rippling through his features.

I reach over and take his hand. I trace the lines in his palm with my finger.

"But it also feels like I've known you forever," I say. "When I'm with you, I ... I don't feel like my world is about to be split in two or that I have to look over my shoulder."

"You don't. I'm already looking over it for you."

The sincerity, the pure genuineness of his words makes my eyes water. Because I know he means it.

I believe him.

And that, in and of itself, is monumental for me.

Oliver takes my hand and urges me out of the chair. He leads me in a half-circle until I'm facing him.

He holds both hands in his and looks up at me.

"Are you positive you can't stay with me today? I don't want you to go," he says.

"I have to."

"Okay." His jaw tenses, but the frustration doesn't reach his eyes. "Can you spare me another hour?"

I bite my lip. "It depends on what you have in mind."

He stands abruptly, scooping me up in his arms. I shriek at the motion.

My legs dangle over his thick biceps as he grins at me.

"I'm not about to let my woman go to work for another man without being completely certain that she's satisfied *in every fucking way.*"

He crushes my mouth with his. His fingers burn into my skin.

My insides ache as we make our way through his house.

I'm not sure where we're headed or what is to come, but I know that it'll be great with Oliver.

And maybe it'll be great after that too.

Just maybe.

Chapter Twenty-Six

Shaye

"Would you like a ham sandwich, Joe?" I know the answer, but I wait for his response anyway.

The little old man from Kentucky slumps on the stool. A knit cap sits lopsided on his head. Strands of hair that resemble a Brillo pad poke out from beneath the edges and through the hole at the top. The tear in the fabric has gotten bigger every day since I noticed it a month ago. I need to remember to get him a new one before the weather turns cold.

Joe's skin is stained with engine grease. I think he does odd jobs here and there—working on cars for people who can't afford to take them to an actual mechanic. But I also suspect those same people take advantage of his kindness and how badly he needs twenty dollars. It's why I didn't take my car to him to be fixed when I damaged it.

"If ya got one back there, I'd take it." He gives me a lopsided, toothless grin. "Maybe some mustard if ya have that handy."

"You know it."

I wave at Travis, a friend of Nate's, as he comes in. Travis did the roofing on The Gold Room when Nate remodeled before I started working for him. Apparently, the place was practically in shambles back then. You wouldn't know it by the looks of the place now.

"Is Nate in his office?" Travis asks.

"I think so."

"Can I head back there?"

"Go for it."

He gives me a little salute and disappears into the hall on the far side of the building.

"Thank God for Sunday evenings," Paige says as I enter the kitchen. She slides a knife through a tomato with the precision of a surgeon. "I think we'd be perpetually behind without Sunday evenings."

"You're right." I reach in the cooler for the ham that Nate keeps for Joe. "I actually look forward to Sunday evenings without the alcohol and the crowd that brings."

Paige's knife hits the cutting board in even intervals. I get to work making Joe's sandwich.

My mind drifts, thinking about how different my job is here than it is during the day for Oliver. I don't think I prefer either one of them. Mason Limited makes me feel accomplished as a professional; The Gold Room makes me feel accomplished as a human.

Besides feeding Joe and providing stability for Murray, this place does so much more for so many people. It's a place for someone to come after work and relax. It celebrates camaraderie. Couples enjoy the steak specials and dance to local live bands on Friday nights. Lonely hearts venture in looking for love ... or a one-night stand.

No judgment.

It feels just as good to be a part of it as it does the team at Mason. *Even if Oliver is a little jealous.*

His broodiness was so hot.

We're exclusive.

"What are you all smiley about over there?" Paige asks. "Oh! You went to the gala last night, didn't you? I saw it on the news this morning."

"I did." I try not to smile but fail miserably. "It was amazing."

"I can't imagine attending something like that. Did you feel like royalty?"

"Um, no. Not royalty." I think of Marius and watching Oliver with the table of women. "More like Cinderella most of the time."

Her cute little face wrinkles. "Why?"

"Oh, just ... you know."

"No. I don't know. But I hope it doesn't mean that something bad happened." She frowns. "You'll ruin my vision."

I laugh as I finish up Joe's sandwich. "Nothing bad happened. Actually, some *really good things* happened."

Her face lights up with interest as the kitchen door swings open. Murray stomps with a frown on his face and a large vase in his hand. In the oversized glass are long-stemmed red roses—probably thirty of them.

"Holy shit," Paige says, setting her knife down.

"Yeah. Someone has money to waste." He thrusts the flowers at me. "Here you go, pal."

It takes two hands to control the weight of the arrangement, so I set it next to the sink.

My heart races in my chest. A dopey smile takes up shop on my lips, and I don't even try to erase it. It would be futile.

"Oh, my gosh." Paige is at my side in a second. "These are freaking gorgeous, Shaye!"

"I know."

My hand trembles as I lower a stem to my nose. The fragrance is heavenly.

You've outdone yourself, Mr. Mason.

"Nate asked me to get some lids for the to-go cups," Murray says, flipping a chunk of hair out of his eyes. "Can someone get me money out of the register? I'm not clocked in."

"I will," Paige says. "Shaye needs to call her man."

I need to do more than that to him.

My stomach fluttering with a thousand butterflies, I spy a little white envelope buried in the greenery. It takes me a moment to fish it out of the center of the flowers.

Shaye Brewer is written in bold, blue ink on the front. I flip it over and slip out the card from inside.

I hold my breath, imagining what romantic or maybe dirty things

Oliver thought up for me. I can't believe he went to the trouble of sending me flowers already. Was he this jealous of Nate? Or maybe he just really wanted to make an impression.

I grin. *You already did that, babe.*

My eyes skim over the words. With each word I read, my heart pounds harder.

My temperature grows hotter.

My palms start to sweat.

Shaye,

I've found myself unable to stop thinking about you. I'll be in town for a few more days. If you'd like to meet up for dinner—or another dance—I would be honored at the opportunity to spend more time with you.

My best,

Marius

"I guess you were right," Paige says, her voice making me jump. "Something really good must have happened."

"Why?" I pull the card to my chest. "What happened?"

She walks around the counter and picks up her knife again. Her eyes narrow. "Well, you got a couple hundred dollars' worth of roses. Red roses, to be exact."

"Oh. Yes." I gulp. "So I did."

She sets the knife down and looks at me suspiciously. "Are you okay?"

"Me? I'm fine. I'm absolutely fine."

A bead of sweat dots my forehead as I look at the flowers again. They're beautiful and sweet, and *Oliver will not take this well.*

Oh, dear God.

I'm not cut out for this kind of drama. I don't know what to do.

Do I tell him? Will it cause a pissing match?

It will *absolutely* cause a pissing match. He didn't even like Nate, and I just said I worked for him. There's no way he'll take this many roses from Marius as a friendly gesture.

But it's not my fault. I didn't do anything wrong.

But it will complicate my new relationship with Oliver. There's no doubt about it.

And I so, so don't need to complicate something so amazing and new.

"Shaye?" Paige's hand rests on my shoulder. "I know you said you're okay, and I'm not calling you a liar or anything, but ... are you okay?"

I turn and face the sweet girl who I haven't known very long.

I should call Lisbeth—that's what I should do. She would know how to handle this. Giving me advice is her job as my best friend. But right now, in the thick of the mess, Paige is here.

"I'm freaking out," I tell her.

She nods. "No offense, but I can tell." She glances up at the roses. "I've never seen someone get so sweaty about a flower arrangement before."

I smile through gritted teeth. *This is so my luck.*

"Well," I say slowly. "This particular flower arrangement is not from the man who I just started seeing exclusively this morning."

This takes her by surprise. "Okay, first of all—yay to you for your new relationship. Second of all ... maybe yay to you for being so interesting that a second guy is also fawning over you?" She laughs tightly. "Or not? I mean, who is guy number two?"

"A guy I met last night."

"So a guy before you became exclusive with the first one?"

I nod warily.

"Then what's the problem?" She shrugs happily. "This is a win-win as far as I can tell."

I lean against the sink and wish I had her optimism. *What if Oliver gets angry? What will he do to me if he finds out? It will be like when Luca thought I was flirting with the—*

Stop. Oliver is *not* Luca.

"I thought about last night at the gala and seeing you with Marius. I thought about having you in my house and in my bed. I thought about waking up and making breakfast ... I want this to be the beginning."

Oliver wasn't angry with me last night because *I* danced with Marius. He was angry because he wants us. *Our beginning.*

I look at the flowers again. They are beautiful and if they'd arrived a few weeks ago, I'd be tripping over myself to touch every single petal. Despite how gorgeous they are, they don't hold a candle to Oliver's smile.

That's what I want.

"Paige, consider yourself the new owner of a bunch of roses," I say, walking to the counter and picking up Joe's sandwich. I grab a bag of chips for good measure.

The decision feels right in my stomach. It's logical. *Why risk upsetting the apple cart—or flower cart, as it is—for one bad fruit?*

"Really?" she asks.

"Really."

"Thank you." Paige smiles. "I've never had that many flowers in my life."

"Me either."

I laugh as I walk out of the kitchen.

I may not have had that many roses before, but I also won't be swayed by an over-the-top gesture. Marius missed the memo last night. That's on him. But I believe my heart is seeing a very clear memo right now.

The man who stole my breath this morning—multiple times— might end up stealing my heart.

CHAPTER TWENTY-SEVEN

Oliver

"We got it!" Holt shoves open my door and marches in my office. "Right fucking here."

"Um, who got it?" Boone makes a face as he follows our brother in. "*I* got it. Me."

Holt fires him a look. "I'm gonna kill you."

I throw my phone on my desk. "I'm gonna kill both of you if you don't learn how to fucking knock."

My gaze slips to Shaye. She glances up at me from her desk and smiles. I'm sure she's thinking what I'm thinking—if they'd have barged in here any day over this past week, there's a chance that they would've found her bent over my desk, lying half-naked on the sofa, or leaning against the wet bar with my fingers inside her sweet little pussy. Since our first night together and our agreement to be exclusive, it's been impossible to keep my hands off her.

I adjust my cock and move my eyes back to my brothers.

"What's so important that you forgot your manners?" I ask them.

"Fine." Boone crosses one ankle over his knee. "Let's not tell him until he's nice, Holt."

Holt tries not to smile. When he speaks, his voice is lowered. "Let's get his EA in here. Bet he'll be nice then."

They both know. They have to. The look they both give me tells me that they know I'm involved with Shaye.

I should just admit it. It would make life a hell of a lot easier. I'm sure Holt would try to convince me to move her to Boone's office or maybe even Wade's, and I'm just as sure I'd shoot that down like a clay pigeon.

Having Shaye next door to me has changed my entire day. I used to work for hours on end, barely going home to sleep. I was anxious, unsettled—looked forward to the next deal and maybe Sunday dinner at Mom's.

But now? It's different. My office, *my life*, has changed. In some ways, it's subtle. It's laughing more in the office and leaving earlier to take Shaye to dinner. In other ways, it's obvious. It's waking up with Shaye in my arms and feeling grounded during the day.

I keep waiting for the shine to dull, for the novelty to wear off, but day after day, it's there. *It gets better.*

"So, we have some news," Holt says.

Boone beams. "I found the owner of the property behind the Jewell project."

I look at him dumbfounded. Then I look at Holt. "Is he serious?"

Holt shrugs. "Apparently so. Legal called and said they'd crafted a proposed contract and said this dipshit sent them the contact information *that they couldn't find.*" He looks at Boone. "How? Just ... how?"

"Okay, so, I used to fuck this girl—"

"Nope." I laugh, opening my drawer for a pen to throw at him if he keeps it up. "We get the idea."

I reach to my right and move my hand around. Instead of finding the hard plastic of an ink pen, I touch something soft. Then something silky. Then the unmistakable shape of a thong.

I don't have to look down to know the soft pair of panties is pink, the silky ones are red, and the thong is the color of Shaye's skin.

My cock gets hard. Again.

I shove the drawer closed. When I look up and into Shaye's office, she's gone.

My attention goes back to Boone and Holt.

"I didn't discuss price," Boone says. "But I know they want to sell— or they will sell if given a solid offer. The old man doesn't use the property for much anymore, and with the city expanding that direction, he doesn't figure his only son that fled the city life to Montana will want to come back and do anything with it."

"That's good for us," I note, pleased. "Good work, Boone."

He grins like a child. "Thanks, Ollie."

A knock raps against the door that separates my office from Shaye's. We all glance in that direction.

"Excuse me," she says, her gaze lingering on me for a second too long before she addresses my brothers. "Hi, Boone. Holt."

They say hello and watch her walk toward us.

Instantly, my instincts are on high alert. *Something is wrong.* Her shoulders are stiff. The smile on her face isn't genuine. Her steps are short and stressed.

"I have the proposed contracts from legal," Shaye says, handing a folder to each of us. "An electronic copy is in your emails, as well. Oliver, please don't forget that you have a call with Greg in ten minutes. I can move that if you would like."

"It's fine. We'll be done by then."

She nods. "Boone, it's your wife's birthday. Please stop and buy her flowers on the way home."

Boone smacks his forehead with his palm. "*Oh, fuck.* I forgot."

"I did not." Shaye pats him on the shoulder. "You have a reservation for three tonight at six at Picante. I figured you wanted to take Rosie."

Boone's hand slides down his face. "You're serious?"

Shaye laughs. "Yes. But all I can do is make the reservation and remind you to get flowers. You will have to figure out how to wow her yourself."

Boone hops to his feet. "I need to call Mom."

"You need to grow the fuck up," Holt calls after him as he heads for the door.

"Thank you, Shaye! Love you!" Boone calls over his shoulder. Then he stops on a dime and turns. He glances quickly at me and then back to a giggling Shaye. "I was kidding. It was just a natural ... You know, you're like a sister ... I'm, um, just gonna stop now."

"Good call," I say, wishing I had the pen to throw at him.

Shaye fixes her gaze on me. *What the hell?*

"I'll check this contract out and get back with you, Ollie," Holt says, standing up. "Thanks for the hard copy, Shaye."

"Of course."

Holt gives me a curious look like *What the fuck is going on here?* before exiting. He shuts the door behind him.

I lean back in my seat and take in the woman in front of me. She crosses her arms. *She means business.*

We haven't fought or disagreed, really, until now, so I'm not sure how to deal with her. What approach will work best? I have no idea—mostly because I don't know why she's pissed.

But she is. That I have little doubt.

I consider telling her that she looks hot as fuck when she's angry, then think better of it. Instead, I choose to play it off like there's nothing to be mad about.

"What?" I ask.

"I don't even know where to start."

"Well, pick something and let's get this over with."

This is not the reaction she wants. She drops her arms to her sides.

"Okay, first," she says, tipping me off that there will, indeed, be a list, "my car was miraculously fixed today when we had lunch."

I hum.

"Do you know anything about that?" she asks.

"I know that you cannot hold a bumper onto a car frame with zip ties indefinitely. I do know that."

"Oliver."

"Yes, Shaye?"

She blows out a breath. "You didn't even ask me first."

"You want me to ask you before I do something nice for you?" I raise a brow. She has to be kidding me. "If that thing fell while you were driving, you would've wrecked. That's a danger not just to you but also everyone else on the road, my lady. I'm not going to know it needs repaired and not have it done."

Her anger wavers.

"You can't be mad at me for that," I say. "It was my civic duty."

"I will pay you back."

"The hell you will."

This relights the fire inside her. "Oliver Mason, you will not start doing this."

"Doing what, Shaye Brewer? Taking care of you?" I stand and walk around my desk. "You are mistaken."

She braces herself against a chair, but I don't go near her. Instead, I walk to the door that opens to the reception room and lock it. Then I close hers and lock it too.

Shaye's eyes go wide as I face her again. *She knows I mean business.*

Still, she's undeterred from her litany of infractions.

Her shoulders straighten. "Second on the list is this." She tosses a folder onto my desk and then jerks out a piece of paper.

Oh.

I recognize the sheet she's holding. It's a cream-colored paper with personal information and tax deductions at the top. The bottom third is a check that I signed yesterday.

Shaye's first paycheck.

In the rush of the day—Fridays are always the worst—I'd forgotten it was payday. And in the distractions of the week—namely, Shaye—I'd forgotten that I instructed Toni to give her a raise.

A substantial one.

Nothing she doesn't deserve and nothing that's out of scale. Executive assistants make this kind of coin. Just usually not a new hire. I don't need the standard three months to know that Shaye will and already does deserve the higher bracket from what we started her on. *Fact.*

I blow out a breath.

"What, *in the actual fuck*, is this?" She shakes the paper in the air. "Are you out of your mind?"

"Maybe."

"Oliver." Her body shakes with anger. "Just ... explain this to me.

Explain what justification you have for paying me ..." She looks at the check. "I won't even say this amount out loud."

"Google it. It's not out of line."

"*Not out of line?*" The laughter that passes through the air isn't one of amusement. "If EAs make this much, I want to know what they're doing to earn it."

I tuck my tie into my jacket. I don't go near her just in case.

I'm not completely surprised at her reaction. It might've gone over better if it hadn't dropped on the same day as Leo answered my call to fix Shaye's car.

"Why don't you have direct deposit, anyway?" I grumble.

"Because I forgot to set it up. But that's highly irrelevant."

"Is it?" I sit. "If you direct deposited that, we wouldn't be arguing right now."

She throws the check on my desk. It flutters daintily onto the wood.

"You will call Toni right now and tell her that you made a mistake." Her tone challenges me to disagree. "Tell her you were drunk or high or that you added a zero where you didn't mean to. I don't care. But fix this, Oliver."

I did. I fixed it by giving her more money. Maybe it's a lot to her, but it's not to me. Besides, she's worth it. She's great at her job. She takes care of me, Boone, and even things for Holt that she catches in the midst of everything else.

Her potential is through the ceiling, and I would happily pay her this, even if I didn't have feelings for her.

The fact that I do have *serious* feelings for Shaye complicates it. So does the hundred-thousand-dollar debt she shoulders.

It's weighed on my mind since she told me days ago. *A hundred thousand-dollars?* I asked a friend who owes me a favor to look into her ex-husband and dig around a little bit. Apparently, the guy was doing business with very bad people. The word on the streets is that his car accident was more of a case of someone not wanting him alive.

"I'm paying you your due diligence," I say. "You don't think it looks suspicious that I'm paying you—"

"Oh, shut up. That is not my due diligence, and you know it."

Woman, just take my help. Trust me.

I can't tell her that I snooped around—not yet. I'm afraid it'll send her running. And I know damn well that she'll reject any attempts I make, any suggestions, to pay off the debt for her—which is what needs to fucking happen.

I'm just trying to figure out how to do that without sending her into a rampage.

"Come here," I tell her.

"I'm not coming there."

"You did yesterday."

She almost smiles. Almost.

I sigh. "Shaye, I'm sorry. I just—"

"You'll just call Toni now or I quit." She crosses her arms over her chest again. "Now, Oliver."

Dammit.

I consider taking a stand, but is this the hill I want to die on? No. I can find a workaround to helping her without making things worse.

"Oliver ..."

"Fine." I stick out my bottom lip like she's won, and I'm pouting. "I'll email Toni."

Her face breaks out into a smile. "Really?"

"I can't let you quit."

She seems satisfied with herself. "Call her now."

"She's gone for the day." I look quickly at the time and am relieved to see that Toni is probably gone. "I'll email her."

"I'll help you."

I scoot back from my desk. "Oh, will you?"

"Yup."

She comes around the corner of my desk and sits on my lap. She wiggles my mouse.

I notice that she pulls up my email and clicks on *new*. Her fingers fly across the keyboard.

I, on the other hand, bury my face in the crook of her neck. Scents of amber and oranges flirt with my senses. My hand goes to her thigh.

She gasps a quick breath as I cup her breast with the other.

I plant kisses behind her ear, feeling her body shake with a chill in response.

"How does this look?" She turns to check my reaction to her draft, but I capture her mouth with mine.

Her hands drape over my shoulders as she twists around to face me. I stand both of us up and sit her on the edge of my desk.

Eyes wide, lips parted, she looks up at me with a grin.

"You're sending that email," she says.

I slip my hand between her legs until I find the thin strip of her panties.

"Oliver," she moans as I run a finger under the fabric.

She's wet—*always so wet*. She leans back, propping her upper body up with her hands. I bend forward and kiss her, rubbing her clit in small circles with my thumb.

My phone buzzes. Shaye breaks the kiss.

"Yes, Kelly?" I ask, continuing my assault on Shaye's swollen bud.

"Hello, Mr. Mason. I have Greg on the phone for you."

Shaye moans again, arching her body to try to maximize contact with my hand.

"*Shh.*" I hold a finger up to my mouth. "Put him through, Kelly. Thank you."

"Of course. Hold just a moment."

The line clicks as Kelly connects Greg to my office.

"Hi, Greg," I say, watching Shaye's eyes flutter. "What's going on?"

"A few things, but I'm mostly concerned with the Greyshell project today. I got a call ..."

He rattles on about an issue that I'm already aware of. I let him talk.

I insert a finger into Shaye's body. She whispers a moan. I shake my head back and forth but don't ease up.

"We're issuing an addendum to their contract," I tell Greg. "Legal is working on it today and the purchasing department was instructed to order the correct material."

"Good." Greg sighs. "That should save me a fight come Monday."

Shaye holds one of her breasts through her shirt as she bites down on her bottom lip. Her legs spread farther apart as she reaches for my hand and slides it to her clit again.

"Greg, can I call you back in ten?" I ask, already unbuckling my belt.

"Sure, boss."

"Awesome." I punch the speakerphone button on the phone and then engage the Do Not Disturb function. "Your little moans nearly got us busted."

"You were the one doing it."

I take her hand and help her off the desk. Then I spin her around.

"Bend over," I say, my cock ready to explode, not helped by the taste of her on my finger as I suck it into my mouth.

She hikes her dress up to her waist and leans her torso flat against my desk—facedown.

Damn.

I drop my pants, roll on a condom, and line my cock up to her opening. I'm fully inside her in one smooth motion.

She moans again, louder this time, and I remind her to be quiet.

"This one is going to be quick," I say as I bury myself deep.

"Good. Make me come, Oliver."

Those words are enough to put me over the edge. It's embarrassing how fast this woman can make me lose control, but I can't stop it.

I palm both ass cheeks, giving one a quick slap before massaging it with my hand. Her back arches, the globes of her behind up in the air, as her juices coat my length.

"There you go," she whispers, her body bouncing against mine. "There you go. *Shit.*"

We climax together—her muscles constricting against me and my body flexing against hers. A shot of bright white light flashes across my vision as I pulse so hard that I think I might pass out.

Finally, after what feels like both an hour and only thirty seconds, I slip out of her. She falls against my desk before standing.

I chuckle. "We're going to have to figure out how to control this."

"Be less attractive." She kisses my cheek.

"I'll try."

She straightens her dress and glances at the clock. "I need to get to the bathroom and then run by home before I go to work."

Irritation sweeps over me like a hurricane over warm waters.

She ignores it.

"Want me to call you when I get off work?" she asks, heading toward her office.

I dispose of the condom and then find a wet wipe in my desk buried under the panties. I give myself a quick cleanup.

"Yes," I say, trying not to focus on her being at a bar all evening.

"Good. Talk to you then."

"Talk to you then. Love you."

My head jerks up at the same time she whirls around. Her eyes are wide—maybe wider than mine.

I drop the wet wipe in the trash and slowly refasten my pants.

Love you? What the fuck?

I don't know what to say because I didn't mean to say that. Do I mean it? Do I tell her it was a joke? Do I admit it was a mistake?

My brain flips into overdrive in its attempt to fix this monster of a fuckup.

"You're funny," she says, flashing me a nervous smile. "I'll talk to you tonight."

She flees from the scene of my crime.

But is it a crime?

I'm not sure what makes me feel worse—that I put her on the spot? *Or that she didn't say it back?*

Chapter Twenty-Eight

Shaye

"He said *I love you*."

I look at the picture of an old lady sitting at a table praying. I found the picture at a flea market the first year I moved out of my mom's house. There was nothing particularly captivating about the white-haired lady with a bowed head over a bowl of porridge, but it spoke to me. It gave me a sense of hope, of family.

It's failed me throughout my life, but I can't part with it.

Lisbeth gasps. "He did what?"

I shrug even though she can't see me.

"Wow, Shaye. How do you feel about that?"

"I have no idea." I take in each stroke of the woman's hair and the way the paint looks white but has gray and a yellow tone to it too. "I don't know how I feel about it."

"Well, *I* love it."

"I'm sure you do."

Lisbeth rattles on about how she knew it—that she called it. That she had a feeling in her stomach since the night I hit his car with mine that something big, something grand, would come of it.

I want to believe her. I do. *But he loves me?*

That word—love—is loaded. What is love, anyway? Sure, I love a frozen Snickers bar—that I'm positive. But loving a cold chocolate candy bar and loving another human are two decidedly different things.

I love Lisbeth. I love Nate. I have love in my heart for Joe and his toothless grin. But none of those things are what I think *I love you* means if you say it to someone you love *like that.*

Like I hope Oliver would say it to me.

Boone said he loved me. He doesn't love me. It was a friendly knee-jerk reflex.

Is that what it was for Oliver too?

"Did you say it back?" Lisbeth asks. "I'm not going to judge you either way. I'm just curious."

"No."

"Shaye!"

"You said you wouldn't judge me!" I pick up a stack of mail and sort through it as a distraction. "What a friend you are."

"I'm not judg—I'm totally judging you." She reconsiders. "No, I'm not. I'm disappointed that you aren't being honest with yourself."

"Oh, please." I toss the envelopes back on the table. The top one is a letter from the loan company regarding Luca's loan. I flip it over. *Screw them.* "I am being honest with myself. He probably just said it like you say it to me when you hang up the phone."

"That's not what I meant when I said that you weren't being honest with yourself."

I groan.

She's not going to let this go.

"You have feelings for Oliver," Lisbeth says.

"I do. I admit that. Happy now?"

"Then why are you being so awkward about his profession of love?"

"Because it's probably not real."

"Why? Because he said it to you? Would you think it was more realistic if he said it to me? To one of the girls at the gala? If he said it to the girl at work who answers the phones?"

My spirits sink.

The answer is that, yes, I probably would think it was more realistic.

I hate this about myself. I hate that my immediate thought is that it will go wrong or that it's not meant to be. I do it all the time.

"Someone sent me flowers, and I didn't tell him," I tell Lisbeth.

"Someone like who?"

"A guy from the gala."

"Shaye."

I groan again. "I know. I know that I should've told him, but I didn't. I didn't want to rock the boat."

"Because he obviously would've blamed you, right?" She scoffs. "He's not Luca, Shaye."

A load of guilt creeps on my shoulders. She's right. I do place Luca's sins on Oliver's shoulders. I let Oliver pay the price for the things Luca has done, and that's not fair—to either of us. Which is why I debated that at The Gold Room.

Today has thrown me, though.

I pace around the kitchen and feel the fog that sits in my head roll slowly away. If I acknowledge that some of my actions, some of my fears, are Luca-induced, it makes it easier to get to the truth about how I feel and what I want.

And what I deserve.

With every step that I take, my head becomes clearer.

I trust Oliver enough to hold me, to listen to my secrets. I respect him as a businessman and as a friend. I appreciate his honesty and openness with me, and even though some of his good intentions are misplaced—like my raise—he means well.

He always means well.

So who am I not to believe him when he says that he loves me? Why do I always feel like there's a game being played behind my back, and I'm the one who stands to lose?

I know the answers to both questions, and none of them are his fault. And I'd be a total jerk—to both of us—if I don't see that and act appropriately.

"Thank you, Lis."

"Oh, you're welcome. It's not like I had anything better to do than to listen to my best friend complain about her rich boyfriend problems." She laughs. "Oh, wait. I do. I could pull up any celebrity magazine and watch my ex-boyfriend stick his tongue down his famous girlfriend's throat."

"Ew."

"*Yeah.*"

"Want me to come over and bring pizza? 'Cause I will. I'll come tell you how amazing you are and how that boy—*boy*—doesn't deserve a woman like you."

She laughs. "No. I want you to go find Oliver and tell him how you feel. You deserve that as much as he does, Shaye."

"Yeah."

"Yeah. I'm just going to be here drinking mojitos, so call me if you need me."

I grin. "Drink one for me."

"I'll drink two for you because that's the kind of friend I am."

I laugh. "I need to be at the bar in twenty minutes, so I gotta go. Stay off the interwebs tonight."

"I'll do my best. *Love you.*"

She chirps the last two words. I roll my eyes.

"Love you, too, sweetie," I say, my voice dripping with sugar.

She laughs at me. "Good night, my friend."

"Night, Lis."

I end the call and turn toward the hallway. I stop when I catch my reflection in a mirror.

My cheeks are rosy, my skin golden. I look healthy. Happy.

I think about all the words of encouragement that I've received from Oliver and am actually wowed. He may have said his *I love you* off the cuff, but I'm beginning to see that he's a man who I utterly feel safe with. The happiness in my eyes is something that I haven't seen for years. I'm standing on my own two feet now, independent of my mom and my ex.

So, I can see this for what it is. *I. Love. Oliver. Mason.*

"You're going to call Oliver after work and tell him the truth. About the flowers and that you love him," I say out loud.

I wait for the words to make me panic, but they don't. They feel right.

But that makes sense because Oliver—and the love that I have for him—feels oh-so right.

Chapter Twenty-Nine

Oliver

Knock! Knock!

I look up from the packet in my hands. The binder clip holding the pages of the financial agreement together clamors against the top of my desk.

I sit back in my seat and take in the one person I didn't expect to see in my office after hours.

Rodney Mason steps into the office that used to bear his name. He hasn't stepped foot in here since the day he retired. In the early days of Holt and me taking over, we'd have meetings with Dad on occasion. Dad met us in the conference room on the first floor.

He looks around the space, his face blank as he takes in what I've done with the place. The bright white walls are now a subdued cream. His desk has been replaced with a darker wood and rounded edges. The sofa is new too. By the look on his face as he observes it, I'm not sure he's a fan.

"Didn't expect to see you here," I say with a sigh.

"I was in the neighborhood."

His features are tight, stressed. *As they should be.* His determination to have this conversation here—where, despite the office being closed, could still be overheard by someone—and not in the privacy of one of our homes is surprising.

But what-the-fuck-ever. Let's get it over with.

He motions toward the chair that faces me. I nod with approval.

He sits gingerly, tugging on the knees of his pants as he unfolds himself in the chair. A grimace sits squarely on his face, and I wonder if he's been having back problems again.

My old man looks tired. There are creases on his forehead that I don't recall seeing before. His skin looks weathered and ashen. His appearance dampens the fire that's been burning inside me since his failure to show up for Rosie's party.

"What's going on?" I ask, figuring the question is as good of an icebreaker as anything. It gives him the floor to tell me why he's here.

He blows out a breath. "How have you been?"

I sit upright. The sudden movements make Dad flinch.

"The last time we spoke," I say, looking him in the eye, "you told me that your family was a giant inconvenience in your life. So let's set aside the pleasantries and get to the reason you're here."

The corner of his mouth lifts.

"That makes you smile?" I shake my head. "I don't understand you, Pops."

He scoots in his chair until his back is resting against the leather. He crosses an ankle over the other knee and looks ... *proud? Relieved? At peace?*

"Coy came to see me," Dad says.

He didn't tell me. "And Holt? Boone? Wade?" I ask.

"I've spoken to all of them briefly."

"I'm sure a brief conversation really answered their questions." I lift a brow. "We're all wondering the same thing."

He stills. "I know. I wanted to talk to you first."

"I called you the other night. The only things you had to say were either rude, cruel, or inciting."

He chuckles. He has the audacity to chuckle.

"If you find this funny, you can see your way out," I say, my jaw tensing. "I've had a shitty afternoon, and I don't really have the patience to deal with you too."

My gaze flips to Shaye's closed door.

It's been a struggle for the last few hours not to pick up the phone or jump in my car and find her. I don't because … I don't know what to say.

Do I recant my admission? Do I save face since she didn't say it back? Do I remove the guilt she might feel for not repeating it back to me?

Maybe she doesn't feel guilty at all. *Why should she if she doesn't love me?*

If only I hadn't said it at all …

But as the hours pass and I have some space between the most honest moment of my life—saying *I love you* to the woman who I'm absolutely sure I love—my instincts tell me *not* to do that.

I do love Shaye. I know I love her because I've never felt this way before. Out of all of my relationships, there's not one person who elevates every level of my life. *Of me.*

My life has changed in the past few weeks. I smile more. I laugh at more than Boone's stupidity. I'm happy to set work aside in the evenings to spend time with her.

The idea of not seeing her, not having her around, fills my soul with a dark, heavy cloud. Every plan I make—from tonight's dinner to next month's work trip to Portland—they all include her. It was one of the reasons that I had her car fixed. I was concerned for her safety, and I couldn't shake it. It mattered. *It mattered because she matters.* My thoughts fall to her constantly. I wanted to show her how much more I care than anyone she's ever known.

My life before made me happy. Contracts, projects, family dinners here and there. But my life now? It's on a different playing field. I still want to accomplish all of the goals I've dreamed of, but I also want to make her life better.

It's so natural. It's the way it's supposed to be. She gives me an opportunity to do even more with my life—with her.

Dad shifts in his seat. I snap out of my thoughts and focus on him again.

"I want to talk to you about something, Ollie."

There's no chuckle, no smile this time. There's nothing but a bead of sweat dotting his forehead.

"Dad?"

My stomach knots. My heart beats hard in my throat. All of my senses are tuned into my father as he sits quietly across from me.

He looks bad. His voice is raspy. His cologne is off, more pungent, and not the usual scent I associate him with.

Suddenly, I'm aware that something *is* wrong. Something more than Dad being a dick or rude or failing to show up to support his kids.

Something is wrong.

"I need help." His lips part, and his breathing gets shallow. "I don't know who else to turn to."

"What kind of help?"

My mind races a million different directions.

He likes to gamble. Has he gotten into financial trouble? Does he owe someone money? Is he sick? He looks ill. Is he going to prison? *Oh, shit.*

What did you do, Dad?

He sets both feet on the floor, only to cross them again. He pushes himself to sit taller in the chair.

"Dad?"

"I don't know how this happened."

"What? You don't know how *what* happened?" A rush of adrenaline kicks in. "Tell me."

He lowers his head. I think he's going to cry.

The man in front of me isn't the strapping CEO that I've always known. Overnight, it seems, he's turned into a frail, scared man.

The scene is hard for me to digest. It's as if the role of parent has been thrust upon my shoulders. It sits awkwardly between us—the shift in our relationship—but he's aware of it just as much as I am.

"It started with alcohol ..." His shoulders slump. "Around the time of my retirement."

Oh, fuck.

"I wasn't ready to quit. Or maybe I was and hadn't made peace with it. Hell if I know now." His voice is broken. *Weak.* It ripples with anxiety and mortification at his confession. "But it was a drink at night, then two, then six or eight with the guys at poker. Then Jim and Jack and then I was telling your mom I was going golfing just to go to distilleries."

"*Dad.*"

He shakes his head, still unable to look me in the eye. "It's not just alcohol now."

I want to ask him what all he's into, what pills or substances he's abusing. That's obviously what he means. But I'm not sure if it will help ... or if it matters.

"I've hid it from your mother," he says. "I don't have the heart to tell her."

He raises his head for the first time and looks me in the eye. Tears stream down his cheeks.

"I've tried to push her away," he says, his voice cracking. "In the few moments in the day when I'm not high or out of it, I know what I'm doing to her. I know the things I've said—you don't forget. And the way she looks at me now ... *I can't, Ollie. I can't do it.*"

Dammit.

I get to my feet and walk around my desk. My heart fractures as I pull the man who pulled me out of a plethora of situations in my life into a deep hug.

He grips me tight, his body shaking as I hold on to him.

"We can fix this," I tell him. "We can get you help."

"You were right the other day. I'm going to hell."

I look at the ceiling and grimace. "I was just pissed."

He pulls away from me and wipes his face with the back of his hand. I find a box of tissues on the bar and hand it to him.

Instead of sitting across from him, I sit next to him. It feels like it makes more sense. Like maybe it will help. I don't fucking know.

No, that's not right. I have countless memories of my parents sitting beside me during my hardest moments. Like when my best friend in college fucked me over. My dad's comment stayed with me for years. *Your friends might disappoint you, Ollie. They might even walk away. But your family will always be beside you—no matter what.*

Maybe Dad's forgotten that lately.

"I'm here, Dad. You're not alone."

He looks up at me, shocked.

"Family will always stand beside you—no matter what," I say.

He wipes a tear away and nods. *He remembers.* "I should've been there for Boone lately," he says, wiping his nose. "Thank God he had you."

"He's had all of us, Dad. Not just me." I sit back in my seat and try to wrap my head around this reality. "And that is because of you."

His eyes snap to mine as if he needs to hear this. It's like it's his only life preserver at the moment. So I throw it to him.

"Why do you think we're all so close?" I ask him. "Why do you think that we rally around each other? Why do you think we've all been so angry that you haven't been there for Boone? For us?"

He holds his breath.

"Because *you* taught us that."

Tears swell in his eyes again.

"It's what a family does," I say. "We pick up the pieces for each other. You're lucky that you have five sons. That's a lot of hands to clean up messes."

He grins sadly. "And my five sons are lucky to have their mother."

We exchange a look that requires no words. A fool could read the room.

"She loves you, you know," I say softly.

"That just makes it worse. I don't deserve her."

My initial reaction is that he's right. He doesn't. He's hurt my mother, and I'll go to my grave knowing that she didn't deserve it. But there's a wiggle of uncertainty that snakes its way through my heart.

Maybe he does.

My father has been an excellent father until recently. He provided, cared, and pushed his sons to achieve things that people only dream of. He loved us too. That was never a question.

He was at our games. Watched practices. Threw the ball with us after games and helped us with our math homework on the weekends. He learned about architecture when Wade became fascinated in middle school and took guitar lessons alongside Coy.

Does the last year or two erase years' worth of love? Isn't he a human too?

I look at the man who raised me and watch him gather himself. He's struggling right now, just like I've struggled before. *Why do I expect more from him just because he's my father?*

Do I think I'll have it all figured out at his age?

When I look into the future, my life is clear. It's me and Shaye, a couple of kids bebopping around the house, and maybe a puppy. The vision sends chills up my spine. That's exactly what I want. What I *have to have*. Nothing else will suffice.

But as I watch Pops, I bet that he, too, had his life pictured. And this wasn't it. He went wrong somewhere, and he deserves the love and support that he's given us.

"I can't speak for Mom," I tell him. "But I'm sure that she'll listen to you. And I'm sure she would want to help."

He frowns. "She used to look at me like I hung the moon, Ollie. How do I let her see me like this?"

"It might be better than her just thinking you don't love her anymore."

He shrugs as if it doesn't matter. "I've not been there for her. I've said things to her that I shouldn't. Hell, I've probably said things that I don't even remember."

"Well, that's for the two of you to handle. And, again, I don't speak for my mother, but she's stuck around for a reason."

"Why, do you think?"

"I honestly don't know. But there's hope for you."

He blinks back tears again. "She's leaving me. She told me. And when her mind is made up ... I can't blame her." He grips the armrests. "You've treated me better than I deserve. What about your brothers? What do you think they will say?"

I get to my feet and walk to the refrigerator under the bar. I pull out two waters and give one to my dad.

"Holt will understand. He's levelheaded that way. Coy's seen a lot of shit like this. He'd be happy to help you. He wants you around to see his son."

Dad smiles.

"Boone will be fine. The kid is softhearted. It's probably to his benefit and detriment."

Dad chuckles. "That boy is something."

"*Something* is right."

I take a drink and look at my father over the bottle. There's a bit of hope sprinkled in his watery irises, and I'm happy to see it. I'm happy I could help put it there.

I don't know what this means for our family, but I know we'll make it through this. It is what families do.

Dad sets his bottle on my desk unopened. He stands.

"I came to see you first because I know you're the strongest out of my boys," he says, his voice somber. "You have always had such a good head on your shoulders. You step up. You don't back down from a challenge."

My mouth goes dry. "Really?"

"I know that if your mother does leave me that she'll be fine because she has you to look after her."

I've never been much of a crier but hearing my father share this with me nearly makes tears gather in my eyes. My heart fills with pride.

"I hope that if you ever find a woman who you love, someone like your mother, I'd hope—I hope that you snatch her up. That kind of woman—strong, honest, loyal—is hard to find. Mark my words."

His words are marked and trigger an immediate thought of Shaye.

I love you.

Her eyes were full of disbelief ... and uncertainty. Obviously, she was unsure. Look at the examples of love she's had in her life.

Shaye is everything my father said. She's strong and truthful. She's beautiful and full of grace. She's a hard worker and loyal—*she won't leave Nate because she promised she'd stick around.*

Shaye is the love of my life. Even though she might not realize it yet, she loves me. And if she doesn't, I'll love her until she does.

"You're going to be a great husband and father someday."

I grin. "Yeah. I will." I walk around my desk and flick my mouse. "But right now, I need to be a good son to my father. He might've tried to fuck up his life, but I'm not going to let him."

I feel my dad's gaze on my face as I search for substance abuse centers. I sense the tears falling down his cheeks.

"Thank you, Ollie."

My hand stills on the keyboard, and I look at him. We still have things to say, fences to mend, but none of that can happen until we jump this hurdle.

And we're family. We'll do it together.

"I love you, Pops."

"I love you, son."

My fingers fly over the keyboard, but my attention slips to Shaye.

We are family too, my lady. Just you wait and see.

Chapter Thirty

Shaye

"You look happy." Nate rolls his eyes as he walks by.

"Why do you say it like it's a bad thing?" I scoop ice into glasses. "I like being happy."

"I like it when you're happy too. Except, when someone is happy, that means they're setting themselves up for being unhappy because the only way to go is down."

I gasp. "You're such a downer."

"More realist, but whatever you think."

He sits across the bar from the drink station and watches me make an order.

I'm thankful we aren't too busy tonight. A nearby festival has stolen many of our customers with their live music and fried foods on sticks.

Can't say I blame them. Fried foods? Yum.

The clock has moved slower than ever since I got here. I swear I look at it every ten minutes. I've almost picked up my phone and texted Oliver a dozen times, but I really want to talk to him in person.

Things were left awkwardly between us. I'm not sure how he feels about that. I didn't return his sentiments for good reason. But now that I know I want to, I want it to be special.

"You look happy," Paige says, slipping by me.

I laugh. "You and Nate. Why do you both say *'You look happy'* like it's a death sentence?"

"You've caught me at a weird moment in my life," she says, tying her waist apron. "But that's a story for another day."

"Great." I make a face at her, undeterred from my quest toward being happy. Forever.

My hand stills over a glass of Coke as I replay my last thought.

Forever.

The thought of forever scares the shit out of me.

I wasn't sold on the concept when I married Luca, but he was a good salesperson. Even if I didn't go all-in on the idea of being with him for eternity, I took out a lease. I hoped I'd emotionally upgrade at some point. After all, it was the best thing that had happened to me.

And maybe it would've been that way for the rest of my life if Luca hadn't changed.

But he did. So there's that.

I place the glasses on a tray.

"Do you know about this mystery boyfriend of hers?" Paige asks Nate.

Nate scowls. "I've heard. Not sure I like him."

"Well, he's not sure he likes you either," I say, laughing.

"Really?" Nate furrows his brow. "What's not to like?"

"Oh, the fact that she works here with you and that you're great friends—if I were a guessing girl," Paige says.

I wrinkle my nose at Nate. "Accurate."

"Well, fuck him. If he has something to say about it, he can say it to my face."

Paige's eyes go wide as she looks toward the dining room. "He might just be here to do that."

"What?" I spin around.

My jaw tumbles to the floor.

I scramble to compose myself—to quiet the thundering of my heart in my ears. But there's no way to play this off.

He's here to see me.

Marius's eyes lock with mine. A slow smile graces his lips.

"Holy shit, Shaye. He's gorgeous," Paige whispers, jabbing me with her elbow.

I unwind my gaze with his and turn to Nate. He's watching me with a careful, knowing eye.

"Need help?" Nate asks, his voice calculated.

"That's ... that's not Oliver."

"My question remains."

I don't know whether to laugh or cry, to run or attempt to defuse the situation that feels more and more like a ticking bomb.

Why is he here? Is he freaking serious?

Nate starts to get up.

"I got this," I say, motioning for him to sit.

"Who is he?" Nate asks.

"Marius ... something or other. I met him at the gala."

"Oh." Nate glances at Marius over his shoulder. "Nope. Don't like him."

"You don't even know him."

Paige giggles. "I like him. I mean, I don't know what y'all are looking at, but if you don't want him, I'll take him."

Nate glares at her.

She winces. "I'll just go check on my tables."

I give her an apologetic smile and turn back to Nate. "I'm going to go talk to him. He sent me thirty roses."

His eyes shoot to the ceiling.

"I know." I groan. "I gave them to Paige."

"How'd Mason take that?"

I hem-haw around the question. Nate doesn't miss a beat.

"You didn't tell him?" He pauses, giving me a chance to answer. "Shaye."

"No, I didn't tell him. I was going to tell him tonight. I am going to tell him tonight. Right after I apparently tell him Marius came to see me." I groan again. "I'm going to tell him to leave me alone. Get my point across."

Nate grins. "I can get that point across."

I smack his arm. "No. You aren't hitting him."

"I didn't say that."

Ignoring him, I walk around the corner. "Murray! Can you take these drinks to table sixteen?"

"Sure thing," he yells back.

I wipe my hands on a towel and then toss it at Nate. He ducks the throw easily, snapping it out of the air and placing it in front of him.

My anxiety creeps up my spine as I get closer to Marius. I have no idea what I could've done, or said, to lead him into believing that I wanted flowers or a date. Regardless, he needs to stop this.

"There you are," he says, his voice smooth. "How are you, Shaye?"

I smile as politely as I can through my nerves. "I'm good."

"Did you get my flowers?"

We step to the side to allow a couple to walk around us.

"I did," I say. "They were beautiful and unexpected."

"I realized that I didn't leave my contact information on the card."

This is true. Use it.

"Right. Um, I tried to figure out how to get in touch with you." I shove a strand of hair behind my ear. "Marius, the flowers were beautiful, as I said, but I'm not sure why you sent them."

"Beautiful flowers for a beautiful woman."

Nate's gaze is heavy on my back as I try not to fidget.

"I ..." I take a deep breath. "I'm in a relationship with Oliver Mason, Marius. And it's not appropriate for you to send me flowers or for me to see you like this."

He looks puzzled. "Is that so?"

"Yes."

"Interesting. Are you sure about that?"

It only takes a second to look in his eyes and know he's screwing with me. Why? Who knows? I don't even care.

"It's really none of your concern either way," I tell him. "Thank you for the flowers and for coming all the way down here to see me. But I would really appreciate it if you would refrain from doing either thing again."

I hold my breath and wait for his reaction. The coolness in his eyes scares me, but a smile spreads on his lips. It's a strange contradiction that I don't care to work out.

He grins. "I'm disappointed, but I respect your choice." He slips a hand inside his jacket and pulls out a business card. He hands it to me. "In case you change your mind."

I don't know what to do so I take the card.

"For the record," he says, leaning in close, "Oliver would be a fool not to see that you're smitten with him." He presses a kiss to my cheek.

"Marius," I say, flushing, "I don't ..."

My voice drifts off as something pulls at my attention from the side. I look up and nearly drop the business card.

Oh. My. Gosh.

Ohmygosh!

Oliver is standing next to the door. His hands are curled into fists at his side. His hair is a mess, his eyes tired yet full of fury.

"Oliver!" I call out and step toward him.

He doesn't move. Twitch. He doesn't even smile.

His eyes stay on me, following me through the dining room despite Marius standing a few feet back. The closer I get, the depths of the emotions in his eyes become apparent.

It was easier just seeing the fury. It shatters my heart to see the sadness. The disappointment.

"What are you doing here?" I ask, my voice sounding like I just ran a marathon.

Every cell in my body vibrates. The hair on the back of my neck stands. A franticness sweeps through me, and I reach for him, only to have him pull back.

He clears his throat. "I came to see you ..." He looks over my shoulder and then back at me. "But it looks like you're busy."

"It's not what you think."

"What do I think, Shaye?"

He says my name like anyone else. Shaye. The warmth, the honey, the kiss that he usually puts on that one syllable is gone.

"I don't know what you think, but—"

"Oliver, how are you?" Marius comes to my side.

The tension between the two of them is palpable. I can almost see the air scattering for safety.

"I just came to say hello to Shaye," Marius says. "I hadn't heard from her and I wanted to make sure she got the roses that I sent."

Oliver's jaw clenches. "Roses, huh?"

Tears lick at my eyes. My vision is blurry through the red-hot water rising quicker than I can blink it away.

"Thirty of them. Kind of hard to miss." Marius laughs. "But she got them. No worries."

"Marius, stop," I beg, my body trembling.

"Stop what?"

"Shaye, don't," Oliver warns, his voice ice cold.

"I didn't want your flowers. I didn't even keep them." I look at Oliver, imploring him to listen to me. "I gave them to Paige. She's over there. You can ask her."

"Perhaps not." Oliver's jaw flexes. "It's clear that I didn't read the room correctly at the gala. Again. My focus and attention didn't satisfy you either. That won't happen again."

Marius steps to the side. "I think I'll be on my way."

Oliver steps in his path. "If I see you anywhere near her again ..."

"What?" Marius asks, glowering down at Oliver. "She didn't even tell you I sent her flowers. You think she tells you everything?"

Oliver's face angers even more. His fist starts to rise.

I shrink back. Please don't hit me.

Another step back.

Please, I didn't do anything. Just don't hit me.

Before I've taken a breath, out of nowhere, Nate is in my space. "It's okay. I got you, Shaye."

He puts his hand on Oliver's arm, holding it down. Oliver's head whips to see Nate begging him to say something.

"You two can piss all over each other," Nate says. "You can either do it outside so I don't have to clean up the blood. Or you can do it in here so I can knock you both the fuck out, which, in reality, is probably what you both need and deserve."

"Is that a threat?" Marius asks.

"No, buddy. That's a fucking promise." Nate's body shakes with anger. "Now hit the road while you have two legs to carry you out."

Marius smirks and disappears out the door.

"What the fuck was that?" Oliver asks as soon as Marius is gone, readjusting his attention to me. "*He* knew where you worked? And that you'd be here tonight. Well played, Shaye. You got the bigger fish."

"Easy on your tone, bud." Nate fills the spot at my side that Marius vacated. "You don't know what you're talking about."

"What do you fucking know about jack shit?" Oliver springs to life, the shock from the moment dissipating. "Let me guess—you're Nate."

He says his name like it's poison.

"I am. Nate Hughes. I'd say it's nice to meet you, but I'll wait and see if that pans out to be true."

Oliver shakes his head and looks at me. "I don't know what to say to you."

A tear slips through my lashes and flows down my cheek. "This isn't my fault."

"The hell it isn't. What else do I not know? What else are you keeping from me?"

"Nothing." My voice breaks. "I'm not keeping anything from you. I should've told you about the flowers, but I didn't want you to be mad."

"I'd only be mad if there was a reason to be."

"Oh, like now? You're mad now, and there's no reason to be."

"No reason to be? I walk in here after telling you that I love you today—something that you didn't say back, may I add—and you're chatting it up with Marius Blast after he sent you thirty fucking roses? I say I have a reason to be pissed the fuck off." He forces a swallow down his throat. "Nate, can we have a minute alone?"

Nate stands in front of me, blocking Oliver. "You okay with that?"

I nod.

He pats my shoulder. "Holler if you need me."

Oliver's gaze lands on the spot Nate touched me. It takes him a long couple of seconds to speak once we're alone.

"All I've asked of you is to be honest with me, Shaye."

It's true. That is all he's really asked of me.

But I've told him as best as I can what I need too. I've told him about Luca and how he controlled me. How he jumped to conclusions. How things got so terribly bad that I was scared for my life sometimes. And, right now, perhaps adrenaline is the only thing keeping me upright. The fear he'd hit me had been momentarily blinding. *Momentarily*. Because Oliver uses words to fight. Not fists.

"I have been honest with you," I say through my unshed tears.

"If you think withholding information like this—if meeting men behind my back at your second job is somehow being honest with me, then I don't think you understand honesty."

I do understand honesty. And I understand fear, something Oliver Mason would know nothing about because he doesn't answer to anyone.

Tears flow uninterrupted down my face as I realize the crux of the situation. It wasn't about the flowers, nor was it about him being angry.

The flowers were a trigger—a situation that brought back too many memories that I don't want to remember. A life of living on pins and needles, of being blamed and shamed. A relationship that required me to overthink every damn situation I was faced with in a day and decide if it was worth fighting over. Because those fights? They didn't end with a kiss and makeup sex.

Maybe I can explain that ...

"I—"

"You know what?" Oliver says, shoving his hands in his pockets. "I don't think this is going to work out."

"What?"

I'm too frozen to allow any of the tears left in my eyes to fall onto my cheeks.

"What did you say?" I ask him. "Oliver, no."

He looks at the ceiling. "I don't have it in me to trust someone enough to have this kind of a ... to do this. You know?"

"Are you kidding me?"

"It's not you, Shaye. It's me."

"Don't use that cliché line on me."

He almost smiles through the sadness that has swamped his beautiful eyes. "Well, it's true. There's a reason I don't have relationships and I'm reminded today of why."

"Because some asshole creeped on me at work?"

"No, because I refuse to expend this amount of energy on someone who doesn't value the same things as I do." He sighs. "I have a lot of things happening right now that need my attention. Maybe we can just take some time apart and … see what happens."

His features are smooth, just like they are when he's in a meeting and doesn't want to tip his hand. He's calm, cool, and collected … only I see the truth. I see the pain and the sadness. And I want to hug him.

"If it gets weird in the office, I can have you transferred to Wade's."

Transferred to Wade's. Every other time I've mentioned that, it's been met with a laugh.

"Do you really fucking think that it would be easier for me to get anything done knowing you were in another office that I could just barge into?"

Oliver has drawn the line. He's closed the door. He's placed me on the other side, no longer within reach.

And that's when I know—*it's over.*

This is no taking time apart and seeing what happens. This is Oliver telling me he's done.

But maybe it's just as well. If it ends now, it can't get worse. It's probably better just to snip it off and not let it get to the point where he controls my life.

I should be grateful for silver linings.

I wipe my face with a napkin that I swipe off a table beside us. "Just so you know, I lied to you today too."

He furrows his brow.

"If omitting things is a lie and we're coming clean, then just know that today, when you told me you loved me? I hadn't realized it at that moment, but I did later. I love you too. *Loved you too.*"

I don't see his reaction. I turn and run to the kitchen.

I'm not sure what happens after that, but I know Nate darted toward the door.

Paige holds me while I cry against the freezer. Murray takes care of the dining room. I sit on the storeroom floor and tell myself that it'll be all right.

Because it will.

I've survived a lot of shit before. I'll survive this.

CHAPTER THIRTY-ONE

Oliver

"Hey," I say, closing the door behind me.

My brothers sit somber-faced around a square coffee table. The lights are low. It creates a chill, mellow ambiance that is probably good for writing music. Which is exactly what Coy uses the space for.

I've only seen the inside of Coy's studio once before, and that was in the building stage. It looks markedly different now, but I'm too fucked up to really appreciate Wade's design.

I sit in a leather chair next to Wade.

My head hurts. My heart hurts doubly bad. I think something broke inside me this evening, but I can't put my finger on what. People say that breakups break their heart, but this feels infinitely worse than that. It's like it broke my soul. *Like it broke me.*

I don't know what I expected to happen. I'm not sure why I allowed myself to get this far into Shaye. It's like I was falling off a ledge and I knew what hitting the bottom was like, but I chose to fall anyway.

The ground is harder and sharper than I ever imagined.

"Mom called," Holt says. "She's dropping Dad off at the treatment center now."

I nod. "That's good."

"What the fuck happened, anyway?" Coy asks.

I take a deep breath. The burden of having to unload my conversation with our father onto my brothers is miserable. In a perfect world, we could all have joined together and had a family chat about it. Hearing this from his mouth would've been the best-case scenario. It just wasn't meant to be.

"He came to see me," I tell them. "I feel like he was probably at his breaking point, and I was probably the closest to wherever he was at that moment."

I don't think that's necessarily true, but I don't want to tell them he specifically sought me out. There's enough pain to navigate without adding more potentially hurt feelings to the mix.

"He, uh, he basically said he had a problem and that he needed help," I say, simplifying the situation. "He was worried he'd really screwed up with you guys and Mom ... and me, for that matter. But he expressed an interest in fixing things so what was I supposed to do?"

"You called Mom?" Boone asks.

I nod. "They're still married. And I knew she'd want to help him."

Wade clears his throat. "How'd she take it?"

"Like Mom takes everything—with grace." I shrug. "I called her and told her what was going on. She told me to bring him home. I guess he hadn't been home in a couple of days."

Coy's face falls. He begins to tap out a rhythm on the coffee table. "*Man.*"

"I drove Dad over, and Mom told me she'd take care of it," I say. "I offered to stay, but I think they had some things to say to each other."

My head falls forward as I replay the scene in my head. The way my parents stood on the porch and looked at each other for a long two minutes. And then Mom opened her arms, and Dad fell into them, and Mom waved me off.

It's a moment I'll never forget. And a day I wish I could.

The drive from Mom's to The Gold Room took entirely too long. I just wanted to see Shaye, to tell her how much I loved her. To tell her that I would be there, that I believed in us.

Where would we be if I were ten minutes earlier?

I rub my jaw. *I'd be in a relationship with a liar.*

The statement is technically true—she omitted a serious fucking piece of information. Omissions are lies. But even though I try desperately to make myself believe it, to sit on the truth and get comfortable in it, I can't.

It was too reminiscent of Kendra. When I walked into Picante for a business dinner and saw Kendra sitting with Charles Gamby's hand around her shoulders and his lips pressed against her cheek, my faith in relationships imploded.

Yet that was nothing compared to today.

Literally nothing.

I got to my car after seeing Shaye with Marius and vomited. It hurt so fucking much. It was a punch in the gut that I didn't see coming.

"You okay?" Wade leans over, his hand covering his mouth. He glances at me out of the corner of his eyes as if he thinks I'm *not* okay and he doesn't want to put me on the spot.

Who knew? Wade does have a heart.

"Yeah." I tap my shoe against the concrete floor.

"Ollie?" Boone says my name like a little kid would call to his older brother. "What's wrong?"

I look at the ceiling. The inevitable is here.

Coy stops working out whatever rhythm he was using as a coping mechanism. He licks his lips. "Is there something else you need to tell us?"

"I know that look." Holt stretches his legs out in front of him. "That look has nothing to do with Dad. Or Mom."

"Shaye," Boone whispers.

Four sets of eyes are on me—three-and-a-half. Wade isn't all-in. He pulls out his phone and pretends to be absorbed with something on the screen.

It's uncomfortable to have so many people in your business but, then again, it helps. It helps to know that I'm not alone. That I have people on my side.

"What happened?" Coy asks.

"I went by to see her at work."

"You work there too, so ..." Coy looks at me confused.

"She has a second job," I tell him.

He seems satisfied with this answer.

"Anyway, I go in there, and Marius Blast is there. *Kissing her fucking cheek.*"

Just saying the words out loud, hearing them float across Coy's studio, is enough to infuriate me again. I shift in my seat in hopes it'll make sitting and not punching something a little easier.

"Blast? How the hell does she know that motherfucker?" Holt asks.

"Landry Gala." I lift a brow as a look of understanding crosses Holt's face. "Apparently, he also sent her a bunch of flowers, and she didn't tell me. She says she sent them home with someone else."

"Ouch." Coy grimaces.

"What's Blast doing sending flowers to our girl—*your girl*?" Boone holds his hands up. "Sorry. *Your girl*. Misspoke."

"She's not my girl anymore."

That admission floats nowhere. Instead, it sinks between us.

My brothers sit quietly, something that's uncommon. They probably know that I need a few minutes to gather my thoughts before I just bleed out on the floor in front of them.

They've all been in my shoes to some degree. They all, except for Wade, have a woman they love. I'm sure they're imagining how I feel.

Like shit.

Used.

Like a fucking joke.

"I'm going out on a limb here and saying that this situation sliced through your trust issues, right?" Holt asks.

"Oh, a little."

"But ..." Boone points a finger at me and then reads my face and puts it back on his leg. "But what did she say? I know Shaye, and I'm sure she has an explanation."

"Yeah. What did she say?" Coy asks.

"I don't know." I rub my forehead, my headache intensifying. "I just

... she said the usual. She didn't want to upset me by telling me. That it didn't matter."

That she loved me.

My stomach recoils. I'm sure it would spew the contents if it hadn't already emptied them.

That sentence is what haunts me. *"If omitting things is a lie, and we're coming clean, then just know that today, when you told me you loved me? I hadn't realized at that moment, but I did later. I love you too. Loved you too."*

Did she love me? Does she love me? Does it make a difference?

"I wasn't there, but I see her point," Coy says.

I fire him a look.

"Think about it," he says. "So some fuckhead sent her flowers. So what? That says a lot more about Blast than it does Shaye."

"How do you figure?" Boone asks.

"Well, Blast isn't stupid. Anyone who's been around Oliver lately knows he's different. I'd imagine that if Oliver was with Shaye at the gala, then Blast knew Shaye was Ollie's girl." Coy looks at me. "Blast wasn't fucking with Shaye. He was fucking *with you.*"

"Why would he do that? I don't have shit to do with Blast."

"Because he's a male, primarily." Wade's voice is resigned. He doesn't want to have this conversation any more than I do. "Look, I'm only sharing my opinion in hopes it puts this situation to bed, and we can all get on with our lives."

"This has nothing to do with you," I tell him.

He sighs. "Oh, but it does. Because when one of us is fucked up, we all pay the price."

My brothers mumble their agreement.

"Blast is used to getting what he wants," Wade says. "I'm sure it was a shock to his system for Shaye to turn him down. *Because that's what she did.*" He watches me to see if what he's saying is sinking in. "If she didn't turn him down, she wouldn't have been with you every day since, now would she?"

He has a point.

"Look at this logically," Wade continues. "He wanted her at the gala. She said no. He sent her flowers. She ignored them. So, he shows up to make a face-to-face play for her. Why? Because he isn't getting anywhere."

"I love when Wade gets all smart," Boone says.

"I'm always smart." He raises a brow at Boone. "You do what you want, Oliver. But I think you're making a huge mistake."

The room grows quiet again.

Wade has a point. *He always has a point.* But I don't know if it's enough.

Whether she wants Marius or not, she didn't tell me. I have to trust her. Relationships are built on that foundation.

Our foundation is cracked, and we haven't started building yet. It seems to me that the temple we were hoping to construct was doomed from the start. Because as I sadly know all too well, if the foundations are not solid, dug deep enough, then the building won't ever weather the storm.

CHAPTER THIRTY-TWO

Shaye

I check my phone again.

Nothing.

No missed calls, no texts, no voicemails.

I sigh, heading to the kitchen because I don't know what else to do. The early afternoon television shows are awful. They aren't nearly as interesting as they were when I was a little girl and would stay with Grandma. Back then, the afternoons were filled with talk shows, pseudo-advice programs, and game shows with glittery wheels. Now, everything looks dull.

Or maybe that's just me.

I called Toni this morning and told her I was sick. She said she'd inform Oliver and to get well soon. That was hours ago and still—no feedback.

He has to know I'm not coming by now.

I sit at the table. An empty pop can from last night rattles next to a magazine. It was a late night—long and dark—and I don't look forward to the sun going down tonight.

My mom used to say that everything felt worse at night. She said that it's because you can't do anything about what's bothering you except worry. I believed her. It made sense. Throughout my life, that's held true.

Until now.

It doesn't matter if the sun is up or down, if I've eaten or not, if I've showered or gotten any sleep—it sucks. Period.

A part of me wants to hope that this can be fixed. Another part of me wants to accept that it can't. I have an inkling to accept reality just so I can start the task of wading through the pain that will come once I accept that this is over.

Because I don't think I've done that yet. I don't think I've really let myself fall into that abyss because it's going to be a long and lonely hole to claw my way out of.

"I need to call Nate and see about getting more hours until I get back on my feet," I mutter out loud. I close my eyes briefly. "Again."

I hate this. I hate being so beholden to situations. *If only Luca hadn't left me with that fucking debt.*

The mail I was going through yesterday is beneath the magazine. I pull them toward me while I figure out what to say to the temp agency when I call them later looking for a job.

"I fucked my boss, and now I'm unemployed," I say out aloud. "Yes, I have a problem with men, trust me, so if you could find me a female boss this time, that would be great."

I roll my eyes at myself.

The top envelope is from Luca's loan company. My stomach sours as I rip it open. The paper inside is perfectly folded and addressed to me.

Dear Mrs. Brewer,

We would like to certify your payment and confirm that your balance of $86,487.09 has been paid in full. Please retain this letter for your records. Should you need addi-

tional information, you may call us during normal business hours.

Sincerely,

Thomas Bjorn

I read it again. And then for a third time. By the fourth time that I read *Dear Mrs. Brewer*, my hands are shaking.

The paper falls to the table as I grab my phone. I have to hit Lisbeth's name twice for it to call her.

"Hi," she says. "How are you feeling today? Want me to come over?"

"Do you know what he did?"

"Um, I'm thinking the *he* you're referring to is Oliver, but if you could clarify—"

"Yes. Oliver." I stare at the letter so hard that I'm surprised it doesn't burst into flames. "Do you know what he did?"

"You already asked me that, and I do not."

My body trembles. Adrenaline pours through me, and I can't quite get a grip on my emotions.

"He paid Luca's loan off, Lis. He paid *eighty-six thousand dollars.*"

The number is staggering. And given that I'd only paid fourteen thousand off over the last three years, it makes me even angrier. There was still so far to go.

"*Oh, wow,*" she breathes.

A small laugh of disbelief escapes my throat as I stand at the head of the table and continue to stare at the letter.

When did he do this? Why?

My memory shuffles to yesterday—to before the Marius incident— and I recall getting the letter in the mail.

So he did this before he broke up with me.

Tears fill my eyes because this is another complication that I didn't want or need. This was hard enough before. I didn't ask for this. And I still owe the money ... just to a different place. A place where I would never have done it. I would never have mixed money with any relationship—*especially this one.*

"Why would he do this?" I ask, my voice breaking.

"Do you want me to come over?"

"No. I really don't. I just ... I don't know what to do, Lis."

Was this his way of making me beholden to him? Was this his way of keeping me under his thumb?

The similarities between my relationship with Luca and with Oliver begin to bleed together.

Both men held things over my head. Both men thought the worst of me. Both men broke my heart.

I close my eyes and feel anger erupting from my core. It's hot— molten—as it flows through my veins.

"Hang on," I say into the phone before pulling it away from my ear.

I pull up my personal email account.

To: omason@masonlimited.com
From: Shaye Brewer
Re: Loan

Dear Mr. Mason,

I just received a letter informing me that a loan in my name was paid in full. I only know of one person who would be able to satisfy that note.

Please be advised that I will be contacting an attorney to set up a repayment plan with you in the coming days.

Best,

Shaye

I hit *send.*

"What did you just do?" Lisbeth asks.

"I sent him an email and told him that I would be paying him back."

"And you did that why?"

"Because I'm not going to owe him a damn thing."

My email dings. I put Lisbeth on speakerphone.

To: Shaye Brewer
From: Oliver Mason, CEO
Re: Loan

Shaye,

Any repayments will not be accepted. Please save yourself the time. Also, I'm sorry I did not have time to explain this in person. That was not my intent.

Best,

Oliver

"Why? Why is he doing this?" I ask, my fingers already typing out a new message.

To: Toni Marquez
Cc: Oliver Mason
From: Shaye Brewer
Re: Two-Weeks' Notice

Dear Ms. Marquez,

Please accept this email as my formal resignation as executive assistant from Mason Limited, effective two weeks from today's date. I endeavor to make this process as painless as possible. However, I am ill and may not make it back into the office. Please let me know if you have any questions or if I can help out from home.

Best,

Shaye Brewer

I read it aloud to Lisbeth.

"Are you sure you want to do this?" she asks.

"Definitely."

"Then send it but I think you should sit on it for a while."

"Sitting on it is what got me in this situation."

Lisbeth laughs. "At least you still have your sense of humor, I guess."

I hit *send*.

Chapter Thirty-Three

Oliver

Well, I've made it two days.

Toni called this morning to ask if I'd like to look at resumes. I changed the subject.

Holt suggested we go look at job sites this afternoon. I deferred.

Boone volunteered to get me a ticket to Vegas. I laughed at him.

What the hell am I going to do in Vegas?

I think he was trying to make a point in his own way. It was as if he were saying, *"You want to be single? Go to Sin City"* because he knows the truth.

I want to be single about as bad as I want a hole in the head.

The sun sits just above the trees. It's the first time I've sat in the wicker chairs since Shaye was here. She was only in this room once, yet it feels odd without her in it now. The whole house is quieter. *It's definitely cleaner though.* Memories of her hair ties on random surfaces and her socks on the living room floor make me smile.

It's sad. I'm sad.

The doorbell rings. I get to my feet and make my way to the foyer.

It's not her. I'd know. I can always tell when she's close.

A quick check of the peephole confirms my suspicions. It's Mom.

"Hey," I say after opening the door. "What brings you by?"

She steps inside and leans in for me to kiss her. I do.

"Want me to fib or tell the truth?" She grins. "Boone told me to come over."

I snort, shaking my head, and lead her into the kitchen.

"He said he was worried about you," she says.

"He needs to worry about himself."

Mom puts her purse on a chair and leans against the island. Her eyes are filled with concern. "Maybe he does. But it's my job to worry about you so it's a good thing he alerted me to a worry need."

"A worry need? I think you have enough of those on your plate right now." I open the refrigerator. "Bottle of water?"

"No, honey. But thank you."

I take one out for myself and close the door.

My stomach growls. The last thing I remember eating was a handful of cashews for dinner last night. Despite the obvious need for fuel, the thought of eating anything is unbearable.

I miss her. God, I miss her.

"Sit, Oliver," Mom says, taking a seat at the table.

I situate myself across from her and take a drink.

"Your father called this morning. I don't know how because it's against the rules, but he did." She smiles. "It was good to hear his voice."

"How are you doing in all of this?"

"I'm okay. Really, I am. It's almost a relief, in a way ..." She plays with her necklace. "So many problems in life aren't fixable. War. Terminal illness. Losing a child. It's a relief that our marriage can be fixed if we choose to."

"Will you choose to?"

She gazes into the distance. "I'm not sure. We'll take it one day at a time. But I've invested decades of my life into this marriage and into this family and I'm not about to let something rob me of that without a fight." She looks at me again. "I love your father. He's a flawed individual, but aren't we all?"

Wow.

"I know I'm not perfect," she says. "And if I would have, or do, I suppose, fall down the wrong path at some point, I would've hoped your father would've rallied beside me. I'll show him the same grace I would want for myself."

I just look at her. How can she take this in stride? She was separating from the man days ago and now she's willing to fight?

"What changed, Mom?"

"What do you mean?"

"You were leaving him and now you're not."

She smiles. "I was leaving him because I had done everything in my power to love him and he didn't want my love. I'm not saying we're not separating now but he's sick. He wants to try to help himself. I know the man who he is, the man who he was. And I know he can be that man again if he chooses to. It might be hard," she admits. "But you give love a fighting chance."

I sit back in my seat, her words washing over me.

"You give love a fighting chance."

Did I give up on Shaye too easily?

As if someone grabs the corner of my mind and spins it in a circle, I suddenly consider Shaye and me in opposite roles. That she walked into my office and one of the women from the gala had come to see me unexpectedly. *What if one of them had kissed my cheek? What if one of them had sent me a gift?*

I would know that their gift, their kiss, meant nothing to me. I'd know that the only one whose presence meant anything was Shaye. *But she would not. She'd look at what she saw ... and have every right to jump to the wrong conclusion.*

The knot in my stomach tightens, especially when I remember the fear in Shaye's eyes. And then ... the resignation.

She's used to not having a voice. *Feeling walked over.* Which is precisely what I did.

Fuck.

"Are you okay?" Mom asks.

"I think I fucked up."

"Well, despite your abhorrent language, I'd like to know why you think that." She grimaces. "I also know everything that you told Boone, so you can skip all of that."

That little shit.

I stand and pace around the table. "It was like seeing Kendra and Charles, you know? I felt played. Humiliated. Like I couldn't trust her."

"That's all very fair."

"Right? Tell my brothers that. They're saying—that it's Blast's fault. Holt said without saying today that I'm overreacting. Boone thinks they're siblings now and has basically written me off." I huff. "Why don't they understand?"

"That's simple. It's not their heart that's bruised."

Mom stands, her chair scooting against the floor. She walks up beside me and lays her hand on my arm.

"Emotions are funny things, Oliver. They influence so much of what we think and do." She pats me and then removes her hand. "Remember what I told you about following your gut?"

I nod.

"What does your gut say?" she asks.

I know the answer. I know exactly what my gut says.

My gut says to go find her, grab ahold of her, and kiss her with everything I have. My gut tells me to fix things. That my brothers are right. That my fear is misplaced and that she's not given me a reason not to trust her.

The fear in her eyes at The Gold Room gnaws at my stomach. For a split second, she thought I was going to hit her. The thought makes me sick. What makes me even sicker is thinking that she could end up with another guy who could harm her and all because I wasn't man enough to fix things between us.

How can I risk that?

"You know," Mom says, heading back to the kitchen. "It would be a damn shame for you to miss out on the love of your life because Kendra was a cheating bitch."

"Mom! Language!" I can't help but laugh. "What's gotten into you?"

She picks up her purse and puts it on her shoulder. Then she looks at me.

"Giving someone your heart is always a risk. What if it breaks?" She gives me a final, lingering smile and heads for the door. "But what if it doesn't?"

Her heels tap against the floor before the door opens and shuts.

Damn.

Chapter Thirty-Four

Shaye

To: Toni Marquez
From: Shaye Brewer
Re: Absence

Dear Ms. Marquez,
I am still feeling under the weather and will not be in the office today.
Thank you for understanding.
Best,
Shaye Brewer

"Does that make you feel better?" Nate sips his coffee at my kitchen table. He lifts a brow. "I do appreciate that you're still being professional despite the circumstances."

I toss my phone at him. It spins in a circle on the tabletop.

My body aches from not sleeping. *Again.*

I had planned on going to the office today and just ignoring Oliver

—keeping the door open and spending a lot of time in the bathroom. But I just couldn't do it. I couldn't see him.

"I have an appointment with an attorney this afternoon," I say. "I'm going to get some kind of contract drawn up or something to put it in writing that I'm paying Oliver back."

Nate whistles through his teeth. "I still can't believe he paid off that damn loan."

"You and me both."

I wish I could talk to him about it. I will. Some day. That day is just not today.

I penned countless emails during the night. I just didn't know what to say. What do you say to someone who did something so outlandish for reasons unbeknownst to you? And then they break up with you over something so silly.

It's not silly. Not really. I can imagine what Oliver felt like when he saw me with Marius. But the fact that he wouldn't even hear me out or give me the benefit of the doubt seals the deal.

"Look, I'm not an Oliver fan," Nate says. "But let's just stay calm for a second, all right, and think this through."

"Let's not."

He chuckles. "Are you at least going to find out why he did it?"

"Does it really matter, Nate? *Really?* Because I don't think it does." I get up from the table. "If he did it because he loved me, which is the dream, right? He wouldn't have walked away from me in The Gold Room. He would have trusted me. He would've known that I wouldn't lie to him or betray him."

"Fair enough."

"So that leaves us with one other option, doesn't it?"

He furrows his brow. "Well, maybe more than one, but I'll let you lead."

"He was trying to control me."

Nate takes another sip of his coffee. "That sounds a little presumptuous."

"I don't think so. Think about it—if he's paid off the loan ... that's more money than most people make in a year. *In three or four years.*

Why? Why would he do that when he won't even have a conversation with me—he wouldn't listen to me? It makes no sense."

"Maybe he was doing you a favor."

"That's a pretty big favor, friend."

He can't argue that.

My phone buzzes and Nate slides it back to me. I open my email.

To: Shaye Brewer
From: Toni Marquez
Re: Absence

Dear Ms. Brewer,

Mr. Mason would like you to know that your email isn't accepting his messages. His calls are also not going through. Please call him immediately.

Best,

Toni

I swipe out of the email app. I don't tell Nate, but it does give me a small dose of satisfaction that he's been trying to reach me.

"You blocked him?" Nate shakes his head. "What are you? Fifteen?"

"No. I'm a woman who feels like she's been put in a position where she owes a man a large sum of money and now he expects her to answer his calls when he feels like it. I'm not doing that, Nate. I did it with Luca in a way and, yeah. No. Not again. Not ever again."

"I—"

Buzz!

The doorbell cuts through Nate's reply. I don't know if I'm thankful or upset about it—mostly because I don't know who is at the door.

"Will you get it?" I ask him.

He nods. "Want me to let him in?"

"Nope."

He rolls his eyes but marches to the door like a man on a mission.

I hold my breath as the door creaks. My eyes dry out as they stay wide as he speaks to whoever is there.

The door shuts.

My heart pounds.

Nate returns with a bag dangling from his arm.

I blow out my breath. "What's that?" I ask, annoyed.

"It's for you."

He sets it on the table, and I peer inside. Multiple take-out containers are stacked neatly in the bag.

"What the heck?" I ask.

I take them out one by one until I spy a note at the bottom. I pick it up.

Shaye,

Since you're too sick to come to the office, I thought you might need some nourishment. A variety of chicken noodle and tomato soups from a place across town that I love.

I miss you. I'm sorry.

Get well soon. And call me. I need to apologize and figure out how to fix the mess I made.

Oliver

"He sent you soup?" Nate laughs. "That's awesome."

I set the note down and look at the display in front of me. *It is kind of awesome.*

"Are you ever going to call him?" he asks.

I miss him. I miss him so freaking much. I wish I could pick up the phone and just pour my heart out, but I tried that already, and he ended things.

"What else do I say, Nate?"

"Maybe you don't say anything. Maybe you listen for a change."

I give him a dirty look, making him laugh.

"He just wants to clean up his mess," I say, glancing at the note again. "He probably wants to smooth it over so he can go on."

"Or maybe he knows he's wrong and wants to actually apologize."

"Fine. I accept. But you know what *I* need? Not to pretend things are fine but know they aren't. I don't live to make him feel better about his fuckups." My heart squeezes. "I mean, I told him that I loved him, and it wasn't enough to fix things for me. I don't owe him anything else."

"Guys are dumb."

"I know."

He laughs. "I mean ..."

He's interrupted again by the door.

"I'll get it," he says, heading more quickly to the door this time. The exchange is executed much faster, and he's back with another bag. "For you."

My heart squeezes in my chest. Hope begins to flutter. I dig through the contents and find the note.

Shaye,

I asked the pharmacist to send you every over-the-counter relief that she had since I don't know your symptoms. I also asked her to send you a Snickers in case you're as sad as I am. I know you like them frozen.

Call me. Please. I'm sorry.

Oliver

Nate stares at me, trying not to laugh.

I sit down, my hand shaking.

"Okay, let's say I do call him," I begin carefully. "What do I say?"

"Probably hello. That's always good."

I smack him on the shoulder.

"You tell him how you feel," he says. "It's not that complicated. You tell him that you have a voice and the right to be heard. Tell him you're pissed about the money because you don't want to be controlled. You tell him that if he ever makes you cry again that I'll break him into so many pieces that they'll never find them all."

I grin.

"You just ... be you, Shaye. But give the guy a chance to explain himself. People fuck up. It happens. Doesn't mean they're a perpetual fuckup unless you're talking about Murray."

"Hey! Be nice to Murray," I say with a laugh.

"Me being too nice to Murray is only hurting Murray at this point." Nate laughs too. "Call the guy, Shaye. I've been him. I've been the guy who did things wrong. At least hear him out."

I study my friend's face. Nate will, without a doubt, always be on my side. And if he—the man who doesn't even like Oliver—thinks it's safe to hear him out, then I should.

"Okay," I say. "Push my phone to me."

He slides it to me. But before I can do anything, my doorbell rings again.

"What can it be now?" I ask.

He shrugs and heads for the door.

I hear the hushed voices. The door shuts. Footsteps tap their way toward me.

"What is it now, Nate ...?"

I gasp as I look up and see Oliver standing in front of my friend. His tie is askew, his hair in waves, and there are bags under his eyes that remind me of my own.

He stares at me like he's seeing me for the first time.

"You blocked me," he says.

My shoulders slump as I let out a breath. "You broke up with me."

This startles him. He moves toward me and sits beside me.

Having his body close to mine, feeling his hand sit atop mine, makes tears form in my eyes.

I've missed you so much.

I look at Nate. "Will you ...?"

Nate winks at me. "Call me if you need me. And you," he says, pointing at Oliver, "behave. Or I'll come for you."

Oliver gives him a half-grin and then watches him walk out.

"I can't decide if I like him or not," he says.

"Why are you here?" I ask, unable to do anything but get to the point.

He hangs his head.

"Oliver."

He looks at me. His gaze is steely. "You said you were sick."

"You know I'm not sick."

"I know. But you said you were, and I'm taking you at your word."

"So you sent soup and meds?"

He grins. "Yes. Because if you're sick, that's what you need." His smile falters. "Shaye, I'm sorry."

"What are you sorry for?"

He pulls his hand away from mine. I miss it immediately.

"I'm sorry for not listening to you. For not giving you the benefit of the doubt. For being so scared that I ran with my tail tucked between my legs." He sighs and sits back. "I know who you are. I hate myself for questioning your loyalty to me."

The pain on his face is evident. I know he means what he's saying. But that doesn't solve everything.

I grab Nate's water bottle and take a long drink, praying he doesn't have any diseases.

"Tell me why you paid off Luca's debt," I say.

He presses his lips together. His chest rises and falls.

"Oliver?"

He looks at me. "When you told me that Luca had left you with such a large loan and you didn't know why and that he had used your mother's house as collateral, something didn't add up. It felt wrong. So I had some people look into it."

I don't know where he's going with this, but I know I don't like it.

"I have their report if you want to read it. But Luca was not a good guy, Shaye. He was into some bad stuff. He owed people money—dangerous people who I would imagine could find themselves in federal prison if they were ever picked up by law enforcement."

My jaw hits the table.

What the actual fuck?

"Am I safe?" I ask, looking around as if someone might be looking through my windows. "I didn't have anything to do with whatever he was doing. Do they know that? Do I need to ... *Shit*. I ..."

"Breathe."

My attention whips to him, and I do—I breathe.

Just looking at Oliver makes me settle. It makes me feel safe. And the fact that I don't have that luxury anymore makes the tears well up in my eyes again.

He takes my hand.

"There are rumors that Luca's accident wasn't an accident. That someone put a hit out on him," Oliver says. "I've heard the coroner was paid off to say he was asleep at the wheel, but from what I've read, that's probably not how things went down."

A chill rips through me.

"The company you were paying off is ... they're legit by a thin definition of the word. They are not anyone you want to be involved with, and when I realized that's who you were paying ..." He wipes a tear off my cheek with his thumb. "I love you. The thought of someone coming after you over a debt that wasn't yours to begin with. I couldn't live with myself, Shaye."

What the hell? Who the hell was Luca dealing with? And possible murder?

I cannot process this. I can't.

"But why didn't you tell me?" I ask through my tears. "Why didn't you ...? Why didn't you say something?"

"It's not an easy conversation to start, Shaye."

My mind sorts through all of my memories with Luca and tries to find any tip-off that this was happening.

"I've had a lot on my plate. My parents were getting divorced, and now my dad is in rehab ..." He shrugs. "There's been a lot of shit. I kept thinking I'd find time to tell you, but they notified you much quicker than I expected. Probably from the strong language my attorney used when sending the payment."

"I'm sorry you had to go through all of this. I really am."

He brushes a strand of hair out of my face. "I'm sorry that I didn't meet you sooner so I could have loved you longer. It would've saved us both a headache."

I smile at him. "Thank you for doing this. But I will still pay you back."

He shakes his head.

"I'm not asking you," I say.

"I'm not taking your fucking money."

"*Yes, you fucking are.*"

He glares at me.

I slip my hand out of his and stand. *There has to be a way to make him understand.*

Walking to the window, I gaze out at the street.

"I know I told you that we were over, but we aren't," he says.

"Not sure I remember agreeing to that." *Even though I want to.* "We seem to have a very different view of how things work between us."

"Is this about the money?"

I turn and look at him. "Yes. Partly. It's also about all that honesty you talk about. This is quite an omission, and I do believe that, according to you, omissions are lies."

He looks at the table.

"I didn't want Marius Blast any more than you wanted to hurt me by getting the information about Luca. We were both doing our best under difficult circumstances, Oliver."

"I know. You're right. One hundred percent."

"And if you want to be with me, I need your trust and honesty as much as you need it from me."

He stands but doesn't walk toward me. Instead, he motions toward the bags on the table. "I'm going to listen to everything you ever say. I'm going to fulfill every need, every wish you have. I'm going to stand beside you, next to you, and help you live your best life."

I still.

"I don't want to hold things over your head. And the money wasn't that—it wasn't me trying to get one over on you. I know that's what you think."

"Yes."

He shakes his head. "It was me trying to help carry a burden for you in a way that I can. Because that's what people do who love each other. They step up. I stepped up as an investment in our future. *Together*. Where we carry each other's burdens, do everything together as a team. Where we have a little girl named Shelby and a cat or a dog or a fucking horse—I don't care. As long as that future is with you." He rushes to me, holding me in his arms. "*I love you*. I want a partnership with you, not some fucked-up power struggle. I don't need power or control. I just need you."

My heart lodges in my throat, making it hard to breathe. My body shakes with an emotion that's not tears and not fear ... but maybe pure happiness.

Hearing him say these things—these beautiful words—soothes something deep in my soul that I didn't know could be reached.

It's not that having Oliver needing me or wanting me makes me feel more valuable or worthy of love. Having Oliver fight for me makes me feel valued. Having a future to build with him is the best gift in the world.

And, in a way, I gave that gift to myself.

I didn't crash when life got hard. I kept going when I didn't think I could. And I learned to trust someone else when all I know how to do is question someone's motives.

That's Oliver's gift to me.

I bury my face in his chest. He palms the back of my head and holds it to him.

"I love you, Shaye."

"I love you."

He kisses the top of my head. "Come home with me. Bring some of your stuff. Bring all of it if you want but let's do that tomorrow because I need to hold you right now."

I lean back and look into his eyes. "On one condition."

"Anything."

"Okay." I smile. "You don't give me any shit about working for Nate—"

"We gotta talk about that."

"Oh, I know we do."

He makes a face, and I extract myself from his arms. He sighs.

"I'm not quitting my job until I'm damn good and ready," I tell him.

"Well, quit there as easily as you quit my company."

I roll my eyes at him. "I'll compromise."

He crosses his arms over his chest.

"Take it or leave it, but this is what I'm offering," I say.

"Go on."

I swallow. "I will work for Nate until I pay you back for the—"

"No."

"Oliver!"

He shakes his head. "I don't know what I'm more against—you working there or you paying me back."

I shrug. "Well, I don't care what you don't like because I'm doing both." I grin. "Where's all that team spirit you were just talking about?"

He's not entertained. Still, the resoluteness on his face eases, and he sighs.

"This is important to you?" he asks.

"Clearly."

He pauses. "Then fine. I respect you, and if paying the loan gives you what you need, helps you understand that I never want to control you, okay. I accept that."

"Oh. Okay." I didn't expect that. I grin. "Thank you. That was easier—"

"I'm not done." He smirks. "I want you to know, however, that when we start a family, I'm going to be completely overprotective. I'll look after you and—"

I silence him with a kiss.

Just as I don't want Oliver to change me, I don't want to change him, either. A part of what I love so much about him is how safe I feel with him. If I argue this point, it would go against one of his best attributes. I have no desire to do that.

I'll just have to figure out how to pay him back in another way. I have time. *Maybe my entire life.*

He rests his forehead against mine. It feels like a semitruck has been lifted off my shoulders.

"We might get this right. We might screw up and get it wrong some-times," he says. "People are inherently imperfect. I've had that rein-forced to me this week."

I run my hands down his tie.

"But I love you, and you love me, and that's worth fighting for," he whispers.

"I think so too."

He grins. "Want to go to my house now?"

"I have one more question," I say, hiding a smile.

"What's that, my lady?"

"Do I still have a job? Or do I have to work for Wade?"

Oliver doesn't answer me. Instead, he sweeps me off my feet and carries me out the door.

Chapter Thirty-Five

Shaye

"What is this going to look like?" I ask.

The sun warms my skin. I stretch out on the chaise beside Oliver's pool and watch him sort through a toolbox.

Steam rolls off the grill in the little kitchenette that I just learned existed. The steaks Oliver prepared after our getting-to-know-you-again romp sizzle, perfuming the air, and I sip a glass of wine and *sigh*.

"Hopefully," Oliver says, plucking a screwdriver from the red metal box, "it'll look like a hinged cabinet door again." He looks at me like I'm nuts. "What do you expect it to look like?"

I laugh. "Not the door. This. *Us.*"

His pace slows as he walks back to the door he just discovered was broken. His forehead furrows.

"It'll look like this, I guess," he says. "What do you want it to look like?"

His voice is confident yet laced with a slight hesitation. I know why. He's trying to be him but also let me be me.

He's afraid to assume anything for fear that I'll feel walked on. And he's right. That fear is legitimate. I've carried that wound for a long time.

And I still have it, festering in a deep part of my soul. Maybe it'll always be there. Maybe I'll never one-hundred-percent be able to let my guard down. I'm not sure.

But what I do know is this: being with Oliver is a safe space to learn. To grow. To set aside my grievances with the past and become a new, whole person again.

"I don't know." I take a sip of my wine. "Maybe like this."

He quirks a brow and bends down behind the cabinet. I can only see the top of his head.

I lean my head back against the chair and think. I think about the reasons that I'm willing to try this with Oliver, the reasons I love him. There are so many—too many things to list, and I'm still getting to know him. I'm still learning what makes him tick, what motivates him, what things are printed on his heart.

What things are printed on his heart beside my name.

The thought makes me smile—it fills me with a wonderful warmth, *a comfort*, that I can't deny. Nor would I want to.

There may have been people who let me down in my life. People who have done me wrong. People who have treated me badly and put me in terrible situations. I'm just realizing that all of that—all of those transgressions—had nothing to do with me.

I know that because of Oliver.

It scares me to think about what my life would be like now had I given up or given in to my fears and the dark days of before. *There were so many of them.* But I kept going, pushed forward—sometimes with the smallest shred of hope that there was a light at the end of the tunnel.

Thank God, I was right.

My light was Oliver.

He rises from behind the counter and wipes a bead of sweat off his forehead. "Fixed it."

I grin.

He walks to my chair. Sitting on the edge, he picks up one of my feet and rubs it in his hands.

"I just want to be clear," he says, working my foot back and forth in his hands.

"About what?"

"As far as I'm concerned, you live here. You don't have to," he says hurriedly. "If you want to keep your place for a while, I get it. There's no rush."

I bite my lip and lift my other foot, wiggling my toes. He laughs and starts to rub it instead.

"Our lives are intertwined. It's you and me," he says. "I'll take that at whatever speed makes you feel good about it. Just don't get confused —I want you living here having babies with my last name as soon as you realize it's our destiny. Not yours—ours."

Oh. My. Gosh.

I don't know whether to laugh, cry, or just get naked. Every part of me says something different. In lieu of an answer, I sit up and motion for him to bend down. Then I kiss him slowly, methodically, with all of my heart and soul.

He leans back with his eyes full of mischief. "Hold that thought."

"What thought? You don't even know what I was thinking."

He winks as he takes his screwdriver back to the toolbox. He fiddles around again until he stands with something behind his back.

Curious, I make a face. "What's that?"

His smile is slow. Seductive. *Sexy as hell.* He brings his right hand to the front. A handful of zip ties dangle from his palm.

I sit up, my mouth dry. My heart pounds like a drum.

Blood pours through my veins with such an urgency that I nearly leap off the chair and into his arms.

"Wanna?" he asks, shaking them around.

"Wanna ... what?" I gulp. "Fix a cabinet or ..."

He chuckles. "How about we go upstairs and—"

"Yes." I scramble off the chair. "Yup. Let's do that."

He wraps his arm around my waist and laughs. "And fix the curtain rod?"

I smack his chest. He catches my wrist and holds my hand to him. His heart races as fast as mine.

"I love you, Shaye."

"I love you."

He takes my hand and leads me toward the door.

"What about the steaks?" I ask, looking over my shoulder.

He stops at the door, groaning, and jogs back to the grill. The steam slows, and the sizzling dies down. Then he turns to look at me.

I study his handsome face.

What does this look like between us? I have no idea. Maybe it's me moving in tonight, maybe it's keeping my house for a year. I'm not sure yet. We'll get there, though, because our love is real. Continuous. Lasting. It's imperfect and vulnerable.

It's relentless.

"I just want to be clear," I say, biting my bottom lip.

"What's that?"

I motion for him to come to me. He smirks but obliges me. I wrap my arms around his shoulders and look into his eyes.

"I really, *really* want to have your babies someday," I say, feeling my body clench at the idea. "Let's—*ah*!"

He picks me up, throwing me over his shoulder, and carries me into the house.

Epilogue

Two months later ...

Oliver

"I'm worried about you." I lean against the fireplace and look at my mother. "Are you okay?"

She laughs, her eyes sparkling. It's been a long time since I've seen this look in her eyes.

"You've been cursing—strategically," I point out.

"I'm old enough to say a few errant words, Oliver."

"And you're letting Boone eat in the living room." I motion toward my youngest brother with a plate full of ribs on my mother's white sofa. "And there's a dog running through your house."

My mom swishes her water with lemon around in a fancy glass. "Fluffy is the very best boy in the whole world."

"Excuse me?" Coy comes up beside her and slings his arm around her shoulder. "I think I'm the very best boy. That is, until my son gets here."

"I'm happy to let him have the title until I get my own boy here."

Mom gasps. "Do you have something to tell me?"

"Me? No." I laugh. "Dammit, I wish I did, though."

Mom's gaze follows mine across the room.

"Maybe soon," she says wistfully. "Maybe soon, Ollie."

"Yeah."

I watch as Shaye talks animatedly with my brothers' wives and girl-friends. They laugh as Bellamy shows them something on her phone. I don't know what Blaire says with her dry sense of humor, but I think Shaye is going to fall off her chair.

It's ... everything.

"I'm gonna go find Wade and Dad," Coy says. He kisses Mom on the cheek before climbing the stairs to the study.

"How's he been?" I ask Mom.

She glances up the stairs. "Your father has been doing really well. Very well. He struggles some days, but he's battling through treatment and is trying. That's all we can ask. I'm really proud of him."

"I'm proud of you too." Her gaze shifts back to me. "Boone told me that you asked him to take over some projects at work so you could spend more time at home."

"Of course he did."

She laughs. "He was really happy."

"Yeah, well ..."

I look back at Shaye.

I always thought I was building this great big life. The more time I put into my job, the more I was going to get out of it. Little did I know that all of the things I hoped to obtain had very little to do with what happens at Mason Limited.

The important parts of my day are dinners with Shaye on the patio. Mornings in the wicker room, as she calls it. It's Saturday picnics at Forsyth Park and *Steel Magnolias* for the millionth time on Sunday afternoons.

It's repainting the living room and having Nate over for a beer and a football game.

Turns out, he's not a bad guy.

I wouldn't say I wasted my life until I met her, but it would be a waste to put *all* of my energy into those things now. There *is* more to life than work, something I'm realizing earlier than my dad. Thankfully.

"Boone is capable," I say before taking a sip of my tea. "He'll do great."

"I know he will. He learned from the best."

"She means me." Holt comes up beside me and pushes his fist into my stomach. "We're going to have to get Boone an EA now. That might set his ego over the edge."

We all laugh, knowing it's true.

Mom's phone buzzes on the end table next to her. She picks it up and frowns. "Poor Riss."

"What's going on with Larissa?" I ask.

"It's Hollis." Mom types out a quick text and then sets her phone back down. "They were supposed to be here for dinner tonight, but he got some bad news about his sister. I just hate this for him."

My spirits sink. "Hollis is such a good guy. What did he find out?"

"I don't know," Mom says. "Riss just said it was bad news, and they wouldn't be here. She said she'll call me tomorrow."

"I'll have Coy check on him tonight," Holt says.

"That would be nice, sweetheart." Mom pats him.

An arm slinks around my waist. I look down to see Shaye sliding next to me.

"Hey, my lady," I say, pulling her in close.

She grins up at me.

"Shaye, honey, I am just thrilled that you're here," Mom says. "Things have been a little ... wonky since you joined the family, but now that they're settling a little bit, I'd love to get to know you better."

"I'd love that, Siggy."

"Maybe I could take all of my daughter-in-laws out for lunch this weekend?" Mom raises her voice so everyone can hear her. "Shaye? Jaxi? Bellamy? Blaire?"

Holt sighs. "I don't know why you're asking Blaire since she won't marry me."

Everyone laughs. Everyone but Blaire. She fires him a look.

"Will you *please* stop it?" she asks.

"Are you going to marry me or not? I mean, come on, B. Damn."

"Come on, Blaire," I say, laughing. "Are you gonna marry him or not?"

Out of nowhere, notes from *Here Come The Bride* filter from the piano upstairs.

"I hate you, Coy!" Blaire yells up the stairs.

He just plays the song louder.

My cheeks ache from smiling as I look down at Shaye. She's practically glowing.

"I guess Blaire will sit this one out—"

"Fine! Six weeks. I will marry you six weeks from today!" Blaire's face is pink as she looks around at each one of our faces. "I mean, as long as that's on a Saturday."

"Somebody get a calendar!" Holt shouts, racing across the room. He scoops Blaire up in his arms and bends her back, kissing the shit out of her.

"It's a Saturday," Jaxi says. "It works."

Mom claps her hands together. "I have some planning to do. Who is throwing the bridal shower?"

Holt releases Blaire.

"It's not necessary," Blaire says. "We have everything that we need."

Bellamy runs a hand over her stomach. "I would, but I'm ready to pop."

Shaye pulls away from me, leaving a hand on my chest. She sucks in a deep breath. "I ... I don't know you very well yet, but I'd like to throw your party." She looks around. "I mean, if that's okay. I don't want to step on any toes. I just thought maybe it would be a nice way to get to know you all."

Blaire smiles. "That would be very sweet of you, Shaye. Thank you."

"Shaye, you must let me help," Mom says. "Think of me as a collaborator with a credit card."

Shaye and Mom join the other girls in the corner. I have no idea what they're talking about, but words like games and cake are repeated.

Wade steps off the staircase and looks around. "What's happening down here?"

"Blaire agreed to marry me in six weeks," Holt says, rounding the corner to the hallway. "Get a tux. You're a groomsman. Both of you."

Wade gives me a look. "I think I'll pass."

"You can't pass. It's your brother's wedding," I say.

"Exactly. What's it have to do with me?"

"Wade!" Rosie shrieks, her voice piercing the room. She leaps over Fluffy and attaches herself to Wade's leg. "I miss you, Wade."

He looks down at her. "I just saw you upstairs. Remember? You shut my hand in the door."

"Oh. Yeah." She screws up her face. "Want to go ride bikes?"

"No. I don't." He looks around the room. "Can't you go play with Bellamy?"

She looks up at him adoringly. "No. I love *you*, Wade."

"Great."

I snicker. "I'm going to leave the two of you to bond."

I slip through the house and make my way to the kitchen. The air is cool, the room quieter. I wait.

It takes a few minutes, but she comes. *I knew she would.*

"Hey," she says, smiling up at me.

"What did you do with it?" I ask her.

She reaches in her pocket and pulls out her ring. It's a blue sapphire that's surrounded by diamonds. The band is thin and gold.

She said it reminded her of my eyes when I gave it to her last night.

"We can't tell them we're engaged now," she says, resting her cheek against my chest. "I can't steal Holt's joy."

I kiss the top of her head. "Maybe we can just elope. Just skip telling them we're engaged and go right to the marriage part of it."

Her eyes twinkle as she looks up at me. "We can talk about that tonight."

"I ..."

Wade storms through the room, waving to us as he passes. "I gotta go. Talk to you tomorrow at the office."

"Everyone too happy for you, Wade?" I tease.

He shakes his head and disappears out the door.

"He's my favorite—besides you," Shaye says.

"Wade? That's interesting."

She runs a finger along my jaw. "I bet when he falls in love someday, he'll fall hard."

I make a face. "I don't think he'll fall in love. He'll be a loner forever."

"Someone will crash into his life and wow him." She raises on her toes and kisses me softly. "Just like I did you."

I pull her up against me, forever thankful that she had to sneeze—four times—and literally crashed into my life. "What do you say we go home and watch *Steel Magnolias* again?"

She smiles. "Sure. Or we could go home and get the toolbox and see if you have any zip ties left."

I growl, making her giggle.

"I love you so much, Oliver Mason."

"I love you so much too."

(Turn the page to read chapter one of Wade Mason's book, Resolution.)

MEET WADE MASON

Romance is not in Wade Mason's portfolio.

This is tragic. It's unfair that a man so maddeningly gorgeous—an architect with a deliciously squarish jaw, adorably dimpled chin, and the hottest black glasses that straddle the line between professional and provocative—rebukes all things love.

I knew this well before I walked into his office.

The man is a conundrum—a complicated, steel wall of a puzzle. On the one hand, he brushes against me in the conference room with a broodiness that sets me on fire. He demands in-person meetings about the house we are working on together. I catch him watching me out of the corner of his eye with a look that's *anything* but platonic. But any talk of hookups, love, or relationships—even in general? Completely off the table.

I'm determined to peel back his layers until I get to the bottom of the mysterious businessman. But my plan is foiled by a surprise that leaves both of us reeling. Neither of us sees it coming, but it changes everything ... forever.

Chapter One
Wade

"Eliza? Please remind me at twelve thirty that I'm needed elsewhere."

I sit back in my chair. Massaging my temple with one hand, I await my assistant's reply through the speakerphone.

"And where might that be, Mr. Mason?"

"It doesn't matter."

"*Oh.*"

I should feel guilty that I'm confusing this poor woman on her third day of work or, at the very least, regretful enough to backtrack.

I do neither. I also don't feel bad about this decision.

"Actually, make it twelve fifteen," I say, further complicating Eliza's confusion.

"Yes, sir. While I have you on the line, I believe your twelve o'clock is walking in right now."

Fabulous.

I squash back a shot of frustration and stifle an annoyed growl. *Do this and get it over with.*

That's the plan. Meet with Curt Bowery and find him and his proposal unreasonable. Then I can tell Oliver I did my due diligence, and now I'm out.

Simple.

"Send him back," I say before the guilt that I should've felt earlier starts to wiggle its way into my conscience. "*Thank you*, Eliza."

"Yes. Of course. You're welcome, Mr. Mason."

Her voice is full of ... happiness. Despite the fact that it's wholly unrepresentative of Mason Architecture, Holt insists that prospective clients prefer a cheerful person at the front desk. Such an oddity, if you ask me.

The line disconnects and I get busy tidying up my workspace. The office is the only place where controlled chaos reigns in my life. Immersing myself in designs, blueprints, clay models—it makes me feel alive.

It's what gets me up in the morning. It's why I work through lunch, and it's the reason I work late most nights. That and insomnia is a bitch.

A knock raps on the door. I run my hand down my tie and click out of the program on my computer. When I look back up, and—*what the hell?*

The human being standing in the doorway is *not* Curt Bowery.

"It *is* you," she says, a wide smile stretching across her full pink lips. *What?*

I do a quick once-over of the woman stepping into my office—the woman who's most definitely *not* my twelve o'clock.

She's about my age with thick, shiny mahogany-colored hair. Her cheekbones accentuate her eyes. They're golden brown, the color of a glass of whiskey when the afternoon sun shines through it, and are framed by long, dark lashes.

She exudes a friendliness, a warm and bubbly vibe that drives home the fact I've never met this woman in my life. I'm sure of it. I don't associate with this kind of person. They're too ... people-y.

The door shuts with a *click!* just before she turns around.

"I know that *Wade Mason* isn't a name you come across daily," she says, moving far too easily through my office. "But I figured that I would get here, and it wouldn't be you after all. I mean, what are the odds?"

Before I can break down those odds for her—about one in one hundred thousand, give or take—she reaches me.

And reaches for *me.*

The scent of coconuts hits me before she does. By the time I get ahold of all of these moving parts—Curt's impending arrival, this random woman in my office, and the encroachment on my personal behind-the-desk space—she wraps her arms around me and pulls me in for a hug.

Oof.

She leans back quickly. Her eyes are sparkling.

"You're a friendly one, aren't you?" I ask, taking a step back in case she has a knife. Because what kind of person hugs another unprompted? Psychopaths. That's who.

Her laughter is light and breezy. "You don't remember me."

Fuck.

I hate when women—*when people*—do this. They think they're special enough to warrant being memorable against the hundred other faces you see through the course of a week. Somehow, regardless of the number of interactions you've had within a certain timeframe, *you* are the asshole who can't remember them.

It's total bullshit.

The woman flips her hair off her narrow shoulder and allows me an even clearer view of her pretty, freckly face. She doesn't look like a psychopath.

Then again, they never do.

"Should I tell you who I am, or should we make a game out of it?" she says, moving to the other side of my desk.

I exhale, confused about so many things—*who she is, why Eliza let her in my office, and where the hell is Curt Bowery when you need him?*

"I'm not much for games," I deadpan, hoping she'll read between the lines and gather that I'm not a fan of … this.

"Really?" She falls back into the brown leather chair facing my desk and laughs. Her gaze settles on me. "Games can be fun, you know."

"I suppose they have a time and place," I say, sitting back down in my chair. I grab a fresh notepad and try to avoid her eyes. "I have an appointment that should be arriving any time, so I'd appreciate it if we could get to the bottom of … who are you? Why are you here?"

I lift my eyes to meet hers. They snap together like the last two pieces of a jigsaw puzzle. She runs a finger over her bottom lip as if she—*and I*—have all the time in the world.

"I thought for sure you'd remember me," she says.

"Isn't that a bit pretentious?"

She narrows her eyes but continues to grin. "No more than your *portentous* assumption that *I'm* not your twelve o'clock."

Confidence oozes out of her as she effectively tosses the banter-ball back over the net. Coupled with her poise at my cool demeanor—a tactic that usually softens whoever is sitting across from me—it's quite a show.

It's also respectable.

"Okay," I say. "Fair enough. But I'm still going to need your name."

She seems satisfied with my capitulation.

"I'm Dara Alden," she says finally. "We had a class together at Georgia Tech. We did a presentation together about intimacy in relationships in a communications class my freshman year."

She pauses, waiting for me to connect all the dots. And I do. Quickly.

Dara Alden was my partner for the worst class and worst project I've ever been forced to participate in. I was certain the professor matched us together just to see me suffer. He had it in for me—no thanks to a speech I presented on why communications classes weren't beneficial to all students and should be eliminated from prerequisites.

I start to respond when my speakerphone buzzes.

"Mr. Mason? You're needed on an urgent call regarding the Greyshell project," Eliza says. "It can't wait, sir."

Internally, I groan and make a mental note to remind her not to call me *sir*. "I'll call them back."

"But, sir ..."

My jaw clenches in both frustration and embarrassment. "I'll call them back, Eliza. Thank you for letting me know."

"*Okay*. Thank you. I'll ... *tell them*," she says before ending the call.

I run a hand through my hair and try to stay calm and focused. But when I glance back up, Dara is watching me with unbridled amusement.

"I'm curious," Dara says, her voice as sweet as honey. "Did your opinions on intimacy change?"

Pulling at the collar of my shirt, I grab a pen. *Have Eliza turn down the thermostat.*

"I don't recall what my opinions were a decade ago," I say, jotting down the thermostat thought in my notepad. "But it's safe to say I've always considered intimacy in relationships …"

Why are we talking about this?

I set down my pen and level my gaze with hers. "Are you really my twelve o'clock? Or was that something you picked up on because I mentioned it, and you just ran with it?" I pause. "Did Boone put you up to this?"

She snickers. "Relax, Wade. I don't even know who Boone is."

"You're the only female in this part of Georgia who can say that with a straight face."

"Heck, maybe I *should* know him." Dara laughs. "Can you introduce us?"

I flip her a look. I don't know what I mean by it, exactly. It just radiates from me without my trying. She seems amused by it and, thankfully, also lets it go.

"All joking aside," she says, running a hand through the air. "Yes. I'm your twelve o'clock. My grandfather is Curt Bowery, and I need an architect."

Well, shit.

It feels like I've been hit on the side of the head a little bit. I'm not sure what to say in response to this news. I knew exactly how I was going to deal with Curt, but this isn't Curt. I don't know why it matters, but it does. Sort of.

"I suppose my follow-up question would be …" I search for the right words. "You do understand what an architect does, right? I design *things* —buildings, houses, hotels. I'm not a therapist specializing in relational intimacy. As a matter of fact, I've said all that I have to say about that topic."

She laughs. It's smooth and loud and sounds foreign in my office.

"That's disappointing," she says, crossing one leg over the other and settling in. "I was hoping we could spend our afternoons discussing intimacy types and debate over whether *true* intimacy is even reachable in modern-day relationships again."

I can't help it. I smirk. "It sounds as though you've lived the past ten years reading a lot of self-help books."

Dara shrugs, teasing me. "And it sounds as though you've lived the past ten years alone and are just as cantankerous as you were back then."

I look down so she can't see my ghost of a smile. It's that gesture—the tiniest splitting of my cheeks—that kicks me out of whatever bullshit distraction was happening between us and back to reality.

There's work to be done. Commitments have been made. Those things aren't happening if I'm sitting here in a verbal tug-of-war with a millionaire's granddaughter.

"I do have another meeting in ten minutes," I say, turning toward my computer. My voice is as detached as I can get it. "Unfortunately, we don't have time to get into your project today."

Out of the corner of my eye, she flinches.

"We don't have time today?" Dara asks, surprised.

"We've used up too much of it discussing ..." *Whatever we were discussing*. I adjust my glasses. "Anyway, seeing if we are a good fit is a part of the process. I don't design many homes because it requires too much ..."

My voice trails off as I turn back to her. The way she's looking at me catches me off guard. Her brows are raised, and her head is tilted to the side. She's silently calling me out, letting me know she doesn't believe a word I'm saying.

We watch each other for a long couple of seconds. It's a standoff of sorts. Neither of us wants to be the first to look away.

It's a case of two strong personalities wanting the other to bend, each of us wanting to control the narrative. What she doesn't know is that I always win that scenario. *Always*.

I stand, adjusting my tie and attempting to clear my head.

"So, what does a person have to do to see if we're *a good fit*?" she asks.

The cheekiness in her question is not lost on me. But I ignore it.

What I don't ignore is the tension between the two of us, nor do I overlook her apparent propensity to try to push my buttons. It's a replay from ten years ago. I almost came unglued over our speech, and it was for twenty class points. This time, there will be a lot more on the line.

Too much to risk, most definitely.

"It has a lot to do with trust." My gaze burns into hers. "*You* have to relinquish control and trust that *I* understand your needs and will deliver everything you ask of me." *Where possible.*

Instead of making her blush as I intended, she grins. It's not the playful one from before or the happy smile that she tossed my way when she walked in. No, this one is darker. Seductive. Not at all what I was expecting.

I smooth my tie with my hand again, running it down my chest. Her eyes flicker to the movement for just a moment before her gaze rises back to mine.

"I think we could get there, Mr. Mason."

My chuckle is soft as I plant both hands on my desk. I lean forward and wait to see if she squirms in her chair. I'm surprised that she doesn't. She sits tall, unwavering—poised despite my efforts to break her resolve.

What the hell?

I'm starting to wonder if Curt Bowery, the hotel magnate worth millions of dollars, would've been easier to navigate than Dara Alden.

"It's not *if* we can get there," I tell her, looking her dead in her eyes. "I'm one-thousand-percent confident in my abilities *to get there.*"

Dara forces a swallow but doesn't blink.

"It's about all the things that lead to that final moment," I say, my voice low and steady. "The journey, if you will."

"That's what they all say." She tucks a small purse under her arm and stands. "But you might be right. I'm not sure you're the man who should be handling ... *my project.*"

Of course, she's right. It's the point I was just trying to make. But hearing her say it pisses me off.

I head to the door. "Think about it. Talk it over with your grandfather," I say, swinging the door wide open. "You can let Eliza know if you'd like to reschedule, and we'll see when I'm available."

She hums as she moseys toward me. "You seem like a very busy man."

I'm not sure if she's being facetious, so I don't respond. I think her statement was rhetorical anyway.

"Busy men always go through the motions and never have time to be creative," she says, fighting a smile. "I'm not sure that fits my needs."

I narrow my gaze.

Much to my surprise *and annoyance*, she laughs as she walks by me. Her elbow grazes my stomach in a move that I think is intentional. Before I can react, she's down the hall and standing in front of Eliza.

"That dress is stunning on you," she tells Eliza as if we weren't in a strained conversation five seconds ago. "Where did you get it?"

"Oh, for fuck's sake," I grumble as I slam my door. The framed copy of the first building I ever designed shakes against the wall.

I lean against my desk and suck in a deep lungful of air. The scent of coconuts only intensifies my frustration.

I open a window and then sit down.

"Busy men always go through the motions and never have time to be creative. I'm not sure that fits my needs."

What the hell?

Relational intimacy.

Loads of rubbish, just as it was ten years ago.

Instead of listening to spoiled, silver spoon-fed women who want their ridiculous projects handled, I have real work to do.

My heart pumps from the interaction with Dara, and I find myself replaying much of our conversation. It's not until I get to *relational intimacy* do I realize how much time I've wasted—and am still wasting.

I put my phone on Do Not Disturb and get back to the only thing I ever want to know *intimately*—my work.

Resolution is live now on Amazon and Audible.

Acknowledgements

I would be remiss if I didn't begin this by thanking my Creator. I'm flawed, unworthy, and make so many mistakes. He loves me anyway.

My family, Saul, Alexander, Aristotle, Achilles, and Ajax give me endless inspiration (and piles of laundry). My parents, Dennis and Mandy, gave me the confidence to shoot for the stars. And my in-laws, Rob and Peggy, pick up the pieces that I drop and pat me on the back when I fall. I love them all more than any words can describe.

I am grateful to have established a wonderful team around me. Tiffany Remy handles the details of all things me. Kari March is one of the most talented humans that I know. Mandi Beck is the best friend a girl could have. Jessica Prince was the reason this book was finished and S.L. Scott never fails me when I need her.

I would like to thank Jen Costa for finally reading this book (I'm kidding), Susan Raynor for cheerleading me throughout the process, and Anjelica Grace for answering my voice messages. Thank you, too, to Brittni Van and Julia Heudorf for your time when it was hard to give. Also, hugs to Atlee Hayes for making me laugh each and every day and for being such a good sport when I torture her over Harlee Hudson.

My Facebook group, Books by Adriana Locke, is the best place on the web. The men and women that pop in every day to make us all laugh, inspire us, and to watch the fireworks that are certain to go down are the reason I haven't lost my mind this year. They are more than my readers; they are my family.

I'm so grateful to Ebbie Moresco, Kaitie Reister, and Stephanie Gibson for their social media support. And a big virtual hug to Marion Making Manuscripts, Jenny with Editing 4 Indies, Michele Ficht, and

Kara Hildebrand for their assistance in the editing and proofreading processes.

My deepest gratitude goes to my readers who never fail to support me. Thank you for trusting me to entertain you for a few hours with my books. I know how many books you have to choose from. You will never know how much it means to me that you choose mine.

Adriana Locke is a USA Today and Amazon Charts Bestselling author with a knack for writing swoony, unforgettable contemporary romances. At nineteen, she traded her small-town roots for big-city life, only to realize her heart beats for quiet mornings and cozy chaos. These days, she's living her happily-ever-after in Ohio with Mr. Locke—her high school sweetheart—four lively sons, and two hilariously hyper Jack Russell terriers.

When she's not penning love stories that will leave you laughing and sighing, Adriana is battling the epic quest of missing silverware, "gardening" (a.k.a. chatting with her plants), or leaving her grocery list on the counter as she heads to the store. Grab a cup of coffee, settle in, and let her books whisk you away to a world of heartwarming romance and irresistible heroes.

Join her reader group and talk all the bookish things by clicking here.

Receive a text alert for new releases, text BOOKS to 740-206-6969. US only.

www.adrianalocke.com